THE ORPHAN GIRL

THE ORPHAN GIRL

AND OTHER STORIES

WEST AFRICAN FOLK TALES

RETOLD BY ***BUCHI OFFODILE***

Interlink Books
An imprint of Interlink Publishing Group, Inc.
New York • Northampton
www.interlinkbooks.com

To my mother, Chiebonem, who first exposed me to storytelling; my wife, Amaka; my children, Buchi Jr., Ijeoma, and Nneka, and their peers at St. Patrick's School who were my first audience for these stories—and all children and story lovers worldwide.

First published in 2001 by

INTERLINK BOOKS
An imprint of Interlink Publishing Group, Inc.
99 Seventh Avenue • Brooklyn, New York 11215 and
46 Crosby Street • Northampton, Massachusetts 01060
www.interlinkbooks.com

Library of Congress Cataloging-in-Publication Data

Offodile, Buchi.
The orphan girl : and other stories, West African folk tales / by Buchi Offodile.
p. cm.
ISBN 1-56656-375-5
1. Tales—Africa, West. 2. Creation—Mythology 3. Tricksters—Africa, West. 4. Africa, West—Social life and customs. I. Title.

GR350.3.O33 2000
398.2'0966—dc21

00-058063

Printed and bound in Canada

Contents

LIBERIA

MALI

MAURITANIA

NIGER

NIGERIA

SENEGAL

Preface

I compiled this volume to help preserve a dying culture. Since I left West Africa many years ago, I have had some occasions to visit. In all of my visits, only one thing remained constant—change. As a storyteller, I felt these changes were taking a turn for the worse. The traditional moonlight storytelling culture of the agrarian society that I used to know has all but disappeared. In its place, a more urban western-type society has taken root. Gone are the measured slow pace and carefree lifestyle I remember. In its place, a fast, and somehow chaotic, lifestyle has been transplanted. The traditional moonlight storytelling hours, when children and their parents formed a human ring around the fire, are now television hours. Television, most of which is foreign, has come to influence the social dynamics and culture of the people as storytelling once did.

In spite of the rapid changes taking place in the cities and the village marketing centers, much of the inner villages has remained intact. Yet most of the social structures I knew have really all but disappeared. Trust is no longer a way of life. People no longer sleep outside in the open air to catch the cool, fresh evening breeze and to be woken only by the splatter of rain, or the ubiquitous *agbusi*, the black stinger ant. Gone is the innocent time when the only fear children had was of ghosts—usually after listening to stories about them, or after a death in the village. Children no longer have enough time to be children and to be told stories. They have different fears, now.

I consider myself lucky to have grown up in an era when storytelling was part of the popular culture and I could learn from master storytellers. Like most first generation immigrants who left their childhood memories, friends, and cultures several thousand miles away, I am nostalgic about my childhood experiences, and especially about the storytelling hours. Those storytelling sessions, when families sat around the fire or under a fruit tree, with the silhouette of the full moon cracking its gaze between its branches, cultivated an unparalleled bond within families. During the non-farming months, boys would spend days following around the *masquerades* (spirits) who were thought to live in the *onu aruru* (ant burrows). To follow the last of them home in the evening back to the burrows, and then prepare to catch the early hours of the storytelling was thrilling for me.

Before this culture, the stories, and their tellers disappear completely, I decided to comb the villages for the elders who could still share these stories. As had always been the case, they were eager to oblige. The stories sounded better than ever to me, each one replete with the narrator's own style. Even the stories I thought I knew well sounded as though I had never heard them before. And the villagers took special pleasure telling them to me—perhaps the fact that I had come from so far away to seek them, after so many years away from the culture, made it even all the more worthwhile to them. They wanted me to know that the white man's culture had not completely subsumed them. They still remembered our roots and culture. Their eagerness to tell the stories remained, though they lacked the captive audience they once commanded.

Unfortunately, these elders will not be here forever. I therefore felt a sense of urgency to record and put some of these stories in print for future generations. I became not only a student of folklore, but also a knowledge engineer who tapped their brains for as many stories and as much history as they had. Now that I live outside West African culture with my own children, who may never experience it firsthand, I wanted to give some of our culture and history to my own children and others like them, to future generations of Africans, and to folktale lovers worldwide.

I have thought about this collection for quite some time. First I imagined picture books and now an anthology. I have known most of these stories all my life, and have been writing and collecting them for well over thirty years. I have also read several earlier works on these stories, which strengthened my drive to compile this volume. But, as a popular saying in Nigeria goes, *Oo mgbe mgbe naara awo odu.* (It was procrastination that deprived the toad of its tail.) Finally I realized that I better formalize my ideas on paper before I lose the ability to do so!

Problems always arise when one culture is translated from its indigenous language to another. Folktales are especially susceptible to this problem. The stories lose some of their meanings and impact. The prose, sayings, and local slang are often either misinterpreted or misunderstood, or both. For an example, to an Igbo of Eastern Nigeria, the mere mention of the word *akwasa* conjures a smile and a lifetime of experience. Yet, *wonderful*, the English equivalent of the same word, probably means very little to him, apart from the obvious. Tell him that the palm oil is "asleep" and it will make sense. Mention the word *ugba* and the Igbo's mouth will begin to water. Call it *fermented oil bean seed*, and it loses its mysticism. As a Nigerian Owerri would say, *Nna taa ugba nuo nmia, ndi moto ha na gbara ma* (Just give me ugba and palm wine, and the world is my oyster.)

Such is the nature of the problem faced by any translation of a people's culture into another language and culture. Nevertheless, the translation must be made. If it is not made for any other reason, it must be made as a necessity, so that the culture can be preserved for future generations. Furthermore, it serves to educate the rest of the world. Yes, as are most folktales, this anthology was written to educate. Education! It is fun. This is the theme of one of the more popular poems in West Africa:

Education is fun
Though the path to it borne
But by a patient one
Education will be won
If the one works hard and dreams

And, if the one has the means.

Akwukwo na aso uso
O na aria ahu na nmuta
Onye nwere ntachi obi
Oga amuta akwukwo
M'oburu na nne ya na
nna ya nwere ego
M'oburu na nne ya na
nna ya nwere ego

—Buchi Offodile

Acknowledgements

This book would not have been possible without my early exposure to folktales. For that I am most indebted to my mother, Chiebonem, and the parents of all my childhood friends.

Also, I am thankful to Dr. Fred Offodile for reviewing the manuscript and offering timely suggestions, which helped to strengthen the stories; and Professor Felix Ekechi for reviewing the introduction and checking my historical facts on West Africa.

For the stories "How the Crab Got Its Shell," "Foriwa's Beads," "The Horse with the Golden Dung" (or "The Cunning of Galonchi"), "The Most Suitable Name," and "Who Is the Greatest Thief?" I am grateful to Jack Berry and the versions he collected in *West African Folk Tales* (Northwestern University Press, 1991).

There are three other authors I must also acknowledge. R.H.K. Williams from whose work "The Konnah People," *Journal of African Society* VIII (1909): 136–37, I adapted "The Origin of War." "How the Pig Got Its Snout" is humbly adapted from Diedrick Westermann's *A Study of the Ewe Language*, trans. A.L. Bickford-Smith (London: Oxford University Press, 1930), 219–21. The story of "Everyone" I based on Okechukwu K. Ugorji's *The Adventures of Torti: Tales from West Africa* (Trenton, N.J.: African World Press, Inc., 1991), 29–35.

The statistics on West African countries punctuating this volume are mostly from the CIA's *World Fact Book 1998.* (See Web site: www.odci.gov/cia/publications/factbook)

Introduction

"Put your money on this sheepskin" said the old man, "and if, by the time I finish my tale, there is one of you awake, that man shall claim everything we have collected."

Young men, old men, children, women, they all put some money on the sheepskin beside the story teller. He waited till they had sat down. He himself settled comfortably on the *catifa* and smiled.

"It is a long tale of vengeance, adventure, and love. We shall sit here until the moon pales and still it will not have been told. It is enough entertainment for a whole night: AN AFRICAN NIGHT'S ENTERTAINMENT."

Thus reads the introduction to Cyprian Ekwensi's epic novel, *An African Night's Entertainment.* Storytellers often started their stories with such a challenge or a tease in the form of an *inu* (riddle). The riddler might ask, "*Kaaram madu abua gara ugbo, nmiri maa otu ma omaghi otu?*" (Can anyone identify the two people who went to the farm in a thunderstorm—one got wet, but not the other?) Any member of the audience who knew the answer responded, "*Nwanyi di ime.*" (A pregnant woman.) The riddles continued until someone, often an elder, interjected with "I have a story to tell you." And the audience, mostly youngsters, responded, "Tell us a funny one." If the storyteller was himself young, the audience might respond, "Tell us, and it *better* be funny. Otherwise we will knock your head." And everybody would laugh nervously and dryly, *Tahee Tahee, Tahee!*

THE STORIES AND THEIR TELLERS

Storyteller: I have a story to tell you.	*Enwere m akuko m ga akoro unu.*
Audience: Tell us a funny one.	*Kooro anyi ka odi uto.*
Storyteller: Once upon a time.	*Onwere otu oge ahu.*
Audience: And it came to pass.	*Otu oge ahu were rue.*

With that, the storyteller proceeded to tell his story while the children gathered around him. They sat on their bare bottoms with legs folded into one another like a jigsaw puzzle. Or, they lay on their stomachs packed like sardines around the storyteller. Some of those who sat down folded their hands and rested them on their laps and listened with their mouths agape. Others pinned their right elbows in their laps and then fanned out the fingers of their right hands like the leaves of a tender umbrella tree, carefully resting their chins on their palms and wrapping their fingers over their mouths as if to force them closed, so as to watch and listen more intently. During the cooler nights the warmth from their bodies provided much-welcomed relief. During the hot and humid nights, beads of sweat began to trickle down their foreheads. But the children were by now so engrossed in the stories that they were oblivious to the discomfort.

In West African culture, storytellers never overstayed their welcome in any home because they had a captive audience in the children. And the stories themselves never grew old because of the unique acting and orating of each individual storyteller. As an actor, the storyteller imitated the characters in the stories, especially animals and ghosts. As an orator, he or she adopted the mannerisms and accents unique to the animals and the ghosts. Assuming a ghost-like character, storytellers would, perhaps, speak through the nose, raising their hands in the air like scarecrows. Their talents were as varied as the individuals and enriched the stories with an element of uncertainty. The storytellers were always ready and able to add different twists to the stories to keep them fresh and entertaining every time.

The storytellers were usually grandparents, uncles, and aunts, for a couple reasons. First, the grandparents' activities were mostly around the homes. They seldom had to travel to distant farms and markets and had more time to share their experiences with the children. Second, they had more experiences to share—and more patience. Children often found these other adults more appealing than their parents for various reasons. Getting away from their parents probably distanced children from their chores! But when all chores were done for the day and everyone was fully fed and relaxed, generally the mothers were the storytellers. This varied, though, greatly depending on the culture, profession of the parents, and the audience. For example, among the Simbas of northern Sierra Leone, men were more often the storytellers. In general, parents who excelled in crafts, such as basket making, were very good storytellers, ostensibly because they could tell stories and work at the same time. Indeed, most fathers told their stories when they were working, or in the company of other men with whom they shared kola nuts, snuffs, and palm wine.

Stories by grandparents were usually the juiciest. They just knew from experience where to put the right types of inflections. When they told scary ghost stories, they knew when to lightly run a feather or broomstick across the children's hair to create the illusion of a ghost touching them. The children got real goose bumps, thus making the stories themselves seem real. Often, the children became even more scared, and got even closer to each other, almost choking off each other's circulation.

Storytellers seldom rushed their art. They usually did not have any concept of time. The man produced his snuffbox, tapped it three times, and helped himself to a hefty mound of snuff on the nail of his right thumb. The nail was unusually thick, dark, and layered with calluses from several years of abuse and neglect on the farms or in the smitheries. Or, he would light his pipe or roll of tobacco with a glowing ember—never a burning one. He wouldn't want to pollute or burn off good tobacco with the bad smoke from a palm-oil flame. He sat at the center with the children forming an impenetrable buffer around him. When the storytelling session was held indoors, perhaps during a thunderstorm, the children gathered around a fireplace with the storyteller, while ears of maize (corn) fresh from the farm, black pears, or coconuts roasted. The maize crackle-popped and the black pear spewed its juice into the fire, teasing it into a frenzy. The aroma of the coconut filled the air, all serving as vivid reminders of the prize that awaited the audience. The suspense became unbearable—and perhaps that was exactly the storyteller's intent.

Eh! Eh! Tihe! He sneezed from the snuff. "*Oburu ogwu dibia gworo ogaghi ere. Ihe onye siri ya mee ya, ya mee ya. Obughi nanim bu* (Name). (Name) *di na* (Village)..." ("If it is by someone's fetish, it won't affect me. Things happen to you if you let them. I am not the only (Name). There is (Name) in (Village)..." By reminding the sneeze that he was not the only one bearing his name, the storyteller was hoping that the sneeze would miss its mark and go looking for its true victim. It was believed that when you sneezed, someone somewhere was calling you, either for good or bad. In this case, the storyteller believed it was for bad.

Storytelling, like a joke, is dependent on the delivery—that is, on the teller, more than the story itself. Experienced storytellers used gestures, songs, mimicry, and varied tones to paint an invisible picture of the story. They knew when to change from one type of story to another, generally beginning the evening with traditional narratives and switching to participatory word games toward the end when children started to fall asleep. As if on cue, the storyteller would start a call and response:

Storyteller: Which creatures can fly?	*One anu na efe efe ee?*
Audience: Can fly!	*Ne efe efe!*
Storyteller: Ducks can fly?	*Obogu na efe efe ee?*
Audience: Can fly!	*Ne efe efe!*
Storyteller: Turkeys can fly?	*Toro toro na efe efe ee?*
Audience: Can fly!	*Ne efe efe!*
Storyteller: Chickens can fly?	*Okuko na efe efe ee?*
Audience: Can fly!	*Ne efe efe!*
Storyteller: Dogs can fly?	*Nkita na efe efe ee?*
Audience: ??	*??*

This is more a game than a story, and so made everyone alert and attentive. The storyteller would name some creatures that could fly, long enough to get everyone into the flow and rhythm of the play. Once the audience got into the rhythm, he would add a creature that did not fit the trait, for example, a dog, and whoever went with the flow and responded "can fly" lost the game and started the next round, perhaps with "Which creatures have four legs?" Songs were also an essential part of storytelling in West Africa. Those half-asleep woke up after the game or song, and the storyteller continued with the narrative stories.

Although stories were told spontaneously at any time of the day and were seldom scheduled, storytelling sessions were usually held at night under the moonlight or naked palm-oil lamps, called *uli oku.* While the palm oil provided the fuel for the lamps, dried palm nut heads or rags served as the wick. It was a test of one's ingenuity and patience to keep the lamp burning. Sometimes one of the children kept guard of the lamp by loosely holding his hands around it to shield it from the winds. Once in a while the wind took offense and retaliated. It changed direction to find a crack between the guard's hands. Then, with a gust, it blew the flame to the guard's hands. When the guard withdrew his hands in retreat, the wind launched a counter-offensive and blew out the flame. It was often a losing battle for the guard! When the stench of burned hair filled the air, the wind had won the battle. If the wind wasn't bothersome, then it was the incessant flapping of the moth and other flying night creatures on kamikaze missions to recapture the lamp.

With the light out and everywhere dark, the stinger ants emerged from their burrows and prowled about, stinging everybody they touched. As soon as the lamp was lit again, often by someone placing the wick close to an ember and blowing until their eyes assumed the color of the ember, everybody would go into a stinger-ant-hunting frenzy. They would crush them with their index fingers as the stinger ants ran helter-skelter trying to escape into their burrows.

Many of the tales West African children heard from their earliest exposure to language are about animals, such as elephants, hippos, lions, monkeys, the ever-scheming tortoise, spider, and hare. These animals usually assume anthropomorphic identities and are cast in fascinating roles in societies that behaved much like our own human communities. (See, for example, "A Bride for a Grain of Corn" and "The Crown Made of Smoke." In others, spirits tempt children, as in "The Orphan Girl.") Fate sometimes punishes folly, as in "The Magic Wand," or rewards perseverance, as in "Animal Language." My favorite stories are those told of the ever-scheming tortoise. As the saying goes, "*A koba akuko ma si akonyeghi mbe mara na nnu atubeghi ya.*" (A folktale without the tortoise is not juicy).

The choice of the tortoise as the central character in some tales is ironic. The tortoise, by all accounts, is the epitome of laziness, or—perhaps more accurately—sluggishness and weakness. To survive in the land of giants like the elephant, speedsters like the cheetah, and mighty beasts like the lion, the tortoise needed its own unique talent. Thus, West African storytellers bestowed wit and cunning upon the tortoise. (See, for example, "The Crown Made of Smoke," "The Tug-of-War," and "How the Tortoise Paid His Creditors.") In other cultures, in a story like "A Bride for a Grain of Corn," the hare or spider plays the role of the tortoise, with the same effects.

Perhaps the most interesting African tales are the participatory ones. For example, see "Why Mosquitoes Buzz," "The Talking

Tree," and "Foriwa's Beads." These almost always involve a song or two and/or a chorus. In certain tales, the songs have specific meanings; for example, they could be used to serenade a lover or demon, as in "The River Demon," or to show grief, as in "The Calabash Child." Though in many stories, they mean very little and are often added just to make the audience part of the story. In "The Latchkey Prince," for example, the song could have been blended in as text without much impact on the story line.

The Functions of Folktales

In a culture without an organized form of schooling, folktales served as a medium for educational advancement. Indeed, folktale sessions were one of the few times when the people gathered as a social group for the purpose of learning (even if the intent of the gathering was more for entertainment). Almost all West African folktales have morals. Many West African customs are preserved through folktales, which are extended versions of idioms and proverbs. As one such expression has it, "Proverbs are the palm oil with which words are eaten." (*Inu bu nmanu eji ata okwu.*) A proverb's very few words, when translated, could fill a book.

West African tales have all the themes and morals that are familiar in the tales of many other cultures: elders must be respected, parents must be obeyed, greed does not pay, neighbors must be treated well, evil is often punished, and so on. Certain characters, however—such as the tortoise, the spider, the hare, and the hyena—are known for their antics and are often allowed to get away with unacceptable forms of social behavior. In general though, the good usually prevailed over evil. Take, for example, "Everyone," a story of how the tortoise got its shell, and a classic case of being punished for one's transgressions. Or "Why the Hawk Preys on Chicks," in which a child goes through many trials and tribulations for disobeying her parents.

Before the Europeans introduced formal education to West Africa in the twentieth century, education was mostly by apprenticeship. There was no benefit of a written language and whatever anyone learned was learned through the spoken language, through observation and listening. Parents taught children about life and acceptable forms of social behavior early in their formative years. As the children grew older, they learned a trade that helped make them productive members of the society. At this point, they were sent to live with a well-established artisan farmer, trader, blacksmith, palm-wine tapper, et cetera. After the apprentice learned the trade and was ready to go out on his own, the master gave him some articles of the trade, such as yam seedlings, to help him get started in his own entrepreneurial ventures. This is what is popularly known as *idu uno* in the Igbo language. Folktales helped to augment this method of education throughout the life of a young West African, serving as the medium for advancing and preserving the customs and traditions of the people.

THE PEOPLE

West Africa is a conglomerate of diverse peoples with very rich and equally diverse cultures. The region covers Cameroon and then cascades westward to include Nigeria, Benin, Togo, Ghana, Côte d'Ivoire (Ivory Coast), Liberia, Sierra Leone, Guinea, Guinea-Bissau, The Gambia, and Senegal along the coastal line of the Atlantic Ocean. In the northern inland and landlocked part of the region are Burkina Faso, Niger, Mali, and Mauritania, with the latter three bordering the Sahara Desert.

Several documented pieces of evidence suggest that humanity, and later our development and use of tools, may have originated in Africa. The Nok culture of Nigeria appears to be the first culture in West Africa to have used tools. With the development of tools and fire, called the Neolithic Revolution, the early people of West Africa learned to domesticate animals and cultivate food rather than hunt and gather them only as needed. They learned to settle in one area for longer periods of time and eventually all their lives, rather than wandering from place to place in search of foods.

Whatever the origin of the earlier inhabitants of West Africa, there is little doubt that they were dark skinned. Indeed, the general area of West Africa south of the Sahara is collectively called the *Sudan*, an Arab word that means, "land of the black men." The temperature is relatively hot all year round, especially in the coastal regions. There is therefore little need for clothing. The main articles of clothing were traditionally strings of beads and raffia, which the adults tied around their waists. The rest of the body was usually left bare, except for the titled elders and chiefs of the villages. Children seldom wore any clothes but during festivities, which took place mostly in the non-farming months. The women decorated their bodies with *uli ogbu* (cam wood pulp) and *nkasi ani*, the juice of special rubber plants.

The original inhabitants of West Africa started trading with the merchants of North Africa as early as the eighth century. Muslims from North Africa established caravan routes to the gold trading posts of the ancient empire of Ghana, which controlled much of West African trade and amassed great wealth and power in the gold and salt trade. By the twelfth century, though, Ghana's power waned as the empire fell victim to more powerful kingdoms.

After the fall of the Ghana Empire, there was a succession of empires like Mali, Songhai, and Kanem-Bornu. Mali emerged as a major force in the struggle for supremacy, surpassing and engulfing ancient Ghana. Its lands included all the area previously held by ancient Ghana and went as far as Gao on the River Niger, which provided the impetus for northeastward expansion and trade with North Africa. At its peak in the middle of the fourteenth century, the Mali Empire had become a major commercial center and economic and political power in West Africa. Soon, its authority extended well beyond Kebbi to Hausaland, in present day Nigeria.

As with most empires, expansion was sooner or later followed by decline and ultimately a fall. West African empires were racked by civil wars when their rulers died. A council of elders within the community would appoint a successor to the throne, with the choice traditionally made from the royal family, either the son (preferably the first) of the ruler or a close relative. But with the conquests, which brought many people with sometimes little or no common heritage under a single rule, the line of succession became blurred. The once simple task of choosing a successor became politically divisive. Powerful leaders, especially those from the military, sometimes took advantage of the confusion at the center to usurp power. Conquered communities, which had been made under duress to pay allegiance to the central government, saw the instability as a chance to regain their sovereignty and go back to their natural states. Natural states were either defined by religion, as in the case of the

Moslem states; language, as in the case of the Mande and Hausa people; or culture, as in the case of the Mandinka people.

Over time the various cultures coalesced and, coupled with ensuing conquests and occupation, the rise and fall of the various earlier empires of the region, the influence of Islam, Christianity, and the slave trade, the present day West African people became a conglomeration of diverse ethnic cultures. Thus, according to John Hargreaves:

> The whole problem of ethnic identity may be extraordinarily complicated. Occasionally it may seem sufficiently established by the inherited physical characteristics of a people like the Fulas; but, in Africa as elsewhere, it is usually necessary to look to acquired, or cultural, characteristics to define differences between people. Each ethnic group normally has its own language (though it may not be wholly different from that of its neighbors) and this is probably the most important single determinant; but ethnicity may also be defined by occupation (the Bozos of Mali are fishermen); by historical experience (common resistance to an enemy, assimilation of a conquered people to the culture and language of a ruling group); by religion. The composition of a group can thus be changed not only by intermarriage but by more or less voluntary decisions comparable to processes of naturalization in more sophisticated legal systems. All this makes it difficult and dangerous to pronounce upon the "origin" of the various African peoples of today (14).

It is not exactly clear when the ethnic groups of present day West Africa settled in their current day locations. As early as the eighth century, however, the Mande, Fulani, and Hausa peoples were already established as inhabitants of West Africa. Other well-known inhabitants of the region include the Yoruba, the Igbo, and the Efik in Nigeria; Akan, Ewe, Guan, Mole-Dagbane, and Ga-Adangbe in Ghana; and the Krous of Côte d'Ivoire. Some of these ethnic groups can also be found throughout West Africa. The commonality of certain ethnic groups across the many cultures and countries of the region is a clear indication of their common ancestry. Quite a few of these earlier migrants may have settled in any country on their own accord as merchants, pastors, or nomads. They have retained their names and cultures, which in turn were assimilated into the host culture.

THE COMING OF THE EUROPEANS

The most important single event that changed the face, tradition, and history of West Africa was the coming of the Europeans in the early fifteenth century. By the fifteenth century, West Africa had become an important region of European trade and exploration. The Portuguese were the pioneers, but by about the sixteenth century, other Europeans, including the French and the British, joined in the trade. They traded in slaves, gold, ivory, pepper, and other commodities. Trading in these commodities led to the establishment of trading posts in Gold Coast (Ghana), Ivory Coast (Côte d'Ivoire), The Gambia, and Dahomey (Benin).

When the Europeans arrived, they signed treaties with West African kings and chiefs, who then provided them protection and granted them permission to trade. The Europeans, for their part, paid taxes to the kings and chiefs in acknowledgment of their political authority. Until the nineteenth century, slaves were the most important commodity. But by 1807 the British abolished the slave trade, and a new economy developed, concentrating on raw materials like cotton, ivory, gum, and indigo. From that point, the Europeans, especially the British and the French, began to penetrate the interior, resulting in the partition and conquest of West Africa between 1885 and 1900. By 1900, all of West Africa was under European rule. A new era thus dawned—the colonial era. West Africa was divided into two major language groups: the French-speaking and the English-speaking. The French-speaking West African nations include Benin, Burkina Faso, Côte d'Ivoire, Guinea, Mali, Mauritania, Niger, and Senegal, known collectively as Afrique Occidentale Francaise (AOF). After the First World War, the former German colonies of Togo and Cameroon became part of the French administration under the League of Nations mandate. The English-speaking countries include The Gambia, Ghana, Liberia, Nigeria, and Sierra Leone. The other West African nation, Guinea-Bissau, was under Portuguese rule.

Under colonial rule, traditional rulers lost their powers to European governments, which outlawed many local customs. The European authorities appointed their own governors, district officers, and warrant chiefs, especially in localities that did not have ruling kings and chiefs. Those kings and chiefs who did not cede power to those appointed by the Europeans were either exiled or dethroned. Thus power, which had once been controlled by the traditional leaders, could belong to anyone who had a warrant from the government, regardless of their age. Warrant chiefs were given certificates of recognition by the ruling governments, which authorized them to judge cases in native courts. Problems arose, naturally, when the warrants were given to persons other than the village's king, chief, or eldest male, who had heretofore possessed the authority to rule and decide cases. The people, for their part, had no choice but to switch their allegiance to the European governments, including their laws and appointees. This inevitably led to a breakdown of authority, custom, and social order. The people, especially the educated ones who had more or less adopted the European system of authority, could now challenge the once revered and respected kings, chiefs, and elders.

The policies of the British and French favored the establishment of churches and missionary schools, which provided them with people who were literate enough to work in their railways, mines, and offices. Some of these early employees were interpreters and court messengers called *kotma*. They were the first among the villagers to wear shoes, talking shoes, so called because they attached metal studs to the heels so that the shoes made noise as they walked on the cement or hard mud floors of the churches and government offices. These individuals were notoriously late to church, just so that they could announce their arrival with their shoes. They loved it when all heads turned in their direction and all eyes focused on them.

Education was geared toward training in the languages (English, French, and vernacular) and the cultures of the ruling governments. This provided the rulers with the clerks, teachers, and interpreters they needed to be able to communicate with the people. Many of the graduates of these schools adopted the cultures of the European governments. Some of them were given privileges comparable to those of their European counterparts. They were appointed to replace European clerks and teachers, district officers and court registrars. This was, of course, contrary to the cultures of the West African people, who regarded age and high moral character as the only qualifications for leadership. Inevitably, there were disagreements between the traditional rulers and the government-appointed officials.

The many languages of West Africa posed great communication problems for the Europeans. It was not surprising that they took immediate steps to "correct" the problem, whether by changing the local names to European ones, or by discouraging people from speaking the vernacular inside the school premises. The outcome of this effort was both positive and negative. On the one hand, it accelerated the assimilation of the English or French language among the pupils and, in countries with several languages it facilitated easier communication among the people, as English or French soon became the lingua franca. On the other hand, it served to perpetuate the belief that anything local, traditional, or cultural about the West African people was inferior. According to Felix Ekechi, "students who spoke Igbo in class on the college premises were made to wear a humiliating cardboard paper bearing the inscription Do Signum (I bear a sign) which identified the wearer as an Igbo speaker!" (226). Furthermore, the inability of the people to speak the language of the colonizer was in many cases misconstrued to signify their level of intelligence. But language development, of course, is a function of the needs of the people. Of course West Africans had no names for the foreign tools the Europeans brought to Africa. In some instances, they translated the names of such tools to the vernacular, based on their functions. Igbo for bicycle, for example, is *inyinya igwe*, or iron horse.

Besides the introduction of formal education, which helped to bring about improvements in the general welfare of the people of West Africa, the coming of the Europeans also helped stamp out some practices such as the killing of twins and babies who were born breech. And perhaps most importantly, although the coming of the Europeans fueled the slave trade, it eventually brought about its end. All these changes in the culture of the West African have come through education and exposure to other cultures.

THE ROLE OF RELIGION

Religion flourished in West Africa in many forms long before the coming of the Europeans. Before the introduction of Islam and

Christianity, traditional African religion predominated. As early as the ninth century, Arab traders from North Africa had successfully introduced Islam to the hinterlands of West Africa, especially the ancient empire of Ghana. Islam soon spread to the Mali Empire in the thirteenth century and later, to northern parts of the coastal countries like present-day Nigeria, Ghana, Liberia, Sierra Leone, Guinea, Burkina Faso, and Côte d'Ivoire.

The vegetation in the Muslim-dominated areas is primarily savanna, unlike the dense forest of the coastal regions, which did not lend itself to easy penetration with the camels and other animals of burden of the Northerners. The coasts were therefore sheltered from the political organizations and religion of the north, until the coming of the Europeans. Thus geography helped divide West Africa into three major religious groups: worshippers of traditional African religions, Muslims in the hinterlands, and Christians along the coast.

The common thread among these local religions, Islam, and later Christianity, is the recognition of an invisible supreme being as the creator. Below the Supreme Being (called Allah, Oluwa, Chukwu, and Obasi in Nigeria; Nyame in Côte d'Ivoire and Ghana) are other lesser gods and deities, with lesser powers. The lesser gods are believed to inhabit waterways, mountains, trees, or even animals. They serve as servants of and intermediaries to the Supreme Being. Among these gods are personal deities—*chi*, which are invoked by diviners or local chief priests through various objects such as amulets and charms. Often these objects, such as cowries or the shell of a baby tortoise, are worn as protection from danger and evil spirits.

Diviners are primarily agents of the social cultures of the people. They provide them with a means for atoning for their transgressions so that they can be at peace with themselves and their neighbors. Divination may be seen more as a mechanism for fostering acceptable social behavior than as a religious practice. For local religion worshippers, the place of worship is a small house usually located at one corner of the compound, where figurines of gods—*okpensi* and *ikenga*—were housed. These figurines were consulted in times of both trouble and celebration.

Myths and legends are immutable parts of the West African local religions. In one myth of the Mande region of northwest Côte d'Ivoire,

God was credited with the creation of heaven and earth. The myth also posits that he created people out of seeds in the form of four sets of twins. These twins populated the earth and learned to grow and cultivate crops, a skill they taught their descendants. They pleaded for rain with their songs and the resulting flood formed the River Niger. In "The Origin of Creation," the Fulanis of Mali tell a similar story of how man was created in God's image and given dominion over all his creations. Similarly, in "The Origin of Death," the Kono people of Guinea tell of why it is that people die. Stories were often spun out of such myths and legends and used to explain the facts of life to children, with the storytellers drawing from the natural scenes that surrounded the villages in which they lived. And so many children in West Africa grew up getting their religion through wonderful stories parents and other adults told to delight them and help explain the ways of the world.

When the Europeans arrived with their own religion, the villagers gave them land in the "evil forests." The forests were called "evil" because they were the dumping grounds for fetishes and other taboos. There, the Europeans built their churches and schools. The new religion accepted and preached acceptance and equality of everyone, especially those rejected and cast away by the local religion. Not surprisingly, the earliest converts of the new religion were people who felt that they had been treated unfairly by the local religion. The converts in turn sent their children to the European schools and churches once they found the teachings of the new religion acceptable. In time other members of the communities started to send their children to the churches and schools, especially those children who were stubborn and less productive in the farms. These churches and schools were seen as reformatories.

Although the new religion and the local religions had divergent views of belief and worship, the latter tolerated the former and believed that they could coexist as long as they stayed out of each other's ways. The new religion, however, was less tolerant of the local religion. It did not recognize the customs of the local religions, and sought to dismantle them. There was a massive effort to translate the Bible into local languages. Several pieces of literature were printed and distributed. Often, the general theme of the preaching in the churches was to discredit local religions as being idol worship, and converts were enjoined to reject them. In many religious education classes recitals that degraded local religion were commonplace. They were usually in a question and answer format. The following, from Felix Ekechi's *Tradition and Transformation in Eastern Nigeria*, was typical:

> Question: *Obu nkafie bu isekpuru alusi?*
> Answer: *Eye, obu nkafie bu isekpuru alusi, makana madu melu fa. Ndu fa enwe, ike ikwu okwu fa enwe, nke fa na afu uzo, nke fa na'nu ife; ije fa eje, mmerube fa emerube, ife ma fa eli, we gabazia.*
> Question: Is it folly to worship idols?
> Answer: Yes, it is folly to worship idols, because they are made by man. They have no life, and they can neither speak, see, hear, walk, move, nor eat, etc., etc. (226).

In their efforts to undermine local customs, the Europeans replaced local names with "religious" (European) names, despite the sacred role of naming within the local cultures. As a baptism welcomes someone into the Christian fold, the naming ceremony in Africa welcomes a child into a family. Names were chosen very carefully, usually based on the parents' experiences. A parent who had difficulty having a child might name her *Ogechukwukanma*, God's time is the best; or *Ikechukwu*, the power of God, if a boy. Furthermore, because of the high infant mortality rate, a child was named only after she has survived her first seven market weeks (28 days) of life. The belief was that after this long, one could be reasonably sure that the child had come to stay, and not to tease. (Those who came to tease were referred to as *ogbanje*, or repeaters.)

Though many in West Africa have embraced Islam and Christianity, many still uphold local customs such as the naming ceremony. People continue to believe that their ancestors, with the gods, are the protectors of the people. Before children reach adolescence, their father consults a diviner or the chief priest of his local religion to determine which of the ancestors reincarnated in the child. The diviner or priest goes through several incantations, calling names of several ancestors until one of them stands out. The title name of this ancestor, who is believed to have reincarnated in the child, is given to the child as his title name. In some cultures, this is done much earlier and the name of the ancestor is given to the child.

The West African people, perhaps due to their reverence for age, attach special importance to the souls of the departed. When they pray to the Supreme Being for protection, they pray through the ancestral spirits. In most circles, these spirits are believed to be superior to the deities. In fact, even where some of the deity worship has disappeared due to Christianity, the consultation or invocation of ancestral spirits persists. For example, during the traditional breaking of the kola nut, pouring of libation, or celebration of important occasions, the ancestral spirits are always called upon to lead the occasion.

The left hand was generally believed to be evil. Even today, some families still regard it as disrespectful for children to hand things over to people with their left hand, especially to their seniors. Consequently, they discourage their children from using their left hands in certain situations, such as eating and writing. If one stubbed one's left foot it was believed to be a bad omen. If it was the right foot, though, it was considered good luck: one might come into a fortune of sorts. If one's right eye twitched, one would see something good like a show. If the left eye twitched, though, one would soon have reason to cry.

Many West African beliefs were advanced through their folktales. In early West Africa, orphans were believed to find special favors with the gods. Consequently, they must be treated well or the gods punished those who mistreated them. (See for example, "The Orphan Girl," from Nigeria.) On the other hand, having twins, in some cultures, was believed to be a bad omen. They were rejected and abandoned in the "evil forests" to die. And, in some other cultures, childlessness was thought to be punishment from the gods. In all the stories, though, if the childless man and woman were true to their course and did not offend the gods, and did all they could to appease them, they were soon rewarded with a child one way or another, as in "Apunanwu" and "The Calabash Child."

THE CULTURE

Because of trade, migration and settlement, conquests and colonization, most of the West African countries share common cultures. Before the coming of the Europeans, the principal occupations throughout the region were farming and trading. In those days, there was no formal currency. People traded mostly by barter as herds of livestock were exchanged for land and other valuables. As time went on, though, precious metals like gold and cowry shells, *ego ayolo*, became quasi-legal tenders. Even salt was traded for gold during the era of the trans-Saharan trade. For those living around the coastal regions, fishing was also an important part of their livelihood.

During this period and through the middle of the twentieth century, families in West Africa were usually large, perhaps as insurance against infant mortality and because extra hands were needed in the farms. As work, farming was a fundamentally social activity and gave families opportunity to stay together: those long treks to and from the fields and long hours working together provided significant opportunities for bonding. The children tagged along with their parents on snake roads that were sometimes barely wide enough to accept their hardened, bare feet. The days started early enough for the dew settled on the tall elephant grasses to have condensed to water. The weight of the water overpowered the grasses, which seemed to be asking for help as they leaned across the path. The leader of the caravan, often the father or eldest male, swatted the water from the elephant grasses. Once the load was relieved, the grasses heaved a sigh of relief as they sprang back up, away from the path. If one listened carefully, one could hear them say, "Thank you," with a smile.

Some of the best stories about animals and nature were often told during these long treks to and from the farms. The stories told during these early morning and late evening treks served dual functions. First, they made going to the farm fun; the long treks seemed shorter, and the heavy loads lighter. Second, they provided another forum and opportunity for learning about nature and the environment. The elder in the caravan would see a squirrel and go into a recital of the traits of the squirrel. "*Osa anaghi akpo na efu*"—the squirrel never cries unnecessarily. And true to form, every time one sees a squirrel calling, one is likely to see a snake (danger) around. "Do you remember the one about the spider and the squirrel?" the leader would ask. Then, he would proceed to tell the story, concluding, "That is why we need roads to the farms, no matter how narrow."

Food

Foods traditionally varied in West Africa according to region. Africans lived close to nature and strove to protect its balance. They grew their crops organically, relying exclusively on the weather for its yield. What is generally defined as West Africa begins just a few hundred miles north of the equator, and so is relatively hot and humid all year round. There are just two seasons: rainy and dry, with the rains heaviest in the coastal region. The rainfall in these regions provides for the growth of heavy forests and the cultivation of plantains and tuberous-type foods such as yams and cassava. Farther north of the equator, the temperature during the hinterlands' dry season is equally hot, but much of the rain replaced by cooler temperatures. The terrain here is mostly savanna and more conducive to cattle herding and the cultivation of grains.

Despite these differences, in general throughout West Africa, protein was derived mostly from meat and beans. The meat came from game animals like antelope, deer, and bush pig, or herd animals like goat, sheep, and cattle, or chicken. Before the Europeans introduced guns, West Africans hunted the game animals with poison-tipped bows and arrows or spears. Once the animal was struck, the hunter tracked it patiently until the poison took effect. In time, guns and traps became part of the arsenal against game animals.

The meat of game or domestic animal was usually divided among the villagers. Any leftovers, which could not be immediately consumed, were smoked over wooden fireplaces and preserved. During the quiet of the nights, the fat from the meats dripped into the fire, sending the red-hot embers spinning. By the time the embers died out, the resonating drips of fat had put the children into a deep sleep, in which they could hardly help but dream of feasts of meat.

The most popular form of transportation in the coastal regions and among the cattle herders of the savanna was walking; the traders in the hinterlands usually rode beasts of burden. Tens of miles could be walked and quite a few calories burned in a day going to the farms and running errands, or riding through the hot desert sun. Of course today much of this is accomplished with more modern vehicles. But nevertheless, the sun, the high humidity, and the work still combine to calories quickly. Not surprisingly, then, food—in quality, taste, and quantity—became and remains very important in West African culture. As a popular saying goes, "The path to a man's heart is his stomach." It is said that some people actually collected their debts in meals—*oji afo eje ugwo.* Because they were likely to collect in foods more than the fair market value of the debt, debtors were better off settling in the agreed tender. Describing such a quantity of food, Chinua Achebe writes in his great novel *Things Fall Apart,*

> The story was always told of a wealthy man who set before his guests a mound of foo-foo so high that those who sat on one side could not see what was happening on the other, and it was not until late in the evening that one of them saw for the first time his in-law who had arrived during the course of the meal and had fallen to on the opposite side. It was only then that they exchanged greetings and shook hands over what was left of the food (32).

Not surprisingly, someone who cooked well became very popular. After a hard day's work the workers converged at the eating-houses of those who had mastered the art of cooking. After a good meal, they lay back on their chairs to expose their overstuffed stomachs as if they were hanging them out to dry. Their stomachs glowed like the back of a *shekere* instrument owned by an aggressive musician. They were unusually smooth and reflected the lone palm-oil lamp generously across the rest of the room. And, unless one was there when the transformation started, he would swear that the stomachs had been worked over by a master masseur who was too liberal in applying an expensive jelly. A drop of water falling on such smoothness lost its viscosity very quickly. It never had time to bead. It gathered tremendous speed and accelerated to the floor with a splatter. All told, these young West Africans are very hard workers. They could cultivate several acres of farmland, even the not-so-friendly ones where their hoes got entangled in the roots of the infamous *ekwe nwunyedi* shrubs, in record time, only to repeat the same feat day-in day-out.

Songs

Yes, West Africans play and eat as hard as they work. After a good meal, they can be heard singing, and pounding their chests—their stomachs by now too full to take any more punishment—and stamping their feet to the rhythm of their music. On a soft soil, their stamping made prints so deep you could bury elephants in them. And, they would rave, they cultivated acres of farmland with their eyes closed.

The African is a natural musician, dancer, and storyteller. He can sing or tell stories about just about any experience or situation. He could, and without the benefit of written music, start or make up an album with anyone, and repeat the same feat with anyone else anywhere with comparable acumen. *Nmadu anaghi aka nka na egwu o mara agba*, they'd say. (One never forgets what he is adept at.)

After a hard day's work on the farms, it was time to unwind and socialize before the next day started, which was usually long before the second cock crowed. At local bars and eating houses where the people *na eli hoteli* and *na anu baa* (eat and drink), the traditional boasts of how one cultivated acres of land or trapped the biggest game in the village could be heard. The rap musicians—progenitors of today's rappers in U.S. cities—told their life experiences in their music with beautiful ballads. Their most important instrument was their own body: mouth, feet, hands, and all its muscles. Sometimes gongs, drums, harps, lyres, flutes made from cow horns or bamboo stems, and guitars made from calabash gourds enriched the music. To untrained ears, the music from all the various instruments might sound like a song from an orchestra without a conductor. For one thing, there were no amplifiers, acoustics, or mixers, and for another, the instruments sometimes seemed to be competing with each other and the vocal. Trained ears, however, could discern all the different instruments and the vocal in no uncertain terms, and along with them, the song's emotion and meaning.

Songs and dance are central to West African culture, and thus its folktales as well. West Africans sing and dance for joy and grief, for peace and war. Songs have even been used to establish social age group lines. Songs invoke magical powers in "The Magic Drum," throw a challenge in "The Talking Tree," and serenade a lover, or demon, in "The River Demon."

Architectural Design

The architectural design of the early West African houses is a special subject all its own. The head of the household built several houses within his compound in natural picturesque surroundings. These houses were mostly thatched and often windowless huts made with earthen walls with varying degrees of sophistication. The head of the household built his main house, or *obi*, at the front entrance into the compound, as a first line of defense. The compound was usually walled with mud and thatched to protect it from the elements.

Behind this main house were littered other houses, usually smaller and occupied by a woman and her many children. A rear entrance into the compound offered the residents of these houses easy access into the compound, especially when the head of the family used the front part to entertain his peers and other dignitaries of the village. The man's *obi* was decorated according to his many titles and societies. It was usually scantily furnished and had a special recliner or easy chair, *oche agada*, made from goatskin or thickly woven cotton fabric, called *agbo*. If the man was titled, the chair or tripod stool was venerated with the markings of his title or society. A goatskin was usually either draped over it or placed on the floor in front of it. In many families, these chairs have been handed down from one generation to another and carry special meaning.

Between the *obi* and the front gate was usually a fruit tree, perhaps an orange tree, where most of the moonlight storytelling took place. During inclement weather such as rain or cold, if the man was leading the storytelling session, the *obi* became the classroom for these stories. If the women and aunts led the stories, the "classroom" reverted to their private quarters, *ogbolodo*. Usually the main articles of furniture in the rooms were mats and beds made of mounds of mud. In other instances, the beds were made from raffia or bamboo stems, ostensibly to escape the wrath of the black stinger ants.

At the village square or playground, rubber plant, oil bean, umbrella, and/or apple (*udala*) trees took the place of the fruit trees. Often, bamboo stem makeshift benches were constructed at the base of the trees to provide much-needed seating decorum, which was easily broken whenever the ripe and succulent fruit of the *udala* tree fell from the drooping branches.

The Family Unit

The West African people's activities always revolved around the immediate and extended families. Under the extended family system, everybody within a village was related, even if outside the nuclear family. Everybody was, therefore, either a brother or a sister—*nwannem*. This closeness made it everyone's responsibility to look out for each other's interests. Thus, although children were born to individual families, they were literally raised by the entire community. Any concerned person scolded a child to remind him or her to behave.

The leader of a household was usually the eldest male; the matriarch was the eldest female. This order was maintained even though these leaders might not have been involved in the day-to-day running of the family. The eldest male was both the moral and political leader of the family. For the village, the leader was the eldest titled male or eldest male in the royal family within a monarchical system. Age, more than wealth or social status, determined the position of the individual in the family and the society. (Though wealth and other individual social achievements were still revered.)

Before the Europeans came to West Africa, there were no schools or churches, and few jobs that forced individuals to work outside of the home. Consequently, much of the social interaction of the individual, especially children, revolved around the family. In such an environment, mothers usually mentored the girls while fathers usually mentored the boys. The boys stayed close to their fathers and learned their traditions. They carried their father's goatskin bags, mats, and/or staff for him when he attended social functions. The girls, for their part, stayed close to their mothers and learned the skills of homemaking, while helping care for younger siblings. Though both girls and boys married outside of the village, the boys came back to the village to retain the family name.

Marriage

The institution of marriage is the most sacred and important institution in the West African culture—the entire social fabric is built upon it. In most West African cultures, if not Africa as a whole, marriage is a bond between two families and two communities, not just the bride and the groom.

Individuals marry outside of their village because a family unit usually started the village. A man grew up and wandered with his family looking for greener pastures. When he settled, his daughters were married to men from other villages. His sons, on the other hand, went to neighboring villages to look for prospective wives. They moved out of the parents' home, several blocks away, to found their own families. In time, the clans grew bigger to become villages. Such villages were often named after the first family. For example, *Umuayom*, literally means "Ayom's children's village." Consequently, one cannot marry from one's village unless it can be proven that the ancestors of one of the parties had migrated into the village and do not in any way have a blood relationship with the other party.

Once a man and woman have consented to marry, the father of the groom brings a gift of palm wine to the parents of the bride. Some men of his immediate family accompany him on this trip. The sole purpose of this initial visit, called *iku aka*, is to inform the parents of the bride of their intentions. It is considered the responsibility of the groom's father to take this initial step. First, it serves to inform the prospective in-laws that he is aware of what his son intends. Second, it affirms his support for those intentions. If the groom's father is deceased, then this responsibility rests with the eldest male in the extended family. This practice supports the general belief that marriages without the blessings of the parents are bad omens and doomed to failure. As with many other beliefs of the West African, folktales perpetuate and elaborate on this idea. (See for example, "The Origin of War" and "The Serpent Groom.")

The importance of marriage is captured in several folktales of the West African people. When a girl is snobbish or particular about whom she must marry, or pays too much attention to her beauty or the material well-being of her suitor, she often ends up getting married to the wrong person, usually a macabre disguised as a prince. Again, see "The Serpent Groom." On the other hand, when she is of humble beginnings, chaste, and open-minded about her suitors, she ends up marrying a prince, as in "The Orphan Girl."

To the West African, one major objective of marriage was procreation. So, a marriage without an offspring was usually an unhappy one. If the couple was pure and honest, however, they were often rewarded in many ways. Sometime the gods gave them children from places they would never have imagined, sometimes magically, as in "The Calabash Child" and "Apunanwu."

Children are the pride and joy of their parents who take the necessary steps to raise them well. They are raised to become productive members of the society and take care of their own families, parents, and extended families too. As I have said, the entire community helped raise the children. Often, when parents could not afford the price of apprenticeship the community contributed to train the child in the chosen trade. This practice of communal education served two important functions. First, it served as a communal investment. When the apprentice was able to stand on his own, he took other children from the village to be his apprentice or perhaps contributed toward their training. Second, the practice served as a social security system that now obtains in a more structured manner in developed countries. The trained child often extended homage to the elders of the community whenever he visited his home during the non-trading or non-farming seasons, now called leaves. Several women's guilds and leagues have composed songs such as *Obughi ma nwa, onye ga enyem* (But for my child, who else would care for me), to extol the virtues and importance of children.

The Role of Women

Although men dominate most social roles in West Africa, women play very important roles within families. They farmed as hard as the men and often played the leading role in managing the family and raising the children. The gods often rewarded women who were treated unfairly by their husband or the community, so long as they remained true to their cause. An example of this is seen in "The Latchkey Prince."

Many different folktales have been told about the place of women in the West African society, especially about their relationship with their husband, family, and children. They were the children's refuge when their fathers raved and ranted. According to an Igbo proverb, mothers feed their children when they are hungry; fathers feed them when their appetite wanes (*Nne na enye mgbe oji agu, ma nna na enye ma oguburu*). Women, as in many places in the world, tend to be the stabilizing force in their families. The importance of this role has been captured in many ways in the culture. Names extolling the virtues of motherhood are popular. Women have been exalted as special and deserving of love and protection in folktales, such as "The Mother in the Clouds." They have also been exalted as angels of mercy, as in "The Magic Wand" and "The Orphan Girl," and despised as angels of wickedness, as in "Fereyel and Debbo Engal the Witch" and "How the Crab Got Its Shell."

CONCLUSION

Before the coming of the Europeans, West African borders, except for those formed by natural landmarks (e.g., rivers) were not mapped. The ruling European governments established the boundaries of West African states as we know them today, as a means of demarcating their lines of authority from each other. Such demarcation facilitated rule and authority over, and "protection" of, the governed. Unfortunately though, some of the boundaries were drawn without regard to the natural and pre-European borders. Some ethnic, religious, and cultural communities were severed from each other while others, who had little in common, were forced together, sometime leading to political instability. A clear example of this is the country of Liberia, which was established by the American Colonization Society (CS) after the abolition of the slave trade. The ruling group, often called Americo-Liberians, was originally from the United States or from slave ships captured by the United States Navy for the purpose of releasing the slaves in Liberia. So Liberia became one of the most conglomeratic of the West African states, the result of Europeans (and later Americans) upending the region's own traditional social, cultural, and political systems.

The grouping of communities with varying origins contributed significantly to the conglomerate character of other West African states as well. Nigeria, for example, has many languages, and thus many cultures. Even within the various languages, there exist hundreds of dialects. Nigeria is not unique, of course. Côte d'Ivoire, one of the French-speaking countries of West Africa, also has many indigenous ethnic groups with equally diverse cultures in language, religion, economic development, and environment. Although this diversity in the people and culture of West Africa is enriching, it makes it difficult to give a complete account of their various origins. Consequently, this volume concerns itself with only the general culture of the people, what binds them together, and the interrelationships of their folktales.

Our choice of "West African" as a subtitle for this anthology of folktales was made for simplicity's sake: tales heard in one African country are most often heard in another. For example, while a given folktale in Ghana might have *Anansi*, the spider, as the central character, the same story told by the Igbos of Eastern Nigeria is likely to have *Mbe Nwaniga*, the tortoise, as the central character. Thus, although I have classified the stories in this volume by nationality, it is at best difficult and at worst impossible to trace their origin to any one country or culture. The stories transcend geographical boundaries and the major differences are mostly in the language and some subtleties unique to a particular culture. I classified the stories to provide an historical perspective, trying as much as possible to present at least a story from each of the West African countries. Nigeria, however, is represented by a disproportionate number of stories, because of my own background. But no one African country can claim ownership of any of the stories; therefore, the categorization of majority of the stories in this volume as Nigerian is purely experiential. In a way, all the stories could have been called Nigerian. By the same token, a writer from another African country and with a different experience might categorize the stories differently. To paraphrase Chief E.P.O. Offodile, writing one's own account of anything "is like giving an account of a war fought in various theaters by various people. Each person will give an account of what happened at his own theater, as he saw it, or as he was reliably informed" (iii). This anthology is but one view of the folkloric elephant of African folktales. And so each reader may decide whether we have found the leg, the tail, the body, the tusk, or the ears, and put them together to form the whole.

Having begun this introduction with the start of Cyprian Ekwensi's epic novel, *An African Night's Entertainment*, I would be remiss, now that my own story is told, if I did not end with the following conclusion of the same book.

> The moon was still shining when the old man completed his tale, but there was not even a glow in the fire. He gathered his robe about his knees and smiled.
>
> "That is the end of my tale," he mused. "A most sorrowful tale, truly. Yes. A sorrowful tale. One must not take it upon oneself to inflict vengeance. But you can see the moral for yourself."
>
> He glanced round at his listeners. They squatted like little cones of white, their heads between their knees. Quietly he rose and reached for the glistening coins on the sheepskin. Had he not warned them that they would all be asleep?

The coins chinked, and a voice said: "Old man, don't do that. Have you won the bet?"

He started. One by one the cones took the shape of bright-eyed men who suddenly roared with laughter.

The old man had no alternative. He, too, laughed (96).

MY STORY IS TOLD

My story is now told and I am tired	*Ike akuko agwulam n'onu ugbua*
The audience is free to be retired	*Nwata eriela ihe o na emuru anya*
When other story times come	*Ubochi nta ozo ka anyi*
The audience will again be bid to come	*Chua kwa na owere nchi*
The audience is retired 'cause I am jaded	*Onye biara ije nwe una*
And not that my stories are ended	*Obughi na uzo di anya*
For from where come these stories	*Ebe akuko ndia si*
Juicier one to be told readies	*Ndi ozo di uto nke ukwu karia di*
I hope you are not sleepy or weary	*Ejim na aka na nti na akorisi unu uko*
For that is proof I have told a good story	*Nihi na obu ya bu na akukom di uto*

WORKS CITED

Ekwensi, Cyprian. *An African Night's Entertainment.* Lagos, Nigeria: African University Press, 1966.

Hargreaves, John D. *West Africa: The Former French State.* Englewood Cliffs, New Jersey: Prentice-Hall, Inc., 1967.

Ekechi, Felix K. *Tradition and Transformation in Eastern Nigeria: A Sociopolitical History of Owerri and Its Hinterland, 1902–1947.* Kent, Ohio: Kent State University Press, 1989.

Achebe, Chinua. *Things Fall Apart.* London: Heinemann, 1958.

Offodile, E. P. O. *A Pedigree of Awka and Its People.* Awka, Nigeria: Chief Ozo E.P.O. Offodile, Kucenda-Damian, 1998.

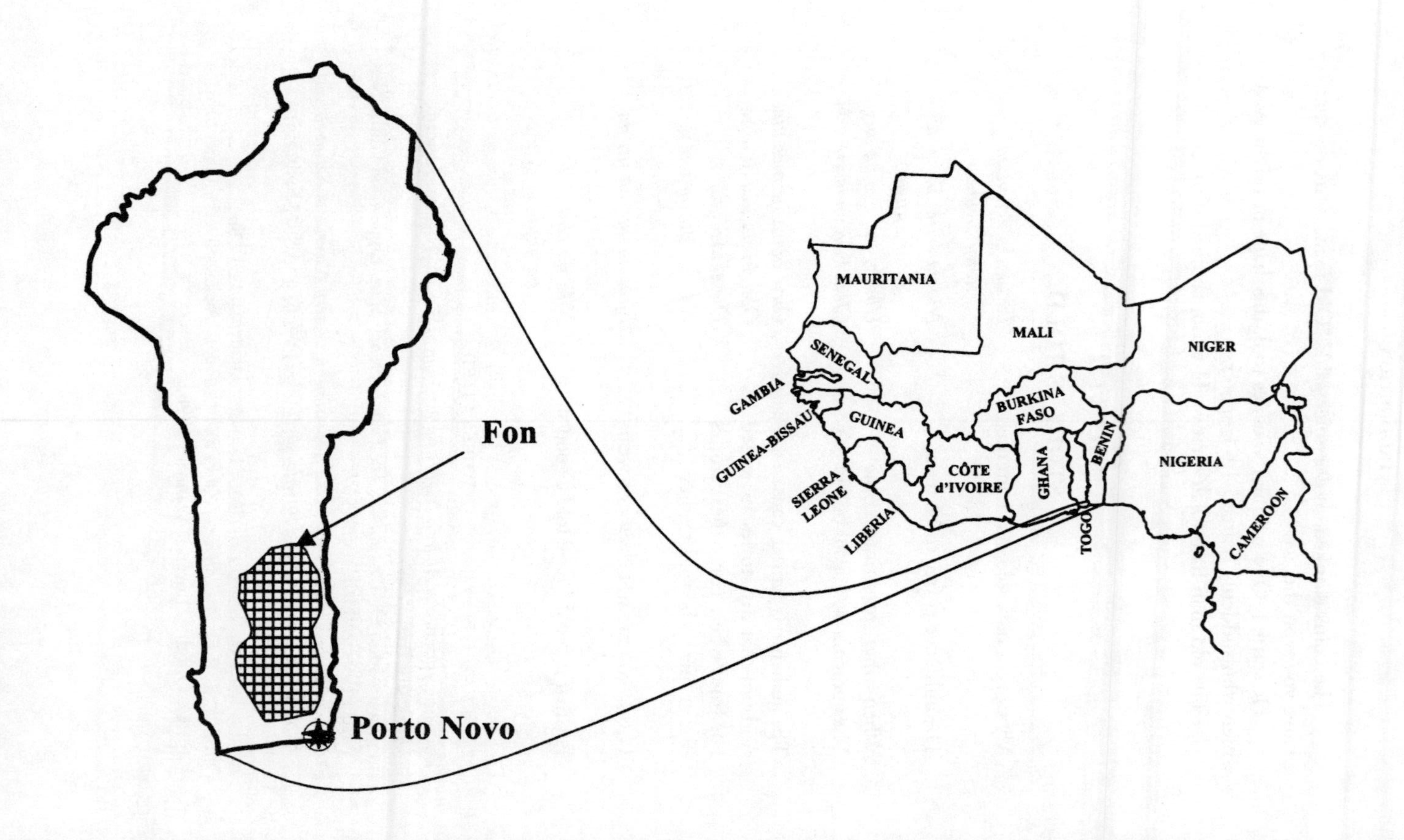
Fon
Porto Novo
MAURITANIA
MALI
NIGER
SENEGAL
GAMBIA
GUINEA-BISSAU
GUINEA
SIERRA LEONE
LIBERIA
CÔTE d'IVOIRE
BURKINA FASO
GHANA
TOGO
BENIN
NIGERIA
CAMEROON

Benin

COUNTRY

Formal Name: Republic of Benin (formerly Dahomey)
Short Form: Benin
Term for Citizens: Beninese
Capital: Porto Novo
Independence: August 1, 1960 (from France)

GEOGRAPHY

Size: 43,500 square miles (112,620 km^2)
Boundaries: Bordered to the northwest by Burkina Faso, north by Niger, east by Nigeria, south by the Atlantic Ocean, and west by Togo

SOCIETY

Population: 6.3 million
Ethnic Groups: The principal ethnic groups are the Fon in the south, the Yoruba in the east, and Adja in the west. The principal groups in the north are the Bariba, Peuhl, and Somba peoples.
Languages: About 55% of the population speak Fon. Other languages include Yoruba, Bariba, and Dendi, among others. The official language is French.
Religion: 70% local religions; 15% Islam; 15% Christianity

The Serpent Groom

From the Fon comes this story about a girl who was nearly destroyed for her obstinacy. The girl was against traditional arranged marriages and insisted on marrying a man of her choice, even though she knew little or nothing about him. When the groom turned out to be not quite what she expected, she had to find a way to escape.

Once upon a time, there lived a man named Alabi and his wife. They were very rich and had several acres of land, many servants, and many herds of cattle. But they had no child. They prayed to their God every day to help them conceive a child. Soon their prayer was answered. They conceived and bore a very beautiful girl. Because they were very rich, the couple spoiled their daughter. They gave her all she wanted. If she did anything wrong, they did not scold her.

When the girl became of age, many men both rich and poor, princes and paupers came to marry her. But she turned them all down. In those days, it was the custom for the father of the groom to arrange marriage with the father of the bride. So it was not surprising that this girl who loathed advice, hated marriage even more—especially because someone else thought it was such a good idea.

"How can I marry someone I haven't even seen?" she asked her father. "Besides, no man is handsome or rich enough for me. They are not even fit to be my servants."

Her attitude toward men worried her parents. They advised her against it, but she would not listen because she had not learned to take advice. So many years passed and the girl still did not marry.

The beautiful little girl became known in the village as "the girl who doesn't want to marry." Men of the village gave up on her, and her attitude rather than her beauty became the subject of discussion throughout the village. Mention her beauty to anyone and the one would respond:

"Sure, she is beautiful. And so also is the guinea fowl, but you do not sacrifice it to the gods, do you?"

Eventually, the general belief in the village became that the girl was not someone anyone would want to marry anyway. Soon her reputation for treating men disgracefully reached near and far. Even to the lands of the ghosts, monsters, and wild animals.

"That is one damsel I must have for dinner," said one Python to his fellows one day.

"As ugly as you are?" teased one of his friends. "She has rejected all the handsome humans that courted her and you think she'd want you?"

"Ha! Ha! Ha! Ha!" they laughed at him.

"Just watch me," he replied.

When the sun rose the next day, the determined Python set out to court the girl. On his way he stopped by his shrine and after several incantations, he was turned into the most handsome young man anyone had ever seen. Then, he donned the best princely outfit he could conjure and strolled majestically into the village. He looked irresistible and almost hypnotic in his charm. His face glowed like the morning star.

"Now," he thought, "it is time to teach that girl a lesson or two about courtship."

When he arrived at the girl's house he met her father drinking with his friends.

"I have come to ask your daughter's hand in marriage," he said to him.

Directly, the girl saw the stranger and rushed toward him. She embraced him and declared: "This is the man to whom I must be married."

"I'd like to marry you, too," pleaded the stranger. "But I need to complete the customary business with your father. I shall send for my people and after that, you and I will be married."

But, the girl was not patient enough for her people to investigate the stranger's background. She packed her things and threatened to run away unless she was allowed to marry him. Her father begged her to listen to the stranger.

"The stranger is wise and understands our custom. Let his people come and we will talk about the marriage."

"I will not wait for his people. I must go with him, now."

Her father tried to dissuade her, and then her mother and the rest of the families tried too. But she would not listen. She took the stranger by the hand, took her little maid and her luggage, and left with him. Her father didn't even have a chance to find out where the stranger came from.

The stranger took the girl and some of her belongings, including her little maid, some chickens, and a goat, and left for his home. They walked for several market days. They passed seven farms and seven rivers and still did not reach the stranger's home.

"How much longer before we reach your home?" the girl asked of the stranger.

"Not much longer," he replied. "We are almost there."

"Your home is awfully far?" she asked rhetorically.

"You might say that," replied the stranger. "But it is all relative, isn't it? For as our elders say, 'a distant village to someone is near to someone else.'"

But they still did not get to the stranger's village until they crossed the boundary between the living and the dead. The girl and her little maid were exhausted. Soon they came to a very thick forest the girl was sure no human had ever set foot inside. But they followed the stranger until they came to the center of the forest.

As they made their way through the thick forest, the girl began to sob. The stranger comforted her, saying, "I love you, remember. And that's all that matters." But the girl continued to sob, for now she feared the worst.

When they reached the center of the forest, they came upon a cave. The stranger led the way and told the girl and her maid to drop their loads. As they did, the stranger went into the cave, and as the girl and her maid looked on in awe, he slowly changed into an enormous python. The girl and her little maid shouted and cried.

"I need some food," hissed the Python. And before the girl could react, the Python grabbed the little maid and swallowed her.

Then the Python seized his bride, locked her in one of the rooms of the cave and swallowed the key. For the next several days, the Python fed on the chickens and goat the girl had brought with her. For as many days, the girl herself was starving—by design, so that she would become thin enough for the Python to swallow her.

Meanwhile, the girl's father was afraid. His fear was heightened when he did not hear from her for so long. So, he went to a diviner to learn more about his son-in-law and the welfare of his daughter.

"Your daughter is in the middle of the river and yet is crying that soap is burning her eyes," said the diviner. "She is in great danger and has only a few more days to live."

On hearing this, Mr. Alabi left hurriedly to summon all the master craftsmen of his village. Among them he selected those who were the best in five unique crafts. First, the Master Seer, who could see through walls and beyond the vision of ordinary human eyes. Second, the Master Rogue, who could steal food from the mouth of a feeding lion. Third, the Master Shot, who could kill a parrot in flight and without any bullets. Fourth, the Master Carpenter, who could craft a boat out of anything within the blink of the eye. Finally, the Master Sailor, who could captain the boat without oars and rudders.

"Your job," he addressed the men, "is to find my daughter and bring her back to me alive. If you do that, I will reward you beyond your wildest imaginations."

The men set out for their adventure guided by the Master Seer. When they reached the river, the Master Carpenter crafted a boat, which the Master Sailor captained. Long before they even reached the thick forest, the Master Seer spotted the Python sunning itself by the beach. On further search, he saw the girl in a corner of the cave where she was locked up, and the key inside the Python's belly.

Now comes the time to employ the services of the Master Rogue.

When the Python rolled over and saw the Master Rogue, the Python was frozen, as if in a trance. The Master Rogue opened the Python's mouth, reached into its stomach and removed the key to the cave. He quickly opened the cave, released the girl, and returned the key to the Python—all before the Python could even move.

Then the men put the girl in the boat and the Master Sailor captained it toward the land of the humans. When the Python came to, he crawled into the cave to devour the girl. When he could not find her, he destroyed much of the cave in anger as it searched the nooks and crannies for her. As he came outside of the cave, he saw footprints and other evidence of human meddling and by the wave on the river, he could deduce that he had been robbed of his most cherished possession.

He immediately chased after the wave, as if he were possessed. In no time, he caught sight of the escapees and lunged at them. Of course the Master Seer had already seen the Python approach and had alerted the Master Shot. But as the Master Shot reacted and fired, the Python already had lunged and broken the boat into several pieces. The shot was fatal and the men struggled to remain afloat until the Master Carpenter crafted another boat, which the Master Sailor captained safely back to the land of the humans.

When they arrived, Mr. Alabi made good on his promise to reward the men quite handsomely. Each one of the men, though, wanted to keep more of the reward for himself.

"If it weren't for me," said the Master Seer, "we would never have seen the girl in the first place."

"But," said the Master Carpenter, "it was me who crafted the boat that got us there. And when we almost drowned, I was the one who crafted another boat to save us."

"What about me?" asked the Master Shot. "If I hadn't killed the Python, we'd all be dead by now. I deserve to get more of the reward."

"Do not forget that I had to risk my life to get the keys from the Python's stomach," said the Master Rogue. "If I hadn't done that we would not be here fighting over the rewards."

"Well," said the Master Sailor. "What can I say? I am just a common sailor. I do not deserve any rewards. So, I will yield my own share of the rewards to all of you. You deserve it more than I do."

As he turned to leave, the rest of the men realized their selfishness and that each one of them played a significant role in the success of their mission.

"Come back, partner," said the Master Rogue. "We are each a piece of the puzzle that when put together solved the mystery of our missing daughter. No one is more important than the other is. Come, let us share the rewards equally among us, for the gun never discharges without all its parts working in unison."

Although the "girl that never wanted to marry" learned her lessons and changed her ways, the men of the village never changed their minds about her. Furthermore, by now she had become so old that her beauty had withered like the flower of a tropical plant in the arctic. And so, she lived up to her name and never got married.

Burkina Faso

COUNTRY

Formal Name: Burkina Faso (formerly Upper Volta)
Short Form: Burkina Faso
Term for Citizens: Burkinabe
Capital: Ougadougou
Independence: August 5, 1960 (from France)

GEOGRAPHY

Size: 105,946 square miles (274,200 km^2)
Boundaries: Bordered to the northwest by Mali, northeast by Niger, east by Benin, south by Togo, Ghana, and Côte d'Ivoire

SOCIETY

Population: 11.5 million
Ethnic Groups: The two major ethnic groups are the Voltaic, which is comprised of Mossi (24%), dominant in the south around Ougadougou; Gourounsi; Bobo, dominant in the north around Bobo Diolasso; and Lobi; and the Mande, which is comprised of Samo, Tougan-Marka, Dioula, and Boussanel. Other groups include the Gurunsi, Hausa, and Fulani, among others.
Languages: The principal languages are Mande, Poular, and Voltaic languages. The official language is French, but English is also used among the people along the Ghanaian border.
Religion: 50% Islam; 40% local religions; 10% Christianity

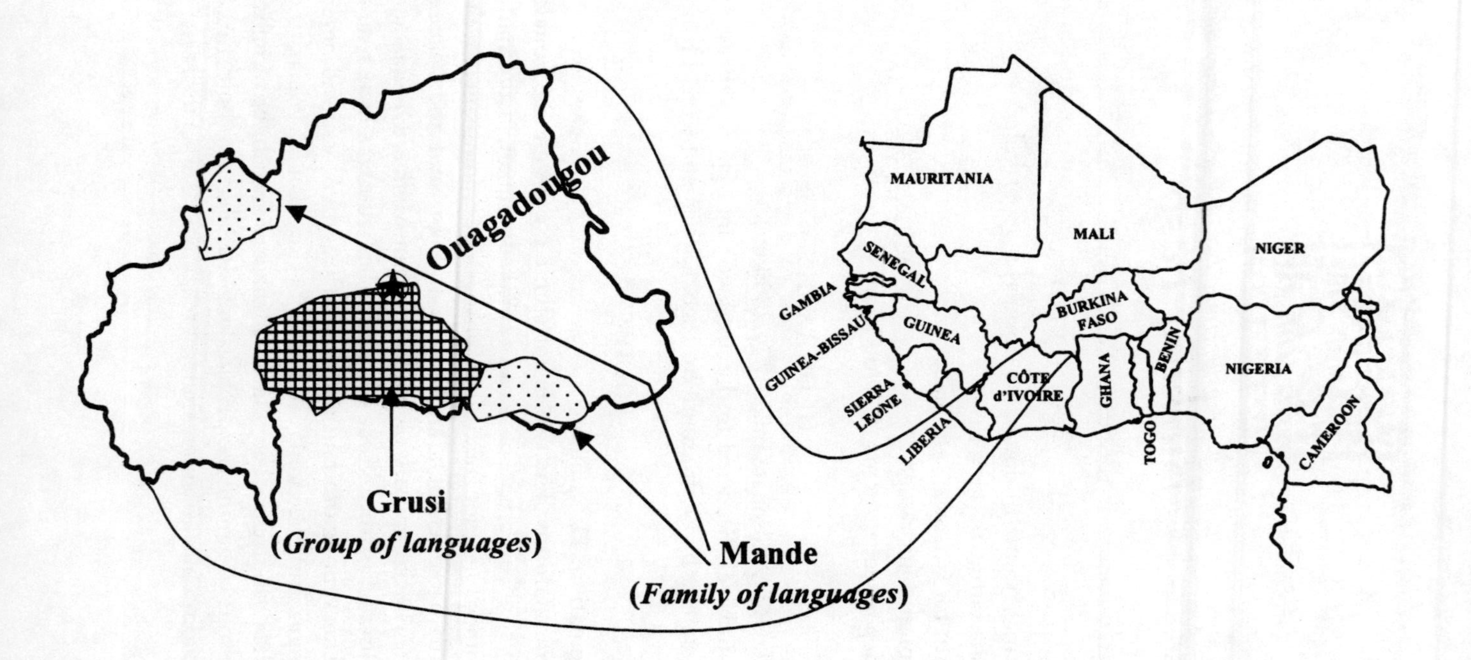
Ouagadougou
Grusi
(Group of languages)
Mande
(Family of languages)
MAURITANIA
MALI
NIGER
SENEGAL
GAMBIA
GUINEA-BISSAU
GUINEA
SIERRA LEONE
LIBERIA
CÔTE d'IVOIRE
BURKINA FASO
GHANA
TOGO
BENIN
NIGERIA
CAMEROON

How the Crab Got Its Shell

The crab's skin, like that of all underwater creatures, used to be smooth and slippery. The Grusi people tell this story about a wicked grandmother who was left to raise her orphaned grandchild. She mistreated the little girl, even depriving her of food. Luckily the little girl got some help from the Crab.

Long, long time ago, crabs had no shells. Their bodies were as smooth as all the creatures who lived in the river. Also in those days, there lived a very wicked old woman and her orphaned granddaughter. The old woman treated her grandchild very harshly. She often sent her to do impossible things so that when she failed, she could justify treating her so badly.

One day she sent the little girl to fetch water with a basket. The little girl went, but when she came back without water, the old woman beat and abused her:

"You lazy fool," she called her. "You will never amount to anything. Don't you know that you cannot carry water with a basket?"

"But you told me to," pleaded the little girl.

"If I told you to kill yourself, would you?"

The little girl was very hurt and angry for she knew that there was no way she could've drawn water with a basket. But if she had argued or reasoned with her grandmother, she would have been punished all the same. She obeyed in order to buy time and delay the inevitable punishment. Her grandmother knew that too.

"Grandmother," the little girl called her one day.

"I have told you," she answered back. "Never call me grandmother again. The day you do, I will beat you more than ever before."

"But you never told me your name," pleaded the little girl.

"That's for you to find out. And, if you don't, you will never get any food in this house."

The little girl was very sad, for she knew that children didn't call grownups by their names. They were always addressed as the mother or father of one of their children or if they had no children, as "our mother" or "our father." The little girl didn't want to ask any grownups either, because she thought they might think she was being disrespectful. And that might make them believe any lies her grandmother told about her.

The little girl became more and more miserable. She soon became quite solitary. Whenever she went to the river, she sat by the bank and talked to her reflection in the river. Then she sang and called out her parents' names. She told them how her grandmother treated her, and asked them to help her cope with the hardship.

One day as she sang to her parents at the riverbank, she scooped a handful of water and poured it on her legs. Then she sang and laughed and consoled herself. Then as she reached down to draw her water and leave, a crab surfaced.

"I have been watching you come here everyday," the Crab told her. "Why do you cry and sing sad songs all the time?"

"Because my grandmother is very mean to me. Now she won't even give me food unless I know her name."

"Your grandmother is a mean, scraggy, and raggedy old woman," noted the Crab. "But why does she want you to know her name?"

"Isn't it obvious?" asked the girl. "So that she can justify her treatment of me. If I don't know her name she deprives me food. If I do, she will beat me for calling her by her name. But, I'd rather be beaten and have food than not be beaten and not have food."

"All right," said the Crab. "I will help you. But promise not to tell her I told you. If she finds out, there's no telling what she would do to me."

"I promise! I promise!" the girl shouted with excitement.

"Your grandmother's name is Sarjmoti-Amoa-Oplem-Dadja."

"Sarjmoti-A... what?" asked the girl, excited and amazed at the same time. She repeated the name several times to the Crab, "Sarjmoti-Amoa-Oplem-Dadja."

What a name! Could that be why she doesn't want anyone to know it? she wondered. "Thank you very much, Mr. Crab. I will never forget you."

With that, the girl filled her calabash with water and set off for home. As she walked, she repeated the name over and over to make sure she didn't forget it. But soon her mind began to wander. She thought about her life as an orphan. Then she compared it to her life with her parents. "I would take my parents any time. No matter how bad I thought they treated me. Mother was right when she told me, 'No one can love you as much as I do.'" When she finally returned from her daydreaming, she realized that she had forgotten her grandmother's name.

"Sargamonti-S..." she said. "Oh! No! I have forgotten her name."

She stood at that spot for a few moments weighing her options. "Should I go back to the river and ask the Crab again, or should I go home and be without food?" Soon her desire for food overcame her lack of desire to make the long trek back to the river. So she quickly put down her calabash of water to the ground and emptied its contents on the hard baked ground. The shrubs breathed a sigh of relief as they soaked up the water. They were so happy that you could here them clapping and cheering as the water drained into the soil through the cracks left by the scotching desert sun.

When the little girl got to the river, the Crab was not as forthcoming with the name as before.

"I believe it was a mistake telling you the name in the first place," said the Crab. "The fact that you forgot it confirms my doubts. Since you left, I have been thinking I shouldn't have told you her name. Your grandmother is really wicked and I wouldn't wish her wrath on my worst enemy. I see your forgetting the name as an omen, a chance for me to save my skin."

"Please," pleaded the little girl. "She will never find out. It will be just between the two of us."

She pleaded some more with the Crab, telling him how she might be treated should she go home without knowing her grandmother's name. Besides, she had wasted too much time at the river, which would only aggravate her problem. She finally broke the Crab down, and he gave her the name once more.

"Alright," said the Crab. "Her name is Sarjmoti-Amoa-Oplem-Dadja! Let me repeat it, because you can *never* get me to say it again. Sarjmoti-Amoa-Oplem-Dadja."

The girl was excited and relieved and set out for her home again. She repeated the name over and over again as she walked home. Soon her mind began to wonder again, "No! Sarjmoti-Amoa-Oplem-Dadja, Sarjmoti-Amoa-Oplem-Dadja..." She repeated the name over and over until she got home.

Later in the evening as she prepared the evening meal, she unconsciously repeated "Sarjmoti-Amoa-Oplem-Dadja," as she had done on her way from the river.

"You evil child," cursed the old woman. "Who told you my name?"

"Nobody," lied the little girl.

"Yes, somebody! Who is it?"

"I got it from the river."

"Who from the river?"

"I don't know! I just got it."

The old woman was filled with rage. She snatched up a calabash pot and ran and speed-walked down to the river without even holding her breasts. She just let them flap against her chest like the popping sound of dried corn placed against a red-hot ember. As the elders say, when a woman runs and holds her chest, she does so out of decency and not because her breasts would fall off. But, decency was not one of Sarjmoti-Amoa-Oplem-Dadja's strong qualities, especially now that she was fuming with rage. By the way she ran and speed-walked, everyone knew she was going to unleash her wrath on someone. She asked everyone she met on the way if they had anything to do with her granddaughter knowing her name.

"Not at all," they all denied.

She continued in this manner until she got to the Crab. Since everyone had denied knowledge of how the little girl found out the old woman's name, the Crab was sure that the old woman knew it was him. He was panic-stricken. His legs shook and knocked against each other as the old woman asked him.

"Did you tell that little thing my name?"

"Ye-ye-ss!" the Crab confessed.

Upon confessing, the Crab knew that flight was his best bet, lest the old woman trample him to death. The furious old lady chased after him. She grabbed her calabash pot and threw it at the Crab. The pot broke and she picked up one half and went after the Crab. When she caught up with him, she stretched out and hit him with the open end of the calabash so that he was pinned to the ground. As she reached to pull out her knife, the Crab ran off into the bush with the calabash stuck to him. That is why even today, crabs still have calabash shells.

Cameroon

COUNTRY

Formal Name: Republic of Cameroon (formerly French Cameroon)
Short Form: Cameroon
Term for Citizens: Cameroonian
Capital: Yaounde
Independence: January 1, 1960 (from UN Trusteeship under French Administration)

GEOGRAPHY

Size: 183,569 square miles (475,440 km^2)
Boundaries: Bordered to the north by Chad, east by Central African Republic, south by Congo, Gabon, and Equatorial Guinea, southwest by the Atlantic Ocean, and west by Nigeria

SOCIETY

Population: 15.5 million
Ethnic Groups: There are several tribes, which belong to either the Sudanese of the north or Bantu of the south. The Sudanese group includes the Peuls, Foulbes, Baboutes, Bayas, and Massas; the Bantu group includes the Fang and Pahouins, Makas, Etons, and Bassas.
Languages: The northern parts speak mostly Hausa. English and French are the official languages.
Religion: 51% local religions; 33% Christianity (mostly in the south); 16% Islam (mostly in the north).

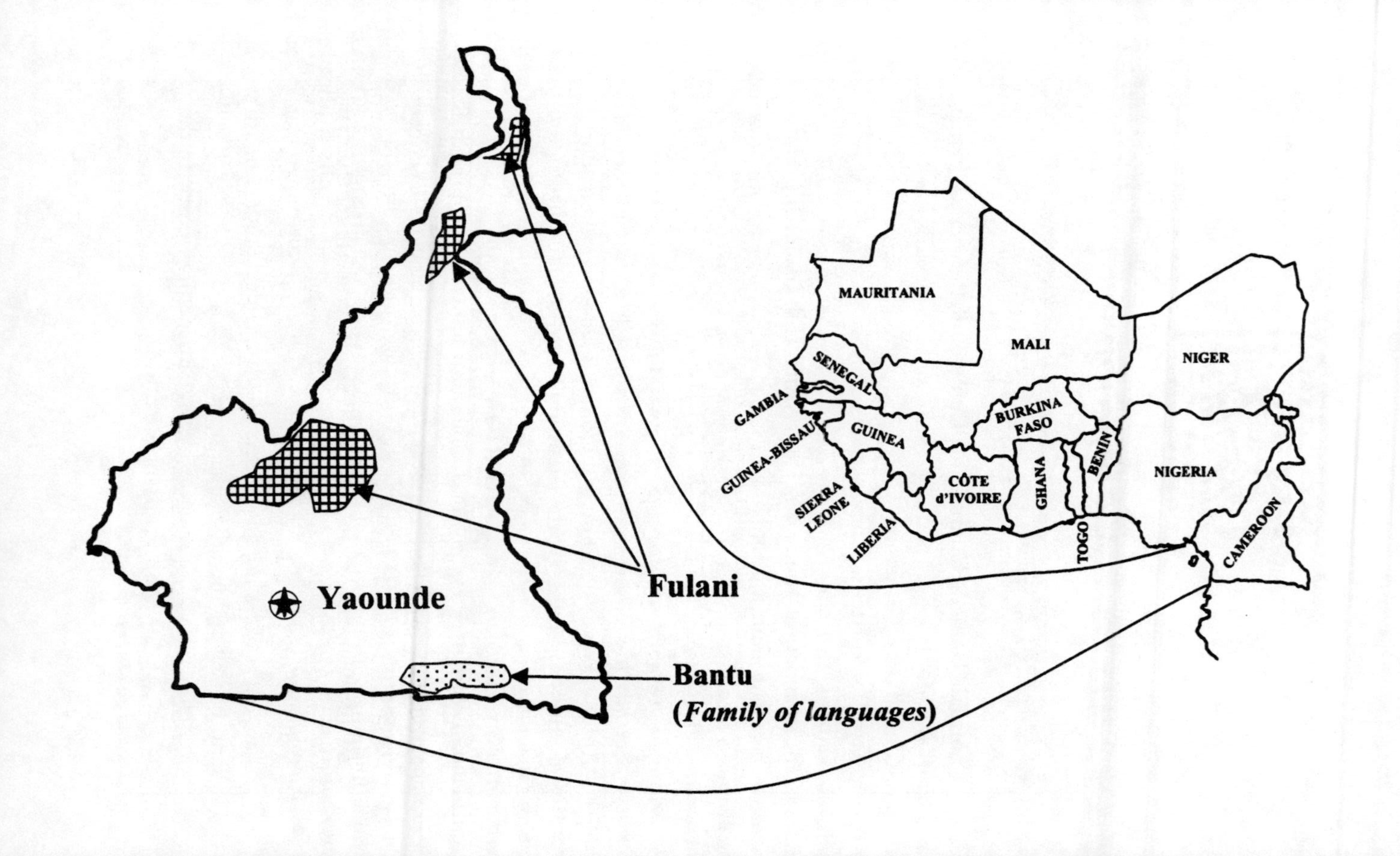
MAURITANIA
MALI
NIGER
SENEGAL
GAMBIA
GUINEA-BISSAU
GUINEA
BURKINA FASO
SIERRA LEONE
LIBERIA
CÔTE d'IVOIRE
GHANA
TOGO
BENIN
NIGERIA
CAMEROON
Fulani
Yaounde
Bantu
(Family of languages)

The Crown Made of Smoke

Be careful when you send someone to do an impossible task, because you might have to do something as difficult yourself. In this game of wits, the Fulanis tell of the Tortoise, who accepted the King's challenge to weave a crown of smoke for him, knowing full well it was impossible. Will the Tortoise turn the tables on the King?

Once upon a time, there lived a very powerful King who ruled his kingdom with great wisdom. The King was blessed with several children, both boys and girls. But there was one among them whom he loved dearly because she was so beautiful. When this daughter came of age, every man in the village came to ask for her hand in marriage. Because the King loved her so dearly, he felt that no one was good enough to marry her. But the king was advancing in age. As much as he hated to, he knew he had to give his daughter's hand in marriage. When he realized that he didn't have much longer to live, he agonized over his dilemma.

"It is no secret that I don't want to give my daughter's hand in marriage," he said to his wife one day. "But I am advancing in age and must do something about it."

"It's your choice," replied his wife. "Either you do it yourself and witness it, or your son will do it for you after you die. What do you want from her husband anyway?"

"It is not money that I want from him. Neither is it strength, or beauty. All I need from him is wisdom. With wisdom, he can have money. He can surround himself with strong people. He can have the whole world, rule it, and keep my Princess happy."

After much soul searching, the King thought of a plan. He came up with a contest and opened it up to everybody, including the animals. Then he challenged them, saying: "I will consider you my equal in wisdom, if you can sew me a crown of smoke. On top of that, I will give you the Princess' hand in marriage and half of my kingdom."

Then the King ordered his servants to set a big fire in the village square for the contest. They set the fire with dried and fresh wood so that it made great smoke. The villagers gathered and waited as the

King and his counselors arrived. They wondered who could be dumb enough to accept such a challenge. "The King doesn't want his daughter married," some of them said. "And he has made that known by this contest."

But the lure of marrying the Princess and inheriting half the kingdom proved irresistible. The first to try their luck were all the men the King had turned away before. They saw it as an opportunity to claim the Princess. They tried to sew the crown of smoke but failed. Then the rest of the men in the village came to try.

"You have been turned down before," said one man to the other. "Don't you know when to quit?"

"You cannot call yourself a hunter," replied the other, "and see a prized game without shooting at it."

After all the men have tried and failed, it was now the animals' turn. First among them to come was the Lion.

"They don't call me King of the beasts for nothing," he bragged. "One has to be wise to rule such a diverse group of animals. I, Your Majesty, will sew you a crown of smoke."

The Lion roared and sprang on his hind legs. He bared his teeth as he wrinkled his nose, clawed, and shadowboxed the smoke. But he couldn't collect enough smoke to sew the crown from it. He tried and tried until he was exhausted. Then he panted and collapsed.

Next came the Hyena, "The qualification was wisdom," said he, "not strength. I, Your Majesty, will sew you the crown of smoke."

The Hyena cried to the smoke. He circled it several times and tried to collect wisps of smoke. But try as he may, the smoke kept going. Tired from the running around, he gave up.

"I am the wisest creature on earth," said the Elephant. "I will sew your crown of smoke." He trumpeted and charged back and forth. He sucked the smoke with his trunk and blew a smoke ring, which soon dissipated. He tried as hard as he could, but failed to sew the crown of smoke.

The rest of the animals tried, but failed. The people jeered at them and laughed. Finally the Tortoise came along.

"The King shall live forever," he greeted the King. "I, your honor, will sew you the crown of smoke."

Everybody in the crowd began to laugh at the Tortoise as some of them kicked sand at him. "How can such a slow poke do what the mighty Elephant, the Lion, and other strong animals couldn't? He is just here to waste our time," they thought.

"I know all your people and the animals have tried and failed. But as much as I hate to admit it, for once I agree with the Hyena: 'The qualification is wisdom, not strength.' That is why I am here."

The King beamed with a wide smile. He hushed the crowd as they murmured.

"Being that you are a wise man, your Royal Highness, you know sewing a crown of smoke will require a lot of time. If it pleases you, your majesty, would you find it in your heart to give me seven market days to sew the crown?"

"Sure," the King replied eagerly, "take your time."

"Oh!" added the Tortoise. "I almost forgot. I will need special materials for the project. Being the King, I am sure that you can do whatever I ask of you. But just to be sure, do I have your word that it is so?"

"Anything you want for the project will be done for you," the King assured him.

"Let it be known that the King has given his word to provide me with anything I want for the project."

"It is written, and so it shall be done," said the King.

Then the Tortoise, the people, and the rest of the animals dispersed. Seven market days later, everyone gathered again to watch the Tortoise make a fool of himself. But the Tortoise was not in the crowd. The people were not surprised. They were sure that he couldn't sew a crown of smoke.

Then the Tortoise crawled gently to the center of the square and approached the King. As they saw that he didn't have the crown of smoke, they laughed and jeered at him so hard that their lungs began to hurt.

"I can see that you have failed like everyone else," said the King. Then he laughed so hard that the rest of the crowd joined him.

"No," said the Tortoise. "You will have your crown."

The King was dumbfounded as the Tortoise continued.

"What you ask of me is special. But it is almost completed. When I divined last night to find out why it was taking me so long to sew the crown, the spirits revealed that a special kind of smoke is required to sew the crown."

"What kind of smoke?" asked the King excitedly, "name it and it's yours."

"You see," continued the Tortoise, "we have been going about it all wrong. The fire with the logs will never do. Start a fresh fire and make all your people shave their heads and throw their hair into it. Then you shall have your crown of smoke as long as there is smoke in that fire."

Immediately, the king ordered another fire started and his subjects to shave their heads and throw their hair into the fire. But, no sooner did they throw all the hair into the fire than the hair burned out. The smoke never lasted long enough for the Tortoise to collect it, much less sew a crown with it.

"More smoke please," asked the Tortoise. But the king's subjects could not grow back their hair fast enough to keep up with the Tortoise's demand. The King had no choice but to call the bet in the Tortoise's favor.

"It is really no use," said the King. "Who needs a crown of smoke anyway, when I have one of gold and silver? But by your actions, I know you are a very wise creature. In keeping with my words, you may have the hand of the Princess in marriage."

Then the King gave the Princess to the Tortoise. He divided his kingdom and gave him half of it. The one he called the kingdom of the people he ruled, and the half called the kingdom of the animals, the Tortoise ruled. That is why even today, the Tortoise is known as the wisest of the animals. And since then he ruled the animals with great wisdom. Sometimes though, the Lion, since he is stronger, usurps the throne. But the Tortoise is the wisest and can outwit him anytime and reclaim his kingdom. As the elders say, men are also afraid of the aggressive bull cattle, but when it comes time to skin it, they find a way to tame its aggression.

Tricks for Tat

When a cunning man dies, a cunning man should bury him. This is the lesson in this Bantu tale of tricks and counter-tricks, ingratitude, and greed. The Squirrel tricked the Buffalo into becoming his source of milk. The Hyena soon tricked the Squirrel out of this milk and eventually killed the Buffalo for food. Now the Squirrel must devise a clever way of reclaiming his prize.

Many years ago, the Buffalo and the Squirrel were very good friends. They gathered food and often farmed together. But the Squirrel was cunning and often tricked the Buffalo into doing things she wouldn't normally do.

It was an unusually scanty harvest season and the Squirrel did not have enough nuts. The Buffalo, on the other hand, had little trouble rustling up a few grasses here and there.

One day the two friends were out hunting and trying to gather some food. It was a particularly hot day and they had little luck. The Squirrel needed food for the night and he was also thirsty. He had always wanted the Buffalo's milk, but he knew that she would never let him have it. They had been gone all day and the more he looked at the Buffalo's udder, the thirstier he became. The Squirrel couldn't wait to sink his mouth into the Buffalo's udder, which was by now quite heavy with milk. So he said to the Buffalo:

"I bet you I can run faster than you."

"With those stunted legs?" the Buffalo asked sarcastically. "I can outrun you even with my eyes closed."

"Okay," said the Squirrel. "You can prove it by taking up my challenge. You see those two big trees? Let's see who can get to the second tree first. We shall run as fast as we can *through* the first tree and continue to the second one. Whoever gets to the second tree first wins."

"That's easy," said the Buffalo. "I will be there to welcome you."

Then the Buffalo pawed the ground and called the race with the wave of her front right leg. By the time she had brought her leg back to the ground, the Squirrel was already gone. He was much faster than the Buffalo. He ran straight to the first tree and immediately ran around it in a flash, then to the second tree. The Buffalo couldn't believe her eyes. She thought the Squirrel actually ran through the tree. So, when she finally lumbered to the first tree, she rammed into it with her horns. The force was so strong that her horns lodged deep into the trunk of the tree and shook loose many of its fruits. She bellowed and tried as hard as she could, but could not dislodge her horns from the tree.

Then the Squirrel came back to the Buffalo.

"I told you," said the Squirrel. "I am much faster than you."

"Yes," agreed the Buffalo. "You won. Help me get my horns out of this tree."

The Squirrel tried and said that he couldn't. (If he did, it would thwart his plan.) So he cleared a small spot on the ground and lay back down to rest, waiting for the Buffalo to become hungry.

The aroma of the fruits scattered all over the ground was irresistible for the Buffalo. She sniffed but could not reach anyone of them. When the Squirrel couldn't hold his own hunger any longer, he went to milk the Buffalo. But before he could touch her udder, the Buffalo kicked him up into the tree. When he recovered, the Squirrel came down to try negotiation.

"There is no sense in you and I dying here of hunger. I know that you cannot wait to sink your teeth into these green grasses and wash them down with these succulent fruits," said the Squirrel as he waved the fruits across the Buffalo's nose. "I can neither eat the grass nor the fruits. I wish they were nuts. But you do have milk I can drink, and I can get you these foods to eat. The way I see it, you need me more than I need you. I can just leave you here and go home. Bye!"

As he started to leave, the Squirrel kicked the fruits that were close to the Buffalo as far away as he could so that she could not reach them.

"You're not really going to leave me here alone, are you?" asked the Buffalo.

"Watch me!" said the Squirrel, as he again started to leave.

"Okay! Okay!" the Buffalo agreed. "Get me some grass and fruits to eat and you can have some of my milk."

The Squirrel went and cut some fresh grasses and picked some ripe succulent fruits for the Buffalo. While she ate the grasses and the fruits, the Squirrel drank some of her milk and collected a bucketful to take home. Then, he went home, telling the Buffalo he was going to get help.

When he got home, his wife prepared a very tasty porridge with the milk. The Squirrel and his family and their guest, Mrs. Hyena, ate very well that day.

"That was such a tasty meal," remarked Mrs. Hyena. "Where do you get such rich milk?"

"My husband," answered Mrs. Squirrel. "He is such a great hunter. He brings home all kinds of food everyday. Today, he brought this rare Buffalo milk. Can you imagine how he managed to milk her? Some hunter, isn't he?"

After dinner, Mrs. Squirrel gave some of the porridge to Mrs. Hyena to take home to her family. When Mrs. Hyena got home, she gave her husband the porridge. He loved it so much he wanted to know where she got it, but his wife teased him.

"Other men hunt or farm all day," she said. "They come back with big game for their wives. Sometime they come home with rich milk, even a Buffalo's, to make porridge soup. But you lay around the house doing nothing. Mrs. Squirrel gave it to me. Her husband got it from his farm."

The Hyena could not contain himself. Before the first cock crowed the next day, he was at the Squirrel's house. He banged at the door and the Squirrel opened it.

"What are you doing here?" asked the sleepy Squirrel.

"Doesn't it bother you that we are neighbors and we never do anything together?" answered the Hyena.

"Not really," replied the Squirrel, eager to close the door.

"Wait!" pleaded the Hyena. "How about you and I go hunting today? Just like the good neighbors that we are?"

The Squirrel tried all he could to dissuade the Hyena. He told him the idea had no merit: Hyenas only hunted in packs of their own kind. But the Hyena persisted and the Squirrel had no choice but to agree to go hunting with him.

The Squirrel's hunt with the Hyena was as fruitless as his hunt with the Buffalo. But the Squirrel knew the Hyena very well and wanted to keep his source of milk away from him. But, he was afraid that if he stayed away much longer, the Buffalo might die of dehydration and starvation. So, he led the Hyena to the Buffalo just to check her out.

"How are you doing?" the Squirrel asked the Buffalo. "I have come with some help."

"Then get to work and free me from this," said the Buffalo.

It has been a little over a day and the Buffalo had not been milked. Once the Hyena saw her udder heavy with milk, he began to salivate. No sooner had the Squirrel tried to extricate the Buffalo from the tree than the Hyena grabbed and bound him. The Buffalo, sensing what was next, began to paw the ground and bellow. Then the Hyena started to milk her as she bellowed some more and kicked at him.

"That will not work," said the Squirrel. "Give her some fresh grasses and fruits to calm her down and you may have your full of milk."

Immediately, the Hyena cut some fresh grasses and picked some fruits for the Buffalo. As she ate, the Hyena gorged his stomach with her milk and filled his bucket.

"Is it fair that I should lead you to food only to be bound here to die like a criminal?" asked the Squirrel.

"No." replied the Hyena. "But life is not fair, is it?"

"You're right. But can you at least untie me and allow me to carry your bucket for you? It is not right for a great hunter like you to carry your own food."

The Hyena thought about the Squirrel's suggestion. The more he thought about it, the more the Squirrel stroked his ego.

"Imagine," continued the Squirrel, "what a reputation you'll have when everybody hears how you stealthily and single-handedly wrestled down the Buffalo to milk her."

"Yeah?" asked the Hyena.

"But you need an eyewitness," said the Squirrel.

That did it. The Hyena untied him.

"Here," he said and handed the Squirrel his bucket of milk. "Maybe I'll let you have some after all."

When the two started for home, the Squirrel took his knife and pierced a small hole in the Hyena's bucket. Then he put the bucket over his own and carried them, slowly draining the contents into his own bucket as they walked. By the time they reached home all the contents of the Hyena's bucket had emptied into the Squirrel's bucket.

When it came time for them to go to their respective homes, the Squirrel carefully lifted the Hyena's bucket, which was now empty of milk but filled with foamy residue, and handed it to him.

"You know," he said to the Hyena. "Fresh milk is like a young maiden: it must be treated with care. Otherwise, it will make faces, fume, and fret. So, make sure that no one greets you when you get home, lest the milk turns into foam."

The Hyena was excited. He took the bucket from the Squirrel and went home full of himself. When he got home, his wife ran out and immediately greeted him.

"Welcome my husband. I can see you brought home some milk."

"No! No!" said the Hyena. "You shouldn't have greeted me. Now you have made the milk turn into foam."

As he complained and blamed his wife, he emptied the bucket. But all that came out was foam. He was very angry with her and they argued all night. When they got tired of fighting, he lay down and thought for a while. Then an idea came to him. He must go back and kill the Buffalo. So at dawn, he went back and did just that. He cut the Buffalo up, brought her meat home, and smoked it over his fireplace.

When the Squirrel went back later in the day for more milk, he found the Buffalo had disappeared. All that was left of her was blood. He knew right away that it was the Hyena who killed her.

As the Squirrel walked home angry, hungry, and dejected, he concentrated long enough to draw up an elaborate plan to reclaim his loot from the Hyena. When he got home later that night, he went to the Hyena's home and lay down at the gate, motionless.

When the Hyena's son went to lock up the gate for the night, he saw a form lying at the gate. Afraid, he ran back to his father saying, "There is someone at the gate. He wouldn't say a word."

His father was very disappointed in him and called his son names. Then, he sent his wife. When she came to the gate and could not get any response from the form, she too was afraid and walked back briskly back to the house.

"Your son was right," she said. "There is something at the gate and it will not move or say a word."

"Then fetch my spear," he commanded. "Whatever it is will have to answer to me."

Grabbing his spear, the Hyena marched to the gate to confront the something. He pushed it with his spear and found out it was the Squirrel. But the Squirrel played dead.

"This must be my lucky day," said the Hyena. "This one I didn't even have to lift a finger to kill." Then he picked up the Squirrel and carried him into his house. He put him in the fireplace where the Buffalo meat was smoking.

As the Hyena and his family slept, they could hear the glowing ember speaking in tongues as the fat from the Buffalo meat dripped into it. They actually did not get much sleep that night. But, the few moments they slept was enough for the Squirrel to haul all the meat out of their house and to his own.

After a restless night and a protracted sleep filled with dreams of Buffalo meat gluttony, the Hyenas woke up to an empty fireplace. The Hyena was very angry. But, with the Squirrel also gone, he guessed that it must have been him who stole his meat. So late that night, he went to the Squirrel's house and lay at the gate.

When the Squirrel's son went to lock their gate later that night, he found the Hyena lying there. He was very much afraid and ran back to his father.

"There is...there is a gigantic monster at the gate," he stammered and shivered with terror. "It wouldn't say a word. It...it looked like..."

"Get a hold of yourself," said the Squirrel. "What is it?"

The Squirrel knew it was the Hyena. So he turned to his wife and shouted loud enough for the Hyena to hear him, "Fetch my magic machete. You know—the one that cuts on its own. Open the door and throw it out to cut whatever is out there to pieces."

When the Hyena heard that, he was much frightened. He quickly got up and ran back home.

So you see, it is best for a cunning person to deal with people of his own kind, so that when he dies they'll know how best to bury him.

Côte d'Ivoire

COUNTRY

Formal Name: République de Côte d'Ivoire (formerly Ivory Coast)
Short Form: Côte d'Ivoire
Term for Citizens: Ivoirian
Capital: Yamoussoukro, since 1983 (formerly Abidjan, which remains the administrative center)
Independence: August 7, 1960 (from France)

GEOGRAPHY

Size: 124,503 square miles (322,460 km^2)
Boundaries: Bordered to the north by Mali and Burkina Faso, east by Ghana, south by the Atlantic Ocean, west by Liberia, and northwest by Guinea

SOCIETY

Population: 15.8 million
Ethnic Groups: There are more than 60 ethnic groups. The major groups are Baoule (22%), Senoufou (15%), Bete (18%), Agni, Mande groups, and non-Ivoirian Africans.
Languages: There are at least as many languages as there are ethnic groups with variants of Mande-Kan spoken throughout the country. The official language is French.
Religion: 60% Islam; 22% Christianity; 18% local religions

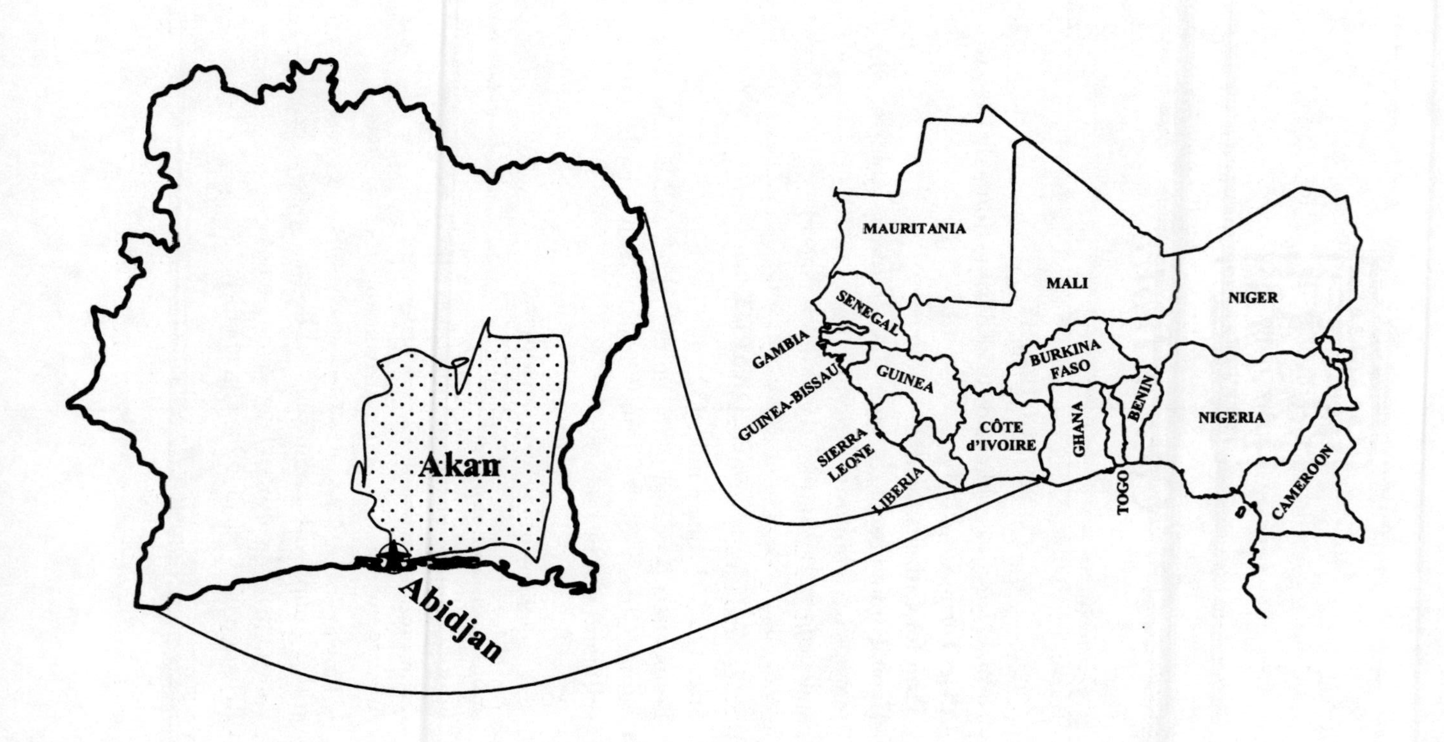

Akan
Abidjan
MAURITANIA
MALI
NIGER
SENEGAL
GAMBIA
GUINEA-BISSAU
GUINEA
BURKINA FASO
SIERRA LEONE
LIBERIA
CÔTE d'IVOIRE
GHANA
TOGO
BENIN
NIGERIA
CAMEROON

Foriwa's Beads

The Akans use this story to illustrate the importance of children obeying their parents. After being displaced from their homes by war, the animals were on the prowl. One by one, they came across a young girl who mocked them. Would the fortress her parents built for her be strong enough to protect her from an animal's anger?

Many, many years ago war broke out between two villages. In the one village lived a man with his wife and daughter. Because the girl was their only child, they were very protective of her. So when the war broke out, they built a thick thatched mud house for her in a safe part of the village and put her in it. They provided her with everything she could ever want while her father went to war and her mother went to the farms. They locked her up in the house, asked her to secure the inside locks, and left. They didn't want her to ever leave her hiding place. They instructed her never to say a word or open the door for anyone else. When her mother brought her more food, she sang to her saying:

Foriwa, my daughter,
It's your mother,
Let me in,
It's time to eat.

Everyday, Foriwa's mother brought her more food and sang the same song. Foriwa would recognize her voice and open the door.

Foriwa, my daughter,
It's your mother,
Let me in,
It's time to eat.

The war lasted for a very long time and Foriwa was becoming impatient with her confinement. The forest animals were by now displaced from their homes in the forests and they prowled even the human neighborhoods for food. They killed domestic animals and even any humans they could find.

One day, the Tortoise searched for food around Foriwa's refuge. *Yaakiin*! *Yaakiin*! The dry leaves rattled under the Tortoise's legs.

Foriwa was startled by the noise. Then she regained her composure and began to sing:

Which animal goes there,
By Foriwa's backyard?
Sala!
Which animal goes there,
By Foriwa's backyard?
Sala!

This must have been a very popular song in the village, because as soon as the Tortoise heard it he responded in kind:

My child it is the Tortoise,
Sala!
My child, it is the Tortoise.
Sala!

When it occurred to the Tortoise that the child must have been put in such a secluded place to protect her from the war, he added:

But be quiet, my child,
Sala!
There is danger all over,
Sala!
Lest you be trampled to death,
Sala!

When Foriwa recognized it was the Tortoise she laughed out loud saying:

I dare you,
Sala!
Vainglorious boaster,
Sala!
With your stunted hands?
Sala!

The Tortoise didn't say a word. He just quietly nibbled on his food and slowly walked away. Before long, the Deer walked by.

Which animal goes there,
By Foriwa's backyard?
Sala!
Which animal goes there,
By Foriwa's backyard?
Sala!

The Deer replied to her as the Tortoise had.

My child it is the Deer,
Sala!
My child, it is the Deer.
Sala!
But be quiet, my child,
Sala!
There is danger all over,
Sala!
Lest you be trampled to death,
Sala!

And just as she had responded to the Tortoise, so Foriwa laughed at the Deer, saying:

I dare you,
Sala!
Vainglorious boaster,
Sala!
You don't even have any horns or sharp teeth,
Sala!

The Deer didn't say a word. He just quietly grazed and slowly walked away. And so it continued when the Goat walked by, the Giraffe, the Python, the Elephant, and then the Lion. The *Lion*!

All the animals just warned Foriwa of the danger and went about their way. But not the Lion. He was furious. "Here I am warning this little girl about the danger," he said to himself, "and what do I get! A dare!"

"Roar! Roar! Roar!" said the Lion, as he bared his teeth and claws. He stood on his hind legs and pounced on the house. He clawed at it furiously with all his might and anger. As he clawed, pieces of the dried mud began to flake off the house. He grabbed some of the fallen pieces and tossed them behind his back. Soon he was so deep into the mud house that all you could see was his tail as piles of mud flew about the forests. He finally got to the girl, grabbed her by the neck and killed her.

The Lion was so hungry that he wasted no time devouring the little girl. There was nothing left of her but the beads she wore on her neck. Meanwhile, a Bird had watched the whole episode from the safety of her perch on a tall tree. As soon as the Lion left, the Bird dove in, picked up the beads, and took them to Foriwa's mother.

"You don't tell a deaf that war is raging," the Bird said as she approached Foriwa's mother.

"She who does not hear will soon hear," she concluded as she dropped the beads at Foriwa's mother, who was busy in her farm.

As soon as she recognized the beads, Foriwa's mother imagined the worst. She ran to her daughter's fortress and broke down. She cried so much that she ran out of tears in her eyes. "Indeed," she cried. "She who does not hear will soon hear."

The Gambia

COUNTRY

Formal Name: Republic of the Gambia
Short Form: The Gambia
Term for Citizens: Gambian
Capital: Banjul
Independence: February 18, 1965 (from United Kingdom)

GEOGRAPHY

Size: 4,127 square miles (11,300 km^2), 11% of which is water
Boundaries: Bordered on all sides by Senegal, except for about 48 miles (78 km) of coastal border to the northwest

SOCIETY

Population: 1.3 million
Ethnic Groups: 42% Mandinka, 18% Fula, 16% Wolof. The rest of the population is comprised of the Joles and Serahuli, among others.
Languages: Mandinka, Wolof, and Fula are the main local languages. The official and commercial language is English.
Religion: 90% Islam; 8–9% Christianity; 1–2% local religions

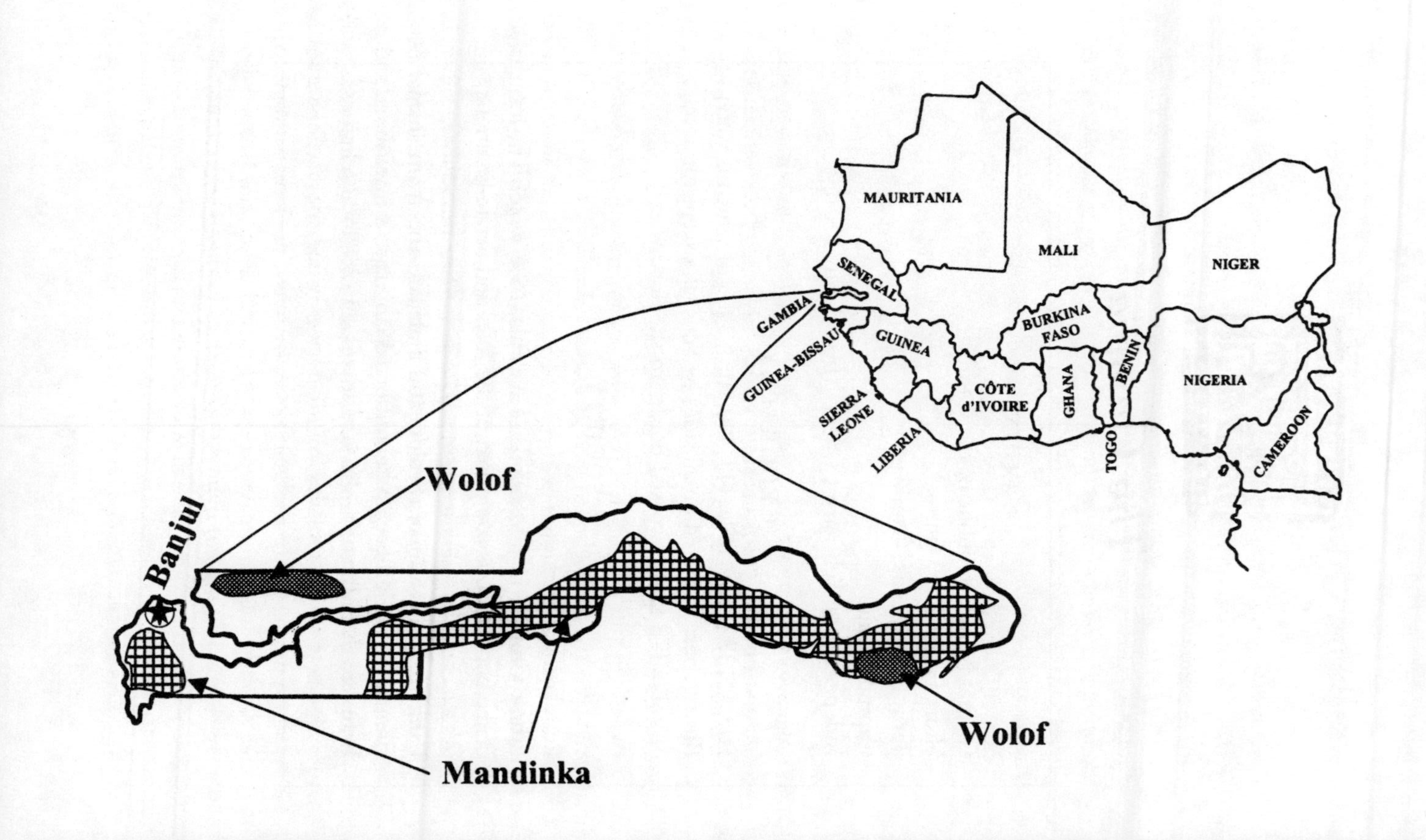
MAURITANIA
MALI
NIGER
SENEGAL
GAMBIA
GUINEA-BISSAU
GUINEA
BURKINA FASO
SIERRA LEONE
LIBERIA
CÔTE d'IVOIRE
GHANA
TOGO
BENIN
NIGERIA
CAMEROON
Banjul
Wolof
Wolof
Mandinka

Fereyel and Debbo Engal the Witch

According to the Fulanis, who live among the Mandikas, there once lived a witch named Debbo Engal, who lived in a distant village with her ten daughters, the most beautiful girls anyone had ever seen. The men of the world wanted nothing more than to marry Debbo Engal's daughters. But, like picking a rose that blooms in a thorny wood, winning the hand of any of these girls was the most difficult of tasks. No man who went to try ever came back to talk about it. Then came the diminutive Fereyel with his ten brothers. Fereyel was no ordinary man. But could he do the impossible and succeed where all others had failed?

There once lived a witch named Debbo Engal. She had ten most beautiful daughters with whom she lived in a big hut in a village far away from the rest of the villages. The beauty of her daughters was known everywhere. Every man of marrying age longed to have one as his wife. Once in a while, young men who could afford the long journey to Debbo Engal's village went to seek the hand in marriage of one of the girls. Strangely, none ever came back. So it was never known whether they married the girls in their village and took up residence there. Or, whether they had ever even made it to the girls' house. But this didn't deter any eager suitors: since the girls were as beautiful as the morning sun, every man had to try to win their love.

Very far away from Debbo Engal's village was a woman with ten sons. When they became of age, they too wanted to claim Debbo Engal's daughters for their wives. The first of the boys thought that it was the will of Allah that they be married to the girls. Said he, "This marriage has been ordained by Allah. There are ten of us, and there are ten of them, so the families don't need to be split."

The rest of his brothers couldn't have agreed more. Then and there, the men made up their minds to make the long journey to Debbo Engal and her daughters. Their mother was not happy with their plan. She begged them to take up wives from the neighboring villages, but they refused and she couldn't change their minds.

"My children," she said, "I am afraid for you. No one that ever went to that village ever came back. That compound is evil."

"Don't worry mother. We will be fine," they assured her.

"Maybe one or two of you can go. When you come back, the rest of you can go and get your own wives."

"No! We must all go at the same time. We believe Debbo Engal will want to have her daughters married into the same family and to handsome men like us."

The young men dismissed their mother's fears. They laughed and said she was a woman and so couldn't understand a man's desires. "How can ten maidens be a match for ten young men like us?" they asked their mother. Then they packed their luggage ready for their trip.

Very early the next morning, before the first cock crowed, they bid their mother farewell and took off for the village of Debbo Engal and her daughters.

The path to Debbo Engal's village was very long and narrow. The young men, with the oldest leading, sang along the way. They were very happy and full of anticipation.

No sooner did the boys leave, even before the sun woke up, than their mother gave birth to her eleventh son. But one could hardly call him a son. He was so small that his mother could hardly see him. While his mother looked around in confusion for the baby, he jumped up and said:

"I am here mother! Where are my big brothers?"

The poor woman was dumbfounded. She was aghast. Somehow, she found her tongue, and said, "They have gone to see Debbo Engal and her daughters."

She opened her mouth again but no more words came out of it.

"I must go and save them," said the diminutive boy. "They are in great danger."

Immediately, he ran off to catch up with his brothers.

"That wicked witch," he mumbled to himself. "All she does is prey on young men. She lays out a welcome mat for them, serves them choice foods and wines, and gets them drunk. While they revel with her daughters, they forget where they were and night falls on them. 'Oh! It is night,' she says. 'Why don't you stay? It is much too dangerous for you to walk now. Stay in the comfort of my home and my daughters. Tomorrow morning you may commence your trip.'

"Young men! They quickly agree, of course. Then, when they fall asleep, the wicked witch pulls her dagger out of its sheath. She sharpens it and creeps into the men's hut and kills them all. Witches! Why do they have to live on human flesh and blood anyway? But not my brothers'. I must..."

As he looked ahead of him, he caught sight of his brothers. He called out to them to wait for him. The young men were surprised that anyone could catch up with them. They looked around for the owner of the voice, but couldn't see anyone. They were about to ignore the voice when the diminutive boy tugged on the last of the ten brother's leg.

"I am here," said the boy.

When they saw the tiny boy, they were shocked. They didn't know what to make of him. A man, or what? He looked like one, but then too small to be one. "Who or what are you?" the boys asked.

"I am Fereyel, your brother," said the tiny boy.

"That shows that you are an impostor," said one of the boys, "for our mother bore only ten of us. Please go away and leave us alone. We have yet a long distance to cover."

"That's why I've come," said Fereyel. "The journey you make is dangerous and I have come to save you from the danger."

The boys were both amused and angered by the tiny boy's bother and audacity. The more they tried to dismiss him, the more he persisted. So they beat him up and left him for dead. Then, they continued on their way to Debbo Engal and her daughters.

After they had covered much ground and the sun had just moved from over their heads, one of the brothers found a beautiful piece of cloth on their path. He picked it up and announced, "Rejoice, my brothers, for this will be a good journey indeed. Look!" he showed them the piece of cloth. "It must have been left here on purpose by Debbo Engal's daughters to lead us to them." Then he flung it over his shoulders. But, before they had walked much farther, he noticed that his shoulders were getting heavier from the piece of cloth. So he begged his brothers to help him carry it.

"Help you carry a piece of cloth?" one of the brothers asked him. "Mother was right. You are the girl she never had."

The brothers laughed over that remark as the one took the piece of cloth from him. But before they had walked much farther, he too began to complain of the weight of the piece of cloth. So, he handed it over to the next brother. In turn, he too was burdened by the weight. They soon passed on the cloth until the tenth brother couldn't carry it anymore. As he took down the cloth, a voice came out of it saying:

"Ha! Ha! Ha! It is me, Fereyel, your brother." Then he jumped out of the cloth. "I was inside the cloth and you carried me all this while. No wonder the cloth was heavy."

The ten brothers were filled with rage. They grabbed Fereyel and beat him to a pulp. "That should teach him a lesson he will not soon forget," said one of the boys. Again they left him for dead and continued on their journey.

Soon one of the brothers stepped on something hard. He looked down and found a piece of silver ring. "It must be my lucky day," he said as he picked up the ring. "Someone must have lost it. Now it is mine." With that, he slipped the ring onto his finger and they continued on their journey.

Not long after, the brother noticed that the ring was weighing down his finger. His finger had become so heavy that he couldn't hold it up anymore. So he passed it on to his brothers. As they had done with the piece of cloth, so they did with the ring, passing it from one brother to another until it was the oldest brother's turn. When he couldn't support the weight of the ring anymore, Fereyel jumped out of it.

"You should have known it was me," said Fereyel. "I was inside the ring."

The brothers were determined to beat Fereyel again and kill him for sure when the eldest one stopped them. "This little thing has taken up much of our time. Let him come along, since he is so determined. Maybe we won't have to bother with him anymore."

The brothers continued on their journey. They walked faster than before, determined to make up for lost time. Fereyel tagged along behind them unnoticed. Soon they reached Debbo Engal's village. When they got to her house, the witch came to welcome them, with her daughters right behind her.

The men were dumbfounded by the girls' beauty. They had never seen beauty such as theirs. They had never believed such beautiful girls lived. They remembered stories their mother told them about beautiful maidens who lived in water, *mammy water*, or who lived in distant places where no one ever went. According to their mother, such a maiden was so beautiful that if a real man passed her on the road without looking back, it was only because he was suffering from whiplash. And, if a man met such a beauty in the evening, he must not accost her for she could be a ghost. He must wait for her to pass by; then, watching from the corners of his eyes to make sure she was not looking, he must bend over to look at her through the arch of his legs to be sure that her heels touched the ground and made footprints. If her heels did not touch the ground, he ran as fast as his legs could carry him, for she was certainly a ghost. So, the boys thought that such beautiful maidens were only figments of the imagination. Yet, here they were, standing face to face with ten of them. They thought they must have died and gone to heaven.

"Welcome, my sons," said Debbo Engal, startling the enthralled boys. "Now that you have seen my daughters, I'd like for you to get to know them. They will make sure that you enjoy your stay with us."

With that Debbo Engal introduced her daughters to the young men and invited them to her guest hut. But she did not see Fereyel, who was lurking behind his oldest brother's foot. In her hut, she wined and dined the men, serving her choicest wines and foods. Finally she noticed Fereyel. She was amused by his size.

"You," she said to him. "Come with me to my hut. You are a darling aren't you? I will make sure that you are very comfortable."

As Debbo Engal planned, night fell upon the young men as they reveled with her daughters. It didn't take much effort for her to persuade them to stay the night. The boys were only too glad to oblige her. She served them more food and wine, and everyone danced some more and drank into the night.

"All good things must come to an end," Debbo Engal announced as she noticed that the twenty young people were tired and beginning to fall asleep on each other. She made their beds, covered the men with white robes and her daughters with blue robes, and bid them goodnight. Then she went into her hut and prepared a nice place for Fereyel.

"Goodnight my little man," she said to him.

"Goodnight my big woman," replied Fereyel. "Tell me one thing, though. How do you sleep?"

"When I am asleep," said she, "you will here me snoring like this:

Hu! Hu! Hu! Hu!
Until daybreak shall I wake!
Hu! Hu! Hu! Hu!
Until daybreak shall I wake!

What about you?"

"When I sleep," lied Fereyel, "I snore like a wild boar, 'Hmmmm! Hmmmm! Hmmmm!'"

"Sleep tight then, my little man," Debbo Engal told him and went to bed.

But Fereyel did not sleep. He just lay as still as he could and pretended to sleep and snore—"Hmmmm! Hmmmm! Hmmmm!"

When Debbo Engal heard him snoring just like he had said, she quietly got out of bed, tiptoed to the corner of the room where her dagger was and slowly pulled it out of its sheath. Directly Fereyel woke up.

"What are you doing?" he asked her.

She quickly replaced the dagger and nervously replied, "Nothing! I am sorry I woke you up, my little man. Here! Let me fluff your pillow."

After she fluffed his pillow, she told him to go back to sleep and she lay down on her bed. Much later, Fereyel began his snoring again. Directly, Debbo Engal got up again and went to get her dagger. Fereyel woke up again and asked:

"What are you doing?"

Again Debbo Engal said she was doing nothing. She fluffed his pillow and begged him to go back to sleep.

Much later, well into the wee hours of the morning, all was quiet. Not even the cricket chirped. Then, as Fereyel lay anxiously thinking about their journey, he was interrupted by the witch's snore:

Hu! Hu! Hu! Hu!
Until daybreak shall I wake!
Hu! Hu! Hu! Hu!
Until daybreak shall I wake!"

On hearing this, Fereyel quietly got out of his bed and tiptoed into the hut where his brothers and the beautiful girls slept. He carefully removed the white robes that covered his brothers and put them over the girls, took the blue robes that covered the girls and put them over his brothers and switched their positions. Then quietly, he tiptoed back to the hut where he and Debbo Engal slept. Gently, he slipped back into the bed and covered himself up. Then he nudged the witch and pretended to snore again: "Hmmmm! Hmmmm! Hmmmm!"

When Debbo Engal heard him snoring, she again quietly tiptoed to the corner of the room where she kept her dagger. She gently drew it from its sheath. She sharpened it quietly and Fereyel didn't wake up. With the dagger at the ready, she crept stealthily to where the young men and women slept. She sought out the sleeping forms wrapped in the white robes and killed them with the skill of a master butcher. Happy with her accomplishment, she went back to her hut and lay down.

Long after Debbo Engal lay down, she began her snore again and Fereyel knew she had fallen into a deep sleep. Immediately, Fereyel quietly slipped out of the hut and went to awaken his brothers. He quickly explained what had happened and showed them the dead young girls. They picked up their things and ran for home.

Before they had gone far through the forest, Debbo Engal woke up. Finding that Fereyel was no longer there, she rushed to where the young men and the maidens slept and found that she had mistakenly murdered her own daughters. Outraged by what she saw and that the boys had gotten away, she enchanted the wind. She flew on it and chased after the men.

Fereyel saw the witch in the wind. He warned his brothers, but they were at a loss about what to do. But not Fereyel. He immediately picked up an egg from the bushes and broke it between them and the wind. Directly, a wide river came between them and the wind so that the witch could not cross. Debbo Engal was furious. She whipped out a magic calabash from nowhere and began to empty the river. Soon the fast flowing river was drained dry and Debbo Engal was able to chase after the brothers again.

As she came again, Fereyel saw her and warned his brothers. He immediately picked up a rock and flung it in her path. Just then, a very high mountain blocked the road. More furious than ever, Debbo Engal pulled out a magic ax and began to chop down the mountain. But by the time she was done, the brothers had crossed the boundary between the living and the witches. They saw their house and ran inside.

The next day, it was the brothers' turn to gather wood for the village. They were still afraid from their encounter with Debbo Engal. But it was a duty they must perform. So they went into the bush scared and always watching their backs. Debbo Engal saw them and turned herself into a log. As they collected their wood, Fereyel noticed the unusual log and knew that it was Debbo Engal. He immediately warned his brothers and they took off and ran for their home again, and got back before the witch could change back to catch them.

But Debbo Engal was not about to give up. She changed herself into different objects so that the villagers couldn't recognize her. Several days later, the brothers were sent to gather some plums from the bushes. All of them had forgotten about the witch, but not Fereyel. While the others searched for plums, he searched for plums and Debbo Engal. When they came to their favorite plum grove, they found that most of the fruits had withered but for the bunch on one tree. The leaves on the tree were especially dark green and the fruits juicy and inviting. The brothers were excited at their luck. They ran to pick the plums when Fereyel realized it was one of Debbo Engal's tricks and warned them. They escaped before she could catch up with them.

When the boys were up and about the next morning, they saw a donkey grazing in the fields. The boys got on it and wrapped their legs around it. "Ai! Ai! Ai!" they urged the donkey. But it wouldn't go and just looked at Fereyel. "Get on," his brothers urged him.

"But there isn't enough room for me," he explained, "as small as I am."

Directly, the donkey grew longer to make room for him.

"Not on your life," protested Fereyel. "Me! Climb a donkey that hears me and grows in length?"

Then the donkey shrank back to its original length. Fereyel knew that it was Debbo Engal and started laughing at her. "You boys have been tricked again. It is Debbo Engal. How can a donkey carry ten men at once and hear what men say?"

As the brothers fell and jumped off the donkey and ran, it changed back to Debbo Engal and chased after them.

"Everything I've tried has been foiled, all because of the diminutive one," she thought. "I must find a way to get rid of him first. Then, I can have the rest of them in the palm of my hand."

Long after the sun woke up the next day, a very beautiful young maiden accosted Fereyel. Her beauty was beyond anything he had seen before. "I have come to visit with you," the young maiden told him. Fereyel was excited. He took the young maiden to his home and entertained her. Fereyel's mother cooked delicious food for them and gave them some choice wines. When dusk fell, she said that she must go to her parents.

"Farewell then," said Fereyel. "I hope to see you again soon."

"Won't you escort me to my path for home?" she asked. "Escorting a friend is a mark of friendship and a matter of courtesy, you know. It is not that the friend cannot find her way."

"Where are my manners?" Fereyel apologized, hitting his forehead with the heel of the palm of his right hand.

Fereyel's mother bid the young maiden farewell as she and Fereyel stepped out into the night. There was a half moon and its weak rays faintly lit the night. The young maiden led the way and Fereyel followed her, but he could hardly see beyond two to three man-lengths in front of him. Suddenly the girl increased her steps and hid behind a very big tree trunk. Before Fereyel could say a word, she reappeared, and now as a huge and vicious looking python. She charged Fereyel.

"I knew it was you, Debbo Engal," he said. "You cannot divine for a diviner you know."

With those words, Fereyel immediately changed into an inferno. The python could not uncoil her heavy and long self in time to turn away from the fire. Before she could react to the fire, she was engulfed.

The python was burned to ashes in the inferno. Then Fereyel returned to the village to tell his brothers and the villagers what had happened. There was a great merriment in the village—eating and dancing and everybody rejoicing that Debbo Engal, the wicked witch, had been destroyed.

The Horse with the Golden Dung

Ahmadu was a ne'er-do-well who preyed on his fellow humans for whatever they had. Now, no one but the Chief in this Mandinka village had much left. Since everyone knew that Ahmadu was never up to any good, he had to resort to trickery to get his equally greedy Chief to part with his wealth. When the Chief discovered that he had been tricked and sought to take his revenge, Ahmadu upped the ante. Now, in order to save himself, he must trick the Chief into abdicating his throne.

When it came to stealing and lying, Ahmadu was the master. He stole anything he could get his hands on. He had become so notorious in the village that nobody dared leave their possessions unguarded. So after a while, Ahmadu became poor. So much so that he barely had enough to eat. Since he could no longer scam what he needed from the villagers, he thought the Chief would be his best ticket to the road to riches.

Ahmadu had only one thing left in this world, his horse. No! Two things, if you count his wife.

"My plan for us to become rich again," he told his wife one night, "must be with you and the horse. You two are all I have and you are priceless to me, especially now. For my plan to work though, I will need to borrow your gold necklace and give it to my horse."

The next day, Ahmadu unstrung his wife's gold pieces from its lace. He buried one of them in his horse's food. Later when the horse passed its dung, the gold glittered in it. Then he fed the horse another gold piece and took it and the golden dung to the Chief.

"The Chief shall live forever," said he, as he genuflected.

"Get up my son," replied the Chief. "What brings you here, Ahmadu?"

"I have a very important news. One that will make you richer than all the chiefs of ancient Ghana and Mali combined."

"Why don't you keep that news to yourself and become rich?" asked the Chief.

"Because riches this great should belong only to a Chief. With all due respect, your Royal Highness, if I became that rich, I am sure that your Highness would want to take it from me. So I thought I'd give it to you voluntarily."

"You are a wise man, Ahmadu. What is this news?"

Then Ahmadu showed his horse and its golden dung to the Chief. The sight of a horse that passed golden dung amazed the Chief. Before he could recover from the shock, the horse passed another dung. Aha! A gold nugget glittered in it.

"What do you want for the horse?" asked the Chief. "Be fair, for as you have said, I could take it from you."

"I am always fair, your Highness. And, as your humble and honorable servant, all I ask for is one hundred gold nuggets and one hundred pieces of silver." Then he clasped his two hands to his chest in respect and waited for the Chief to beat down his price.

"Rise, my child. One hundred pieces of gold and one hundred pieces of silver you shall get." With that, he ordered his servants to settle with Ahmadu.

Ahmadu was beside himself and could not believe how forthcoming the Chief was. "To be sure that no one steals the gold," he said, "you must quarantine the horse and put some of your most trusted men to stand guard over it for four moons. After that, you must gather some of your workers to separate the gold from the dung, under the watchful eyes of the guards."

Four moons later, the stable where they had put the horse was filled with dung. The workers beat the dung to harvest the gold. But there was nothing.

The Chief was enraged. He sent his messengers to summon Ahmadu. "Bring that rogue to me alive, and if he resists, kill him and bring me his corpse that I may throw his carcass to the vultures."

When Ahmadu got the news he was ready, for he had been expecting to be summoned by the Chief. Then he told his wife that she must go with him.

"Here is the plan," he told her. "When we get to the Chief, you must argue and contradict everything I say. We will get into a fight and I will take it from there."

Ahmadu took a gold piece and bought a rooster that was full of life. He killed the rooster and poured its blood into a snake leather pouch and tied it around his wife's neck. Then, they set off to answer the Chief.

"The Chief shall live forever," greeted Ahmadu, as he prostrated in obeisance. "You called for me, your Royal Highness?"

"You told me that your horse passed gold in its dung. I have had it for four moons and haven't got any gold."

"Not only did I tell you," Ahmadu said emphatically, "I *showed* you."

"He tricked you, your highness," his wife said. "There was no gold."

"Shut up, you liar," shouted Ahmadu.

"You are the liar," his wife said.

Ahmadu pretended to be really angry and tackled his wife to the ground. He drew his switchblade and cut the snake leather pouch around her neck, spilling its bloody contents all over the floor.

"You killed your wife, Ahmadu!" exclaimed the Chief.

"You summoned me? Tell me why. Quickly too, so that I may restore the life in her."

"You just committed a capital offense," said the panic-stricken Chief, "and you want to know why I summoned you? Forget about why I summoned you. You've killed your wife."

Immediately, Ahmadu requested a calabash of water. He took it and muttered some words. Then he soaked his cow-tail switch in the water. He lashed seven times in the air with the cow-tail switch, making an eerie sound. He sprinkled some of the water on his wife and commanded her.

"Lacerated throat be healed, I command you. Get up, woman."

Directly, there was no visible gash on his wife's throat and she got up and embraced her husband. On seeing this, the Chief imagined how powerful he could become with the cow-tail switch. He could bring his men who had fallen in battle back to life.

"I never thought I would live to see such great supernatural powers with my own eyes. You know, I think I prefer that cow-tail switch to the gold. What do you want for it?"

"Now, as I am sure you know," said Ahmadu, "the switch is worth a lot more than the horse. But for you, I am asking for only two hundred pieces of gold nuggets and two hundred pieces of silver."

The Chief paid his price and took the cow-tail switch.

One day, when the Chief and his advisers were eating and drinking, he wanted to show off his latest powers. So, when one of his wives came to replenish their food, he told them that he could kill her and bring her back to live. Then directly, he tackled her to the ground and slashed her throat.

"You have killed her," one of his advisers said, panicking.

"That's alright," said the Chief. "Let's eat and drink. I will raise her soon."

But his advisers were worried and urged him to raise her. Then the Chief soaked the cow-tail switch in a calabash of water. He chanted like Ahmadu did, and slashed the cow-tail switch in the air seven times and sprinkled the water on his wife's body. Then, like Ahmadu, he commanded the laceration and the woman. But she just lay there, dead. He sprinkled the water again, but still nothing happened.

"Go and get that rogue Ahmadu for me. This time he will die for sure."

They brought Ahmadu to the Chief. He ordered his most trusted and strongest men to tie him to a sinker with his hands behind his back, wrap him in a big leather bag, and throw him into the deepest part of the river to drown.

The men tied Ahmadu with the sinker and leather as they were directed. Then they took him to the river to drown him. They traveled from early morning to late morning, until they needed to answer the call of nature. Leaving the load by the roadside, they went into the bush. Before they could come out, a poor kola nut trader on a donkey rode by.

"Who could leave such a load by the roadside unattended?" the stranger asked.

"Please help me," said Ahmadu from inside the bag. "Help me! Help me! I don't want the gold. They said the Chief wants to give me his riches for saving his life. I don't want any riches. I want to remain poor!"

"You must be crazy," said the trader. "Everybody wants to be rich."

"Take the riches. It has always been trouble for me. You can untie me and take my place. I don't want it."

Quickly the trader untied Ahmadu and took his place. Then Ahmadu tied him up in the bag and rode off in the trader's donkey with the bag of kola nuts.

Soon the Chief's men returned and hauled off the cargo. "Finally, Ahmadu," one of them said. "Finally we have you in our hands. No longer will you trick people. Now you die. We will throw you in the river."

"No! No! No!" the trader shouted from the bag. "I am not him. It is I. Untie me!"

"Yes! Yes! Yes!" replied the men. "It is you! It is you!" Then they threw him into the river and returned to the Chief.

Before they had finished reporting to the Chief, there came Ahmadu on the donkey. He urged the donkey on and came before the Chief, who was speechless.

"Your great, great grandfathers send their greetings," Ahmadu said to the Chief. "They send their regards and this bag of kola nuts. It would be nice for you to go see them and show your respect and appreciation. Where they are, they have tons of gold and silver and would like you to come and fetch them yourself. You must go to where I have been to claim them. Meanwhile, I will stay here until you return."

On hearing this, the Chief summoned the villagers. He told them how Ahmadu had seen his forefathers and that he must go to see them too. While he was gone, Ahmadu was to assume his throne until he came back.

"You must serve him just as you have served me. He is your chief until I return."

Ahmadu gave instructions for the Chief to be tied, just as he had been tied. Then the men took him to the river and threw him into the deepest end.

Ahmadu ruled the village for four moons. And when the Chief never came back, Ahmadu remained the Chief of the village.

Ghana

COUNTRY

Formal Name: Republic of Ghana (formerly Gold Coast)
Short Form: Ghana
Term for Citizens: Ghanaian
Capital: Accra
Independence: March 6, 1957 (from United Kingdom); became a republic July 1, 1960

GEOGRAPHY

Size: 92,098 square miles (238,540 km^2)
Boundaries: Bordered to the north by Burkina Faso, east by Togo, south by the Atlantic Ocean, and west by Côte d'Ivoire

SOCIETY

Population: 18.9 million
Ethnic Groups: Akan (44%) mostly in the western part of the country; Ga and Ga-Adangbe in the coastal belt around Accra; Ewes (13%) in the Volta region
Languages: Ga, Twi, Ewe, Fante, Dangme, and Dagbani, among others. The official language is English.
Religion: 38% local religions; 30% Islam; 24% Christianity; 8% others

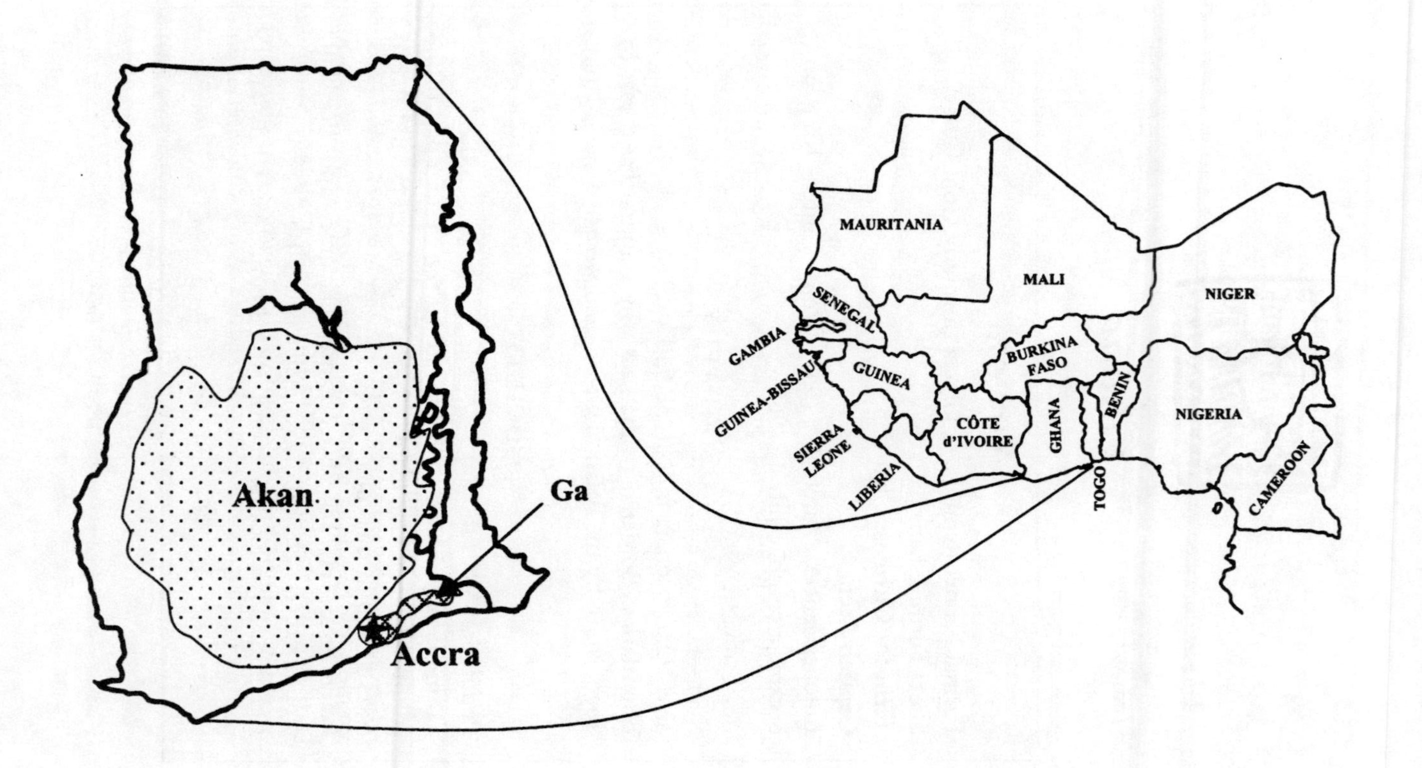
Akan
Ga
Accra
MAURITANIA
MALI
NIGER
SENEGAL
GAMBIA
GUINEA
GUINEA-BISSAU
BURKINA FASO
CÔTE d'IVOIRE
GHANA
BENIN
NIGERIA
SIERRA LEONE
LIBERIA
TOGO
CAMEROON

A Bride for a Grain of Corn

Nyame, the Great One, challenged all the creatures of an Akan village to a contest of wisdom. No one was brave enough to accept the challenge except the Spider, who was determined to prove he was the wisest of all Nyame's creatures—even after he learned that to prove it, he must pay a bride price with a grain of corn.

Long, long time ago, Nyame, the sky god, wanted to test the wisdom of his creatures. So, he issued a challenge to both the animals and the people. He told them that he would bestow wisdom and riches on the one who proved himself the wisest of all his creations. To make sure that the creatures were not out to waste his time, they had to pass a qualifying test.

The creatures found the challenge rather callous, for they were afraid of what the outcome would be if they failed. They gathered at the village square with everyone else and discussed the situation among themselves.

"How can we prove our wisdom to the Great One?" asked the Lion. "He already knows what is in our hearts."

"We cannot fake it, then?" asked the Hare.

"Maybe he wants only the humans for the contest," said one man. "That must be why he challenged our wisdom."

"The least he could've done is tell us what the test is," complained the Monkey, "that way we can decide whether or not we want to compete."

Thus the creatures and humans argued among themselves. Soon a great crowd formed before Nyame's court. But no one was willing to step forward and accept the challenge. They all withdrew to the periphery of the court. Just then the Spider approached the crowd.

"What's happening?" he asked the Elephant.

"You must be the only one who didn't hear the challenge," replied the Elephant.

"I heard the challenge," the Spider corrected him. "That's why I am asking why everyone is leaving. Who accepted it?"

"You must be crazy. No one in his right mind would dare accept the challenge."

The Spider brushed past the Elephant and the rest of the animals that were in his way and went to the center of the court.

"Oh! Great One!" said the Spider as he bowed. "I am the wisest of all your creations. And I have come here to accept your challenge to prove it."

The rest of the animals were dumbfounded. Some of them tried to shut him up but failed. And still others covered their eyes to keep from seeing what Nyame might do to the Spider. For his part, Nyame was surprised and amused that of all his creations it was such a funny-looking creature that accepted his challenge. A creature that he said was the result of a botched experiment. But he was impressed by the Spider's bravery, if not his wisdom.

Happy that he finally found a contestant for his challenge, Nyame called his counselors. Then he addressed everyone gathered: "Before you today," intoned Nyame, "the Spider has accepted my challenge. Be it known that should he not prove himself to be the wisest of my creations, as he has claimed, then I will unleash my wrath upon him."

As everyone murmured and urged the Spider to back out, the Spider himself simply bowed in obeisance to Nyame, saying, "Be it done unto me as you wish if I am not equal to your challenge."

"Because I am a fair and loving God, and would not want one of mine to suffer, you must prove to me that you are equal to my challenge."

"At your service," said the Spider.

"Here," said Nyame as he handed the Spider a piece of rock. "Break it that we may eat. It is customary that every occasion such as this begin with the breaking of kola nuts."

The Spider was blue with embarrassment, but soon recovered. He immediately reached for a throw-on loincloth worn by one of the ladies in the crowd. Then he rolled it up and gave to Nyame.

"What is this for?" asked Nyame.

"With this cushion, I want you to carry the village square on your head."

"Impossible," replied Nyame. "You can't carry the village square on your head. It is land—not a load to carry."

"As your Nyameship knows, this is rock—not a kola nut to crack."

"Alright," said Nyame. "You have passed my first test." Then he reached into his pocket and pulled out a grain of corn. "Now the ultimate test. To prove your wisdom, I give you this grain of corn. With it, you must pay the bride price for a very beautiful maiden and bring her to my court. You have seven market days to do so."

The Spider accepted the grain of corn from Nyame. He genuflected and left for his home. There he told his wife to pack his luggage for a long trip. His family was afraid, for they knew the challenge he had accepted. They pleaded with him to just disappear but he was undeterred. Early the next day he picked up his sack and flung it around his neck and left on his journey. Although he was sure the task at hand was a formidable one he dared not show it by wearing his thoughts on his face.

"I must protect my pride and reputation," he said to himself. "And I do not need any pessimists to keep me from thinking clearly and mapping out my plans."

As he walked absentmindedly on a long, lonely, and winding road to nowhere, he concentrated long enough to think through a strategy for the task at hand. Late into the afternoon of the second day of his journey, he arrived at a village. He had by now eaten all of his provisions. He was hungry and tired and, when he came into the village, he sought a poultry farmer. He found one feeding his chickens and begged him to shelter him for the night, with the promise he would continue on his journey the next day. The man was sympathetic and welcomed him.

After they had eaten dinner, the Spider brought out the grain of corn and showed it to his host.

"This is the most wonderful corn you ever saw. You plant it and it is guaranteed to yield seven bushels at harvest time. I never let it out of my sight and have protected it with my life all these years. I cannot wait for the planting season."

His host was very impressed that such a corn existed. He helped the Spider hide it for the night. But early the next day, the Spider demanded the corn:

"I need to dry it some more," he said.

His host brought the corn and the Spider put it out to dry. Almost immediately, one of the man's chickens ate the corn.

The Spider broke down crying. He refused whatever recompense the man gave him. Finally, he agreed that the only solution was to take the chicken he had seen eat the corn, so when he got home, he could kill it and recover the corn. Of course, he took the healthiest rooster in the man's poultry.

The Spider thanked his host and took off for another village. There he sought out a shepherd. He begged him to shelter him for the night and gave him his rooster to put in his sheep's corral. Late at night, the Spider went into the corral and killed the rooster.

In the morning, when he was ready to leave, the Spider went to his host and requested his rooster back. When they went to get it from the corral the shepherd noticed it was dead.

"You don't mean it," gasped the Spider. "That was a special rooster. Don't you see how matured and red its head and comb were?"

"What can I do to repay you?" asked the shepherd.

"You have been very good to me," said the Spider, "but he who lives by the sword must die by the sword. Give me the sheep that was responsible for the death of my rooster."

"But I don't know which of them killed it," pleaded the shepherd.

"It must be that one," said the Spider as he pointed to the fatted ram. "Look at those horns and vicious eyes. It must be him."

The shepherd gave him the ram and the Spider tied a leash around its neck, and the ram trailed behind him as he continued on his journey. By nightfall, he arrived at yet another village. There he sought out a cattle herder and begged him to shelter him for the night. But the cattle herder needed a little convincing.

"You must not know me," said the Spider. "I am Anansi the Spider. I am a messenger of Nyame. He has sent me to a distant village on a mission. If you harbor me, you will find favor with Him."

Upon hearing that, the cattle herder welcomed him into his house. He fed him and gave him his guestroom. When it was time for them to go to bed, the Spider told his host to put the ram with his herd of cattle.

"It is a special ram and he does not sleep with its kind," said the Spider. "It only likes to sleep with cattle."

Directly, the cattle herder put the ram in with his herd of cattle. Late that night, the Spider went into the barn and clubbed the ram to death. When he was ready to leave the next day, his host noticed that the ram had died. He pleaded with the Spider who, out of the goodness of his heart, decided to settle for nothing less than the best of the cattle herder's bulls. This he took to the next village.

On his way, he heard a group of people crying. He went over to learn what they were crying about. There he found they were crying because one of theirs had died.

"Who is it?" asked the Spider sympathetically.

"It is a little girl," replied one of the mourners. "Those are her parents."

"I am really sorry," said the Spider. "Perhaps I can help. I am Anansi the Spider, messenger of Nyame. You are in luck. I must take the girl's body to Nyame's kingdom where she can have everlasting life. Take this bull. Kill it and use it to entertain the mourners for Nyame has smiled on you today. Just give me the body to take to Nyame."

The little girl's parents pondered the idea for a moment. Then they called the elders who met to discuss the Spider's offer. After much deliberation, the elders thought that the Spider's offer was a good one and accepted it. After all, Nyame might restore the girl's life and the mourners needed something to wash down their sorrows. So, they gave the Spider the dead girl's body. He borrowed a loincloth from one of the mourners, tied the body to his back and carried it to the next village as if she were sleeping.

The Spider passed two villages, but not wanting to settle until nightfall, he continued. When he came to the third village, it was nightfall and he asked the villagers to take him to their Chief. When he met the Chief, he told him that he was the messenger of Nyame. He carefully laid the child on the floor and asked for a special quarters for her.

"She is Nyame's daughter," said the Spider. "Please, no one should disturb her. We have been on a long trip and she must get some rest."

On hearing this, the Chief prepared the guestroom for the Spider and the girl. He entertained him and killed the fattest calf for him.

When the Chief asked him to go and wake up the child so she might eat, he replied that she would not eat if woken and that it was best for her to wake up on her own.

When it was time for everybody to retire to bed for the night, the Spider went to the Chief and asked him to let the child sleep with the rest of his daughters.

"You know children," said the Spider. "They are the same everywhere, even in Nyame's kingdom. She would never sleep with other children. She only sleeps with adult maidens. With so many wives, oh Chief, I hope you have some maidens who wouldn't mind sharing their place with Nyame's daughter?"

"Of course," replied the Chief, eager to find favor with Nyame. "Bring her along and I will have her sleep with my daughters."

Carefully the Spider picked up the body and took it to the room where the Chief's eldest daughters slept. When he got there, the girls were already asleep. He pushed the eldest daughters apart and lay the body between them.

Early the next morning, the Spider was fed a sumptuous breakfast before he prepared to leave. Then he asked the Chief's servant to check whether Nyame's daughter was awake so she could eat and get ready for their long journey. But! Alas! When the Chief's messenger went to get the girl, she was dead.

"She cannot be dead," reassured the Spider. "She must be sleeping deeply." So he went into the room with the Chief. He ran the back of his hand across her nose and feeling no breath he shook the body. But there was no response. He tried again, then the Chief tried, but there was no response. Directly the Spider went into an uncontrollable fit of wailing.

"Nyame's favorite daughter," he cried. "Your daughters must have rolled over and smothered her. What am I to do? How can I face Nyame? His wrath is sure to descend on the one responsible for the death of his favorite daughter, starting from their parents and throughout their kingdom."

The Chief was panic-stricken. He didn't quite know what to do. He pleaded and prayed to Nyame to kill him and spare his daughters and his kingdom.

"Please don't let the wrath of Nyame come upon my people. I will do anything to atone for this evil done against Nyame."

"The only way, I think, that this may be remedied is for you to give me the responsible daughter so that I may take her to Nyame to do with her as He pleases. No other form of atonement will do. That way he will spare your people and your kingdom."

"If that's indeed all it will take," said the Chief. "Take her with you."

Then the Chief gave the second daughter to the Spider, but he refused her, saying that he was sure it was the first daughter who crushed Nyame's daughter to death. She was the one big enough to kill Nyame's daughter under her weight. So the Chief let him take the first daughter, and the second as well, if he wished. But the Spider took only the first daughter.

The Spider took the maiden and the body of the little girl and went back to Nyame. When he arrived, he told Nyame of his adventure. On hearing it, Nyame was very pleased by the wisdom of the Spider. He breathed on the little girl and she came back to life, and he returned her to her parents. He also returned the Chief's daughter to him.

"As for you," said Nyame to the Spider, "you have shown me that you are the wisest of all my creations. I will therefore keep my word."

So Nyame gave the Spider more wisdom. That is why even today the Spider is regarded as the wisest creature in the animal kingdom. Also, Nyame gave the Spider riches beyond his wildest dreams. But what happened to these riches, no one knows. Somehow the Spider became so poor that the only way he survives is by his wisdom in crafting webs. In fact, he is the only animal in the whole animal kingdom who knows how to spin webs and set traps to catch his food.

Animal Language

From the Akan people comes this story of a man who was down on his luck. Everything he touched turned to disaster, until he chased a deer who had stolen from him. As reparation for his losses he was given a rare gift—the ability to understand the language of the animals. With the gift came one condition: if he were to reveal it, he would die. At first, the man saw the gift as a worthless burden. But when his fortunes began to improve miraculously, his view changed.

There once lived a very poor man and his wife. They were so poor that they had neither enough to eat nor enough to wear. Not only was the couple poor, they were also unlucky. So unlucky were they that *nothing* they did ever turned out right. If they bought goats or cattle or chicken or pigs to breed for food and cash, the animals died. If they farmed, the crops died or the animals dug them up and ate them.

One day as they sat in their old beat-up house that let in water when it rained and sun when it shined, the man said to his wife, "I think I might just have the answer to our poverty."

"Please do not tease me, Kofi," she warned her husband. "Nothing can get us out of this poverty. Everything we've tried has failed and I have given up."

"We should not give up, Araba. You told *me* not to—now you are?"

"Alright—what is this wonderful idea?" asked Araba.

"I have an idea. I don't know that it is wonderful, though. I am thinking of going to Chief Kumah to beg him to let me tap his palm trees for wine. And you, my wife, can take the wine to the market and sell it."

"That is a splendid idea," assured Araba. "But would he oblige you?"

"I don't know, but there is only one way to find out. I have nothing to lose anyway. Besides, he has so many palm trees in his farm that I am sure he will not mind my tapping a few of them. People say that he is a very rich and generous man. That is why they call him the Money Chief."

Meanwhile, Araba was counting her chicks before they were hatched. She closed her eyes and fantasized about how she would spend the money from the wine on new sets of clothes and thatching for her leaky roof. "Oh, that cloth Mrs. Nattey wore yesterday would be great in blue. Yes! Blue. That is the color I want," she thought.

Very early the next day, Kofi left for the Money Chief's villa to ask him for some of his palm trees.

"What is in it for me, my son?" asked the Chief. "I am a businessman you know, and I didn't get this rich by giving away all my wealth. As our people say, 'a chicken does not feed into its neighbor's stomach,' so let us make it a business proposal. I wash your hands and you wash mine."

"I know you to be a fair man," said Kofi. "Whatever you say will be alright with me."

"Take ten of my palm trees and tap them. Then whatever money you make from selling the wine from them, we shall share equally. I will even give you the calabash for collecting the wine. There, take what you need," Chief Kumah concluded, pointing to neat rows of calabash containers.

Kofi was overjoyed and took as many calabash containers as he could. When he arrived back home and told his wife about the deal he had struck with the Chief, she was ecstatic. She knew now that all her fantasies were about to become realities.

The next day, Kofi was up before everybody else in the village, eager to get to work. He fell the palm trees and tapped them for wine. He worked tirelessly all day and into the late evening, even as his stomach growled for food. "Once the wine comes in and it is sold, I will eat all the food I want," he thought.

Later that night, Kofi and his wife were talking and chatting like they never had before. They were very happy all of a sudden; they were filled with anticipation of the next morning. They played games, counting the number of full calabashes of wine they'd collect in the morning.

First thing the next morning, Kofi was off to the farm to collect the wine.

"Oh no!" he exclaimed as he approached the first tree and saw that the calabash container was broken. "Who did this?" he asked. But confident that the other containers were still there anyway, he didn't dwell much on the lost wine. He ran with hope and anticipation to the next tree. But that container was also broken. One by one he visited the rest of the trees. And one by one, the calabashes had all been broken, and the wines gone. All that remained, as evidence, was a swarm of bees and flies fighting over the spills on the ground. Dejected and in tears, Kofi ran back home to his wife.

"What is the matter?" asked his wife.

"Lightning has struck us again," replied Kofi in disgust. "I told you that everything I try is bound to fail. There was no wine and all the calabashs were broken."

"Do not talk like that," admonished his wife. "You are a very hard worker and our god is bound to look kindly on us someday. You must keep trying. I am sure there was wine from the trees. My guess is that someone must have stolen it, and broken the pots to cover their tracks."

"You are right," said Kofi, "I must not give up and should try again."

"Perish the thought of giving up," said his wife. And as Kofi spotted a smile of encouragement, she added, "Now, that's the man I married."

Encouraged by his wife, Kofi went to Chief Kumah to borrow more calabash pots. After making fresh cuts on the palm tree for the wine to run, he tied the calabash under the cuts and went home.

By the next morning, all the pots had been broken again. Once again, only the flies and the bees were left, fighting over the drips. Kofi was now convinced that indeed this was the work of a thief and not just his bad luck alone. So, he went back and borrowed more pots. This time he set them up to collect the wine and decided to keep watch over them. He took up position at a strategic location in the palm tree plantation and waited patiently.

Tired from the long wait, Kofi was about to doze off, when the buzz of mosquitoes awoke him. Rather than slap the mosquitoes against his chin or ears, he just gently warded them off with his hand. He was afraid that swatting the mosquitoes might alert the thief to his presence. For the next several hours Kofi waited patiently. But the mosquitoes were also frustrating him. He was about to call it a night when he heard a twig snap a few yards behind him. For just an instant, he began to wonder why he was out there in the deep forest. "Are these pots of wine worth my life?" he thought. "Suppose the thief is some wild animal I cannot subdue—then what? Or—"

His thought was interrupted as he heard the breaking of a pot. Straining to see in the weak moonlight, he made out what looked like a deer by one of the calabash pots. As he watched, the deer pulled Kofi's pot from under the palm tree and emptied its contents into its own pot, then smashed the empty pot to the ground.

Kofi dove after the deer, aiming at the antlers. The deer, though, leapt away in the same instant. But Kofi chased after the Deer, determined not to lose it. The chase continued into the early morning as the sun began to provide some daylight. The chase took them up over the crest of a very high hill, until suddenly, upon descent, Kofi found himself in the middle of an assembly of animals. In the center of the assembly was the Lion, and Kofi could tell that he was their king.

Kofi stopped in his tracks. "Now, I have really done it," he said to himself. "Walked into an ambush of wild animals."

The Deer ran straight to the Lion. He stretched out his forelegs with his head between them as if prostrating.

"What is the matter?" asked the Lion. "Is it not bad enough that we have to avoid you in the open forest, now you chase us in our own homes?"

Before the Lion could conclude his remarks, the Deer, almost out of breath, quickly told his version of the story. The Monkey, who must have been the Lion's assistant, asked Kofi to tell the Lion why he was chasing after their friend.

Kofi wasted no time telling the animals his life story. He began with how he was down on his luck, and how he hoped the palm wine would be his ticket to riches, and ended with the discovery of the Deer stealing from him. He then apologized to the Lion for disrupting his council and asked to be allowed to go back to his wife.

"I am a fair judge," said the Lion, "and it is obvious to me that it is the Deer who is at fault. He was given enough money with which to buy wine for my court, and he chose to steal from you instead. What he did with the money I don't know. We shall deal with him later. For you, I will give you a special gift that could pay for your troubles ten fold. From today onward, you will have the power to understand the language of the animals."

Kofi just stood there, still waiting for the gift that would pay for his losses ten times over.

"Be gone then," said the Lion, "while we decide on the fate of our friend here."

"What could be more ridiculous?" Kofi thought, as he bowed to take his leave of the animals. But not wishing to offend them, he thanked the Lion and was about to leave when the Lion said:

"One more thing about your gift."

"What?" Kofi asked in frustration.

"You must never tell anyone about it. If you do, you will surely die."

Kofi thanked him again, even though as he left he was more disappointed than ever. "What a gift!" he thought. "How can understanding the language of the animals pay for my losses? That is too ridiculous to imagine and talking about it to someone else is even worse. I'd *rather* die than talk about such a gift."

Tired from the long chase and his disappointment, Kofi went back to his house afraid that his wife might be mad that he had been gone for too long. But to his amazement, she was very understanding and thrilled to have him home.

"Where have you been?" she asked frantically. "You look horrible. Are you all right? Did you catch the thief?"

"It was the Deer who had been bringing bad luck to us. I chased after him but couldn't catch up with him."

Later that night Kofi went back to guard the palm trees to be sure that the Deer did not come back. But the Deer did not come back, and by daybreak he found all the calabash pots full of palm wine. He quickly brought them home and prepared them for his wife to take to the market. Every morning he came back with pots full of palm wine, which his wife sold for lots of money.

Kofi's luck seemed to have changed after that night he chased the

Deer. He now had a little bit of money to buy many of the things he needed such as cattle, goats, and horses. He was now able to fix up his house to keep out the rain and sun. His wife was now happier than ever. She was able to buy the clothes she needed to make herself presentable in public.

Meanwhile, Kofi understood what the animals said, and so often just chuckled or laughed out loud, and felt awkward since no one knew what he laughed about. One hot afternoon after tilling his farm for planting, Kofi went to the river to take a bath. Then he heard a hen with a brood of about ten chicks say to them, "How stupid can he be? Strip all his clothes only to get water on his body? That figures. No wonder he does not know that there is a box of gold behind his house. I saw it last time I was scratching for worms, but covered it up before his evil dog chased me out."

"Ha! Ha! Ha! Ha!" Kofi started to laugh. But he startled the hen and quickly stopped. Then he ran his palm several times over his face to make sure he was not dreaming. Sure enough he wasn't. He stuck his pinkies into his ears to clear them. Then he heard the hen rebuke one of his chicks.

"Leave that worm for your brother. I gave you the first catch, didn't I? You have to learn to share."

Convinced of what he heard, Kofi continued with his bathing as if nothing had happened.

Later that night after everybody had gone to bed he took a hoe, went behind his house and dug up the box of gold.

Gold! Gold! Gold! Gold everywhere. There was enough gold in the box to set Kofi and his wife up for life. But he couldn't tell his wife how he knew the gold was there in the first place, much less where to dig. So he hid it away in a safe place and brought home a little piece at a time, as he needed them.

Soon Kofi and Araba were the richest couple in all the land. Araba was very generous to the poor and tried to help them get back on their feet. Kofi was equally generous. But he concentrated his efforts on making more money and making himself more famous. Life couldn't have been better for the couple. They were very happy together. Soon they were blessed with a son, whom they loved very much.

As Kofi and Araba lay down one evening to sleep, he heard two mice gnawing at the door and one mouse said to the other.

"These people are now rich. They fortify everywhere with iron doors. Things were better when they were poor and had wooden doors you could gnaw through."

"Yeah! Such is life," replied the other mouse. "When you gnawed through the wooden doors, you found nothing. Now that they are rich and you are sure to find something in their home, you cannot gnaw through the doors."

"Ha! Ha! Ha! Ha!" laughed Kofi, forgetting that he was there with his wife.

"What's so funny, Kofi?" asked Araba as she woke up with a start. "Are you laughing at my snoring again?"

"No! Nothing! I was just dreaming," he lied. "Go back to sleep."

But the laugh was loud enough to wake up the baby too, and Araba didn't take kindly to that.

"This laughter of yours will get you into trouble one of these days you know. I have tried to ignore it, but one of these days you will laugh at a corpse in a crowd of mourners and make a fool of yourself. Now I will have to nurse the baby to sleep all over again. I wish you were equipped to nurse him yourself."

"Sorry dear. Ha! Ha! Ha! Ha! Go back to sleep."

According to one ancient saying, when a dog is about to die, somehow it loses its sense of smell, especially of meat, its most favorite food. Though Kofi was a very rich man, he was content with just one wife. But because polygamy was one of the true signs of wealth in Kofi's village, he decided to take a second wife.

Kofi married a woman whose beauty could only be matched by her jealousy. She couldn't stand to see Kofi and Araba together. When they laughed, she claimed they were laughing at her, and when they talked, she claimed it was about her. She was happy only when Kofi and Araba were fighting.

One day as they cooked in their backyard, Kofi's second wife walked by. Then Kofi heard his dogs talking about her.

"There she goes again," said one dog to the other. "Since she came our portions have become smaller."

"And one would think that if she ate our portions she would be bigger," replied the other.

"Ha! Ha! Ha! Ha!" Kofi burst out laughing.

"What are you laughing at?" asked Araba. "Don't you know that one-man laughter weakens the jaw muscles?"

"Do not pretend that you don't know on account I am here," added Kofi's second wife. "I hear you two talking and giggling all night about me. Now you have to do it even in my presence. Only God knows what you talk about when I am not here."

"Honestly I do not know what he is laughing about," Araba tried to explain. But Kofi's second wife did not want to hear of it.

Kofi came to Araba's defense, only making matters worse. His second wife now concluded that it was Araba whom Kofi loved all along and would do anything to get her out of trouble.

This was how Kofi lived with his two wives for a very long time until one day his laughter really went overboard.

Kofi had called a two-day party to celebrate the coming of age of his son. He had selected and tethered two cows, two goats, and chickens for the occasion. He sat in the crowd and watched his wives' women's league put on their specialty dances. Then he heard one of the cows tell the other.

"Boring. When will this be over? I am famished and cannot wait to get out of here."

"You better enjoy it while you can because your bones are mine tomorrow," said one of Kofi's dogs to the cow.

Unfortunately, it was just at the point when Kofi's second wife was performing a solo number for her husband and his peers.

"Ha! Ha! Ha! Ha!" Kofi went into an uncontrollable bout of laughter.

"That's it," said Kofi's second wife, as she stopped dancing and started crying. "As everyone here is my witness, you are laughing at me because I cannot dance."

"No! No!" protested Kofi. "I was just laughing at a wild thought."

"What kind of wild thought could you be having at a time like this?" she asked.

But Kofi would not tell for fear that he would die. In order to get the ceremony completed without further incident, Kofi promised to tell her about his wild thoughts later.

For days Kofi's second wife bugged him to tell her what he laughed about during the festivities but he always dismissed her. When his wife couldn't wait any longer, she took the matter to their Chief.

"This matter has gone on for so long, my friend, that if I were you, I would just get it over with," the Chief advised him.

"I am sorry. But I cannot tell, for if I do, I will die," Kofi told the Chief.

"Now that's funny. Ho! Ho! Ho! Ho!" bellowed the Chief. "Who ever heard of someone dying for saying what he thought?"

Kofi stood there confused. If he told the source of his laughter, he would surely die. Then again, if he didn't he would die too, albeit slowly, from the nagging of his wife. So, he decided on the former method of death. He called all his friends, family, and the Chief to assemble in his house the next day for a feast for his death, for he had led a good life. When they were assembled, Kofi addressed them.

"People shouldn't cry for me," he said. "To you Araba, I give all my gold. To you son, I give the rest of my estate." Then bowing to the Chief, he told the people gathered about his encounter with the Deer and the Lion King and the gift they had given him for his losses. Then he told them what he was laughing about during the celebration of his son. No sooner did he finish telling his stories, than he fell down on the ground, dead.

The feast turned to mourning. The villagers were so grieved and angry that they hardly knew what they were doing when they seized Kofi's second wife and killed her. They cremated her and put her ashes in a sack and gave it to the Crow to dump into the river. But the Crow was very curious and opened the bag in flight to see its contents. The ashes spread all over the place. Wherever they fell, hatred and jealousy were sure to sprout. This marked the beginning of bad things and bad people in the world; before then, kindness, love, and unselfishness had thrived.

Finders Keepers

Every farm must have a road that leads to it, even if it is seldom used. The Akan people tell this story of Anansi the Spider, who sought to steal the Squirrel's farm by presenting this logic before the Lion's court. But what if the farm is a Squirrel's? The Squirrel has no use for roads—he just makes his way through the trees. In this story, neither the Lion nor the Spider has the final word.

The Squirrel was a very good farmer and farmed large fertile lands during the farming season. And come harvest time, he gathered his crops and saved them in his barn for the dry season. The following farming season, he did the same thing all over. When he had gathered enough for his barn, he sold the rest for money.

Eventually, the Squirrel realized that the lands that were close to all the animals had been over-farmed. The yield had become scanty. So he decided to go away to a richer virgin land.

Now, we know the Squirrel. He climbs the trees. He could jump from one tree to the next and cover a wide distance. From the treetops, he could see far and choose which way to go. So it was that the Squirrel was on top of a very tall tree. He saw at a distance a land he knew to be very rich for his corn. Hop! Cham! Cham! He went through the branches until he came to the land. Just as he thought, the soil was very black with richness. He went down to it. Dug up a bit of dirt and was satisfied with its quality.

"This is it," said the Squirrel. "This is where I plant my corn this season. I am sure it will be the best corn ever planted. Now comes the hard part—clearing these thick bushes."

But being such an industrious animal, the Squirrel went to work immediately. He cleared the forest and burned the brush. Several days later, he tilled the land and planted his corn. In not very long, the corn grew. Their leaves were green and full of life. In time, the corn matured and was ready for harvest.

Because the Squirrel traveled through treetops, he never bothered to build roads to his farms. No matter where his farms were located, he reached them through the treetops.

One day, the Spider went out hunting. He canvassed as much of the neighboring forest as he could, but killed nothing. He went deeper into the woods with the hope of finding something to bring home for the evening meal. Then he stumbled upon the Squirrel's corn farm.

"What a marvelous work of nature," the Spider said to himself. "This is the best corn farm I have ever seen. Who could it belong to?"

Then he walked around the farm looking for an entrance, a road that connected the farm to its owner. But he couldn't find any.

"That's strange," he said. "Such a bountiful corn farm without a road to it? How can that be? Who could be so careless as to toil so hard to cultivate such a farm but could not spend a little time to make a road to it?"

Then the Spider began to look into how he could claim the corn farm for himself. He thought about different ways of legitimizing his claim. When he went to bed later that night, he couldn't sleep. He just tossed and turned, weighing his options to lay claim to the corn farm.

"I cultivated it during the night," he said in his dream. "No. Nobody would believe that. I…"

"Wake up!" said his wife. "You are talking in your sleep. What is it now?"

"I've got it!" he exclaimed. "How would you like to get the benefit of several months of labor for a day of labor?"

"You know me," his wife replied. "I take the easiest way out. Just tell me what to do."

Then the Spider called his family together. First, he told them how he had come upon this corn farm. "It must be providence," he said. "When I woke up this morning getting ready for my hunt, my right eyelids twitched as though they were going to fall out of their hinges. And, when I couldn't figure out why, I went and asked the diviner who told me that my eyelids twitched because I was going to see and bag a big one. But I searched far and wide and couldn't kill even a rat. Then! Wow! I ran into the farm. Our god works in mysterious ways. When he closes the door of opportunity, he opens the window. But we must secure the farm before anyone else does."

Then the Spider told his family of his plan. First thing in the morning, they must all go and build a path to the farm. After that, they must waste no time harvesting the corn and storing it in their barn.

Before the first cock crowed, the Spider and his 100-member strong family took off to the cornfield with their machetes and hoes. They made a path through the bush, connecting their home to the corn field. They worked harder than they ever did before. Then they scattered some broken pieces of pots and dried shrubs about the path, to make it look old and in frequent use.

Immediately after they made the path, they harvested some of the corn and hauled it to their barn. Every day they came and harvested more corn and hauled it home to their barn.

"I'll be!" exclaimed the Squirrel, when he noticed that someone had been stealing from him. "Who would do a thing like this? I labored to farm this land and planted the corn, and now someone has the nerve to steal it. I must find out who it is."

The Squirrel hid between the brushes by the end of the farm where the Spider stole. His machete drawn and at the ready, he waited. Just like clockwork, the Spider and his family came first thing the next morning. They wasted no time cutting down some ears of corn and bagging them.

"Caught you," the Squirrel shouted as he pounced on the Spider. "So! You are the one who has been reaping where you didn't sow?"

"Let me go," said the Spider as he tried to free himself from the Squirrel. "What do you mean reaping where I didn't sow? This is my farm."

"*Your* farm?" asked the Squirrel, shocked. "It is *my* farm and you are stealing my corn!"

"Ha! Ha! Ha!" laughed the Spider. "Ha! Ha! Ha! Ha! Your corn? Can you show me the path to this your farm and corn?"

"What do you mean path?" asked the Squirrel. "You know that I don't need a path. I use the treetops."

"Gather the harvest, family," said the Spider. "Don't mind the intruder. How can one claim a farm for his own without a road to it?"

Frustrated, the Squirrel left the Spider and his family and went home swearing and cursing at them. "I will see you in King Lion's court. You must return my corn."

Several days later the Spider was summoned before the Lion, king of the jungle. The Lion invited the Squirrel to state his case and then the Spider.

"It is my farm your honor," claimed the Spider. "How can he claim it is his farm when he doesn't even have any road to get to it. How can it be possible that he farmed and tended this farm for so many months without a path to it? Send your messengers, your honor, and they will find that the only path to the farm leads from my house. It is my farm."

So the Lion sent his messengers who came back and reported that indeed, the only path to the farm led from the Spider's home. The Squirrel even admitted that it was the only path, and that he had never needed one. The Lion had no choice but to rule in the Spider's favor.

"I feel that the farm belongs to you," he told the Squirrel. "However, I have no choice but to rule in the Spider's favor. In all my life, I have never seen a farm without a road to it, especially one that far from home."

No sooner did they get the favorable verdict than the Spider and his family decided to harvest the rest of the corn. First thing the next day, they went and cut down all the corn. They worked all day harvesting and bagging the ears. The Squirrel could do nothing but watch and cry.

"This is justice?" he cried.

When the Spider and his family were done, they tied the ears into large bundles. They helped each other put the loads on their heads. Then they started the long walk back to their home.

"Looks like rain," the Spider said to his wife, as he noticed the sky becoming darker and darker with clouds.

"I'll say," replied his wife. "A heavy one too. We'd better hurry up before it gets here." But before she could finish her sentence, a heavy drop of water landed on her nose, almost tipping her over.

By the time they had taken a few more steps, the rain came in a heavy downpour. They struggled to walk, but the rain was so fierce it blinded them. The flood of rain made their heavy loads even heavier. So, they dropped their corn by the roadside and ran into an abandoned hut for shelter.

The rain lasted from when the sun was overhead to when it was about to go to sleep. It poured and thundered with dazzling and frightening lightening. When it was finally over, the sun smiled again. And the Spider and his family came out from their shelter to pick up their corn. Because of the severity of the rain, they wondered if all their corn hadn't been swept away by the flood.

As they approached the spot where they had left their load, they saw a black mass of something in the place of their loads. On closer look, they noticed it was a giant crow.

"How thoughtful of you," the Spider said to the Crow who was brooding over the corn. "You protected my corn from the rain and flood. Now I do not have to worry about drying them."

"You either have a good sense of humor or a great imagination," said the Crow. "This is my corn. Please go away so that I can haul it to my home."

"It is my corn," cried the Spider. "I left it there to escape from the rain."

"How can anyone leave their bags of corn on the roadside and not watch over them?" asked the Crow. "It's now my corn. I found it and protected it from the rain. Please be gone."

When the Spider realized that he was fighting a losing battle, he stood back and watched the Crow gather the bags of corn in its huge talons. Then he balanced them very well and with one flap of his huge wings, flew off. The Spider and his family were left without anything to show for their efforts.

Why Man and Fox Are Enemies

In the beginning, the Man and the Fox and the rest of the animals lived together. In a Ga village the Fox and his friend the Spider often visited the Man's house for food and play. Being industrious, the Man had many chickens in his coop. He sometimes cooked them and shared them with the Fox and the Spider. One day the Spider's greed led him to steal Man's chickens. The Spider must now find a way to frame the Fox and pit the Man against him. The Fox, for his part, just wants to eat the Man's chicken before the Man kills him.

Long, long ago, people and all the wild animals were neighbors. They were very happy together and looked out for each other's interests. When one needed something, he borrowed from the other. The animals had no fear of people and people had no fear of the animals.

During this time, the Fox and the Spider were the best of friends. They often went to the Man for food. After eating, the Spider told funny stories to the Man's children and everybody laughed and had a good time. After the stories, the Fox and the Spider went back to their own homes.

In those days, as now, the Man farmed a lot. He had chickens, pigs, dogs, goats, and cows. Sometimes he had the meat from some of these animals, especially the chicken, in the soup he served the Spider and his friend the Fox.

As our elders say, "All wild dogs are carrion eaters. It is the one that leaves the evidence on his mouth that is called the glutton." So, the two friends loved these meats, especially chicken meat. The Spider loved the chicken as much as his friend the Fox did. But, he wasn't as vocal about it as was the Fox, lest whatever he said come back to haunt him. He often wished privately he could have some of those chickens all to himself. The Fox, on the other hand, salivated whenever he saw the chickens. He'd stay and stare at them as his mouth watered and saliva flowed from it. Then he'd say out loudly, "I wish I could have those chickens all to myself."

One day the Spider went to visit the Man. But, when he got

there, no one was home. As he turned around to leave, he heard the chickens clucking in the barn behind the house. Directly, his mouth began to water.

"If no one is home," he thought, "maybe I could..."

His mind wandered as he faced the door again. He reluctantly knocked again, more to reassure himself that no one was home than to make sure they were. Satisfied that no one was at home, he turned away to leave, but his desire to have the chickens overcame him. He swung back toward the barn, then away from it. The more he resisted, the more he seemed to be drawn by an invisible force toward the barn. When he found it was easier going toward the barn than away from it, he obeyed his instinct.

"Wow!" exclaimed the Spider as he saw what seemed like thousands of chickens in all shapes and sizes. "That red one would really make a nice pot of soup."

The Spider grabbed as many chickens as he could and sneaked out of Man's compound. Then he looked around, just to be sure that he was not being watched, and went home using the bush path. When he got home, he made several pots of chicken soup and had himself a wonderful dinner. When he was done, he had some palm wine, laid down to rest and dozed off.

"My goodness," exclaimed the Spider, as he woke up with a start. "I must have dozed off. I need to figure out what to do with all these feathers since that is the only thing that can connect me to the chickens."

Immediately the Spider scurried out of his recliner and gathered all the feathers. He put them into a big sack and went to dispose of them, making sure to pass by the Fox's den. The Spider knew that the Fox was quite curious and that he was sure to accost him once he saw him with the load.

As the Spider approached the Fox's den, he did a quick search for the Fox and when he could not find him about, he let go of his voice and did one of his solo whistling numbers just to be sure that the Fox was around.

"Hello, my friend!" greeted the Fox, as he trudged out from the back of his den to checkout the sound. "Leave the singing to the canary. Why are you so happy carrying such a heavy load that it is about to pull off your neck? What is it?"

"Oh!" said the Spider. "It's nothing."

"Come on," insisted the Fox. "Since when did we start keeping secrets from each other? We are friends, remember?"

"Sure! But this is different. It is nothing, really."

The more the Spider tried not to tell the Fox what he was carrying, the more the Fox wanted to know. The Fox became even more curious when the Spider refused his offer to help him carry it. Finally, when the Spider felt he had the Fox where he wanted him, he said: "Alright! I should've known that I couldn't get by you without telling you. You got it out of me. It is corn dough. I am going to use it to make some cakes. Also, there is some meat for groundnut soup. After such a dinner, I plan to wash everything down with fresh palm wine. You know, the type that has not been diluted with water."

The Fox's mouth began to water. He smiled euphorically as he replayed what the Spider told him over and over in his mind. "If I hadn't run into you, you mean you wouldn't have told me?"

"Forget about my telling you," said the Spider. "Are you going to work for the meal or just talk?"

"Sure! Sure!" replied the Fox, excited.

"Here! Take the load off me. You carry it and I will let you have some for yourself."

The Fox carried the sack with such zeal that the heavy load felt so light. He started to leave for the Spider's home and waited for the Spider to follow him.

"Go ahead," said the Spider. "I need to catch my breath. I have been carrying that for a long time." Then he heaved a sign of relief as the Fox left. "I will catch up with you soon," he told the Fox.

The Fox was very excited. He bid the Spider a good rest and took off. Not long afterwards, the Man came by. On seeing the Spider so exhausted, he asked, "What is wrong with you? You look like you have been on the farm all day."

"Nothing is wrong with me," said the Spider. "I am just here wallowing in my thoughts."

"What could you be thinking about?" asked the Man.

"The Fox just passed by," continued the Spider, "and he was

carrying a very heavy sack of what looked like feathers."

"Feathers?" asked the Man.

"That was what I asked myself," answered the Spider. "Yes! Feathers."

The Man bid the Spider good rest and raced after the Fox. The thought of the Fox carrying a bag of feathers, and a heavy one at that, made his heart race and his mind think the worst. The only way that someone could have feathers was if they had raided his chicken barn. Soon he caught up with the Fox and asked him what he was carrying.

"Corn and meat, of course," replied the Fox naively.

"Corn and meat?" asked the Man.

"Yes," insisted the Fox. "Corn for making cake and meat for groundnut soup. I got them from a friend."

"Then you wouldn't mind opening the sack, would you?"

"Of course not," said the Fox.

By the time the Fox put the sack down, a crowd had gathered around them. Then the Man drew his knife and cut the sack open. Feathers filled the sky. The Fox was embarrassed and just looked on with mouth agape. As he tried to explain, the Man drew his knife in anger and chased after the Fox to kill him.

"You rogue and liar," he shouted and cursed at the Fox. "You have betrayed my trust and friendship and must pay with your life. I knew you would do this as often as I saw your mouth water at my chickens."

The Fox ran faster than he ever had before. And even till today, the Man still chases after the Fox to kill him. The Fox, on the other hand, keeps coming after the Man's chickens. "If I am to die for what I didn't do, I might as well do it," he says to himself.

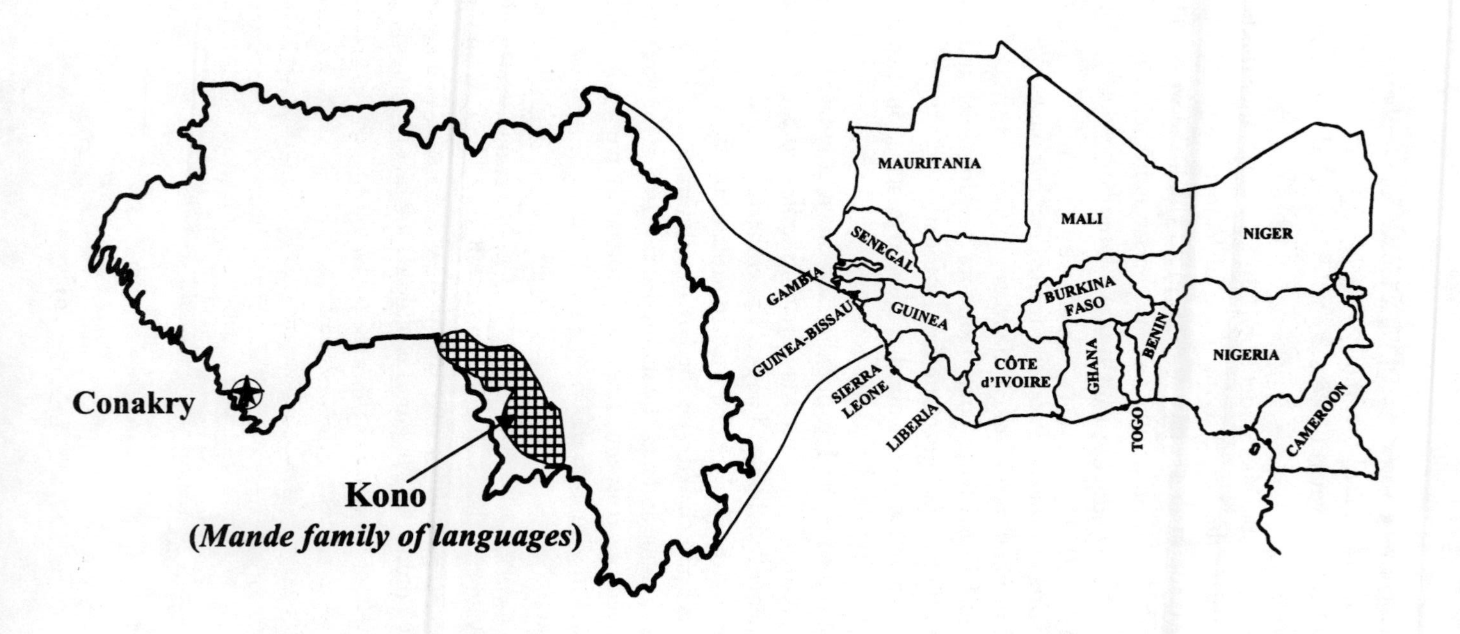
Conakry
Kono
(*Mande family of languages*)
MAURITANIA
MALI
NIGER
SENEGAL
GAMBIA
GUINEA-BISSAU
GUINEA
SIERRA LEONE
LIBERIA
BURKINA FASO
CÔTE d'IVOIRE
GHANA
TOGO
BENIN
NIGERIA
CAMEROON

Guinea

COUNTRY

Formal Name: Republic of Guinea (formerly French Guinea)
Short Form: Guinea
Term for Citizens: Guinean
Capital: Conakry
Independence: October 2, 1958 (from France)

GEOGRAPHY

Size: 94,926 square miles (245,860 km^2)
Boundaries: Bordered to the north by Senegal and Mali, southeast by Côte d'Ivoire, south by Liberia and Sierra Leone, west by the Atlantic Ocean, and northwest by Guinea-Bissau

SOCIETY

Population: 7.5 million
Ethnic Groups: The principal ethnic groups are the Peuhl (40%), Mandingo (30%), and Soussou (20%); the Kissi, Toma, Kouranko, and other smaller tribes comprise the rest.
Languages: The principal languages are Mandingo, Kissi, and Poulah. The official language is French, though English is also spoken.
Religion: 85% Islam; 8% Christianity; 7% local religions

The Origin of Death

The Kono people use this story to explain why people die. Sa (Death) was a good friend of Alatangana (God). Since he was magical, Sa conjured up mud, from which Alatangana created the world as we know it. But Sa had a beautiful daughter with whom Alatangana eloped without even so much as a dowry. For Sa's revenge, he takes Alatangana's children whenever he wants them.

In the beginning, before anything was created, there was only darkness. But there also lived Sa (Death), with his wife and daughter. Sa was very magical and could conjure weird things as he pleased.

One day Sa decided to create a sea of mud. Soon after, Alatangana (God) visited him, saying, "What a dirty place you have made here. How can you live in such a place? You have no light. You have no plants. You could drown in the mud."

But Sa told Alatangana that he did what he could and had no way of making his creation better. So Alatangana helped Sa to make the world look better. He made the mud stronger, so that it could be stepped upon. But the mud alone had no life. So he created the stars, the plants and trees, and all kinds of animals.

Then said Sa, "That is indeed remarkable. Now the world is greener and filled with life. I like the improvements. You and I should be great friends."

Sa became friendly with Alatangana. He entertained him and they talked and ate. The two visited each other regularly and their friendship grew. Over time, Alatangana, who was a bachelor, asked Sa for the hand of his daughter in marriage. But Sa was reluctant to part with his only daughter. He made all sorts of excuses why Alatangana should not marry his daughter. But Alatangana and the girl were very much in love. Finally, since Sa would not give his consent to the marriage, Alatangana secretly married the girl.

Alatangana and the girl were very happy together. They had fourteen children—seven boys and seven girls. Four of the boys and four of the girls were of the same race, but the other three boys and three girls were different.

The parents were surprised that their children looked so different. Furthermore, they spoke different languages among themselves. Their parents didn't understand them. Alatangana was annoyed with this and went to ask Sa why this was the case.

"Why is it that my children with your daughter are different?" Alatangana asked Sa. "They speak in different languages that we cannot understand. Is this of your making?"

"Yes," replied Sa. "It is of my making that they are different and speak different languages. That is your punishment for taking my only daughter without my consent and without any dowry. You shall never understand what they say."

"You have to remove your curse on my children," said Alatangana.

"Sorry," replied Sa. "It is too late. But, because they are also my children, I will give them gifts to help them live a happy life. To some of them I have given paper and ink and wisdom. They will be able to put down what they think so they can help their brothers, sisters, and children. To others, I have also given wisdom, strength, and tools they need to help their brothers, sisters, and children. Go then and have them paired up, a boy of a kind to a girl of the same kind and disperse them to populate the world."

Alatangana was happy that Sa was patient enough to talk with him, given how he had eloped with his daughter. So he accepted what Sa said. He immediately set for his home, paired up his children and dispersed them to all parts of the world. They procreated and gave rise to the different peoples and races of the world.

But the world was still living in darkness. So Alatangana sent the Rooster to Sa. "When you get there, ask him what we should do for the stars are not enough and the world is still very much in darkness."

When Sa saw Alatangana's messenger, he remembered his daughter again. He was angry all over. But for the love of his daughter, his anger subsided.

"You have come on a very long journey," Sa told the Rooster. "Get some rest while I think of what Alatangana should do about the darkness."

When the Rooster had rested, Sa sent him back to Alatangana

saying, "When you get back, you should face the east and sing this song, 'Koko ro Oko o!' On hearing you, the King of the Stars shall wake up so that the day will come and the people can go about their business in full light."

The Rooster was very happy that he had the power to wake up the King of the Stars. He thanked Sa and hurried back to Alatangana with the message. When he rested from his long trip, he faced the east and sang his song, "Koko ro Oko o!" Directly, there was a faintness of light in the sky. A few moments later, the Rooster sang his song again, "Koko ro Oko o," and there was something that looked like an outstretched hand, then the King of the Stars, the Sun, woke up. Thus the first day was born.

The Sun was answering the call of the Rooster. He traveled across the sky answering the Rooster as he called all day. When the Rooster became tired and quit calling him, the Sun went back to sleep on the other side of the earth and darkness came again. Directly, the stars and the moon came to help people see when the Sun went to bed.

Then one day Sa called on Alatangana.

"In spite of what you have done by taking my only daughter away from me, I have given you light. But you have not given me anything for my kindness. Not even a dowry for my daughter. In return for all my deeds, you owe me a service."

"You are right, Sa," said Alatangana. "I owe you what you shall ask."

"All right," replied Sa. "Since you have taken my daughter without as much as a dowry, I have no more children. In return, you must give me one of my grandchildren, any time I call for one. Whenever I want one of them, I will call the one by the sound of my calabash. The one will hear the rattle of my calabash in his dream. When he does, he must come running and answer to my call."

In keeping with his promise, Alatangana had no choice but to let his children go and answer Sa, whenever he called. Thus even today, Alatangana's children still answer the call of Sa. All because Alatangana didn't pay a dowry when he married Sa's daughter.

Guinea-Bissau

COUNTRY

Formal Name: Republic of Guinea-Bissau (formerly Portuguese Guinea)
Short Form: Guinea-Bissau
Term for Citizens: Guinea-Bissauan
Capital: Bissau
Independence: Declared September 24, 1973, but not officially recognized by Portugal until September 10, 1974

GEOGRAPHY

Size: 13,948 square miles (36,120 km^2)
Boundaries: Bordered to the north by Senegal, south-southeast by Guinea, and west by the Atlantic Ocean

SOCIETY

Population: 1.2 million
Ethnic Groups: Balanta (30%), Fula (20%), Manjaca (14%), Mandinka (13%), plus other smaller African ethnic groups and Europeans
Languages: Local languages include Criolo and other vernaculars. The official language is Portuguese.
Religion: 50% local religions; 45% Islam; 5% Christianity

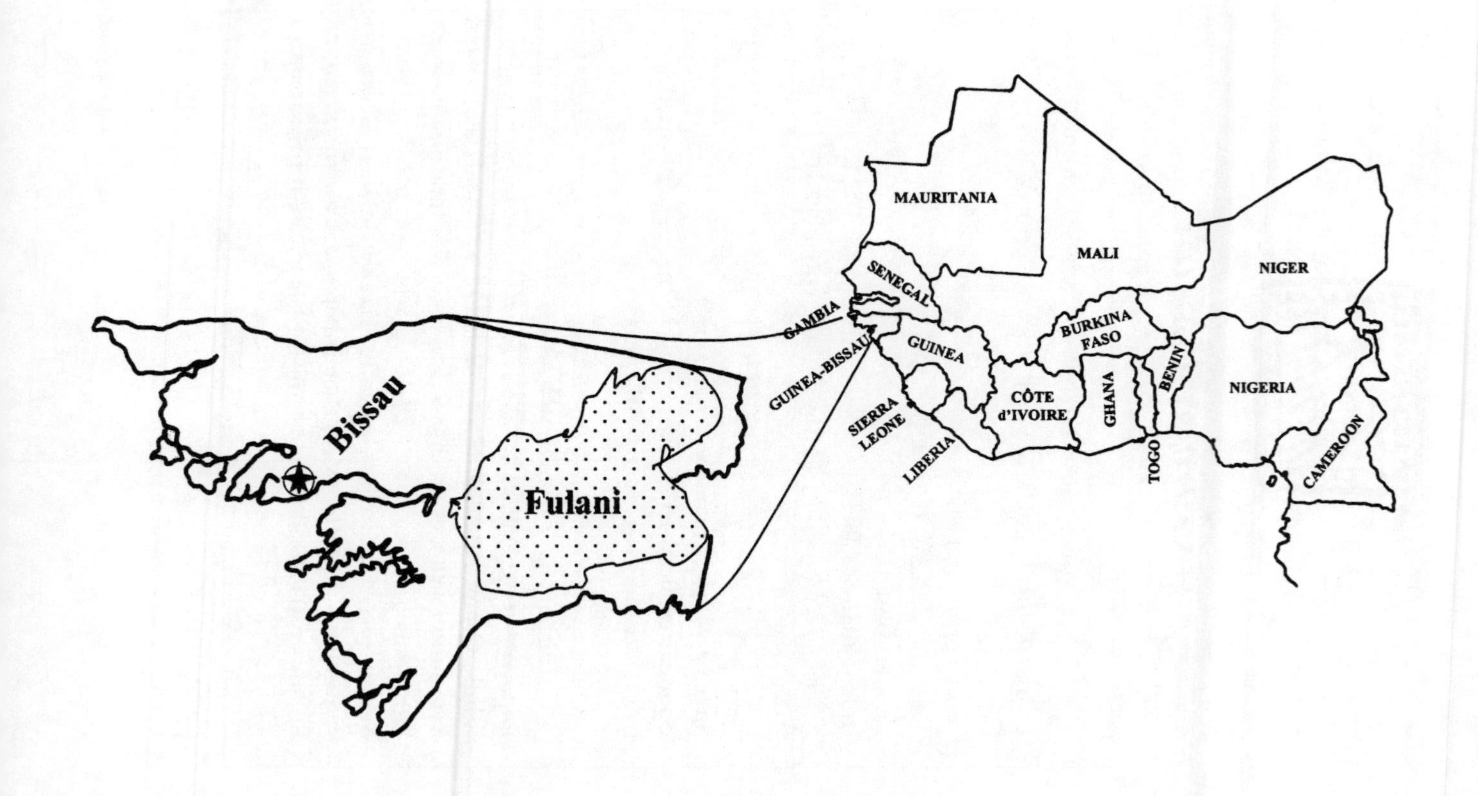
MAURITANIA
MALI
NIGER
SENEGAL
GAMBIA
GUINEA-BISSAU
GUINEA
BURKINA FASO
BENIN
NIGERIA
SIERRA LEONE
LIBERIA
CÔTE d'IVOIRE
GHANA
TOGO
CAMEROON
Bissau
Fulani

The Most Suitable Name

The Fulanis were usually herdsmen and adventurers. In this story they tell of three gentlemen who tried to outdo each other with their respective expertise. Greedy made the glutton sick, Stingy denied his child milk, and Nosy stuck his nose in everything whether it involved him or not. When one day Greedy claimed to be greedier than Stingy was stingy, Nosy decided to keep an eye on them to call the bet.

There once lived in a village, three men who thought that they were the best. They were so sure of themselves that they each took a name befitting their specialty. The one named Stingy believed no one could be more of a scrooge than him. The one named Greedy thought he could make a glutton sick. And the one named Nosy? He could stick his nose into the back of his head, just to know whether it smiled at anyone behind his back.

Because of their rather unique qualities, the three men became friends and always argued about who could outdo the other. One day in such an argument, Stingy said to Greedy, "I don't really know why we keep on with this argument every time. What makes you think that you are greedier than I am stingy?"

"Because I am," replied Greedy.

"Prove it," said Stingy.

"Alright!" said Greedy. "This village is too small an audience. Besides, knowing you, you would rig the ballot. So, you and I must travel the world to determine who can best live up to his name. You can't get a fairer bet than that. The world will be a neutral and objective audience and we can know once and for all who is the boaster among us."

Meanwhile, as they argued and laid their bet, Nosy was eavesdropping. When they separated to prepare for their journey, Nosy ran home and got himself ready too. He told his wife to pack him enough food for a very long journey.

"Where are you going?" asked his wife.

"Stingy and Greedy laid out a bet," said Nosy. "I am going to keep an eye on them. They need a neutral observer to call the bet."

"Sticking your nose in everyone's business again?" teased his wife. "If you were part of that bet, I am sure you'd be the winner. Nobody can poke their nose into anyone else's business quite like you."

Very early the next morning, Nosy was at the rendezvous spot for Stingy and Greedy.

"What are you doing here?" asked Stingy.

"I figured you needed someone to call the bet," replied Nosy.

Soon Greedy arrived and the three men set out on their journey. Now you know Greedy, he loves to beg. So he did not bother to pack food for the trip. "I am sure Stingy will have enough for both of us," he thought. "Even though he won't want to part with it, I am sure to make him, as long as I am greedier than he is stingy."

The three men traveled along a narrow and winding road on their wild adventure. It was not long before the sun woke up. Soon, it was midday and the men were becoming hungry and thirsty. Stingy was famished. But he did not want to eat his food when Greedy was looking.

"Oops!" said Stingy. "I've got to go. You wait for me here; I will only be a moment. I need to go and ease myself."

Greedy didn't trust Stingy. He suspected he must be up to something.

"You took the words right out of my mouth," said Greedy. "I need to go too. I'm about to explode. Let's go do it."

As the two men disappeared into the forest, Nosy went after them. "Someone needs to see what these men are up to, easing themselves or not."

After the three men eased themselves, they sat down to rest. With Greedy always watching him, Stingy could not eat his food. Instead, he slowly brought out his millet cake and quietly laid it behind him. Then he faced Greedy and they talked as if nothing had happened.

"How much farther is the next village?" asked Stingy of Greedy.

As Greedy looked and pointed in the direction of the next village, Stingy slowly tried to reach his millet cake for a pinch into his mouth. But as he reached for the cake he startled a deer, which was helping itself to the cake. As he turned around, the deer ran off with what was left of the cake. Stingy ran after the deer, hoping to get his cake back.

By now Greedy had figured out what had happened. He stopped long enough to lick the crumbs of the cake the startled deer had left on the ground and ran after Stingy and the deer. "Mm, mm," he said. "That is some good millet cake. I am famished and must have more of that cake before I die of hunger."

Nosy, who observed the whole episode, ran after them saying, "It will be fun to see how Stingy recovers his cake from the deer. I know he is stingy, but I don't think he is fast enough to catch up with the deer."

Chakam! *Chakam*! *Chakam*! They went in the brush and meadow, chasing the deer and each other. They were at this for a very long time before Stingy felt he was close enough to tackle the deer. The deer tripped, dropping a very small piece of the millet cake it had not eaten.

Stingy grabbed the cake. Then Nosy grabbed Stingy and tried to pry his hand open to see how much of the cake was left. Meanwhile, Greedy put the deer in a headlock. He stuck his hand into its throat and tried to force it to throw up whatever part of the cake it still had there. Now, which of these men—Stingy, Greedy, and Nosy—do you think lived up to his name the best?

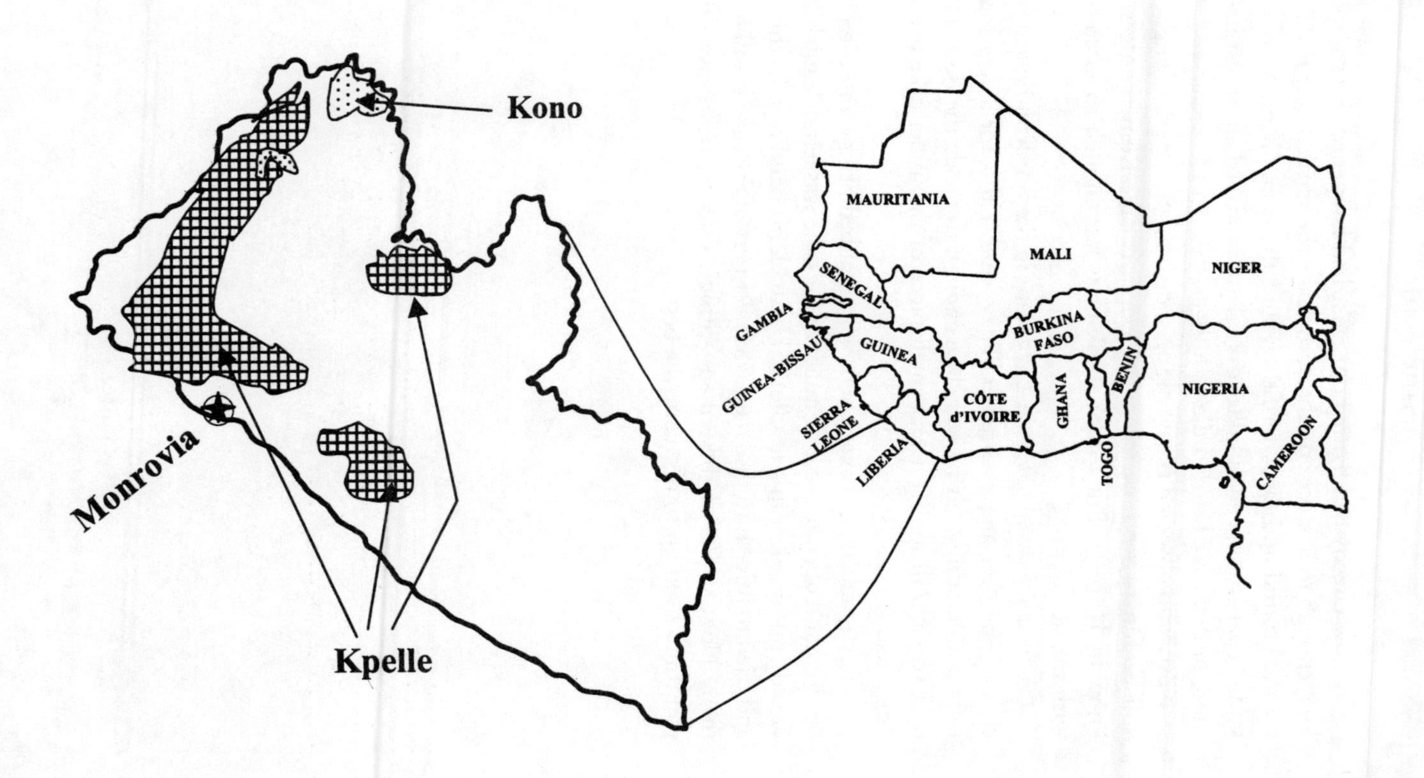
Kono
Monrovia
Kpelle
MAURITANIA
MALI
NIGER
SENEGAL
GAMBIA
GUINEA-BISSAU
GUINEA
SIERRA LEONE
LIBERIA
CÔTE d'IVOIRE
BURKINA FASO
GHANA
TOGO
BENIN
NIGERIA
CAMEROON

Liberia

COUNTRY

Formal Name: Republic of Liberia
Short Form: Liberia
Term for Citizens: Liberian
Capital: Monrovia
Independence: Founded in 1822; adopted a constitution that made it a republic on July 26, 1847

GEOGRAPHY

Size: 38,250 square miles (111,370 km^2)
Boundaries: Bordered to the north by Guinea, east by Côte d'Ivoire, south and southwest by the Atlantic Ocean, and northwest by Sierra Leone

SOCIETY

Population: 2.9 million
Ethnic Groups: The African ethnic groups make up about 95% of the population and include the Kpelle, Bassa, Grebo, Gio, Kru, Krahn, Belle, Dei, Gbandi, Mandingo, and Mano, among others. About 5% are Americo-Liberians.
Languages: There are several local languages including Mende-Tan, Mende-Fu, Kru, Kpelle, and Bassa. The official language is English.
Religion: 70% local religions; 20% Islam; 10% Christianity

The Origin of War

According to this story from the Kono people, the first war on earth was waged when a son took a bride without his father's permission. Because she was very beautiful, the father exiled his son, in order to take his son's wife for himself. Then, to regain his wife from his father, the son sought the help of the King of his village of exile. When the father refused to give up the woman, the King made war with him and killed him. But the King then took the woman for himself. When a King mightier than he came along, he defeated him and took the woman. And so this vicious cycle of wars continues.

Long, long time ago, there was no war on earth. People lived in harmony with one another. When two people disagreed on anything, they resolved it amicably. There was never any exchange of harsh words that could lead to wars. No one ever as much as hit his neighbor. Whenever someone made his neighbor lose blood, it was always by accident. Then, it was necessary to divine the gods so all would be forgiven.

At this point in time, there were many more men than there were women. So all women of marrying age were already married. All a young man could do was wait and hope that when other young girls became of marrying age, they would consider him for marriage.

In this village, there lived a certain man, his wife, and their son. Soon, the woman died, leaving their son, named Samba, to be raised by her husband alone. Before long Samba grew up to be a very handsome young man.

Although Tamba, his father, was advanced in age, he felt he still needed a female companion. So he got married to a very young and beautiful maiden. Not too long after the maiden arrived at Tamba's house, Samba took a liking to her. Tamba was very mad and cross. In his anger, he beat Samba severely.

"I need a wife father," pleaded Samba. "You must find me a wife."

"No!" said his father. "You will get married when I know you are ready."

"But I am ready. All my mates my age have taken their own wives."

"Yes! But they are not living with their parents. You take a wife when you can support her."

So it was that Tamba refused to get Samba a wife. Samba was angry and disappointed. Once in a while he'd go back and ask his father for a wife. But his father refused. The more his father refused, the more determined Samba was to get married.

Samba resolved to get himself a wife no matter what. He worked hard to save enough so that he could have his own place. He prayed every day to his God to help him.

One day his father went on a long trip with his wife and left Samba to himself. One night after a long and hard day, Samba prayed for a wife as he always did. Then, God appeared to him.

"Go and cut some wood and make a fire for me," God told him.

Samba did as he was instructed and made the fire for God. Then God came and stayed with him. For several days God stayed with Samba. Samba begged and begged God for a wife of his own. Someone he could come home to everyday. Someone he could call his own.

The more Samba prayed, the more God became sympathetic to him. Then one day, God put Samba into a deep sleep. He told him not to wake up or speak until he told him to.

While Samba slept, God took a stem of banana tree, the size of a human being, and laid it beside Samba. He covered the stem and Samba with a piece of cloth and left. Then very early the next morning, God came back.

"Lango! Lango!" God called. "Wake up."

Immediately, out of the log of banana stem rose a beautiful maiden. Her beauty had never been seen in the village before. Samba, who was also awakened by the call, looked on with mouth wide open. He tried to speak but no words came out of his mouth.

"Samba," God called him, "Take Lango as your wife. You must support her and protect her honor at all times."

"It shall be done," Samba promised. "Thank you, my God, for answering my prayers."

A few days later, Tamba came back and saw Lango. Immediately, he began to lust for her. He tried all he could to drive Samba away from home so he could have Lango to himself. He discredited Samba. He never liked anything he did.

When Samba noticed what his father was trying to do, he became very angry and lashed out at him.

"If I find you interfering with my wife," warned Samba, "I shall take your life."

Tamba was shocked at such an uttering from anybody, especially his son, for it had never been uttered before. Angered by his son's threat, Tamba saw it as an excuse to drive him away from his house. So he did, and Lango stayed back and lived with Tamba.

But Samba could never forget Lango, for he loved her so much. He traveled for many days until he came to a village where he settled in exile. The loss of Lango gnawed at him daily. So, he went and told the village's Chief Momodu his story and begged him to help get his wife back.

Chief Momodu sent his messengers to Tamba to return Samba's wife. But Tamba would not heed his request. Instead, he killed the messengers to keep them from going back to Chief Momodu. Thus, the first murder in the world was committed.

When Chief Momodu did not hear from his messengers, he went with more messengers to Tamba. When Tamba refused to give him Lango, Momodu took her by force and made war with Tamba's men. Momodu defeated Tamba and killed him.

Momodu, on seeing Lango, fell in love with her immediately. He took her as his wife and chased Samba out of his village, threatening to kill him if he stayed around.

Samba ran away to another village, this one ruled by Chief Fabamba. There he told the chief his story. He begged the chief to help him get his wife back. When Fabamba went to Momodu, he would not give him Lango. So they made war. Momodu was defeated and killed.

And Fabamba was taken by Lango's beauty. He wanted to keep her to himself and sought a way to drive Samba away. "The reason for all these wars is because of Samba," he said to himself. "If I killed him instead of driving him away, all these wars would stop."

On that thought Fabamba lured Samba away to a distant forest and killed him.

Fabamba's claim to Lango was short lived though, for when other chiefs more powerful than he saw Lango, they made war with Fabamba and took her from him. This cycle continues till today. For as long as there are Langos of any kind in this world, there will continue to be wars.

The River Demon

The Kpelle people tell the story of a River Demon who feeds on children who lie. This story is one of many used to teach children to follow socially acceptable forms of behavior. In this particular situation, a mother suspects her two daughters of stealing from her. When they deny the accusation, she takes them to the River Demon for judgment. If the girls are innocent, the River Demon will wash them ashore. But if they are guilty and do not confess, they will be swallowed by the river.

Once, in a remote village, there lived a woman and her two daughters. The sisters took turns preparing the meals for the family. When their mother went to the farm, one of the girls prepared the meal. She saved it in a calabash and kept it on the earthen mound. There the food stayed. Then, the girls went out and played until their mother came home, so they could all eat the meal together.

This village was an island, surrounded by waters so wide that you could not see the end of them. Now, in this water, there lived a demon who fed only on people who have done wrong. When someone was accused of any wrongdoing, he was taken to the center of the river to swear by it. If he was innocent, the river left him alone. But if he was guilty, the River Demon opened his wide mouth and swallowed him.

It happened that whenever this woman left her food in the house, one of the daughters ate it. When she asked them about it, they denied it. One day the woman came back from the farm with a rabbit she had killed. She singed the rabbit and cut it up. Then she gave some of it to the first daughter to make soup. The rest of the meat she dried over her fireplace. That night, they ate like they never had before. They were full and happy. The next day, the mother went back to the farm leaving the girls at home.

When their mother came back later that day, she found the rest of the meat was missing. She was furious.

"Food I can understand they ate because they were hungry," she thought. "But meat! That's outright greed and any child who grows up with such lofty taste buds will never amount to anything. She is likely to end up a rogue in order to satisfy her tastes for meat and such."

With that analysis she decided to confront the girls.

"Who ate the rabbit meat?" she asked them.

They each denied knowledge of the meat. "I didn't even know that it was out there on the fire," said the first daughter.

"Neither did I," denied the second daughter. "I thought we ate it all up last night."

Their mother was not happy with the situation. She begged them to tell the truth.

"I am not going to punish you," she begged them. "Just tell the truth. You know how much I hate people who steal. I hate people who lie even more. You must ask permission before you take anything. But, should you take it without permission, you must admit that you did."

"I didn't touch the meat, mother," denied the first daughter, "honest!"

"I was out all day playing," denied the second daughter. "I didn't even know we had any rabbit meat."

Poor woman. "And I thought I was raising very good children," she said to them. "Now, not only am I raising thieves, I am also raising liars."

For several days she weighed her options. She thought, "Should I beat the truth out of them? Should I deny them food?" But she concluded that none of the options was viable for she would be punishing the innocent girl as well. "Could they have colluded and eaten the meat together?" she wondered. After much debate with herself, she called the daughters together and announced her plan.

"Since I cannot get the truth out of you," she told them, "I will take you to the River Demon. But I will give you one last chance to confess. To make it easier for you, you can come and tell me privately and I will not let the other know you did. But if I do not hear from either of you by daybreak, we will let the River Demon have you for dinner."

With that she went to bed and her daughters went to their room. There, they both lay on their backs. Each stared at the wall geckos stalking the night moths on the ceiling of their thatched house. They couldn't get any sleep.

"Why don't you admit it," said the first daughter. "Why do you want to shame everybody tomorrow?"

"What about you?" retorted her sister, "Why don't *you* admit it?"

They went at each other for most of the night until they finally fell asleep. When they woke up the next morning, their mother had already left for the farm. The girls were relieved that at least they would survive that day. "Before she comes back," thought the second daughter, "it'll be too late to go to the river."

Later that day, before the sun was barely past overhead, they saw their mother coming back in the distance. Their jaws dropped. Their hearts began to race and beat monotonously against their ribs. They were so beside themselves that they didn't know their mother had reached them.

"Won't you welcome me?" she asked them.

"Welcome ma," they responded nervously.

They helped their mother put down her load. They served her food and after she ate, she asked whether they were ready to confess. But they said nothing. So she took the girls to the river. When they got there, she put the second girl in a big calabash bowl and pushed her to the center of the river.

"Serenade the River Demon," she instructed her. "If you are innocent, he will let you be, if you are not, then goodbye, my daughter, for this is the last I will see of you."

When the calabash flowed to the center of the river the girl began to sing:

River Demon! River Demon!
If it was I that ate the rabbit meat
Then here I come I am yours
Open your mouth that you I may entreat
But if the meat was eaten by someone else
Then forever keep your mouth shut that I may retreat...

After two to three verses of the song, nothing happened to her. The river reversed its course and the girl was washed ashore to her mother. Then her mother removed her from the calabash and put her sister, the first daughter, in it. She pushed her to the center of the river telling her to serenade the River Demon.

River Demon! River Demon!
If it was I, that ate the rabbit meat
Then here I come I am yours
Open your mouth...

When the number one daughter started to sing to the River Demon, the river began to swirl. It carried her into the whirlpool and began to swallow her. Her mother pleaded with her to confess. But she still would not confess. Soon the water was up to her neck. Her mother pleaded with her again to confess. But she denied it and continued to sing until the river covered her completely.

After that, the woman cried for her daughter. When she could not cry anymore, she took her second daughter and went back home. There the two of them lived for a very long time. Whenever they went to the river, they'd remember the girl and cry again.

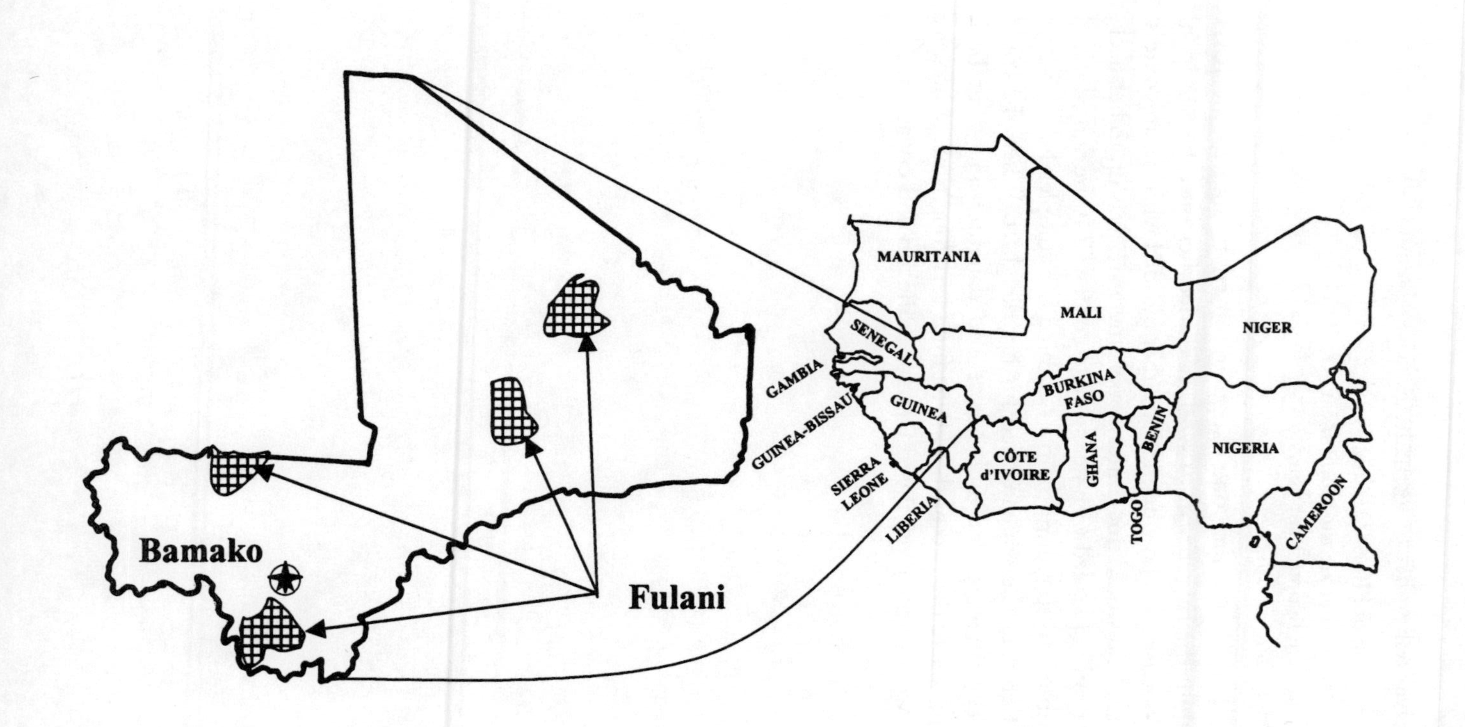
Bamako
Fulani
MAURITANIA
MALI
NIGER
SENEGAL
GAMBIA
GUINEA-BISSAU
GUINEA
SIERRA LEONE
LIBERIA
CÔTE d'IVOIRE
BURKINA FASO
GHANA
TOGO
BENIN
NIGERIA
CAMEROON

Mali

COUNTRY

Formal Name: Republic of Mali (formerly French Sudan)
Short Form: Mali
Term for Citizens: Malian
Capital: Bamako
Independence: September 22, 1960 (from France)

GEOGRAPHY

Size: 482,077 square miles (1,248,500 km^2)
Boundaries: Bordered to the north by Algeria, east by Niger, southeast by Burkina Faso, south by Côte d'Ivoire, southwest by Guinea and Senegal, and west by Mauritania

SOCIETY

Population: 10.4 million
Ethnic Groups: Mande (50%), comprised of Bambara, Mandingo, and Sarakole; Peul (17%); Voltaic (12%); Tuareg and Moor (10%); Songhai (6%); others (5%)
Languages: Bambara and other local languages are spoken by about 80% of the population. French is the official language.
Religion: 90% Islam; 9% local religions; 1% Christianity

The Origin of Creation

The white of clouds provides the basis for this tale by the Fulanis about the creation of the world. The world was at first a vast ocean of milk and clouds until God improved his creation with vegetation and stone. When these became unruly, he created iron to check them. In turn, he created fire, water, sun, and man, with each creation stronger than the one before.

In the beginning the world was an ocean of milk. And God was satisfied with his creation. All was a white ocean of milk and cloud. But there was little difference between heaven and earth. So God wanted to add color to his creation. He said, "Out of milk shall come forth plants and stones."

Then there were plants and stones.

So, in the beginning God created milk
Then for color, he added plants and stones

But stone was too strong for milk and plants, squashing them as it rolled along. So God wanted to create something stronger to counteract the strength of stone. He said, "Out of stone shall come forth iron."

Then there was iron.

So, in the beginning God created milk
Then for color, he added plants and stones
And then iron to put a check on stone

Iron, as one can imagine, became too powerful for stone. Something mightier was needed. Thus God took it upon himself to create fire. "Let there be fire," he said.

And there was fire.

So, in the beginning God created milk
Then for color, he added plants and stones
And then iron to put a check on stone
But iron was too strong for stone
So, he created fire

Soon the fire was out of control, burning everything in its path, in a wild rage. So God said, "Let there be water." And there was water, which controlled the rage of fire.

So, in the beginning God created milk
Then for color, he added plants and stones
And then iron to put a check on stone
But iron was too strong for stone
So, he created fire
And then water to control fire

"Water, water, why have you refused to cease? For with my hands I made you to control fire. Now you pour and pour unending." So, God made sun to put a check on water.

So, in the beginning God created milk
Then for color, he added plants and stones
And then iron to put a check on stone
But iron was too strong for stone
So, He created fire
And then water to control fire
Then came sun to control water

Then God thought to himself, "I have created all these things. I need a rest. I need a shepherd to watch over these creations." So God created man, thinking, "My shepherd should be in my image so my creations will pay heed to him."

So, in the beginning God created milk
Then for color, he added plants and stones
And then iron to put a check on stone
But iron was too strong for stone
So, he created fire
And then water to control fire
Then came sun to control water
And man he gave dominion over all creations

But man became proud. He ruled without compassion. In order to humble man, God created afflictions. Man, in trying to fight the afflictions of sickness, hunger, worry, and jealousy became weaker. But then these afflictions became too proud of their control over man. So God created death, which controlled afflictions and with it, man.

So, in the beginning God created milk
Then for color, he added plants and stones

And then iron to put a check on stone
But iron was too strong for stone
So, he created fire
And then water to control fire
Then came sun to control water
And man he gave dominion over all creations
But man was proud and ruled without compassion
So, God created afflictions to humble man
And death to control afflictions and with it man
But death killed every man in its way and wanted to eliminate man

However, God didn't really intend that man should be eliminated, seeing that he was in his own image. So said he, "I must make someone special. A man who can conquer death." So God sent his son to the world.

So, in the beginning God created milk
Then for color, he added plants and stones
And then iron to put a check on stone
But iron was too strong for stone
So, he created fire
And then water to control fire
Then came sun to control water
And man he gave dominion over all creations
But man was proud and ruled without compassion
So, God created afflictions to humble man
And death to control afflictions and with it man
But death killed every man in its way and wanted to eliminate man
So, God sent his son who defeated death.

Mauritania

COUNTRY

Formal Name: Islamic Republic of Mauritania
Short Form: Mauritania
Term for Citizens: Mauritanian
Capital: Nouakchott
Independence: November 28, 1960 (from France)

GEOGRAPHY

Size: 398,000 square miles (1,030,700 km^2)
Boundaries: Bordered to the north by the Western Sahara, northeast by Algeria, east by Mali, south by Mali and Senegal, and west by the Atlantic Ocean

SOCIETY

Population: 2.6 million
Ethnic Groups: The major ethnic groups are mixed Maur/Black (40%), Maur 30%, and Black 30%.
Languages: The official languages are Hasaniya Arabic and Wolof. Other local languages include Pular and Soninke.
Religion: Almost 100% Islam

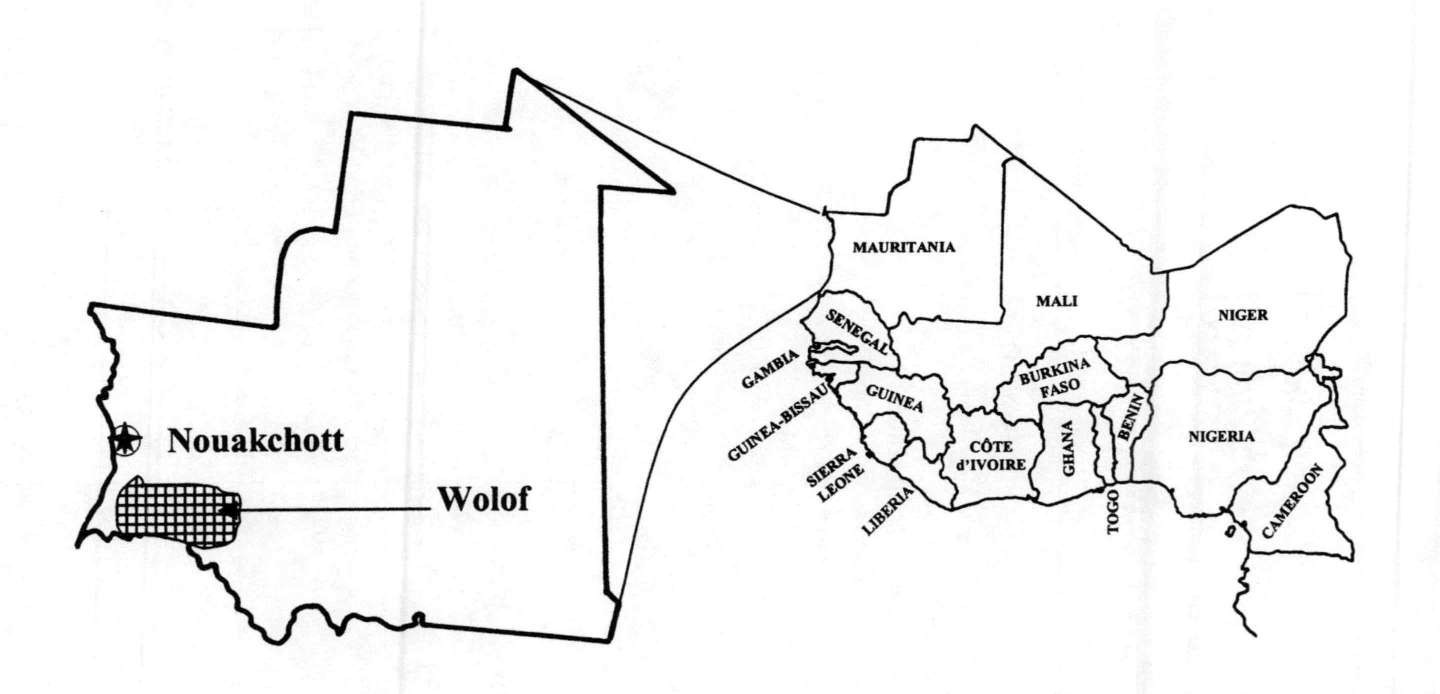
Nouakchott
Wolof
MAURITANIA
MALI
NIGER
SENEGAL
GAMBIA
GUINEA-BISSAU
GUINEA
SIERRA LEONE
LIBERIA
CÔTE d'IVOIRE
BURKINA FASO
GHANA
TOGO
BENIN
NIGERIA
CAMEROON

The Magic Silk Cotton Tree

The Wolofs tell this tale of a child raised by a Duck in a silk cotton tree. When humans discovered the child, they tried to destroy the Duck and its habitat in order to rescue the child. But the Duck had magical powers, which it used to stymie the humans.

Once upon a time, there lived a man and his two wives. His first wife had no children, but the second wife had two and was pregnant with a third. The first wife was jealous of the second wife but she was sure that she would one day have her own child. "I am still young," she'd say to herself. And since her co-wife's children were both girls, she hoped that she'd be the first to have a baby boy. Unfortunately for her, when the second wife had her third child, it was a boy.

"There goes all I wished for," she said to herself one day. "It is bad enough for me that she has children, it is even worse that she now also has a baby boy. Now my husband will love her even more."

Since the birth of this boy, the first wife had searched for a way to discredit her co-wife. She planned all sorts of schemes, but none of her plans worked. Then she thought, "Since this baby boy is the only guarantee that she will continue to find favor with my husband, I must kill him."

One day, as the second wife was not looking, the first wife stole the child and buried him in a shallow grave. While she was burying the boy, a wild Duck circled overhead, searching for food. The Duck saw what the woman had done. After the woman left, the Duck swooped down and dug up the child. It took the baby to its nest atop a big silk cotton tree by the bank of a river.

The Duck fed the baby wild berries. It brought him water from the river and food from people's compounds. Two years later, the baby had grown into a very handsome little toddler.

The Duck and the Boy were very happy together living in the silk cotton tree, which was quite far away from the village so that the boy hadn't seen another person for two years.

One day, a Hunter was searching for game. He wandered too far away from home and came upon the silk cotton tree. As he searched for game, he noticed what looked like a monkey in the silk cotton tree. He pulled out his bow and arrow, took aim and was about to release his arrow when he noticed something unusual about the game. To his amazement, it was a little boy. He squinted his eyes to get a better view of the figure. Then he shaded them with his hands, constructing an imaginary telescope. But he came up with the same conclusion: "It is human," he said. "Thank you God. How could I have convinced my people that I didn't mean to spill his blood? Who would have believed that a small boy like this could have climbed this big cotton tree in the middle of the forest?"

For a moment, he was very confused and just rattled in his mind. It was bad enough to kill a fellow human being, but it was even worse to kill a defenseless child. He replayed the consequences of killing a human being in cold blood over in his mind. The likelihood of a banishment to a foreign land, the shame, the…

"Quack! Quack! Quack!" said the wild Duck as she dove for the Hunter, in defense of her nest.

The Hunter ducked. By the time he collected himself and his bow and arrow, the Duck was out of sight. He tried to climb the tree to rescue the boy, but the trunk was much too big for him to get a good grip. Then he tried talking the boy down from the tree. But the little boy would not listen to the Hunter. So the Hunter ran back to the village to tell the Chief what he had seen.

"Order the talking drums," said the Chief. "Everybody must be assembled at the market square first thing tomorrow morning."

Very early the next day all the villagers were gathered. They knew that it must be something serious for the Chief to summon them so quickly without warning.

"What could it be?" a villager asked his neighbor.

"I heard that a hunter visited the Chief with some kind of news."

"What kind of news?"

"I don't know. But those who were there said that after he got the news, the Chief exclaimed, 'Please gods, don't let me see my ears unless it is through a reflection.'"

"It is very serious then," concluded the villager.

After the villagers were gathered, the Chief addressed them. First, he introduced the Hunter, whom he had quarantined in his palace since he brought the news.

"All of you know Musa the Hunter," the Chief said. "He said that he saw a little boy sitting in a nest atop a silk cotton tree by the river bank. He doesn't know how he got up there. He tried to talk him down but a giant Duck chased after him. Is anyone among you responsible for the boy being up in the tree?"

A wave of murmur passed through the audience. Each one asked his neighbor if he knew anything. After a few moments the Chief reassured them that he was going to get to the bottom of the mystery. He summoned the elders to approach him for a short council. After the council, he requested audience from the villagers again.

"As I was saying," he continued, "I am resolved to find out who put the boy up there. Since the silk cotton tree is too tall and big for a human to climb, we shall cut it down."

"Impossible," said a man to his neighbor. "I heard the tree is so big it would take about four market weeks to fell it."

"No tree is that big," his neighbor corrected him. "Just call Alhaji Bello, the tree nemesis. Pay him his fee and he will fell it before the sun is overhead."

"I heard he has a magic ax and machete so sharp he shaves with it."

"Not only that," added his friend. "I hear the ax and machete even cut on their own."

As the two men raved about Bello, the Chief continued. He called on Alhaji Bello and gave him nine other able-bodied men. He paid them handsomely and charged them to cut down the silk cotton tree to rescue the boy.

"Go in peace," he said. "Through your hands we shall solve the mystery of the boy in the silk cotton tree. We shall know the parent among us who defaced the name of Allah by putting his child up in the tree."

Very early the next morning, Alhaji Bello and his men took off for the river. They arrived and found the boy atop the silk cotton tree just as the Hunter had reported. They immediately got to work chopping down the tree. They had chopped the tree until just a very fine slab of wood held it. Bello was sure that the tree would fall with the next blow of his razor-sharp ax. He surveyed the tree and its likely direction of fall. He scurried his men to safety and, with all his might, dealt the tree its final blow.

Then a voice from the boy sang:

Quack! Quack! Mother duck, it's your ducklin'!
Quack! The silk cotton tree is getting thin.
Quack! It is about to fall!
Quack! It is thin and is about to fall!

As Bello looked in amazement at the boy, another voice came from the riverside and sang back in response:

Quack! Quack! Silk cotton tree!
Quack! Tree trunk, enlarge!
Quack! Keep your stand, silk cotton tree!
Quack! Tree trunk, enlarge!

It was the wild Duck. And as she sang, the trunk of the silk cotton tree grew back to its original size. The men were astonished. They again started to chop down the tree, more determined than before. But as soon as the tree was about to be felled, the boy sang to the Duck. And as the Duck sang back, the tree trunk assumed its original size. After several tries, the men determined that they could not cut down the tree and gave up. They went back to the Chief to report their frustration.

"The Chief shall live forever," said Bello, genuflecting. "We couldn't cut down the tree. Whenever we came close to felling it, the boy sang and something by the riverbank sang back. Then the tree trunk went back to its original size. We have tried several times with the same result. And, as our people say, 'It is only a crazy man who does the same thing over and over expecting different results.'"

On hearing this, the Chief ordered his medicine men to give the men some magic powder. He advised them to split themselves into two groups. While one group tried to cut down the tree, the other should go upstream and sprinkle the magic powder into the river.

Very early the next day, the men set off to accomplish their task. When they got there they did as they were instructed. Five of the men started chopping the tree and the other five went upstream to poison the river. As the tree was about to be felled, the boy started to sing again:

Quack! Quack! Mother duck, it's your ducklin'!
Quack! The silk cotton tree is getting thin.
Quack! It is about to fall!

Quack! It is thin and is about to fall!

The men looked on, eager to see the result of the magic powder. Then the wild Duck sang back, but very slowly and painfully:

Quaaackkk! Quaaackkk! Siiillllk-cootton tre-ee!
Quaaackkk! Tre-ee trrr' ennnlaaarge!
Quaaack! Ke-eep yo staand siiilllk-co' tre-ee!
Qua...

"It must have died," said Bello. "Aiyerere!" he exclaimed with joy as only a portion of the tree trunk returned to its original size. Then with a few more blows, the tree fell. They caught the littel boy and took him back to the Chief.

Again the Chief summoned the villagers. The talking drum was beaten as before. When they were gathered, the Chief addressed them.

"At last we can put to rest, the puzzle of the boy in the silk cotton tree," said the Chief. "Each one of our women must come and claim this child. And by the power of the gods and blood, we shall know the rightful mother."

One by one all the women came to claim the child, but he would not go to anyone of them. Finally, it was the turn of the boy's true mother. When she came forward and stretched out her hands to the boy, he immediately ran to her.

Directly the talking drum sounded. All the villagers were happy that the child's true mother had been found.

"Now," said the Chief. "What kind of mother is she that throws her child away?"

"The Chief shall live forever," said she. "My child was lost, but now is found. He was dead, but now lives."

Since nobody knew how the child ended up with the Duck, the diviners were summoned. They threw their strings of cowries and seashells and determined that it was the woman's co-wife who had kidnapped the child and buried him alive. The Chief ordered for her to be imprisoned and punished for her wickedness.

As for the Duck, she staggered back to her feet the next day when the effect of the medicine wore off. She had cried all day and night for the boy and the silk cotton tree, but her cries seemed to have lost their magic. Since then, ducks dislike trees and prefer to build their nests on land or float them on water.

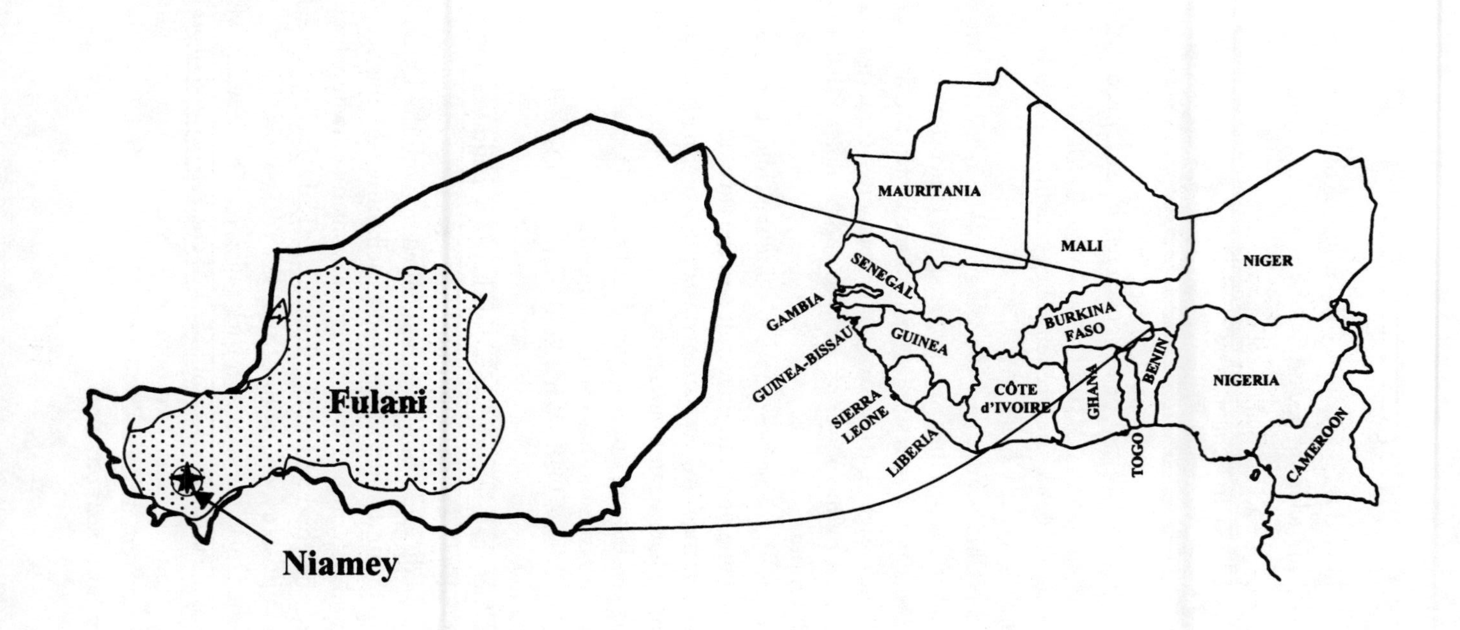
Fulani
Niamey
MAURITANIA
MALI
NIGER
SENEGAL
GAMBIA
GUINEA-BISSAU
GUINEA
SIERRA LEONE
LIBERIA
CÔTE d'IVOIRE
BURKINA FASO
GHANA
TOGO
BENIN
NIGERIA
CAMEROON

Niger

COUNTRY

Formal Name: Republic of Niger
Short Form: Niger
Term for Citizens: Nigerien
Capital: Niamey
Independence: August 3, 1960 (from France)

GEOGRAPHY

Size: 496,900 square miles (1.3 million km^2)
Boundaries: Bordered to the north by Algeria and Libya, east by Chad, south by Nigeria, southwest by Benin and Burkina Faso, and west by Mali

SOCIETY

Population: 9.9 million
Ethnic Groups: Hausa (56%), Djerma (22%), Fula (8.5%), Tuareg (8%), and Kanouri (4.3%). Others include Arab, Toubou, Gourmantche, and French.
Languages: Local languages include Hausa and Djerma. Official language is French.
Religion: 80% Islam; 15% local religions; 5% Christianity

For Your Ears Only

The Fulanis tell this story to illustrate the importance of trust. A Hunter came upon a Chameleon who sang and played the harp in a secluded part of the forest. The Chameleon made the Hunter promise not to tell anyone else about him, and in return promised to be the Hunter's personal entertainer for the rest of his life. The Hunter agreed, but soon he could no longer bear to keep his find to himself.

There was once a Hunter who lived in a West African village. One day he shot a deer with his bow and arrow. After a very long chase that took him through several woods and across several rivers, enough time for his poison to take effect, he recovered the deer. He was on his way home when he heard a very sweet and melodious song coming out of the woods near the bank of a river.

Man is the king of all animals
Man imposes his will on them
It is not man that is ruled by the animals
Animals cannot impose their will on him

"Ah!" he exclaimed. "What a sweet voice! What good manners! I would give anything to have that girl for my wife."

After the music ceased, he started toward the corner of the woods where the music came from, but stopped. "Suppose that is a mermaid?" he thought. "There have been stories of mermaids in this part of the woods. I better run back home with my kill."

As he turned away for home the sweet music started playing again.

Man is the king of all animals
Man imposes his will on them
It is not man that is ruled by the animals
Animals cannot impose their will on him

With his desire overcoming his fear and reasoning, he tiptoed to the edge of the woods. Then he peered into the corner from where the music came. To the Hunter's surprise he found a Chameleon with a harp hung around his neck.

"Do not tell anyone," the Chameleon begged the Hunter, "and I will play my music for you only."

The Hunter was startled, for he had never seen a Chameleon who talked before, much less one who played such beautiful music. "A Chameleon? My own Chameleon to entertain me alone?" The thought of that got the Hunter even more excited and he settled down to listen to the Chameleon play for him some more. After the Chameleon was done, the Hunter picked up his deer and went home.

Everyday the Hunter went to the forest to listen to the Chameleon sing for him. On a successful hunting day, the songs made the hunt even more rewarding, and on not so successful days, they made him feel like the day was not a total loss.

After several market weeks, the Hunter could no longer keep the secret of the Chameleon to himself any more. He just had to tell someone.

"Get out of here," his wife told him.

"You must be crazy," his friends told him. "Where is this Chameleon?" asked one of them.

"Out in the woods," he replied.

"I bet he ran so fast that you couldn't catch him?" they teased him. "Ha! Ha! Ha! Ha!" They laughed so hard at him that he felt embarrassed.

"Why don't you tell the King?" suggested the other. "That's who people go to when they have unusual stories like that. That way, the King can give them what they need to confirm the story."

"Of course if you are lying, you could pay with your life," said the other.

The Hunter knew he was telling the truth. And, since the Chameleon liked him so much, he thought that he would let him show him to the King. So he set out to tell the King what he had seen. On his way to the King, the Hunter thought of how great he would be, being the only one that the Chameleon befriended.

"What do you want?" asked the King's guard.

"I have a very important message for the King," he replied.

"The King is in his court," said the guard, "and cannot be disturbed. Tell me and I will deliver it to him later."

"I know of a place where the King can find a Chameleon who sings and plays the harp," said the Hunter. "It also extols the virtues of man in his song."

"You must either be crazy," said the guard, "or have a weird sense of humor. In either case, you chose the wrong person to joke with. Get out of here."

"But I am serious," insisted the Hunter.

"Then maybe you should tell him yourself."

The guard took the Hunter into the King's court where he was in conference with his chiefs. "Long live the King. Here is a man who insists he must have your audience."

"The King will live forever," greeted the Hunter.

"What can I do for you, my son?"

"Several market weeks ago, I came upon a Chameleon that played such a melodious song, I have been listening to him every day since. But I thought I'd let you know of him since I can no longer stand to keep the discovery to myself."

"Is that why you have decided to interrupt my court?"

"No, your honor. The Chameleon actually sang and spoke to me," replied the Hunter. "Isn't that amazing?"

"Indeed, it is amazing!" agreed the King. "A Chameleon that sings and talks. That is amazing. Where is this Chameleon?"

"Way in the deep woods where I hunt. I will bring it to your court tomorrow."

"Not necessary. I will give you four of my best men to go now and get that Chameleon. If there is such a Chameleon, I will make you rich beyond your wildest dreams. But if there is not such a Chameleon, you will pay for this lie with your life."

"So be it, my lord," agreed the Hunter.

So the King sent four of his guards with the Hunter. He gave them instructions to kill the Hunter if he was lying, otherwise, to come back with him and the singing Chameleon.

After a long walk that took them from the time the first cock crowed to about the time the sun was overhead, the Hunter and the guards came upon the woods where the Chameleon lived. The Hunter led the guards to a corner of the woods. There, he cleared the brushes with his hand to expose the Chameleon. Sure enough, the Chameleon was still there with his harp hung around his neck.

"You see. I told you," said the Hunter.

"I see a Chameleon alright, but he is neither playing, singing, nor talking," observed one guard.

"Hello, good ol' pal," said the Hunter to the Chameleon. "These men are from the King and want to make sure I was telling the truth about you. Strike some notes and sing for them so they can tell the King what I said was true."

The Chameleon just sat there and looked on. No song came out of him or his harp. It didn't even as much as move a muscle. The guards just waited patiently to give the Hunter enough time to convince the Chameleon to talk and play. After waiting for what seemed like eternity, the guards became impatient.

"I think this charade has gone on long enough," one of them remarked.

"Please pal," pleaded the Hunter to the Chameleon, "forget about the song. Just say something. Anything at all."

Still the Chameleon wouldn't say a word. It just stayed perched on a twig like a Christmas ornament. As the Hunter looked at the Chameleon in desperation it seemed to have a sinister look about it. The once friendly look seemed to have given way to that of glee.

By now the guards couldn't wait any longer. So they carried out their orders to kill the Hunter. As they turned around to head back home, a voice came from behind them.

"I told him not to tell," said the Chameleon.

The guards froze on their tracks as they looked back and saw the Chameleon adjusting his harp.

"The Hunter spoke the truth," concluded one of the guards.

"And we killed him," added another.

"He brought about his own death," said the Chameleon. "He shared my little secret because of his greed. I told him not to tell anyone about me and he was not content to come here and listen to me. He had to tell the world about me so he could be rich and famous."

The guards were shocked and started to run back home. As they ran they heard the Chameleon singing.

Man is the king of all animals
Man imposes his will on them
It is not man that is ruled by the animals
Animals cannot impose their will on him

Guess what they told the King when they got back home?

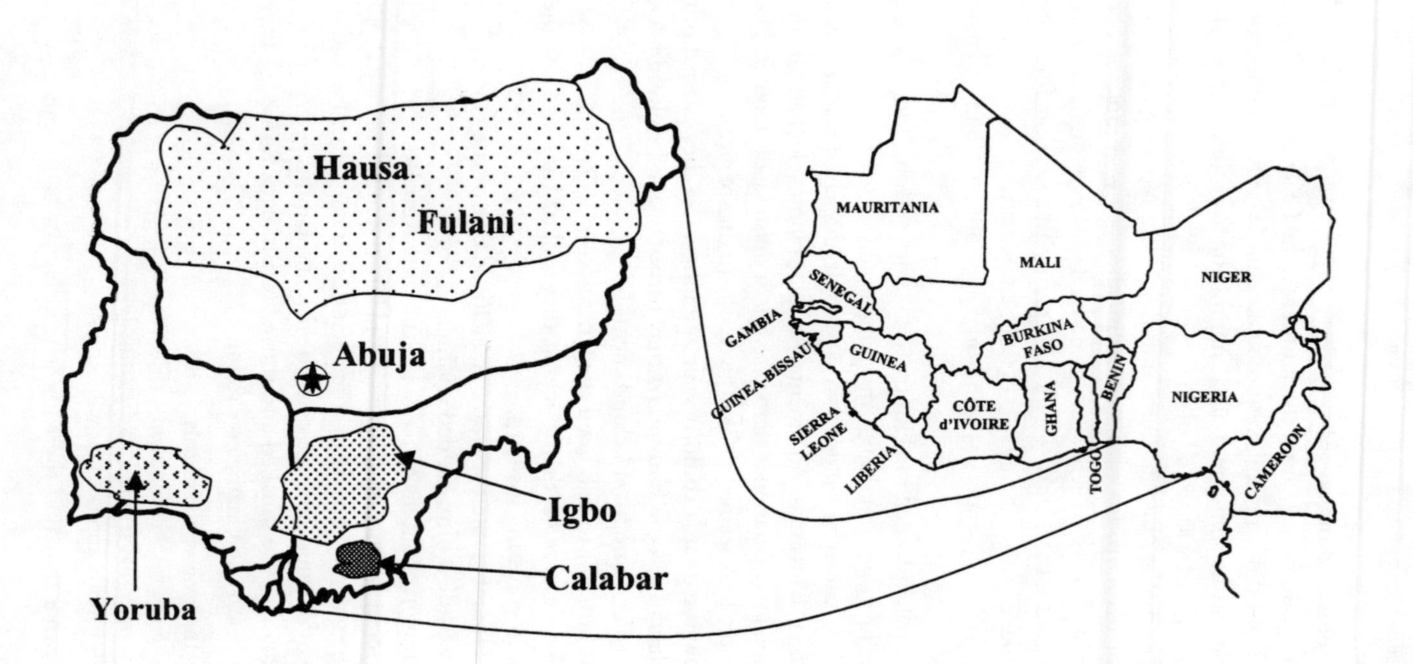
Hausa
Fulani
Abuja
Igbo
Calabar
Yoruba
MAURITANIA
MALI
NIGER
SENEGAL
GAMBIA
GUINEA-BISSAU
GUINEA
SIERRA LEONE
LIBERIA
CÔTE d'IVOIRE
BURKINA FASO
GHANA
TOGO
BENIN
NIGERIA
CAMEROON

Nigeria

COUNTRY

Formal Name: Federal Republic of Nigeria
Short Form: Nigeria
Term for Citizens: Nigerian
Capital: Abuja (formerly Lagos)
Independence: October 1, 1960 (from United Kingdom)

GEOGRAPHY

Size: 356,669 square miles (923,770 km^2)
Boundaries: Bordered to the north by Niger, northeast by Chad, east by Cameroon, south by the Gulf of Guinea, Bight of Benin, and the Atlantic Ocean, and west by Benin

SOCIETY

Population: 113.8 million
Ethnic Groups: There are several recognized ethnic groups, but the most populous are the Hausa and Fulani in the north, Yoruba in the southwest, and Igbos in the southeast. Others include Kanuri, Ibibio, Tiv, and Ijaw.
Languages: There are as many languages as there are ethnic groups. The most widely spoken are Hausa, Yoruba, Igbo, and Fulani. English is the official language and language of instruction in educational institutions.
Religion: 50% Islam; 40% Christianity; 10% local religions

APUNANWU

The Igbos have several versions of tales of a girl named Apunanwu. In this version, a childless Chief's prayer is answered when his pot of palm oil turns into a beautiful girl. Because of the girl's beauty and origin, the Chief named her Apunanwu, which means beautiful and averse to heat. He ordered her never to do anything that might make her hot. Jealous of Apunanwu's popularity and beauty, one of the King's wives refused to feed her. Apunanwu had no choice but to cook for herself.

There once lived a very popular Chief in a certain West African village. He was a Chief with many titles, one of which was Ifemelunma. Chief Nma, as he was popularly known, had several wives. But none of them bore him a child. He prayed most days and nights for a child, but still could not have any.

Chief Nma was very industrious and, like most chiefs, farmed several lands. He also raised several herds of livestock, and had several servants. One day after a bountiful harvest of palm nuts, Chief Nma was very pleased with his harvest. His servants had finished pressing the oil out of the palm nuts when he came to inspect the yield.

"Ifemelunma," his chief servant greeted him, using the Chief's full name, which means something done right.

"*Onaghi awa na afa*," Chief Nma replied, which means that it never requires an interceder.

Many title names are short forms of a statement for which the titleholder responds with the remainder of the statement.

"So why is it that I do not have a child to succeed me when I die?" Chief Nma asked rhetorically. "I have done right by my forefathers. I sacrifice to them and observe the laws of the land, yet I have no heir to continue my good deeds."

As Chief Nma was inspecting the pots of oil, he beamed with pleasure at their quality and aroma. The oils were redder than usual and he was sure that they would never go to sleep, that is, congeal or settle. Chief Nma tilted the pots to reassure himself of the quality of the oils. They flowed like water. It was the kind of oil that the villagers used to eat roasted dwarf yams during the new yam festival.

Even though all the oils this time seemed of exceptional quality, the oil in one of the pots stood out from all the others. It had a special glow about it and seemed lifelike. Chief Nma looked at it a second time. He was taken by its quality and, as he gazed at the oil, he unconsciously prayed, as had become his custom, asking God for a child.

"Chineke," he called his God. "You have blessed me again with a bountiful harvest. You always do. Let all praise and glory be to you." Then he added, "If it is your will, you will one day also bless me with a child. If you will it, this pot of oil will be turned into a child for me."

Just as he finished his prayers, the pot of oil slowly began to take on human form. As the Chief looked on in amazement at the metamorphosis of the oil, a very beautiful girl emerged from it. She was full of health and shone like the morning sun. She was the most beautiful girl the villagers had ever seen.

"Father," called the young girl. "I have heard your cries and am here to comfort you."

Chief Nma was dumbfounded. When he finally collected himself, he stretched out his hands and embraced the girl. He was very happy that his prayers have been answered at last.

Although the girl was not a baby, Chief Nma still regarded her as one. He therefore didn't name her right away. He waited for the traditional seven market weeks to pass. Meanwhile, he kept her indoors, just like a little baby.

After seven market weeks, Chief Nma presented the girl to the village for the naming ceremony. There was dancing and feasting in the village. Word about her beauty reached all the lands and everybody from far and near came to see the Chief's new daughter. Everyone related to Chief Nma, from his brothers and sisters to his wives, was invited to participate in the ceremony. Each one of the relatives was given a chance to name the child. They all came forward and called out names for her according to their desires for her.

"*Ogechuckwukanma*," Chief Nma's last wife and the girl's stepmother called out. "God's time is the best," she explained.

"*Chinyere*," Chief Nma's brother called out. "Indeed she was a gift from God."

After everybody had his or her turn naming the girl, it was finally Chief Nma's turn. When he came to call out a name for his daughter, Chief Nma looked up to the heavens, thanked the gods and the villagers, and called her, "*Apunanwu.*"

Because of Apunanwu's background, Chief Nma gave orders to his servants never to allow her out in the sun. Indeed, her name literally means "averse to heat." But it also signifies beauty. Thus she was to step out only in the early morning before the sun became harsh, or in the late evening after the sun goes to sleep. To be sure, Chief Nma provided her with personal servants who waited on her hand and foot.

Several moons later, one of Chief Nma's wives had a baby girl. Her mother called her Ada-Nma, or the first daughter of Nma, even though her given name was Nwa-Nma or Nma's daughter. Nwanma and Apunanwu, as siblings, did lots of things in common and grew up together. But Nwanma's mother was not happy that Apunanwu was always looked upon as Nma's first daughter. Or the fact that everyone was always talking about Apunanwu's beauty, with little mention of her own daughter's.

One day Nwanma's mother sent all the servants to the farm very early in the morning. She gave them instructions to make mounds for the yams and to finish the portion of land she showed them before they could come home. After the servants left, she took her own child aside and fed her, leaving Apunanwu without food or water. When Apunanwu could no longer bear the hunger she went to Nwanma's mother to get some food.

"What a lazy girl you are," she scolded her. "All I hear about is your beauty—as if one could eat beauty. Why don't you fix your own food? You can't even pick up a broom to sweep the floor much less cook food. Are you ever going to live with a man and cook for him?"

Apunanwu was quite embarrassed and saddened. But she knew that she could do the chores. So, she went into the kitchen to prepare her own food.

Apunanwu set up the tripod and made a fire. She peeled some yams and washed them for cooking. As she prepared the yams and put them in the pot of boiling water, her body began to melt. First, the hand with which she put the yams in the pot. Then, the leg nearest the fire began to melt. Soon both her legs were melting and the floor of the kitchen was turning red with palm oil.

Meanwhile a black weaverbird making a nest in a nearby palm tree saw Apunanwu melting and shrinking in size. Directly, it flew down to the kitchen floor and dipped its neck on the oil. Then it flew to the village square where the Chief was in a meeting. In order to get the Chief's attention, the bird flew over him and made a dropping on him.

"My God," said the Chief. "Whichever bird that dropped on me, I should have your head for dinner."

"Then I will not tell you what I meant to tell you," replied the bird.

"Please tell me," pleaded the Chief.

Then the bird began to sing:

The beautiful oil in the Chief's house melted!
The beautiful oil in the Chief's house melted!
Whoever brings a container can get his share!
Whoever brings a container can get his share!
I have my own stock!
You can see it around my neck.

Immediately the Chief understood the message. He left the meeting and ran to his house. But by the time he got home, Apunanwu was already melted from the waist down. When the Chief saw her, he cried with rage and sadness. There was nothing he could do. He stretched out his hands to her, but her hands had already melted. He grabbed her, but she slipped from his hands. Chief Nma could do nothing but watch his beautiful daughter melt away.

The Chief was very distraught. He put himself in seclusion and mourned Apunanwu. Then God decreed that no longer could one wish for a child to come out of an object. That is why nowadays, no one can get a child unless by natural means. Also, that is how the black weaverbird came to have a red band around his neck.

Everyone

The Igbos tell this story of the Tortoise who took the nickname "Unu Dum," or "Everyone." The Tortoise in this story is the epitome of wit and greed. With food available only in the sky, the birds contributed feathers to help the animals make their own wings so that they could go with them to get some food. No sooner did he receive his own pair of wings than the Tortoise engineered a plan to claim all the food and drink for himself. The birds became angry at the Tortoise and took their feathers from him. How will the Tortoise find his way back to earth?

Famine, famine everywhere. The animals were really skinny because they didn't have food. They thought perhaps the gods were angry and were punishing them for their follies. The animal kingdom was in a state of chaos, with all the animals questioning each other for answers. (Also during this time the Tortoise's shell was smooth.)

"What have we done to deserve this?" asked the Lion.

"Yes! What have we done?" asked the Elephant. "That is the question."

"What haven't we done is more like it," answered the Cougar.

Although the animals were starving, the birds looked fresh and well fed. In spite of the fact that they needed to eat more than other animals, in proportion to their bodyweight, they did not seem to have suffered at all. Indeed, some of them, especially the male birds, seem to have gained weight and their plumage seemed to have taken on a totally new ravishing color. Even the Tortoise's neighbor, the Crow, had more baby crows. Some animals thought, "Perhaps the birds look so healthy because we are looking so pitiful ourselves that everything else looks good to us." But the Tortoise did not accept that explanation. He had to find out why the Crow was flourishing when other animals did not even have enough to feed themselves.

"Hello there, Ebony, my friend," said the Tortoise. The Tortoise called everyone by a pet name, especially when he wanted something from them.

"'Ebony'? 'Your friend'?" responded the Crow. "Since when?"

"Relax, my friend," said the Tortoise. "I just wanted to compliment you on your new arrivals. How are the new baby crows?"

"Very well, thank you," replied the Crow, "and the baby tortoises?"

"Haven't you heard?" asked the Tortoise. "Most of my family has died because I don't have any food. But not you, Ebony. Every time I see you, your plumage is something to behold, and I say to myself, 'That's a hardworking friend. But how can she sleep through the night feeding fat while her neighbors are losing their families to the famine? Doesn't she feel any sense of guilt?'"

"I did not bring about the famine, so why should I feel guilty?" the Crow defended herself.

But not to lose the moment, the Tortoise continued. "Even the Lion who shares all he has with everyone has to beg for food too. If that isn't the end of the world, I don't know what is."

By this time the Crow was beginning to feel guilty, which is just about where the Tortoise wanted her. She took a second look at the Tortoise and noticed that his smooth shell has lost its luster due to poor diet. So she confessed to the Tortoise that there was a place out in the sky where the birds had discovered food.

"And you have been going there for food without your four-legged friends?" asked the Tortoise, in shock.

In order to make up for their mistakes, the Crow and the other birds decided that they should take the animals with them the next day, which was the feast of the New Yam Festival for the sky kingdom.

There was a problem, though. The animals couldn't fly. So the birds came up with a plan: They donated some of their feathers to make wings for the animals. The Elephant, the Tiger, the Monkey, the Crocodile, the Pig, and every animal in the kingdom now had a pair of wings and could fly.

"Pooooh!" trumpeted the Elephant after testing his wings. "I really can fly."

"Watch out, Chip," warned the Monkey to the Chipmunk, "he could trigger a tornado, and guess who would be the first to be blown away?"

"I know," added the Ostrich. "And since I am the only bird that is close to him in size, I had to donate most of my feathers, and now I can't even fly."

"Cut it out fellows," admonished the Lion. "This is a memorable day for all of us and we should not be teasing each other."

"Mooooo!" said the Cow. "I can fly too."

"Oink! Oink!" said the Pig. "Me too."

"Roaar," said the Tiger. "Me too."

All the animals tested their wings and were now ready for the trip. As they were about to take off for the sky kingdom the Tortoise went in front of the group as if to lead the way.

"Do *you* know where we are going?" asked the Hippo. "Why don't you let the Crow or one of the birds lead the group?"

"No, I am not leading us," the Tortoise corrected him. "I just have this great idea. As the Lion pointed out, this is a special day for us. So why don't we take on special names?"

"Special names?" wondered the Crow.

"Yes, nicknames," explained the Tortoise.

Neither the birds nor the animals saw anything wrong with that. Indeed, they thought that it would be fun. So, they all agreed with the Tortoise's suggestion and each took a nickname for the trip.

"I have always wanted to be a fireman, so I will be Fire Chief," said the Lion.

"I will be Bogeyman," said the Gorilla.

After all the birds and the animals had taken their names, the Tortoise said, "My name is Everyone."

All the animals burst into laughter. "Ha! Ha! Ha! Ha!" They laughed so hard their lungs began to hurt.

"'Everyone'? What kind of name is that?" asked the Hippo.

"Yes! Everyone!" said the Tortoise emphatically. "Just my nickname for the trip."

Since it was only a nickname and none of the animals and the birds had any reason to suspect anything, they did not question the Tortoise further and set out on their trip to the sky kingdom full of anticipation. As they flew higher, and higher, they could smell delicious food. Something they had not experienced on earth for such a long time.

When they got to the sky kingdom, they found it more beautiful than the birds had described. The gardens were filled with food. There was greenery everywhere and the kingdom seemed to be overflowing with life. Their hosts were especially friendly and gave them the royal treatment. The animals were dumbfounded.

"How can there be two worlds?" the Tortoise wondered. "Here they have so much food. But down on earth, we have no food and die of hunger. If only I can stay here, I could live forever."

"Does this place always look like this or did you set up all these to impress us?" he asked one of the ushers.

"Yes, this is the way it is all the time," answered the usher.

As the Tortoise salivated and thought about the prospects of taking up residence in the sky kingdom, he found himself sitting in a majestic place with the birds and the rest of the animals. His mouth watered, as he smelled the food being set out for them. Food filled every inch of the table. Then four pages carried the Sky King in on his carriage to address the guests.

"Welcome, everyone, to our small and humble place," said the King.

"If that is not the understatement of the century," the Tortoise thought, "I do not know what is."

"Thank you for joining us in our New Yam Celebration. The tradition started..."

The Tortoise tried very hard to follow the King's welcome address, but his concentration was continually broken by the smell of the most sumptuous food he had ever seen, and by the rattling of wine cups. Out of the corner of his eye, he could count all the different dishes that had been set up for them. The more the king spoke, the hungrier the Tortoise became. "Yuuummy! Those look so mm, mm good that I cannot wait to taste them," he thought.

"In closing," said the King, "welcome to our kingdom." Then he stood up and the servers told the guests to do the same. "Now," said the King, "everyone is welcome to join us in our feast."

The animals and the birds couldn't wait to start eating. But the Tortoise moved ahead of them and spread out his hands to restrain them. "Remember, I am 'Everyone,'" he said. "It is me whom the King invited to feast with him. Wait your turn. Maybe he will invite you too."

The animals and the birds sat back and watched the Tortoise gobble the food. Starting with the most delicious and tastiest of the dishes, he stuffed himself until he could hardly get up. When he had nowhere else to put the food, he invited the rest to share the leftovers.

After dinner, the Sky King ordered the most delicious wines for the guests.

"Oh, the aroma of that wine," said the Lion as he looked up to the ceiling and waved his head while sniffing loudly as if to savor the entire aroma.

"Drink wine on an empty stomach?" asked the Monkey. "That would really make your day."

"I will settle for anything now—I am so hungry that I want to make it up with the wine."

"That is, if he will let us get a taste of it," the Crow added.

"Oh, he wouldn't do that again, would he?"

"Everyone is welcome to drink with us," said the King. "The wines are special. They were made from the fruits of my orchard. I am sure everyone will enjoy them."

The animals and the birds tried to grab their cups. But the Tortoise restrained them again. "Remember, I am 'Everyone,'" he said. "The King is inviting me to drink with him."

The Tortoise drank and drank the wines until he couldn't drink anymore. Then, he asked the rest to join him.

The animals and the birds became even hungrier and angrier. The leftover foods and drinks only teased their tummies. Frustrated by the whole charade, the birds, led by the Crow, decided the joke had gone too far and demanded their wings back from the Tortoise. And one by one all the birds plucked the feathers they donated to the Tortoise for the trip.

Of course, at first the Tortoise didn't mind losing the feathers. After all, he wanted to stay in the sky kingdom forever. But the Sky King told him they didn't let anyone live with them. They welcomed everyone, but didn't let them stay forever.

"How can I get back to earth?" the Tortoise thought. "Jump. Jump!"

But, the Tortoise needed to fall on something fluffy. So, he begged the animals to tell his wife to make a pile of leaves for him, but they refused. Finally, he begged the Crow.

"Ebony, good ol' friend. You are not going to leave me behind, are you? Please tell Mrs. Tortoise to make a bed of leaves for me. So when I fall, I don't hurt myself."

The Crow felt sorry for the Tortoise. But, at the same time, she wanted to pay him back for his greed. So she agreed to send the Tortoise's message to Mrs. Tortoise.

"Hello, lady Tortoise! I have a message from your husband," the Crow greeted.

"Where is he?" asked Mrs. Tortoise. "That ne'er-do-well. I bet he decided to live up there. He can stay there and see if I care."

"No, no. It is not what you think. He will come back when you do what he asks of you. He wants you to lay a bed of rocks on the market square for his landing," the Crow lied.

"Why?" asked Mrs. Tortoise, "Didn't he fly up there like everyone else? And why does he want a bed of rocks anyway?"

"Yes! But he wanted to bring lots of food back to you. So, he took a bet with the Sky King that he could survive a fall on a bed of rocks. If he does, the Sky King will give him all the food he wants."

The thought of food made Mrs. Tortoise's mouth water so much that she didn't think much about the implications of the message and made the bed of rocks.

After the bed of rocks was made, the Crow graciously flew back to the sky kingdom to inform the Tortoise that his bed of leaves was ready for his landing.

The Tortoise bid farewell to his host and took a dive for earth. Without the fluffy leaves or anything else to break his fall, he fell like a ton of bricks onto the bed of rocks. What a crash he took! The crash was so loud it was heard throughout the animal kingdom, and all thought the Tortoise had died.

"He survived!" exclaimed the Crow, disappointed as the Tortoise wiggled his leg.

Although the Tortoise didn't die, his shell was broken into several pieces. Mrs. Tortoise was very scared. She cried and begged the animals to help her put the Tortoise together, but they refused. By this time all the animals had boycotted the Tortoise and the best craftsmen in the kingdom would not help him. Finally Mrs. Tortoise was able to recruit the services of the Snail and the Crab. They could not use the best tools in the kingdom, though, on account of the boycott. So the Snail used his saliva for mortar while the Crab did the best he could to piece the Tortoise back together with her crooked claws.

This is why nowadays the Tortoise's shell is a bunch of crooked patches—and rough at the joints, as if a committee of apprentice craftsmen had put them together.

How the Tortoise Paid His Creditors

He that borrows and pays shall live to borrow again. But the Tortoise is not just any creature—when he cannot pay, he devises a way of making his creditors pay for their generosity. Once, at the height of a famine, broke and with no food, the Tortoise decided to borrow building rods, which were at that time of little value to the rest of the animals. How will he convert the rods to food? From the Calabar people comes this story of intrigue.

Once upon a time there was a great famine in the land of the animals. Food was very scarce and only the strong and the wise survived. Those who had food hoarded it and guarded it with their lives. It was a very bad time to have young ones.

The Tortoise was known as the wisest animal in the kingdom. He was also known as the slowest, the laziest, and the most cunning. The famine affected him more than it did the average animal, because, as could be expected, the Tortoise had not farmed or gathered food in anticipation. Because food was so scarce, he could not figure out how to borrow enough to weather the famine. So he decided that he should borrow something else.

"I should go and borrow some building materials from my neighbors," he said to himself one day. "If they are really my neighbors, good neighbors, they should lend me a measly rod for my hut." Confident, the Tortoise first went to the Worm.

"Hello there, Slink," he greeted the Worm.

"Hello, old man," responded the Worm. "To what do I owe this honor?"

"Mind if I borrow a stride length of rod from you? I am putting up a house and ran out of rods. I will pay for them before long."

"Rods?" the Worm asked, surprised. "All the creatures are dying of hunger and you are putting up a house? Where do you get food?"

"I don't," the Tortoise corrected him. "But, the way I see it, no one will lend me food anyway. I might as well finish my house, so when I die of starvation it will be what I have left for my family."

The Worm wasted no time lending him the building rods, lest

the Tortoise change his mind and beg him for food. "Be sure to pay," he warned the Tortoise.

"My word is my honor," the Tortoise promised. "You shall have your money, with interest, exactly seven market days from now. I shall be waiting for you in my house."

Then the Tortoise thanked him and left. He took the rods home. Then he went to the Rooster's. There he used the same line as he had with the Worm. It worked like magic. He took the rods home and went to the Fox, then to the Leopard, and then to the Hunter. Seven market days later, at about the same time the rods were borrowed, the Worm was at the Tortoise's to collect his money.

"Hello, old man," the Worm greeted the Tortoise. "I am here to collect my money."

"You came just in time," said the Tortoise. "It was a stride length of rods, wasn't it?"

"Yes! A stride length of rods, with interest."

"Of course! With interest," the Tortoise agreed.

Then he gave the Worm a seat in his guestroom. He asked him to wait there while he went to get the money. The Worm was very excited that the Tortoise was going to come through after all. He thought of what he could buy with all the money. While he was salivating over the types of food he could buy, the Tortoise went into the inner chamber of his hut. Then he went out the back door. He came around to the front gate and waited for his next guest. Just then he saw the Rooster strutting toward his house.

"Welcome, Red," the Tortoise welcomed him. "I have been waiting for you."

Then he led him into his house and pointed to the guestroom, saying, "Go in there and wait for me while I go to get your money."

The Rooster opened the door of the guestroom and went in. There he saw the Worm and before the latter could say a word, he ate him.

The Tortoise was again at his gate waiting for the Fox. Just as he expected, he saw him at a distance jogging merrily toward him.

"Welcome, Sly," he welcomed the Fox. "I know you are a creature of time. Let's go inside so I can fetch your money."

"Give it to me now," demanded the Fox.

"What makes you think I carry that kind of money on me? You are here already. Let's go in and I will fetch it."

Reluctantly the Fox followed the Tortoise into his house.

"Wait in my guestroom while I fetch the money and some kola nuts to serve you."

As the Fox walked into the room, he saw the Rooster and chased him around the room. He soon caught him and ate him.

Next to come was the Leopard. The Tortoise was, as usual, at his gate. He chuckled as he saw him striding majestically toward him.

"Welcome, Spot," said the Tortoise. "I have your money ready and will fetch it shortly. But to show you I am a man of my word, I have your interest in my guestroom."

"What is it?" asked the Leopard.

"A surprise. But to give you a hint, it tastes yummy."

The Leopard couldn't wait to get to the Tortoise's guestroom. He opened the door and saw his natural enemy and food source staring him in the face. Hungry, but without working up a sweat, he caught the Fox and devoured him. Then he lay down to relax while he waited for his money. "What a lad the Tortoise is," he said to himself. "I never knew he had it in him. I guess I always judged him hastily."

As the Leopard waited for his money, the Tortoise was at his gate, welcoming the Hunter. "I see you always come prepared, eh!"

"Yes, why?" asked the Hunter.

"I mean, with your gun always loaded. You didn't mean to shoot me if I defaulted, did you?"

"That's an idea. But, no! I am a Hunter. I always carry my gun loaded just in case I run into some game. Besides, the jungle is not exactly friendly. So it doubles as protection. But enough of the queries. Where is my money?"

"Sorry, my friend," the Tortoise apologized. "I almost forgot. But as our elders say, 'He who asks questions never misses his way.' Go into my guestroom and wait while I fetch it. Meanwhile, feel at home and I will get you some fresh palm wine."

When the Hunter went into the room, he disturbed the Leopard, who had been taking a catnap. Directly on seeing the Leopard, the Hunter aimed his gun at him. But on seeing the Hunter, the

Leopard had charged him. Just as the Hunter was pulling his trigger, the Leopard was at his throat. The gun discharged, hitting the Leopard. The Leopard had already taken enough of a bite out of the Hunter to kill him.

Once the Tortoise heard the gunfire, he knew that his plan had worked. He ran into the house and eavesdropped at his guestroom door for any sign of life. Realizing that none of his guests was still alive, he went into the room. He laughed himself silly.

When the Tortoise recovered from his amusement, he picked up the Leopard and cut him up. The Hunter he buried in his backyard. Now the Tortoise has enough food to weather the famine.

The Calabash Child

A childless Igbo King was finally blessed with a child. This child, however, was no ordinary child. She grew out of the bud of a calabash plant and hated to be reminded of that. If anyone called her a calabash child, she told the King and Queen, she would no longer be their child.

There once lived a King and his wife. They had been married for several years but had no children. As the King was advancing in age, it worried him that he had no child to assume the throne after him. His wife was very worried too. Other women teased her behind her back because she had no child. Every day and night, she and the King prayed to their *chi* for a child.

The King, like most kings, farmed several acres of land. His wife, unlike most royal wives, took part in tending the farms. Every day she took several servants and hired hands to the farms. As a lady, she cultivated mostly cocoa-yams, beans, and calabash.

This was a particularly good year for the crops at the farm of the King's wife. All the cocoa-yam leaves were greener and broader than usual. The beans and the calabash plants lived up to their nicknames as their tendrils grew beyond the boundaries of her farm. The King's wife was especially happy and expected a bountiful harvest. In time, the plants bloomed, turned into buds, and then plump fruits.

One day, long before the first cock crowed, the King's wife woke up and said her morning prayers. She, as always, asked God for a child and went to her farm to tend to the crops. Then to her surprise, she saw a very beautiful little girl squatting next to one of the mounds of calabash plants.

"*Ojiefi*," said the little girl. "Good morning."

"Good morning my child," replied the King's wife. "What is a little girl like you doing in the farm this early in the morning? Where is your mother? She should know better than leave you here unattended."

"This is my home," replied the little girl.

The King's wife was confused. The farm was too far from any homes and she thought that the girl was not sure of what she was saying.

"But it would take a strong man from the second cock crow to when the sun stands overhead to get here from the closest home," she corrected her. "For you, my child, it would certainly take much longer."

But the girl only smiled. Then she muttered a few words to herself. All of a sudden she became a calabash, which rolled to the foot of the King's wife and turned back into the little girl again.

The King's wife was now both shocked and afraid. But her desire to have a child of her own overcame her fear. So, she begged the girl to follow her home. She promised to take very good care of her, if only she would agree to be her child. The girl was happy that the King's wife asked her to be her child. But she was not sure it was such a good idea.

"I'd like to be your child," said the girl. "I know that someone who can take such good care of ordinary plants would make a very good mother. But I have lived with people before, and I didn't like my experience. That is why I have decided to live here by myself."

But the King's wife was persistent. She pleaded with the girl to come with her. She promised to treat her very well and not to be like those other families.

"I will go with you," said the girl. "But under one condition. I know I came from a calabash. But I *hate* to be called a calabash child. The day anyone calls me a calabash child will be the last day you see me."

"You have my word, my child," said the King's wife. "Nobody will call you a calabash child. I am the King's wife and what my husband says is the law."

Then the little girl agreed and followed her home. The King's wife was filled with joy. She hugged the girl as she cried for joy. Finally, she has a child of her own. Someone she could hug and cook for, someone who would make them happy in their old age.

When they got home, the King's wife told the King of her experience and how she had found the girl. The King was very happy. He called all his people and there was great merriment. The King finally has a child, an heir to the kingdom. The King named the girl Onunaeliaku (born to consume wealth) and the King's wife named her Ifeyinwa (nothing like a child). Then he warned everyone never to call her a calabash child. Anyone who did would be put to death.

The people received the news of the King's new daughter very well. They feasted and danced for several days. The King was finally happy and for his next title, he took the name Obiajulu (finally at peace).

Onunaeliaku grew into a very beautiful girl. Princes from far and wide courted her. But the King refused to offer her hand in marriage.

"She is my only offspring," he explained. "I want her to remain and succeed me when I die."

Although some people were not happy with the prospect of having a female king, they had no choice but to rejoice in the good fortunes of their King.

The King never let Onunaeliaku out of his sight. He had servants who waited on her hand and foot. He gave her all she wanted. Onunaeliaku eventually adjusted very well to the village and was unquestionably the princess.

One day the King and his wife needed to go on a trip. They called all their servants together and gave them strict instructions. They must never let the princess out of their sight. They must do all she asked of them and must not let any harm come to her.

Long after the King and his wife were gone, Onunaeliaku became hungry. She asked the servants to prepare her meals. They agreed and told her that the food would be ready soon. She waited and waited, but the food was never served. She became even hungrier and went back to find out what was wrong.

"I am famished," she announced. "Isn't the food ready yet?"

"What food?" asked the servants, "Ha! Ha! Ha! Ha!" they laughed at her. "If you want any food, you cook it yourself. We have always looked forward to the day the King and his wife would go out so that we could enjoy ourselves. Isn't it bad enough that they ordered us around? Now you too, a *calabash* child?"

Onunaeliaku was very saddened. Her eyes became red and heavy with tears. She went back into her room and cried. She stripped herself of all the things that the King had provided for her. She changed into the scanty clothes she had worn when the King's wife found her. Then she quietly walked out of the compound through the back door.

Before the sun went to sleep that day the King and his wife came back from their trip. But there was no Onunaeliaku to welcome and hug them.

"Onunaeliaku! Onunaeliaku!" the King called.

But there was no answer. The King thought that maybe she was asleep. He went into the house, then her room, but could not find her. Her room was the same as always.

"Onunaeliaku!" he called again. But there was still no answer.

"Ify," the King's wife called as she ran back out to the compound, "answer me wherever you are."

Immediately, the King called all his servants together to ask of them what had happened to the princess he left in their care.

"We have not seen her," answered one of the servants. But the King insisted that they must know what had happened to her. One of the servants finally admitted to seeing her in her old clothes, headed toward the farms.

Immediately, the King and his wife chased after her. They caught up with her several villages later.

"What is the matter, Ify?" asked the King's wife.

But Ifeyinwa was too sad to talk. Her eyes were red with tears. She wiped off the tears with the back of her hands and started to sing:

My mother bore me	*Nnem amutam o*
Tumangwe	*Tumangwe*
And named me consumer of wealth	*Bua m nwonu na eli aku*
Tumangwe	*Tumangwe*
My father bore me	*Nnam amutam o*
Tumangwe	*Tumangwe*
And named me consumer of wealth	*Bua m nwonu na eli aku*
Tumangwe	*Tumangwe*
My own servants saw me	*Oru agbatara m ahum o*
Tumangwe	*Tumangwe*
And called me a calabash child	*Kpom nwonu ugu akpatara na agu o*
Tumangwe	*Tumangwe*
Calabash child or not	*Akpatam n'agu o*
Tumangwe	*Tumangwe*
I am going back to my roots	*Na anajekwem bem o*
Tumangwe	*Tumangwe*
Calabash child or not	*Akpataghim n'agu o*

Tumangwe	*Tumangwe*
I am going back to my roots	*Na anajekwem bem o*
Tumangwe	*Tumangwe*

The King and his wife were very saddened. They pleaded with Onunaeliaku to go back with them.

"Come with us," said the King. "A servant in my own house dared to call my daughter names? That cannot be. Come with us and show me which servant, and I will teach him a lesson or two about respect, whether I am there or not."

But Onunaeliaku was insistent on going back to where she came from and could not be swayed.

"The servants have broken my trust and ruined my honor. I don't see how I can be in the King's home anymore. Let me go back to where I can be happy and nobody knows my secrets."

Seeing that he had lost his daughter for good, the King's eyes became red with tears, which began to roll down from the corners of his eyes. We all know that it is very hard for a man to cry. The welling up of a man sends goose bumps over all those who see it. And here was crying not just a man, but a King who had the power to do anything, yet didn't try to force a little girl to go against her will. This really moved Onunaeliaku. And, seeing the sincerity of the King's love, she decided to go back with them.

This made the King and his wife very happy and they took Onunaeliaku back to the village. When they got back to the village, Onunaeliaku showed the King the servants who had called her names. The King's anger grew again, to the point of rage, and he ordered all his servants killed.

By killing all his servants, the King hoped to restore Onunaeliaku's honor. But by killing the servants, the King also broke the spell that had been cast on Onunaeliaku. "You shall be bound to remain a calabash," a spirit had said to her, "Until human blood has been shed for your sake."

When the King and his wife died, Onunaeliaku became the *Eze Nwanyi* of the village. Her people respected her very much and she ruled them with compassion, as had her father before her. This marked the beginning of female leadership in the village, which had been traditionally ruled by men.

The Hunter and the Lion

The Yoruba people tell this version of how the Hunter and the Lion became mortal enemies. After the Hunter saved the Lion from imminent death, his act of mercy almost cost him his life, but for the quick-wittedness of the Hare.

Many years ago, there lived a Hunter in a certain village. One day he took up his bow and arrows and went into the woods to hunt. He spent almost the entire day in the woods, and succeeded in killing a deer and two rabbits. The Hunter was very happy. He hung the deer about his neck and tied the rabbits around his waist. He was merrily whistling and calculating how to share the kill among his people when he was interrupted by a cry for help from what sounded like a Lion. He was startled and afraid. "It must be after my kill," he said to himself.

He quickly turned in the direction of the cry. But, he could not see what made the cry for help. Then came the cry again. This time he was able to pinpoint where it came from. It was the Lion all right, hanging like an understuffed pillow between a fork of branches in a tree. "Just as I thought," muttered the Hunter in disappointment. Then he slowly lay the deer down and drew his bow and arrow. Slowly, he pulled backwards as he watched the Lion. But the Lion did nothing.

"Please help me," said the Lion. "I am stuck."

The Hunter slowly lowered his bow and arrow and cautiously walked toward the tree. Then he very carefully surveyed the Lion to be sure he was not playing a trick on him. From what he could see, the Lion seemed to be stuck and in pain.

"Who did this to you?" asked the Hunter.

"Help me down and I will tell you," replied the Lion.

The Hunter helped the Lion out of his trouble. He unstuck him and brought him down from the tree.

"Thank you very much," said the Lion. "It was the Elephant. He was the one who stuck me up there for three days running."

"Be gone then," said the Hunter. "I need to return home to my family."

Now, the Lion had been stuck in the tree for three days, and he was hungry, tired, and thirsty, so he begged the Hunter for yet another favor.

"You have been very kind to me," said the Lion. "But what good is it that I should be left here to die. I am too weak to catch my own food. Would you kindly also give me something to eat?"

"Where can I find food?" asked the Hunter.

"That deer is big enough to share with me, wouldn't you say?" asked the Lion. "I know you to be a true friend that I can count on during my time of need. Help me now and when I regain enough strength to hunt my own food I will repay you for your kindness."

The Hunter thought for a while. Then he cut the deer into two equal halves and gave one to the Lion. "You do not owe me a thing," he reassured the Lion. "So, never mind repaying me. I shall be going now."

The Hunter had barely finished talking when the Lion swallowed his share of the deer in one gulp and asked for more. Then the Hunter gave him the other half. The Lion ate it up and asked for more, eyeing the rabbits around the Hunter's waist.

The Hunter gave him the two rabbits, which he devoured, and then demanded even more food.

"I am not full, my friend," the Lion said. "Remember, it has been three days."

"But I am without anymore to give you," pleaded the Hunter. "I have given you all I have caught today." Meanwhile the Lion eyed the Hunter's dog.

"No! Not my dog."

"But I am still hungry," said the Lion. "I must have more to eat."

The Hunter had no choice but to let the Lion have his dog. When he finished eating the dog, the Lion still insisted that he needed more to eat. Then he and the Hunter began to argue and make palaver. "This is the gratitude I get for saving your life? How is it that the gods allow me to be punished for my kindness?" the Hunter pleaded, confused.

While they were talking, the Hare came by. "What seems to be the trouble?" he asked.

As if the Hare was the juror he had been waiting for, the Hunter stated his case to him. Then the Hare turned to the Lion to corroborate the Hunter's story.

"That is true," said the Lion. "But I am still hungry and need more to eat."

"Show me how you were stuck in the tree," said the Hare.

Then the Lion started to describe how he was stuck in the tree. But the Hare said he couldn't understand it.

"The way you describe it is confusing. It is not possible that you could be stuck like that for three days. If you are lying, I will have no choice but to rule for the Hunter. I believe I will understand it better and pronounce better judgment if I could see you in the position you describe." Then he turned to the Hunter and said, "Put him back where he was in the tree so that I may see."

So the Lion played dead and the Hunter picked him up and forced him back between the branches.

"This was the way I was stuck," said the Lion with much pain.

"Then," said the Hare, "Mr. Hunter, a grasshopper killed by the hornbill is deaf. You are a man and the Lion an animal. Why did you save him? You already gave him all you have and he wants even more—you. Shoot him."

Then the Hunter shot the Lion and took him home for food as reparation for his deer, rabbits, and dog. He vowed to do henceforth what comes naturally, and he has been doing it ever since, whenever he runs into a Lion.

The Latchkey Prince

The motif of this story is similar to that of many Igbo stories that involve Kings. Such stories may involve several wives, childlessness, or the lack of a son. The King in this story has everything but a son. When he finally gets a son, it is by the lesser of his wives.

There once lived a very wealthy and powerful King. He was so powerful that kings from neighboring villages paid him homage. For that, he protected them from their enemies. This King had almost everything he wanted. But still he yearned for the one most important thing he lacked: a son.

As was the tradition in this land, the King had four wives. Though they had fifteen children between them, none of them bore him a son. Although he officially had four wives, he was influenced by his first wife to treat the one named Mebu very badly. In his very big estate, he built very beautiful homes very close to his mansion for the other three wives. For the fourth wife, he built a shack at the farthest corner of the estate. Whenever he bought things for his wives, he only remembered the first three. The fourth wife was so poor in the King's estate that she barely had enough to eat.

Everything the King did to have a baby boy failed. By tradition, none of his girls could take over the reign of his village after his death. As a last resort, the King went to a chief priest of the shrine of his forefathers, who gave him four rare palm kernels for his four wives.

"Have each of your wives crack these kernels," he told the King. "But, instead of eating the nuts, they must eat the shells and discard the nuts."

"That I shall tell them to do," agreed the King, and left for his palace.

When he got home, he gave the palm kernels to his three wives with the instructions from the chief priest. The fourth kernel he threw away, into the river. But the King's three wives were very proud people. They couldn't understand why anyone would eat palm nuts, the staple food for paupers, much less the shells.

"How can I be in an ocean of water and cry that soap has entered my eyes?" asked the one.

"How can I eat the shell of a palm kernel?" asked the other. "I have never even eaten the palm nut, much less the shell."

"I never heard anything so ridiculous," answered the third.

So they all cracked the palm kernels and threw away the shells. As a compromise, they ate the nuts.

"Yuck!" said the one.

"Pooh! Pooh!" said the other as she spat out the chaff.

"I can imagine what the shells might taste like," concluded the third.

The King's servant who was sent to deliver the message to the women never liked the way the King treated Mebu. He sneaked food to her whenever he could. So when he saw what the other wives had done, he picked up the palm shells and gave them to Mebu.

"You must eat them," he instructed her. "I am sorry, but that was all I could sneak by for you today."

"That's okay," she replied. "You have been my savior and *chi* to this point. Besides, the yam that a father gives his daughter on the palm of her hands never burns her." Mebu then threw the shells of the palm kernels into her mouth and ate them all.

The King was so sure that his three favorite wives would bear baby boys that he decreed that henceforth all baby girls born to his household would be thrown away. And when the King's three beloved wives gave birth, one by one, to baby girls, they were all immediately thrown away. When it was Mebu's turn to have her baby, the King's head wife was appointed to be her midwife. Popularly known by the servants as Ajo, or Meany, she lived up to her name. When the baby came, it was a boy. But Ajo tossed him into the river and told Mebu that it had been a stillborn baby girl. Poor Mebu. What else could she do but go back to her lonely hut and mourn her misfortune?

The God that looks after babies must be different from the one that looks after grown-ups. For instead of drowning, the baby floated down the river to where a lonely old woman was washing her clothes. There it settled as it hit her around the calf.

"What kind of fish is without fear that it should hit me like that?" the old woman wondered.

As she turned around to reach for her machete to spear the fish, she realized it was a baby.

"A baby! Oh ooooo! Where could its mother be?"

She picked it up and nursed it with water.

"It must be a baby thrown away by mistake on account of the King's decree," she thought.

After several hours of waiting in vain for the baby's mother to come and claim him, she took him home to nurse and raise him.

"My God has answered my prayers at last," she said to herself as she went home.

This baby grew up to be quite a handsome lad. His stepmother became very fond of him and at the same time worried that someone could come to claim or even steal him from her. So whenever she went out, she made sure that the boy had enough to eat and drink. Then she locked him up in the house while she went to run her errands. The abandoned baby had now grown into a very handsome latchkey boy.

One day as the King's dog was chasing a squirrel, he ran after it into the backyard of the house where the boy lived. After losing sight of the squirrel, the dog casually sniffed its way into the compound through a dilapidated bamboo fencc, to the part of the house where the boy was eating his lunch.

"Here doggie, doggie," the boy said as he offered the dog some food and bone. Then he petted the dog. When the dog finally started to leave, the boy started singing.

King's dog you found me oo!
　La la. La la do!
My fa-ther decreed oo!
　La la. La la do!
Ba-by girls must be tossed away oo!
　La la. La la do!
Ba-by boys must be groomed oo!
　La la. La la do!
He bore me and tossed away oo!
　La la. La la do!
The King is a meany oo!

Nkita eze ichota m oo!
　La la. La la do!
Nna m eze mali iwu oo!
　La la. La la do!
Amuta nwanya si tufuo oo!
　La la. La la do!
Amuta nwoke si dote oo!
　La la. La la do!
O mutam tufuo oo!
　La la. La la do!
Eze anyi bu onye ilo oo!

La la. La la do!
King's first wife is a meany oo!
La la. La la do!
King's servant is my savior oo!
La la. La la do!

La la. La la do!
Nwunye eze onye ilo oo!
La la. La la do!
Odibo eze a zogom oo!
La la. La la do!

After this song, the dog ran back to his master and started waggling his tail at him very hard. But the King only petted him and sent him outside.

The next day the dog went back to the latchkey boy, whom he now saw as a friend. As before, they played and ate and the boy petted him. And when he was about to go home, the boy sang his song for the dog again.

King's dog you found me oo!
La la. La la do!
My fa-ther decreed oo!
La la. La la do!
Ba-by girls must be tossed away oo!
La la. La la do!
Ba-by boys must be groomed oo!
La la. La la do!
He bore me and tossed away oo!
La la. La la do!
The King is a meany oo!
La la. La la do!
King's first wife is a meany oo!
La la. La la do!
King's servant is my savior oo!
La la. La la do!

Nkita eze ichota m oo!
La la. La la do!
Nna m eze mali iwu oo!
La la. La la do!
Amuta nwanya si tufuo oo!
La la. La la do!
Amuta nwoke si dote oo!
La la. La la do!
O mutam tufuo oo!
La la. La la do!
Eze anyi bu onye ilo oo!
La la. La la do!
Nwunye eze onye ilo oo!
La la. La la do!
Odibo eze a zogom oo!
La la. La la do!

The dog again ran home and wagged his tail for his master. This continued for several more days until finally the King said to the dog, "Why is it that you come to me every day at this time to waggle your tail?"

"Mm mm mm mm," the dog gave a friendly insistent sound. "Woof! Woof!" he barked at the King and waggled his tail in a frenzy. He then headed toward the door and waited for the King to follow him.

"Okay! Okay! Come and show me what you are getting excited about."

The King then followed the dog to the latchkey boy's house. When he saw the handsome boy behind the fence, he was dumbfounded. The boy's bearing pleased the King so much that he grew fond of him and loved him immediately. In fact, the boy was every inch his father. The King felt as though he were seeing himself as a boy. He then made up his mind to find out who the boy's parents were, so he waited for them to come home.

"If only they would just let me be close to you and treat you like the son I never had," said the King. "I would be satisfied."

As he was talking to the boy, the old lady came back. After a very long conversation with her, she told him everything she knew about the boy. How she had found him in the river and raised him to be such a fine young boy. How a diviner had told her that he was indeed the King's son. Yes—a latchkey prince.

"Which of my wives is his mother?" the King asked.

"I do not know. But there is one way to find out."

"How? You name it and your price and I will pay you," said the King.

"No. It is not a matter of money. It is a matter of love. And love conquers all."

As the word got to the wives that the King's lost son had been found, each of them claimed him and wanted him for their son. But the only way to determine the boy's true mother was for them to prepare a meal. From whichever dish the boy ate, the King would determine the boy's true mother.

On the judgment day, the King gave his three favorite wives money to buy and prepare the best dishes they knew. To his fourth wife, Mebu, he gave nothing, as usual.

All the three wives spared no expense. They prepared the most delicious and lavish meals money could buy and set them on the plushest tables they could find. Meanwhile, Mebu picked up the dregs from her house and leftovers from the King's dumpster and whipped up a meager-looking meal. Without any table to set the dish on, she set it on the grass at the corner of the estate near the King's stable.

The die was cast. The King dressed his son, now the Crown Prince, in the best royal regalia, as befits an only prince. As the

Prince stepped out of the mansion to the judging arena, his grace, royalty, and elegance amazed the whole village.

"The Prince shall live forever," they said and prostrated themselves as he walked by majestically.

When he came to the first dish, everybody was filled with anticipation. The air was so tense and thick that you could cut it with a knife. He looked the food over and walked on by.

He walked past the rest of the tables without tasting any of the food. Turning then to his father he said, "My King. You officially have four wives, but I have seen only three tables set for your Prince."

So the King's servants pointed to the stable where Mebu had set her own dish. The Prince then walked to the stable and without hesitation, devoured the food Mebu had set on the grass.

Everybody was filled with joy and merriment. But they were surprised that it was the lesser of the King's wives that bore his Prince and their future King. Because of the circumstances of the birth of his son and how he almost lost him, the King then decreed that he should be divorced from all his wives except Mebu. Further, he decreed that henceforth no one in his kingdom could be married to more than one wife at a time.

"Take her and bathe her in the best oils in the estate," the King addressed his female servants as he hugged and kissed Mebu. "Dress her in the best clothes. Sprinkle her with the best perfumes. Then put the crown befitting a king's wife on her head, for she will forever be my true wife."

From that day, the King and Mebu lived happily ever after. And when the King died, the latchkey Prince, who was once abandoned for dead, became King and ruled over the land.

WHY LEOPARDS HUNT DEER

The Deer borrowed the Leopard's billy goat to sire his nanny goats. But, when he returned the billy goat after the breeding season, the Leopard would not accept it. Instead, after several breeding seasons, the Leopard claimed half of the Deer's herd. When the Deer refused, the Leopard sued him before King Lion. The Lion was about to rule on the case when the Hare rudely interrupted him. This story comes from the Igbos.

Many, many years ago, the Leopard and the Deer were very good friends. They lived in the same neighborhood and often played hide-and-seek together. In the Leopard's backyard was tethered a he-goat, which he had won in a wrestling contest several days earlier. The Deer, for his part, was quite a farmer and had a few she-goats and he-goats. His he-goats, though, were still underage. So, during the breeding season he went to the Leopard and asked him to loan him his he-goat so that he could breed it with his she-goats. Since they were good friends, the Leopard quickly agreed.

"Thank you, neighbor," the Deer said to the Leopard. "I will return him happier and in good health after the breeding season. Also, I will return him with a she-goat, so that you may start breeding your own goats."

"Splendid," said the Leopard. "I could use all the goats I can get."

The Deer took the Leopard's he-goat home to his she-goats. He built a larger pen and put him in there with all his goats. After the breeding season, the Leopard took a young nanny goat and Mr. Leopard's billy goat back to him.

"Hello, neighbor," the Deer greeted the Leopard. "Here is your billy goat, as promised, with interest—a very healthy nanny goat. Now you can start breeding them so you can also have your own herd."

"That's very good of you," said the Leopard. "But I cannot take them now. As you can see, I have not built a pen for them yet. Keep them. I will come for them as soon as I have built the pen."

So the Deer took the goats back to his pen. He fed them and watered them as he did his own flock. After the second breeding season, the Deer took the Leopard's he-goat and the she-goat back to him. But the Leopard sent him back with the goats saying, "I am yet to build a pen."

This continued for several more breeding seasons. Meanwhile, the goats crossbred and had many more young ones. After about ten breeding seasons, the Deer's pen was now littered with goats, as many as the stars in the sky, according to the Leopard's estimate. Then one day, the Leopard came knocking at the Deer's home.

"Hello, neighbor," said the Leopard. "I can see that our flock has grown quite a bit. I think it is time to share it so you don't have to feed them alone."

"Our flock?" asked the Deer surprised. "Share our flock?"

"Yes! Our flock," reaffirmed the Leopard.

"As far as I know," said the Deer. "You have a billy goat and a nanny goat in my pen. Let me go and fetch them for you."

"Ha! Ha! Ha! Ha!" the Leopard laughed at the Deer. "All these years you have been breeding with my he-goat and she-goat and you think all I get is the pair! What about all their offspring? I was trying to be generous by asking to share them—I should have asked for the whole flock."

The Deer refused to share the flock, claiming that they all belonged to him and that he was just being fair returning the billy and the she-goat.

"I returned your he-goat and the nanny-goat," the Deer explained, "but you refused to accept them. I should have left them outside for the wild animals to devour. But I brought them here and fed and watered them for you all these years. Now, to show you I mean well, I will give you your he-goat and she-goat, and four more she-goats."

But the Leopard refused the offer. When the Deer also refused to share the herd, the Leopard sued him before the Lion, the king of the animals. The Lion called a meeting of the animal kingdom to come and judge the case between the Leopard and the Deer.

The Lion sent a special notice to the Deer through his messenger, saying: "You have been sued by the Leopard for equal share of a herd of goats. You must appear before the King first thing tomorrow morning. You must not tamper with the evidence and all the goats in question must also be at the trial."

The Deer was distraught. He paced about his pen talking to himself. His voice was cracked and he seemed to be fighting a losing battle holding back tears. "Maybe if I give him more goats he'll be happy and withdraw the suit. But share? No! That's out of the question. I won't share. How can he call himself my friend?"

"Talking to yourself again?" asked the Hare, who was just passing by. "If you need to have your head examined I can call the Tortoise to divine for you. He owes me a favor and it will not cost you much."

"Go on your way, Hare! I have no need for a diviner," said the Deer in a broken voice.

"Crying too?" asked the Hare. "Then you really need help. What is it?"

Then the Deer told him why he was unhappy and that he was even willing to increase his offer to five she-goats. What he refused to do was share the goats equally.

"You don't have to," reassured the Hare. "Let me represent you before the Lion and you won't have to share the goats. It will cost you only..."

"Get away from here before I make you," the Deer interrupted. "I don't need anybody to represent me. The case is clear and I will win it."

"So why are you crying if the case is that clear and you are sure to win? Why are you increasing your offer? Why...?"

"Out of here," shouted the Deer.

Realizing that the Deer was bitter and serious, the Hare hopped away. The next day the Deer gathered all his flock and herded them to the Lion's court. By the time he got there, the place was filled with the rest of the animals. The Leopard was seated on one side of a large rubber plant, which provided much needed shading for the gathering. He beamed with a sinister smile and tapped the nails on his right paw on the ground when he saw the Deer at a distance herding the goats to the square.

"Now let's see," thought the Leopard. "If I eat one goat every other day, how many days would fifty goats last me? Fifty days? No. Eighty days? Forget it. All I know is I will eat one goat every other day until they are finished."

A few moments later, the Lion walked in and the Baboon called the animals to order. The Lion assumed his spot and the Baboon asked the Leopard to present his case. After the Leopard had done so, the Lion asked the Deer:

"Is that the case the way you see it?"

"Yes. But..." said the Deer as he was interrupted by the Hare.

"The King shall live forever," greeted the Hare. He seemed rather in a hurry and didn't bother to genuflect to the Lion. Instead, he just hopped about singing merrily to himself.

"Who is it that greets me from a distance and interrupts my court, without even as much as a bow?" asked the furious Lion.

By the tone of the Lion's voice one would have mistaken the Hare for a trusted and popular war hero who was challenging his king's authority. Immediately the Lion's messenger ran after the Hare and brought him before the gathering.

"Bind him," roared the Lion. "He must be taught never to interrupt my court."

"What did I do? What did I do?" asked the Hare nervously. "What did I do that I should be bound like a criminal?"

"Respect! Does that word mean anything to you?" asked the Lion. "First, you pass by me without genuflecting. Second, you interrupted my court, whistling merrily about. Third, you were supposed to be in court like everybody else. Need I say more? What do you have to say for yourself before I think of more charges?"

"Yes, I mean No," said the Hare. "Yes, to the first question and No, to the last. I am just happy because this morning when I woke up, there they were. Ripe clusters of palm nuts growing out of the fronds of my palm tree. And, as if that weren't enough, my father is having a baby and the ground fell on the sky. I was just hurrying to go fetch my mother from the war so that she could see these phenomena for herself."

"Impossible," said all the animals.

"If you lie to me," the Lion threatened, "I will kill you. Palm fruits do not grow on palm fronds. Don't you mean your mother is having a baby and your father is at war? The ground fell on the sky? You must be crazy."

"No! I mean what I said. Why do you say it's impossible and that I must be crazy?"

"Because, knuckle head," said the Elephant, "men do not have babies. That's why!"

"Then what charges are there between the Deer and the Leopard?" asked the Hare.

The Lion's messenger explained the charges that the Leopard had brought against the Deer.

"Unbind him," said the Lion. "The lawsuit has been decided."

Then the Lion turned to the Leopard and the Deer, saying respectively: "You own a he-goat, and you the she-goats?"

"Yes, your Lordship," the two animals answered.

Then to the Leopard, "Take your he-goat and the five she-goats he has given you and go back home."

Then to the Deer, "You must not divide the flock with him because he-goats do not give birth."

And so it was that the case was decided in favor of the Deer. But, the Deer was afraid that the Leopard might want to take the law into his own hands and take the goats by force. So, he herded them to a distant market and sold them off. Meanwhile the Leopard ate up his own goats and decided to seek his revenge.

When the Leopard sneaked into the Deer's pen to steal the goats he was surprised and angry to find that they were all gone. He tore down the pen in a rage and growled back to his own house. On his way, the Leopard saw the Deer coming back from the market and immediately chased after him.

"If I cannot have the goats," said the Leopard, "maybe I can have the shepherd."

Since then the Leopard and the Deer have been enemies. And even today the Leopard chases after the Deer to eat him.

The Magic Drum

A King had a drum with magical powers and everybody, especially the Tortoise, coveted it. While everybody merely wished they owned the drum, the Tortoise did something about it. He developed a scheme that allowed him to take ownership of the drum. The Tortoise, however, did not know that the drum's magic came with an important secret. The Igbos use this story to illustrate the repercussions of greed and covetousness.

There once lived a king named Obioma, or Kindhearted. He was very sick and his people were sure he was dying. But a voice came to him in a dream.

"King Obioma!" the voice called him. "Because you are kind, I will spare your life and give you a special gift. There is a magic drum at a corner in your private room. Whatever you ask of it, it will give to you. But you must never wash the drum."

When the King woke up he walked into his private room and came out with the magic drum hung around his neck. He admired the drum and its special leather finish. And, because food was scarce at the time, he asked the drum for food and beat it with the skill of a master drummer, singing:

Pam putu! Pam putu!	*Kpam putu! Kpam putu!*
My magic drum!	*Igba nri na nmanya!*
Pam putu! Pam putu!	*Kpam putu! Kpam putu!*
Give me food and drink that are yum-yum!	*Igba nri na nmanya!*

Suddenly, the most delicious food and drinks came out of the drum. The King and his people ate to their heart's content.

One day, another village came to fight King Obioma. Their soldiers carried spears and arrows. Their faces were painted with red ink and their eyes ringed with white chalk. Their commander wore an elephant-like mask. The rest donned hats with ostrich and cockatoo feathers, and chanted war songs.

Quake them shake them!	*Kwekem kwekem!*
Quake-shake the enemy!	*Ebunu ji isi eje ogu!*
Trample, trample!	*Nzogbu nzogbu!*

Trample the enemy! *Enyi mba enyi!*

King Obioma heard their war songs. Then he beat his magic drum. Everywhere was filled with the most delicious food his enemies had ever eaten. They dropped their spears and arrows and gobbled the food. When they were full, they thanked King Obioma and went back to their village without making war.

Everybody, including the animals, especially the Tortoise, wanted the King's magic drum, but the King guarded it very well. Then the Tortoise developed a master scheme for conning the King out of his magic drum. Every day he took off very early in the morning and climbed a palm tree by the river where the King's wife and daughter fetched their water and waited for them to show up.

One day, the King's wife and the Princess went to the river for a bath. The Princess stood by the riverbank enjoying the cool sea breeze. The Tortoise was atop a palm tree picking palm nuts. Then he dropped a palm nut beside the Princess' foot.

"Mother!" said the Princess. "The palm nut I wished for has come to me. I was looking at it while I was bathing. I guess my eyes must have plucked it out of its socket. May I eat it?"

"Yes," said her mother. "But wash it first. This must be your lucky day. That must be why the palm of your right hand itched a while back."

"Yes! I should expect more fortunes today, then?" concluded the Princess.

As soon as the Princess ate the palm nut, the Tortoise came down the palm tree.

"Give me my palm nut," he said. "Where is it?"

"In my tummy. It was yummy," answered the Princess.

"No! You stole my only palm nut for feeding my family," said the Tortoise crying. "How could I have stared death in the eye to climb that tall palm tree and pick these nuts for my family only for you to eat them?"

"But I didn't know it was yours. I picked it," pleaded the Princess.

"No harm done, stranger," the King's wife intervened, "my husband is the King. He will pay you whatever price you ask for your palm nut. My daughter did not know it was yours."

"Yes, let us go to the King," said the Tortoise. "I am sure that he knows how serious a crime it is for people to steal from their neighbors in this time of hardship; he wrote the law himself. Now his family is in violation of that law. Let us see whether that law is only for us poor creatures or for everybody in the land."

When they got to the King, the Tortoise told him how the Princess stole his palm nut. Being a kind and honest man, the King wanted to make sure that the Tortoise was compensated very well for his troubles. So he asked him to name his price.

"I am sorry you feel the Princess stole from you. How can I pay for your loss? Do you want cattle, goats, gold coins, or food? I will repay your loss a hundred times over. Just name your price."

"Thank you, my King," said the Tortoise. "But I will have only the magic drum."

The King's heart skipped a few beats. He looked at the Tortoise with an evil look. But he was a man of honor, and he could not go against his word in front of his people. So he gave the magic drum to the Tortoise.

The Tortoise was very excited and chuckled inside, happy that his plan worked. Then he took the magic drum and went home, called his family together and told them how he had tricked the King out of his magic drum. After reveling in his success, the Tortoise beat the magic drum.

Pam putu! Pam putu!	*Kpam putu! Kpam putu!*
My magic drum!	*Igba nri na nmanya!*
Pam putu! Pam putu!	*Kpam putu! Kpam putu!*
Give me food and drink that are yum-yum!	*Igba nri na nmanya!*

Suddenly, all types of delicious food came out of the drum. The house was filled with foods. His family ate like they never had before. They were proud of the Tortoise and called him all sorts of glorious and flattering names.

"*Omenuko aku*," his wife called him.

"*Ono n'ikpo gbuo agu*," his brother called him.

"*Nna anyi ukwu, i mee*," his children called and thanked him.

"*Akpa Uche*," his father-in-law called him.

For several days the Tortoise provided food and drinks for his family with the magic drum and gloated as they showered him with praise. But that was not enough for the Tortoise, who wanted all the animals to respect him. So, he invited all to the village square to share his food.

The animals did not trust the Tortoise and only a few of them honored the invitation. When they settled down, the Tortoise came out with the magic drum. He sat at the center of the square and beat the magic drum.

The square was filled with all sorts of sumptuous food. The animals could not believe their eyes and the Tortoise's generosity as they gobbled up all the food. They loved the Tortoise for his kindness. He was now wealthy, kind, and respected. Other animals invited him to their homes and he was quite popular.

For several moons the Tortoise provided food and drinks to all the animals. But after so much use, the drum had become dirty. So the Tortoise took it to the river and washed it.

At dinnertime, he beat the magic drum as before.

Pam putu! Pam putu!	*Kpam putu! Kpam putu!*
My magic drum!	*Igba nri na nmanya!*
Pam putu! Pam putu!	*Kpam putu! Kpam putu!*
Give me food and drink that are yum-yum!	*Igba nri na nmanya!*

Instead of food, a troop of angry warriors came out of the magic drum. They were donned in their traditional war regalia. But, instead of their swords and bows and arrows, they were armed with cow-tail switches that made eerie noises as they cut the wind to lash at its victim.

"Phew! Phew!" went the switches.

"Wow! Wow! Wow!" went the warriors.

They lashed at the Tortoise and his family so hard that some of the switches were stained with their blood. The Tortoise and his family were covered with bumps and bruises. When they could not move anymore, the warriors left them for dead and disappeared back into the magic drum.

It took the Tortoise and his family until the morning of the following day to come to, and even several more days to recover from their wounds. Meanwhile, his wife boiled some water, and with the help of some home remedies, was able to nurse every member of her family back to health.

"I wonder what went wrong with that drum?" the Tortoise

thought. To be sure though, the Tortoise cautiously tapped the drum again, but the same result. The warriors came out of the drum again and beat him mercilessly.

Convinced that the drum has lost its magic for sure, the Tortoise in his wicked ways decided it was not only his family that would suffer the bad fate from the magic drum. "If the animals enjoyed the wonderful meals with me, they should also take the punishment with me."

With that, the Tortoise decided to invite the animals for yet another feast. Since word of the Tortoise's generosity had spread throughout the animal kingdom, he did not have any problem getting all of the animals to honor his invitation this time. Some of the animals passed up breakfast and lunch just so that they would have a voracious appetite for the tasty foods they had come to expect from the Tortoise.

The Tortoise sent his family away for safety and hired the Bush Rat to dig a burrow for him from his house into the village square. Then he sat at the center of the square with the magic drum as the animals gathered around him.

"I'll let you beat my magic drum," said the Tortoise to the Monkey. "I already ate. Just return the drum to me after you are done."

The Monkey was excited. He took the drum from the Tortoise and the animals watched him as their mouths watered. The Tortoise escaped into the burrow.

Pam putu! Pam putu!	*Kpam putu! Kpam putu!*
My magic drum!	*Igba nri na nmanya!*
Pam putu! Pam putu!	*Kpam putu! Kpam putu!*
Give me food and drink that are yum-yum!	*Igba nri na nmanya!*

The troop of angry warriors appeared again. The feast turned into shrieks and cries as the warriors lashed at the animals with their switches. The village square turned into a war zone. The animals were thrown into a stampede as they ran helter-skelter.

"Phew! Phew!" went the switches.

"Wow! Wow! Wow!" went the warriors.

Some of the animals were too hungry and tired to run for safety. While some of the bigger animals like the Elephant trampled some of the smaller animals like the Rabbit, some others were killed by the lashings of the warriors. Those who could run away did, calling the Tortoise all sorts of names. When the warriors thought that all the animals had died, they went back into the magic drum.

When all was quiet, the Tortoise came out of hiding. He picked up the dead animals and took them to his house and he and his family made a feast of them. Believing he had exhausted the utility of the magic drum, the Tortoise decided to take it back to the King.

Meanwhile, the story about the warriors and the magic drum had spread, so the King was expecting the Tortoise. As he lay down to sleep and anticipated the Tortoise's return of the drum he pondered about what to do with it. Then, the voice came back to him again and said, "To restore the magic to the drum, you must sing the magic song backwards."

When the day broke, the Tortoise brought back the drum as the King had anticipated.

"Here is your drum. O, King," the Tortoise said. "I am a fair creature. I believe I should not keep your drum forever."

"Indeed!" replied the King. "You are a fair creature, thank you. How about a feast before you leave?" Then he raised his hand as if he was going to beat the drum.

But the Tortoise withdrew into his shell, then crawled out again, and scampered back to his home when he didn't hear the drumbeat.

The King went into his private room. There, he gently beat the drum and sang the magic song backward and restored the magic:

Putu pam, putu pam!	*Putu pam, putu pam!*
Drum magic my!	*Nmanya na nri igba!*
Putu pam, putu pam!	*Putu pam, putu pam!*
Yum-yum are that drink and food me give!	*Nmanya na nri igba!*

From then on, food became plentiful again for the King and his people. King Obioma reigned and ruled his people better than ever before. The word of his kindness spread far and wide. His enemies no longer wanted to fight him. And everybody lived happily ever after.

The Magic Wand

Greed, wickedness, and kindness are the subjects of this tale from the Igbos. The King's wife rewarded one of her subjects, Okoma, with a magic wand that made him very rich. But, his wicked friend, Ozuru, attempting to gain the same riches for himself, killed the King's wife and framed Okoma. Now Okoma must devise a plot to force a confession from Ozuru.

There once lived a King and his wife. Unlike most wives of kings, this King's wife was very industrious and powerful and did most of her chores by herself. She went to the market to buy her own food. She washed her own clothes. And she cooked her own food, just like an ordinary person.

There were two men who lived along the route the King's wife took to the market. The one named Ozuoruonye (no one has it all), Ozuru for short, was wicked and greedy, while the one named Nwokeoma (a kindhearted or good man), or Okoma, was kindhearted and poor.

Whenever the King's wife went to the market, she stopped to get a drink of water from the men. Water was very scarce in those days, more so because the stream was too far away from home and it took a long time to go and fetch the water. Often children went to fetch water and tripped and broke their calabash of water on the hilly and treacherous road. They cried not as much for the broken calabash, but for the spilled water and the effort expended in fetching it. Worse still, they were often given another calabash and made to go back and fetch the water again.

Ozuru always refused to give water to the King's wife. Everybody knew Ozuru as a very wicked man, who not only refused strangers kindness but also sometimes robbed them of the little they had.

"Rich people, you think you own me and my water too?" Ozuru teased the King's wife.

"No, I just wanted a drink of water to quench my thirst," she replied.

"You've got the money. A drink of my water costs two herds of cattle."

"But I do not have two herds of cattle with me," pleaded the King's wife.

"Ha! Ha! Ha! Ha! Now tell me, who is richer? You, or me? When you die you are going to leave all that wealth here anyway. And you cannot even buy a gourd of water? Ha! Ha! Ha! Ha!" Ozuru went into an uncontrollable bout of laughter.

The King's wife left Ozuru and went on her way thirstier than ever. Then she walked for quite a distance to get to Okoma's house. Okoma gave her water. He always did, even though as a poor man, he barely had enough for himself. He respected the King's wife and genuflected to her. In fact, everybody knew Okoma as a very kind man and had told tales of him giving away his last water and food.

The King's wife went through this experience with the two men for many market weeks. She always swallowed her pride and royalty and went home, never telling anyone about it, not even the King. But, of course, the King's wife was very impressed by Okoma, who continually gave her water whenever she asked for it. So, she wanted to reward him for his kindness.

One day when the King's wife went to the market, she took along a magic wand. This wand could do whatever its owner commanded. When she got to Okoma's house she gave him the wand and asked him to hit her on the back with it.

"No! No! Your Royalty," he protested, bowing to her.

"But you do not understand," she replied.

"Yes, I do. Mine is to protect and serve you but not to hurt you."

"Yes. Then you must do as I say, for if you do, you will become richer than you ever imagined," she reassured him. "It is my way of paying you back for your many kindnesses."

Okoma then took the magic wand and tapped her gently on her back. All of a sudden, his house was filled with all sorts of beautiful goods. His yard was filled with cattle, yams, and everything any rich man would have. Except for the King, Okoma was now richer than every man in the village.

Everyone in the village soon knew about Okoma's sudden wealth. Wealth didn't spoil Okoma, though. He even became kinder to people, especially those less fortunate than he was. The kinder he got the more popular and wealthier he became.

Ozuru was of course very angry and envious of Okoma. He wanted to know how he came about his sudden wealth and fame, so he decided to pay him a visit. Okoma was always eager and proud to tell people about the source of his wealth, and how he earned it, so he told Ozuru what had happened.

The next day when the King's wife was on her way to the market Ozuru ran out of his house to accost her.

"Good day, my Lady," he genuflected.

"Good day Mr. Ozuru," responded the King's wife. "To what do I owe this courtesy?"

"My Lady. It would be an honor for me to serve the wife of my King. It is such a beautiful, but muggy, day that I thought you might want a drink of water."

"No, Mister. I am mighty fine. A thirst with the hope of satisfaction farther down the road never killed anyone before," she replied.

"But, my Lady. Why wait until down the road to drink warm water when you can have pure and cold water here?"

"My son. The sparrow said that since hunters have learned to shoot without missing, she has learned to fly without perching. You never offered me water before, so I have learned not to be thirsty around your house."

But Ozuru insisted that she should come to his house for a drink of water. The King's wife realized that the only way she could get Ozuru off her back was to follow him to his house for a drink of water.

While the King's wife was taking her drink of water, Ozuru went behind her back. "Okoma became so rich with just a puny wand and a tap on her back," he thought. "I could be even richer with a club and a whack on her head."

With that, Ozuru took a club and hit the King's wife as hard as he could. Now he did not know what to do, for he had killed the King's wife. Meanwhile Okoma was enjoying his riches, unaware of what had happened.

Late that night, Ozuru took the body of the King's wife to the woods and leaned it against a shrub. Before the first cock crowed he was at Okoma's house.

Knock! Knock!

"Who is there?" asked Okoma.

"It's your friend, Ozuru."

"The last time you came I wondered why it took you so long to come after you heard about my good fortune. Now you are visiting me a second time in as many days?"

"Sure pal, open up. It is your lucky day."

"Indeed! But it is too early, man. What can I do for you? My family and I are still in bed. Leave the list of what you want on the door and I will make sure that you get them at day break."

"I don't want anything from you, Mr. Big Shot. I just want to do you a favor," he lied.

"What is it?"

"You remember that trophy deer you have always wanted? You can get it now."

"Uh?" exclaimed Okoma. "How?"

"I just saw Mr. Nweke with two deer bulls. They must have weighed a ton each. Their antlers must have been six feet long. He said that a herd of about two hundred deer had been sighted at the north wood. All he had to do was go and pick which one he wanted."

"But he is a lousy shot," noted Okoma.

"That is my point exactly," replied Ozuru.

Okoma wasted no time getting into his hunting gear. With his gun dangling about his shoulders like a dog on a leash, he swung open his door, eager to go and hunt for the trophy he had always wanted.

There is nothing more fulfilling to a hunter than bagging the biggest game in the village. Okoma had always wanted to hunt big game but never could because he was poor and his gun was very low quality and could barely kill a squirrel. Hunting with it in the north wood where the lions and the hyenas also hunt would have been very dangerous. Now that he had a more powerful gun with double barrels, he couldn't wait to go hunting in the north wood.

When they got to the north wood, Ozuru pointed in the direction where he hid the body of the King's wife and whispered.

"There! There! Shoot! Shoot!"

Boom! Boom! Okoma fired in anxiety.

No sooner did the bullets leave Okoma's gun than Ozuru rushed to the scene to pick up the "deer."

"Oh nooo," lamented Ozuru.

"What? What? Did I destroy the antlers?" Okoma asked naively.

"You have killed the King's wife."

"The King's wife? But what could she be doing here this early in the morning?" asked Okoma.

"Do you want to ask that of the King?" replied Ozuru.

Okoma was very distraught with himself. How could he, the doer of good deeds, now be known in the village as the one who killed the King's wife? Especially after all she had done for him. He had become not only the proverbial dog that bit, but also killed, the hand that fed him. Ozuru was of course very happy that his trick had worked to his satisfaction.

While he thought of how best to relay the accident to the King, Okoma took the body to his house and covered it with clothes and mats. In his mind, he replayed the sequence of events leading to his shooting those fatal shots. "I couldn't have been the one who killed her," he thought. "But who did and how do I prove that I didn't?"

Meanwhile a day had passed and the King was looking for his wife. "To him who finds her," he decreed, "I will reward abundantly and make rich beyond his wildest dreams. But to him who as much as held her all this while, much less harmed her, I will give the ultimate punishment: death."

After a restless and thoughtful day, Okoma came up with what he thought was a good idea. He spent most of the money from his wealth to buy the most beautiful clothes, jewelry, and shoes of a quality that no one in the land had ever worn. By late afternoon he dressed up in them and went to Ozuru.

When Ozuru saw Okoma, his jaw dropped.

"I know you are rich," he told him, "but I didn't think you were that rich."

"I am now," replied Okoma.

"Where did you get all that from?" asked Ozuru.

"The King," replied Okoma.

"The King? First, his wife and now the King himself? Why?"

"For killing his wife. Apparently he had been wanting to get rid of her but did not quite know how. Who would have thought? I guess some of us are just born lucky," teased Okoma.

"Born lucky, my foot! That was my luck," Ozuru murmured to himself.

"Excuse me?"

"Nothing. I said you are lucky indeed."

Before the sun went to bed that day, Ozuru was at the King's castle banging on his door.

Bang! Bang!

Ozuru was let in by a page who led him to the King.

"What can I do for you, my son?" asked the King. "I am sorry I am not receiving visitors until I find my queen. Unless your visit is related to her disappearance."

"It is, my King," he replied. "The King shall live forever. All the gifts you gave to Okoma are mine."

"What are you talking about?" asked the King, confused.

"I was the one who killed your wife and I deserve my gifts now."

So Ozuru told the King how he had killed his wife and why. How he had made it look like it was Okoma who killed her.

"It hurts me that you are not only wicked but also greedy. Those who live by the sword shall die by the sword."

The King was very angry and ordered his servants to imprison and then kill Ozuru. To Okoma he gave gifts beyond his wildest dreams. When the King died, the villagers made Okoma their king, and his good deeds and powers were known all over the land.

The Orphan Girl

Chika was an orphan girl left to the care of a cruel stepmother. Her stepmother made her do all the work while her own daughter, Enuma, did little or nothing. In their Igbo village, the villagers drew their water from the river on only three of four market days. The fourth market day, Eke, was reserved for the ghosts, who lived on the other side of the river. A disagreement between Chika and Enuma on the eve of Eke market day resulted in their spilling the last water in the house. First thing in the morning, Chika was made to go and fetch water from the river, amid all the dangers of the ghosts and their antics.

There once lived a man and his two wives and two daughters. In time one of his wives died, leaving her daughter, named Chika, to be raised by her co-wife. This co-wife was very wicked to Chika. She never loved her. She treated her worse than she would a servant. She was partial toward her own daughter, Enuma, whom she seldom allowed to do anything. And so, Enuma was spoiled rotten, a braggart with no respect for anyone.

Chika was made to do most of the work in the house, though the work should have been divided equally between the two girls. She did all the work with grace, however, never complaining. When they ate, she was given mostly the leftovers.

"If I ever hear this from anyone," her stepmother warned, "I will kill you." So Chika never complained. She was just content that she even had something to eat.

Now, it was the custom in this village that no one could go to the river for water on Eke market days. The river was just at the border between the lands of the humans and of the ghosts. Through the diviners, the people knew that the ghosts went to the river for water on Eke market days only. The other three market days belonged to the humans.

On one Nkwo market day when the family came back late from the farms, Chika discovered that they were low on water. Since the next day was Eke, she decanted a sizable portion of water and saved it for the Eke day. After dinner, Enuma wanted to take the water for a bath. But Chika refused and told her that it was the last water in the house.

"What is left is barely enough for tomorrow," she warned, "and you want to take it for a bath?"

"I *need* to take a bath," said Enuma.

"But you and I took a bath at the farm this afternoon," reasoned Chika.

The two girls tugged on the gourd of water back and forth with all their might. As if her life depended on it, Chika wrapped both her arms around the gourd as Enuma tried to wrestle it from her. As they argued and tugged on the gourd back and forth and spilled much of its contents, Enuma's mother came to intervene. When the girls heard the door, Chika reluctantly released her grip on the gourd. This sent Enuma flying backward until she landed on her bottom, breaking the gourd and spilling what was left of the water.

"Tahe! Tahe! Tahe!" Chika chuckled nervously like any average child.

"You found that funny?" screamed her stepmother.

"No ma," pleaded Chika, trying very hard to hold back her laughter.

"What is going on here?" her stepmother inquired.

Then the two girls explained their sides of the matter, which to an observer were surprisingly corroborative testimonies. But Chika was not surprised that Enuma did not lie about the incident. Enuma always told the truth about matters concerning the two of them. She had no reason to lie, especially if her mother was the judge. Enuma knew that no matter what, her mother would rule in her favor.

"I knew it must be you," Chika's stepmother said, pointing at her. "So you mean you did not make sure there was enough water in the house? And you want to deprive her of taking her bath? Make sure that your father does not wake up to look for his bath water, nor me wake up to look for water to cook his meal."

"But tomorrow is Eke market day," pleaded Chika.

"That's news to me," said her stepmother. "It's your problem, isn't it? Just mark what I told you. Otherwise I will spread your meat to the vultures." Then, she turned around and went back into the house.

Meanwhile, Enuma tried to squeegee and wring the water off her clothes. She slapped the sand off her bottom and followed her mother to the house. Just as she was about to enter the house, she stuck her tongue out at Chika, saying, "Now whose turn is it to laugh and whose is it to cry?"

The next morning Chika was up before the second cock crowed. She picked up the largest water gourd she could carry and started to the river. As she went she trembled and prayed to her *chi* for protection. "If this is what a mother would wish for her child, then I deserve whatever bad that comes my way. But if this is not what a mother would wish for her child, my *chi* will protect me from all evils."

As she walked, she cringed at every step she took. All the grasses seemed to have eyes staring at her. The cries of the cricket sounded more like the roar of a lion. Soon she came upon what looked like a host of scorpions covering the road. She held on to the gourd as tightly as she could with her left hand. Then, she ran the back of her right hand over her eyes to be sure she was not dreaming.

When she realized that what she saw was real she begged the scorpions to let her by. She told them her life story and sung:

Mr. Scorpion, gentle scorpion,
Have mercy on a poor little orphan
It wasn't by my own will that I am here
It was my stepmother who sent me here
Although diviners said no one should,
But disobey my mother the gods also forbid

On hearing her story, the scorpions disappeared from the path and she continued on her way. Not much farther, she came upon a cluster of snakes. They were entangled with each other in a massive heap. Chika was petrified. She screamed and jumped as the leaf of an elephant grass touched her bare legs. When she regained her composure, she pleaded with the snakes. She told her story and sang to them. On hearing her story, the snakes also disappeared and she continued on her journey.

Relieved that the snakes were out of her way, she went on with renewed determination. Just as she was counting the different types of snakes she had seen in that heap, her concentration was broken by the roars of a pride of overgrown lions. As a lioness trudged toward her, the stories about how the lioness is the real killer in the pride flashed through Chika's mind. Just then, her song came to her. Soon after she sang, the pride disappeared.

Chika continued on her way, meeting all sorts of weird looking things. She met an old woman who walked on her head, two coconuts that tried to crack each other open, and several pieces of clothes that washed themselves at the riverbank. When she stepped into the river to fetch her water a nasally voice asked, "What are you doing here child?"

Chika looked up. But she couldn't see anyone about. Before she could respond, the voice continued. "No need to look," it said. "You will not like what you see."

But Chika was more determined to see the owner of the voice than she was afraid. All this while she had encountered only dangerous animals and weird things. Finally, a human being who spoke—or so she thought.

"*Iputago ula?*" Chika greeted the voice, asking whether it slept well.

"*Eh, Nwam! Iputago,*" the voice replied in the affirmative. "This is not a place for a sweet girl like you to be on a day like this. Doesn't your mother know better than to send you here to die?"

Then Chika turned to the direction she was sure the voice came from. To her amazement, she was facing a very scraggy old woman with one eye, one hand, and one leg. Much of her nose had been eaten up by leprosy, which made her sound nasal. She had a gourd that was about four times smaller than Chika's. Chika took pity on the old woman and helped her fill her gourd. Then Chika offered to carry the water for her. As she hopped and Chika followed her to her home, Chika became more comfortable with her and told her all about herself. She told her how her mother died, and her stepmother was raising her. How she did all the work and about the incident with the broken gourd of water, which brought her to the river on an Eke market day.

When they got to the old woman's home, she gave Chika a stone for yam and tree barks for fish and asked her to cook them for food. Chika took these items and put them in a gourd the old woman gave her and lit a fire under it. Moments later, she went to examine the pot and found it filled with delicious fish and the tastiest yams.

She served it and she and the old woman ate. After they had eaten, Chika realized that she had lost quite some time and begged her leave of the old woman.

"I am sorry," she said. "But I have to go now, lest my mother think that I am lagging in my chores. I hope you will be fine. I will come again to see you."

"Before you go," said the old woman, "take one of these gourds for yourself. It is a token of my gratitude for all your help." Then she presented Chika with two gourds. One was bigger with beautiful natural designs on it. The other was smaller and seemed to have been harvested out of season from an untended farm. Chika reached out and took the smaller gourd and thanked the old woman.

"Then go well my child, and peace be with you. When you get home, call your parents together. Tell them to clear a spot for you. When they have done so, break the gourd. But first—on your way home, you will hear 'Doom! Doom! Doom!' and 'Cham! Cham! Cham!' At the first sound, run into the bush and let the evil spirit pass. At the second, run back out and continue on your way."

Just as predicted, on her way Chika heard "Doom! Doom! Doom!" and "Cham! Cham! Cham!" She did exactly as she was instructed. Finally she got home and told her parents to clear a spot for her. Just as her stepmother was about to scold her for being tardy, she broke the gourd. Immediately the house was filled with all sorts of beautiful things like gold, silver, foods, herds of cattle, and so on. Her father was overjoyed. First, that his daughter came back home safely, and second, that she came with all sorts of riches. His love for Chika was now stronger than ever.

But Chika's stepmother was not happy. She wished that her own daughter had brought home the riches. So to remedy the situation, she waited until the next Nkwo market day. When everyone went to bed, she went to the back of the house and turned over all the pots of water.

Before the first cock crowed on the next day, which was Eke market day, Chika's stepmother woke up her own daughter, Enuma, and sent her to the river.

"You good for nothing," she abused her. "You want to stay here and sleep yourself to death while this other girl gets all of your father's affection. Go and get your own gourd right now and make your father proud. Make sure that you come home with a much bigger one."

On her way, Enuma met all the dangers and weird things just like Chika. Unlike Chika, Enuma was very rude and nasty to them.

"Get out of my way," she told the scorpions, snakes, and lions. She found the incidents of the coconuts and the clothes rather amusing. She laughed at them and the old woman who walked on her head. When the old woman at the river accosted her, she covered her nose in disgust. She never offered to help her with her water. When the old woman invited her to her house, she went only because she expected to get the magic gourds. She never offered to carry the old woman's gourd for her. When the old woman gave her the stone and tree barks, she fretted:

"How can someone live like this? Don't you know that gourds burn and should not be used as cooking pots? Who ever heard of eating stones and tree barks anyway? I don't do my own cooking, why should I cook for you?"

Enuma complained about everything. She did only things that were easy and beneficial to her. Finally, when she was about to leave, the old woman presented two gourds to her.

"Take one of these gourds. When you hear 'Doom! Doom! Doom!' on your way run into the bushes. But when you hear 'Cham! Cham! Cham!' come back out and continue on your way. When you get home ask your mother..."

"I know what to do," interrupted Enuma. She looked at the gourds, sized them up, and snatched the bigger and better-looking one. "I will take it from here."

"Go in peace my child," said the old woman, her voice trembling. "But I am afraid for you."

Enuma went home. On her way she heard "Doom! Doom! Doom!" and continued on. Then she heard "Cham! Cham! Cham!" and ran into the bush. When she got home, she asked her mother to clear her house and lock her doors and windows so that they could keep all the riches to themselves.

"Clear it mother," she said, "for I have got the big one."

Her mother quickly cleared her house. Then she locked the doors and windows and asked Enuma to break the gourd. But, instead of the riches they expected, they were overcome with smallpox, leprosy, and other diseases in epidemic proportions. When the woman's husband could not find her and Enuma, he went to her room. When he opened her door, all the diseases escaped into the world. That was how diseases, which are still with us today, came to be spread all over the world.

Meanwhile, Chika remained an industrious and well-mannered young girl and when she became of age, she was married to a very handsome and wealthy prince and they lived happily ever after.

The Power of One

According to a popular proverb, a journey of a thousand miles starts with a single step. In this tale by the Calabar people, the Tortoise took advantage of this idea to become rich. While every other creature, when given the choice of how much gold and silver coin he wanted from the King, chose hundreds or thousands of coins, the Tortoise simply chose the number "one."

Many, many years ago in Africa there lived a King named Etukudo. He had everything that a King could have: yams, cattle, goats, sheep, silver coins, and gold coins. He also had thousands of acres of farmland and hundreds of farmhands that helped him tend his farms.

King Etukudo was also very generous and known to often reward his workers for more than their daily wages. One year after a bountiful harvest and triumph over his foes, he wanted to reward everyone for their hard work.

"Akpan," he called his head servant.

"Yes Sir, my King," answered his head servant.

"Go to the vault and bring those things you counted up last night. I hope that nobody tampered with them."

"No one, my King. I made sure of that," the servant said and disappeared into the back room.

Several moments later, the servant returned with an entourage of about twelve other servants, each carrying a basketful of coins.

"Here are the coins, my King," said the head servant.

"Go to the village square and distribute them to all the inhabitants of my village, for they have worked very hard this year. They deserve to share in the fruits of their labor. As our people say, 'When good fortune befalls a medicine man, it trickles down to his medicine bag.'"

"My King is a wise and generous king," echoed the head servant.

The head servant, with the help of other servants, loaded up the baskets of money on their donkeys. Then, they set out to the village square. By the time they arrived at the village square, everyone, including the animals, was already assembled and waited anxiously.

For previous gifts, the King had rewarded individuals according to their performance. This time, he decided to give anyone whatever amount he asked for. So when the caravan of donkeys arrived, the head servant made the announcement to the crowd.

"The King has decreed that everyone should be given whatever amount he asks."

"Wow!" exclaimed the Elephant. "I think I will ask for an uncountable number of gold coins. You know—a number so large that your jaws would break before you could count to it."

"That figures," said the Rabbit. "You are going to need that much to be able to feed that tummy. I just need one hundred silver coins."

"I want two hundred silver coins," said the Lion.

"I think that five hundred gold coins will be alright for me," said the Monkey.

"How about two thousand silver coins?" said the Gorilla.

"You've got it," said the head servant as he made marks on the ground at the foot of each person or creature to identify their request.

Finally he came to the Tortoise. "How many do you want, old man?"

"One!"

"One what? Thousand? Hundred? What?"

"Just the number one."

"Alright, Mr. Know It All. Whatever you say."

The rest of the crowd couldn't contain themselves laughing. For once, they thought the Tortoise was modest and contented, or outright crazy.

"We shall see who gets the last laugh," the Tortoise said to himself.

"Wait a moment!" said the Leopard. "You mean with all this money here you just want one coin?"

"Yes. Just ONE," answered the Tortoise rather emphatically.

"Okay! Okay!" agreed the Leopard. "This I've got to see. You are not up to something again, are you? What..."

"Ahem!" the head servant cleared his throat to get everyone's attention. "I will now distribute the monies according to your wishes."

As he went back to the beginning of the line, the Tortoise followed him with his basket. When the head servant got to the Elephant, he reached into the basket of gold coins and started counting.

"One, ..."

"That's me," the Tortoise said and took the money from the head servant and put it inside his basket.

"One, ..." the head servant started again to count out gold coins for the Elephant.

"That's me again," said the Tortoise. He took the money from the servant and put it in his basket.

"One, ..."

"Mine again."

The crowd was by now impatient. Some of the bigger animals were closing in on the head servant and the Tortoise, nudging the latter to give everyone else a turn.

"When he calls out two thousand," the Tortoise said to the Gorilla, "then you can have a turn. Right now he is calling out 'one' and it is still my turn."

"One," said the servant.

"Here sir," the Tortoise answered, stretching out his hand for the coin.

By now the crowd understood the game and was beginning to disperse. The Tortoise collected all the coins one by one and when he could not carry them all, he borrowed the King's donkeys to haul them to his house.

THE RUBBER MAN

This popular Hausa tale is about why the Tortoise withdraws into its shell when threatened. The Tortoise, lazy and cunning, did not farm when the rest of the creatures farmed. When it was harvest time, however, he reaped where he did not sow. When the King's servant noticed someone was stealing from the King's farm he set a trap to catch the thief.

The Tortoise was a lazy and slow animal who relied mostly on his wits to survive. One planting season, the rains came back with a vengeance after a long draught. Everybody worked harder than ever plowing the land and planting their crops, but not the Tortoise. While everybody was busy, the Tortoise ate the little bit of food he had and slept all day. Worried that they were wasting valuable time, his wife could not help but intervene.

"Aren't we going to plant anything this year?" asked Mrs. Tortoise. "The rains have come and our neighbors have plowed hundreds of acres."

"Of course!" answered the Tortoise. "Sure the rains have started, but hardly. Never mind those braggarts who plow long before the rains have wetted the soil. We have all the time in the world. Besides, it's not how fast or how soon you start a race that counts. It's how you complete it."

"Alright. But remember that once the rains are gone, they are gone," pleaded his wife.

Now not only did his wife remind him to plow the farm, his neighbors also got into the act.

"What's with you this planting season, old man?" asked the Chimp. "I see you want your family to starve again this year. Just don't come asking to borrow from me again."

"I won't," said the Tortoise, "so you have nothing to worry about."

"Don't go to the Crow either," continued the Chimp. "She has enough mouths to feed as it is."

Time passed and most of the animals weeded their farms. Still, the Tortoise had neither plowed nor planted. Meanwhile, most of the crops were now planted and the barns were bare. The Tortoise's barn was bare just because he had eaten all he had. Mrs. Tortoise was now worried and impatient with the Tortoise not only because they didn't have much to eat, but also because come harvest time, they still wouldn't have anything to eat. Then the Tortoise decided on a plan.

"The time is now right for me to plow the soil for our farm," he said to Mrs. Tortoise. "Buy some baskets of peanuts, roast them, and salt them to get them ready for planting."

"Who ever heard of planting roasted and salted peanuts?" asked Mrs. Tortoise.

"Trust me. I know what I am doing. These are instant peanuts. You plant them roasted and salted and, come harvest time, you harvest them roasted and salted."

Mrs. Tortoise did as she was told. She bought some peanuts, salted and roasted them for planting, just as she was instructed. Meanwhile, the Tortoise went to the farm. When he got there he ate his lunch, rested and sunned himself. Later that evening he came back pretending to be tired from plowing the farms.

Before the first cock crowed the next day, the Tortoise was up and ready for the farm again, this time to go and sow the peanuts. Mrs. Tortoise was quite impressed by his dedication and wasted no time packing the roasted peanuts for him. The Tortoise tied the bags of peanuts on his back. Then he went to his favorite spot in the forest and made a feast of the peanuts. He sunned himself and slept. At dusk he came home pretending to be tired from a hard day's work.

"I am home!" he announced. "Where is my dinner?"

"Welcome, my hero," replied Mrs. Tortoise. "Dinner will be served in a moment."

For the next several days the same thing happened. The Tortoise woke up and carried bags of roasted peanuts to the forest and ate them. He came home and lied to his wife.

When harvest time came, the rest of the villagers harvested their crops—but not the Tortoise. For the next several days, he just lay about the house and watched the villagers haul their harvest to their barns.

"Isn't it time to harvest our peanuts?" asked Mrs. Tortoise. "Surely they must be matured by now. The others have pulled up most of their harvest."

"Remember, these are special peanuts. They went in late and will come out late," the Tortoise lied.

By now Mrs. Tortoise was beginning to think that all was not well. "But what could have happened to all those peanuts he hauled to the farm all those days?" she wondered. Just to be sure, she offered to help the Tortoise with the harvest. But, he refused her offer of help.

"In a few more days I will harvest the peanuts myself," he said.

While the Tortoise lied to his wife in order to buy time, he was hard at work in his mind looking for a way to bring back a harvest of peanuts to her. Since he did not have any farm to speak of, the only way the Tortoise could harvest any peanuts was to steal them. So, when his wife went to bed, he crawled out. He searched for a farm large enough to still have peanuts that late in the harvest season.

And there it was: the King's farm, full of acres of unharvested peanuts. The Tortoise went to work immediately and pulled out as many peanuts as he could and stuffed them into his bag. Then, he hid the bag in a safe place and crawled back home.

"Wake up," said the Tortoise to his wife. "This is the day I will harvest our peanuts. I will be back by dusk. Have my dinner ready. Harvesting is a hard job and I will come home tired and hungry."

"All right. I cannot wait to taste those peanuts," said Mrs. Tortoise.

The Tortoise picked up an empty bag and his lunch and went to the farm. When he got there, he rested under the big oak tree. He ate his lunch and had his fill of water, and then he sunned himself and slept. At dusk, he picked up the peanuts he had stolen the night before. He went home and threw down the bag of peanuts for his wife.

Mrs. Tortoise was very excited. She grabbed a handful of peanuts, cracked one open and tossed it into her mouth. "These are raw!" she said as she made a face and spat it out. "You said they would be harvested roasted and salted!"

"You must be out of your mind. Who ever heard of peanuts that were harvested roasted and salted?" asked the Tortoise.

"I must have misunderstood you," Mrs. Tortoise apologized.

"Sure you did," said the Tortoise.

From that night on, the Tortoise went to the King's farm and stole bags of peanuts. The following mornings, he went back to haul them to his wife at dusk.

Meanwhile, the King's servant noticed that the peanuts were being harvested faster than he could account for. "Someone has been stealing from the King," he said to himself. "I must find out who it is, or else the King might think I am the one stealing from him."

The servant collected some clay and molded it into the statue of a man. He placed it in the spot where the Tortoise had stolen the peanuts. Then, he covered it all over with thick and sticky rubber sap. "I am sure by morning I will know who the thief is," he said.

That night, the Tortoise sneaked out as before to steal more peanuts. The moon was by now half size and the moonlight faint but bright enough for one to find his way around the farms. The Tortoise got to work immediately stealing the peanuts. He was about to fill his second bag with peanuts when he noticed the shadow of a man.

"Oh!" the Tortoise said, startled. "It is not what you think. I was just inspecting the peanuts to see if they were mature enough for harvest so that I may tell the King." Then he stood up straight, turned, and faced the figure. "What are you doing here by the way?"

But the figure did not say a word. It just stood there.

"Who are you? And what are you doing there, I said?"

Again there was no answer from the rubber man.

"Do you know that this is the King's farm?" the Tortoise asked.

But the rubber man did not answer.

The Tortoise was now as scared as he was mad. But determined to prove his innocence by intimidation, he walked cautiously to the rubber man.

"Answer me now before I slap your face," threatened the Tortoise.

When the rubber man didn't answer his queries, the Tortoise decided to get rough with him.

"Why don't you answer me?" the Tortoise asked, and in the same breath he slapped the rubber man with his right hand. But the rubber man, who has been standing in the hot sun all day was now so sticky that the Tortoise's hand stuck to his left chin. Yuck!

"Let go of me right now," said the Tortoise. "If you don't let go of me, I will slap you with my left hand. Believe me, it is more dangerous than my right."

And with that, the Tortoise slapped the rubber man with his left hand. It got stuck to the rubber man's right chin. Yuck! Yuck!

"I see you want to play rough! If you want it rough, I will play it rough and if you want it cool, I will play it cool. I am good at both," the Tortoise boasted. "And you are really going to get it now. If I give you a hard kick, I could break your bones."

So the Tortoise kicked the rubber man with his right leg. Of course, it also got stuck. And finally, the Tortoise tried to free himself. He pressed his left knee and his head against the rubber man. They, too, both got stuck. Now the Tortoise had nowhere to go. He had been caught.

The next morning the King's servant came to check his trap. "Ha! Ha! Ha! Ha! So it was you who stole from the King. I should have known. It is only you, who prefer to cultivate lands that have been tilled by someone else, who would have the audacity to steal from the King. Now you are going to be punished for your laziness and for stealing."

In order to humiliate the Tortoise, the King's servant carried him through the market square stuck to the rubber man. People laughed and teased the Tortoise. He was ashamed and he hid his face inside his shell. For several moons the Tortoise didn't show his face in public. Whenever he saw anyone he withdrew into his shell.

Since that time, Tortoises have been shy. They hide their faces in their shells when they see people. They think people will laugh at them because their great-great-grandfather stole peanuts from the King.

NIGERIA

The Talking Tree

The Tortoise wanted to con the other animals out of their food. So, he hid in a tree hollow to scare them into abandoning their food. He yelled daring words at them and beat his war drum. When the animals discovered that it was the Tortoise, he had to devise one last trick—a disappearing act—to save his skin. This story from the Igbos also explains why the Praying Mantis walks as he does.

The animal kingdom went to war and came back with a lot of loot. The Elephant led the troops as they marched back in triumph from the battle. As they marched, they were startled by a booming sound from a hollow in a huge oak tree.

If it's the Elephant, let him come and yell.	*Oburu Enyi ka m zogbue*
And I will trample him to death!	*Anu ngwomili koto ma ngwo!*
My loincloth *yagham* on my shell.	*Mbe n'ukwu yagham n'okpulukpu*
And I will trample him to death!	*Anu ngwomili koto ma ngwo!*

The Elephant was visibly shaken and walked backward in retreat. "I have been through a lot of wars in my life. I have also heard all types of war songs. But I have never heard one that sounded quite as bold and daring as that one," he said.

"Who could be so strong that he challenged even the mighty Elephant?" asked the Lion.

As they looked on and wondered, a branch of the tree shook in their direction.

"It is the tree! It is the tree! The tree is talking and is about to attack us," the Giraffe shouted in a panic.

"Trees don't talk," observed the Hippo. "The war song is coming from that hollow in the tree."

"Maybe I can use my paws to strangle whoever is in there," said the Lion. Then he pounced forward in a rage. But the drum and the war song sounded even louder.

If it's the Lion, let him come and yell.	*Oburu Agu ka m zogbue*
And I will trample him to death!	*Anu ngwomili koto ma ngwo!*
My loincloth *yagham* on my shell.	*Mbe n'ukwu yagham n'okpulukpu*

And I will trample him to death! — *Anu ngwomili koto ma ngwo!*

"Rrrrrroar," the Lion roared and stood on his hind legs baring his claws. He then tucked his tail between his legs and ran back to the rest of the animals.

"How can we show our faces in public if we cannot defeat whoever is beating that drum?" asked the Hippo.

"But we cannot see who it is," observed the Cheetah.

"It might be the ghosts of all our enemies we have defeated in battles coming back to haunt us," concluded the Monkey. Then he approached the oak tree to try to get a glimpse of whoever was in there.

As the Monkey started to climb the big oak tree, the drumbeat intensified. The beat was so loud that the oak tree began to shake again, throwing the Monkey off balance. He soon lost his grip and fell in fear.

If it's the Monkey, let him come and yell.	*Oburu Enwe ka m zogbue*
And I will trample him to death!	*Anu ngwomili koto ma ngwo!*
My loincloth *yagham* on my shell.	*Mbe n'ukwu yagham n'okpulukpu*
And I will trample him to death!	*Anu ngwomili koto ma ngwo!*

All the animals tried their luck at challenging the intruder. Meanwhile, the Mantis was gingerly scaling the oak tree on the other side in the rhythm of the drumbeat. The higher he climbed, the louder the drumbeat, and the slower he went.

For what seamed like eternity, the animals tried to challenge the intruder but were always scared away. And for that length of time, the Mantis was forever trying to get to the top of the oak tree. When he had made it halfway up, the intruder saw the Mantis. The beat of the drum and the war song grew even louder. All in an attempt to scare the Mantis down the oak tree. But the Mantis would not fall down. Then, in a loud and scary voice the intruder continually beat his war drum and sang his war song:

If it's the Mantis, let him come and yell.	*Oburu Okolingodo ka m zogbue*
And I will trample him to death!	*Anu ngwomili koto ma ngwo!*

My loincloth *yagham* on my shell.	*Mbe n'ukwu yagham n'okpulukpu*
And I will trample him to death!	*Anu ngwomili koto ma ngwo!*

The Mantis slowed down, but he wouldn't budge. He continued to climb the oak tree to find out who was scaring the animals. Finally, he reached the hollow at the top of the oak tree. As he peered into the hollow, he saw the Tortoise banging on his drum.

"It is the Tortoise! It is the Tortoise!" shouted the Mantis.

Yes, who else could it be but the Tortoise? The Tortoise with his cunning and greedy ways had decided to take all the loot for himself. So, he disappeared ahead of the troop and climbed into the hollow atop the oak tree. With his drum, he threatened the animals, hoping they would abandon their loot in fear.

Within a blink of the eye, the Monkey was atop the oak tree. He dragged the Tortoise out of his hiding place.

The animals tried the Tortoise and convicted him of treason.

"What form of punishment should we give to him?" asked the Elephant.

"Kill him! Kill him!" suggested the Monkey.

"Yeah! Smash him on the treason rock as we do all our traitors," said one animal.

And in unison, all the animals agreed that the Tortoise should be smashed on the big treason rock.

"Your Commandership," the Tortoise addressed the Elephant. "I know that I have sinned against my people and deserve whatever punishment you give me. But I'd like to remind you that I have survived a fall from the sky onto a bed of rocks. So I am sure that I will survive a smash on the treason rock."

"That is true," agreed the Lion.

"I have betrayed my people and cannot show my face in public anymore. I am not worthy to be among my people anymore. Why don't you just banish me to the never-never land to die?"

"No! That is too easy," said the Gorilla. "Besides, how do we know that you will not come back to play another trick on us?"

"I am so mad at myself that I want to get this over with as soon as possible. I do not deserve to live. And if you want proof that I will not bother you any more and that I want to die for my greed, just smash me on that muddy water at the edge of the river," suggested the Tortoise.

"No!" protested the Hippo.

"Yeah!" the Tortoise continued. "As soon as I hit that mud, all that gooey and slimy mud will cover my eyes and nose and suffocate me to death."

After a short debate the animals decided to smash the Tortoise on the muddy water. Just to make sure he took a hard fall the Elephant was elected to do it.

The rest of the animals stood back and watched as the mighty Elephant picked up the Tortoise. He held him by his neck with his big trunk and swung him around and around several times. And with one big heave smashed the Tortoise into the muddy water.

"Thump," the Tortoise was smashed into the muddy water.

Quickly the animals ran forward to the edge of the muddy water. They looked in, hoping to find the Tortoise choking to death. But he was nowhere to be found. The Tortoise had clawed his way through the mud to the sea where he swam to safety. He had fooled the animals once again. The Elephant stuck his long trunk into the mud. He reached way down in search of the Tortoise. But he was long gone.

"Get off me! Get off me! Shoo. Shoo. Ha! Ha! Ha! Ha!" the Elephant ran and laughed, swinging his trunk as he tried to shake off a Crab who had clung to his snout, tickling him.

"That will teach you not to disturb someone trying to have a quiet nap in his house," the Crab warned as he fell off the Elephant's trunk.

After searching all over for the Tortoise, the animals gave up and went home. It was a day most of the animals have tried to forget. But not the Mantis. Today, the Mantis walks very slowly and in a shaky gait, for the vibration he absorbed as he climbed that big oak tree is still with him. He keeps his hands in a fighting position, always ready to fight an intruder. Since that fateful encounter, the Mantis has come to be known as Oche Ogu (one who is always poised for a fight) by some Igbo people.

The Tortoise and the Pig

The Tortoise and the Pig were once such good friends that they even owned a business together. After they got their payment for a job, the Tortoise persuaded the Pig to loan him his share of the payment. When it was time to repay the loan, the Tortoise came up with excuses instead of money. Eventually the Pig became tired of this and got rough with the Tortoise. But the Pig's anger backfired. This story from the Igbos explains why the Pig digs up stones with his snout.

Long, long time ago the Tortoise and the Pig were very good friends. They did quite a lot of things together, including sharing a small rototilling business. One day the King hired them to rototill his farm and promised to pay them handsomely.

"Good morning, my Lady," the Pig greeted the King's wife as he and the Tortoise arrived at the King's house on the appointed day.

"Good morning gentlemen," responded the King's wife.

"We have come to till the King's land. All we need is someone to show us to the farm," requested the Tortoise. "Our fee is ten silver coins, with food, or twelve without."

The King's wife sent one of her servants to take them to the farm. As the King's servant mapped out the land, the Tortoise couldn't help but wonder why he ever got into the rototilling business in the first place. The longer he stared at the open field, the lazier he became.

"That is an awfully large lot," he thought. "There is no way anyone could be expected to till even a fraction of it, let alone the whole thing."

The Pig, being an industrious creature, wasted no time at all. He went to work on the farm right away. "We had better get going if we plan to get the work done in time to collect our fees," he told the Tortoise. But rather than do his fair share of the work, the Tortoise was busy hatching a scheme to avoid the work as much as he could.

As the Pig worked, the Tortoise excused himself for one reason or another. Usually he went to the big oak tree near the farm to bask in the sun. When he came back, the Pig asked where he had been.

"Just went to answer the call of nature," he lied.

"I notice you are not keeping up with me. We really need to hurry it up, you know."

"You can hurry all you want. What's important is not how fast you start but how fast you finish. This is a marathon and not a sprint. Slow and steady will win the race."

This continued for a while until the Pig finally figured out that the Tortoise was up to no good. The Pig concluded that the Tortoise was devising a master plan to get the Pig to finish the work all by himself.

"I think I could use one of those calls of nature myself," the Pig told the Tortoise. "I am not made of wood, you know." He then went into the meadow and lay down under the shade to take a well-deserved rest.

"Good enough. But hurry it up—there is still quite a bit of work to be done."

As the Pig rested, the Tortoise heard the King's wife and her servants coming to the farm. He immediately started working as hard as he could in order to impress them. When the King's wife got there, she stood for a while watching the Tortoise. Every so often the Tortoise, who was aware of their presence, wiped off the sweat from his face with effort, feigning tiredness.

"Where is your partner?" asked the King's wife.

"I wish I knew," replied the Tortoise. "He is either answering the call of nature or resting. And I am left alone to work my bones to death. It is easy to see that he is quite lazy. All he does justice to is the dinner plate. Just open up the dish, I am sure he will come running as soon as he smells the food."

Angry at the Pig, the King's wife divided the food she brought for them into three parts. She gave two parts to the Tortoise and left the third for the Pig.

"If he learns to do his fair share of the work, I will give him his fair share of the food," explained the King's wife. She then thanked the Tortoise for his effort and left.

The Tortoise wasted no time devouring his share of the food and waited for the Pig to come back.

When the Pig returned, the Tortoise brought out the third of the food the King's wife had saved for him.

"Let's eat, partner," the Tortoise invited the Pig.

"Eat what?" asked the Pig.

"You took the words right out of my mouth," said the Tortoise. "Can you believe this? You are seeing it with your own eyes. The food the King's wife brought for two strong men is not even enough to feed my baby."

The Pig became very mad and decided to forgo lunch rather than eat to provoke his stomach.

"Let us manage it, partner. It is better than nothing at all. Besides, she might be really disappointed and mad if she learns that we did not eat her food. Who knows—she could be testing us. You don't want to upset her, do you?"

"Of course not. But it's really very cruel of her. If we knew they'd skimp on the food, we would have just charged them twelve silver coins and brought our own lunches."

After lunch, they went back to work. The Pig was becoming increasingly tired from hunger and the hot sun. On the other hand, the Tortoise seemed to have just found his second wind.

"I told you, didn't I?" said the Tortoise. "'It is not how fast you start, but how well you finish that matters.' It is when the lightening strikes that one sees what is lurking behind the bushes. It is during the heat of the sun that the best is brought out of a plodder, not early in the morning. Heck, anyone can work hard then."

At dusk the two friends headed to the King's palace to collect their money.

"The work is done," the Tortoise told the King. "And as agreed, our fee is ten silver coins. As the senior partner, you hand them over to me." And turning over to the Pig he asked, "Isn't that right?"

"That is right," replied the Pig.

On their way home the Tortoise, in his greedy way, was busy hatching a plan enabling him to take all the money for himself. "We shall split our fee now," he said to the Pig. "To start with, I will take two coins, one for collecting the money and the other for holding it. The balance we shall split equally."

The Pig couldn't believe his ears. But he accepted the terms because he knew the Tortoise would take all the money if he argued.

"Are you really a true friend?" asked the Tortoise.

"You know I am," replied the Pig.

"Then you will not mind going to the market with me. I need to buy a present for my wife."

The Pig followed the Tortoise to the market. The Tortoise picked a very beautiful dress for his wife, which he bargained down to ten silver coins. Of course he didn't have enough money for the dress, so he begged the Pig to loan him his share of the money. The Pig agreed and the Tortoise paid for the dress.

"It is not really wise to come home with me now because I had a fight with my wife. That is why I bought this dress for her. Come back tomorrow. Then, we will have made up and your money will be waiting for you."

The Pig agreed and went home. The next day he went to the Tortoise to collect his money. But the Tortoise was not home. So, he left a message with Mrs. Tortoise that he would be back the next day to collect his money. The next day, the Tortoise dodged again. The Pig became very mad and swore to collect his money the following day whatever the cost.

When the Tortoise came back, his wife gave him the Pig's message. First thing the next morning, he instructed his wife to turn him over and paint him with mud.

"Now, I am your grinding stone. When the Pig comes back, tell him that I am sick in bed and that you are grinding some medicine for me."

By the time the sun was overhead, the Pig returned fuming with anger.

"Where is that lazy husband of yours? Tell him I have come to collect my money *right now*."

"I am sorry, my husband is sick in bed. It is for him that I am grinding this medicine," replied Mrs. Tortoise.

"Will you stop grinding that thing and go and get him out here."

Mrs. Tortoise pretended not to hear the Pig and continued with her grinding. The Pig became even angrier. In his rage, he picked up the grinding stone and threw it over the fence.

The Tortoise got up and cleaned himself of the mud. He picked up a stick and walked back to the house through the back door. Then he limped out to meet the Pig, pretending to be sick and in pain. Meanwhile the Pig was still scolding Mrs. Tortoise to go and get her husband.

"What is the matter?" asked the Tortoise. "Is it your money? Please leave her alone to mix my medicine and I will give you your money." Then turning to his wife he said, "Mix my medicine while I get his money. Where is the grinding stone?"

Then the Tortoise's wife told him that the Pig threw away the stone in a rage.

"No problem. Just go and get the grinding stone so that I may pay you. I have my money inside it. Besides, I need my wife to mix my medicine."

The Pig then ran back to the backyard to get the grinding stone, but he could not find it.

"Oh! No! Not only have you lost my money, you are also depriving me of my right to get well again. I want to pay you, but I need to be alive to do so. Find my stone and I will give you your money."

The Pig went out again to look for the stone but could not find it. He dug up every stone and mound he could find looking for the grinding stone and money but still could not find it.

That is why even today you can see the Pig digging around with his snout. He is looking for the Tortoise's grinding stone, so the Tortoise can pay him back his money.

THE TUG-OF-WAR

The Calabar people, like many other ethnic groups in West Africa, regard the Tortoise as both witty and cunning. In this story, the Tortoise's desire for recognition as an animal of valor led him to put himself in a very precarious position. After challenging the Elephant to a tug-of-war contest, he must devise a clever way of rigging the contest.

The Tortoise, the slowest of all animals, never got much respect. He soon tired of being the laughing stock of the kingdom. He envied the rest of the creatures who all seemed to be known for their good qualities.

"Speed," the Tortoise said to himself, playing a solitary word association game. "The Cheetah. Flight—the birds. Strength—the Lion. No! The Elephant. Slow—the Tortoise. Nooo! I must put an end to that. I must be known for something else. Something of valor."

To make sure that he got the respect he thought he deserved, the Tortoise decided to challenge the animals to a game of tug-of-war. Starting from the smallest of them to the biggest. When some of the animals heard his challenge, they laughed at him. "How can the Tortoise beat anyone in tug-of-war?" They all asked.

"Even the Lion?" asked the Rabbit.

"Even the Lion and the Elephant," answered the Tortoise.

"And the Hippopotamus, the Giraffe..."

"You heard me," the Tortoise interrupted the Rabbit. "All the animals, and I'll start with you."

"Don't worry about me," the Rabbit quickly excused himself from the contest. "Worry about the Lion, the Elephant, the Hippopotamus..."

"Go get them," the Tortoise said emphatically.

The Rabbit ran off to inform the animals of the Tortoise's challenge. When he got to the Lion's den, he was filled with such excitement that he almost ran into the den. Just in time his better sense of judgment overcame his excitement, and he stopped several yards away from the den and shouted, "Lion! Lion! Have you heard the one from the Tortoise?"

"I hear it all the time," said the Lion. "Nothing he says or does surprises me any more."

"This one will," continued the Rabbit as his tail shook and his whiskers stroked his chin fervently. He was nervous as a fly. "He is challenging you to a tug-of-war."

Then the Rabbit ran off chuckling as the Lion came out roaring with anger. From the Lion's house he went to the Deer, to all the other animals, and finally to the Elephant and to the Hippo. All the animals assembled at the play square for the Tortoise to formally launch his challenge.

"Before now," said the Deer, "I thought this was a misunderstanding. You are serious?"

"Dead serious," said the Tortoise.

The Lion got up and started to walk away, saying that he'd thought the challenge over and wouldn't dignify it with a response.

"I knew you'd feel that way," said the Tortoise. "I know how easy it is for your ego to be ruffled. You go about bullying all these helpless deer and rabbits. Sneaking behind their backs, killing them,and thinking you are strong. Come for a fair fight; let's see how strong you are."

The Lion thought that the Tortoise had really overstepped his bounds. He pounced on him, as the Tortoise waved his finger and said, "Ta! Ta! Ta! Ta! *Fair* fight! Remember? That means it has ground rules. Put me down."

The Lion reluctantly put him down.

"I know that you believe you can take on all the animals," the Tortoise continued. "And, although you and the Elephant and the Hippo have never been in a fight, even *you* will agree that it will be a toss-up between the three of you."

"For once you are right," said the Lion. "But get to the point. I am running out of patience."

"Here is my challenge. I will take on the Elephant and the Hippo. Since they are the biggest, I believe they are also the strongest. If I beat them, as I am sure I will, then you and I are equal, a toss-up. We can then rule the kingdom together."

As part of the rules, the Tortoise sent all the animals away while he and the Elephant, and then the Hippo, worked out the details privately. The Elephant lumbered back to his house ranting and raving. So did the Hippo. "I hope for his sake that he never follows up with this madness," the Elephant said to himself.

Several days passed, and neither the Elephant nor the Hippo heard from the Tortoise. Meanwhile, the Tortoise went to his house and twirled a very thick rope from vines he had strung together.

One day as the Elephant was grazing along the bank of the river where the Hippo lived, he came upon him wallowing in the sandy beach. Not knowing that the Tortoise was spying on them from behind the bushes, the two animals talked about the Tortoise's challenge very casually.

"Have you heard anything yet?" asked the Elephant.

"Nothing," said the Hippo. "I hope I never do. Just for his sake. He's just a fly trying to perch on my eye. How do I kill it without giving myself a black eye?"

"You're so right," the Elephant agreed. "I consider the matter closed unless I hear from him again. He must have been drunk when he made the challenge."

So the Elephant went about his business while the Hippo rolled about on the warm sand. A little while later, he was about to get up when he heard a voice behind him.

"The Elephant tells me that you are not taking my challenge seriously," said the Tortoise. "You should have, because we are going to have the tug of war right now."

"I can beat you any time, even in my sleep," said the Hippo. "I don't need to pray and seek divine powers to fight someone I am sure to beat."

With that, the Hippo got up. He sneezed to clear his nasal passages and the Tortoise found himself in a hurricane. The Tortoise was blown into the bushes, but as soon as he collected himself, he came back out and faced the Hippo again. He looked up at the Hippo as if he were looking into the heavens. He was a mass of flesh.

"You are right," the Tortoise said. "In your sleep."

The Hippo thought the joke has gone too far and became angry with the unwelcome guest. But, just so that the other animals wouldn't think that he had run from a fight, he stretched out his neck and asked the Tortoise to tie the rope around it.

After the Tortoise was done, he passed out the instructions: "Now, you go back into the water. Wait until I tug on the rope three times. After the third tug, pull as hard as you can. Better brace yourself because by the third tug, I will pull you out."

The Hippo nodded and dragged the rope into the water. Then the Tortoise took the other end of the rope and ran after the Elephant. Taking a short cut, he soon caught up with him.

"Good day to you, Mr. Elephant," greeted the Tortoise. "The Hippo tells me that you didn't take my challenge seriously. So, you really think that you are stronger than me?"

The Elephant was both amused and angered. He chuckled and flung his trunk about to chase the flies. The wave from it almost swept the Tortoise off the ground. For a moment the Tortoise thought that maybe, he had made a mistake challenging him. "Not if my plan works," he thought.

"I don't and I am," said the Elephant. "It will be no contest. I could throw you to the heavens by merely shaking my body to drive off the flies."

"Then prove it," said the Tortoise. "Here! Take the rope and tie it around your neck. I will go and tie the other end around my waist. When you feel three tugs, do your worst because I will do mine."

As the Elephant tied the rope around his neck, the Tortoise crawled back into the bush. Now, this bush separated the Elephant from the river where the Hippo was waiting for his signal. When he was clearly hidden from the Elephant's view, the Tortoise gave the rope one, two, and by the third tug, the rope was as taut as an iron rod.

The Elephant and the Hippo tugged on the rope as hard as they could, with all their might. The Elephant bellowed and moaned while the Hippo groaned and moaned. Neither was able to pull the other far enough. Just as the Elephant seemed to be getting the upper hand, the Hippo doubled his efforts and regained some of the edge. He groaned even louder and pulled with renewed vigor when it seemed that he was about to be dragged out of the water. Then it was the Elephant's turn to be pulled nearly into the bush. He bellowed and pulled with renewed strength. The two animals were so equally matched that none of them gained advantage for long.

The Tortoise was very proud of himself. He just sat back and enjoyed the spectacle. The Hippo and the Elephant went at it for a very long time. When the sun was about to set, the Tortoise drew his knife and cut the rope.

The Elephant was sent falling over all the trees in his way. Those too small to sustain the force were crushed under it. On the other side, the Hippo fell into the deep end of the river in a big thundering splash. The splash was so huge, it beached some unfortunate fish, who had been watching the Hippo tug and moan at the rope.

The Tortoise then followed the rope to one end. There he found the Elephant collapsed on the ground, panting. The Elephant was not only surprised that the Tortoise could keep up with him at all, much less for as long as he did, but that he did so without even working up a sweat.

"It is not size that counts," explained the Tortoise. "It is strength." Of course the Elephant had to agree. And from that time on, he always said that he and the Tortoise were equally matched in strength.

As soon as the Tortoise got this approval from the Elephant, he scampered in the opposite direction to the Hippo, hoping to settle the matter before the Elephant recovered.

As he approached the riverbank, the Tortoise saw the Hippo slowly coming up for air.

"I'm exhausted," he said. "I give up—you are indeed as strong as I am."

"I am surprised that you lasted that long," bragged the Tortoise. "I expected to have pulled you out sooner. That rope was your savior. At any rate, for now, I will accept the fact that we are equally matched."

And so it was that the Tortoise, the Elephant, the Hippo, and the Lion ruled the animal kingdom. Because they are the rulers of the kingdom, we have more tales of them than we do of other animals.

Why the Hawk Preys on Chicks

The Igbos tell this tale of a young girl, Nma, who did not heed her mother's advice. Nma's disobedience spelled trouble for her. Will she be rescued from the land of the ghosts?

Once upon a time there lived a childless woman and her husband. Time after time her neighbors teased her because she was childless. One day one of her neighbors with whom she was quarreling teased her so much that she became brokenhearted. When she went to bed that night in tears, she prayed to her *chi* to give her a baby of her own. This time, her prayer was answered, and she was blessed with a very beautiful baby girl, whom she named Adanma.

Adanma, or beautiful girl, was known as Nma, or beauty. Her name fit her like a glove, for she was truly beautiful. When she became of age, every man in the land began to court her. Adanma, though, had one flaw that always worried her parents. She had an insatiable appetite for *udala*, or apples. As a beloved only child, she was never in want and was always well provided for. But her greed, for apples, soon got her into a very big trouble.

One day when Nma's parents wanted to go on a trip they stocked the house with food and several baskets of the tastiest and juiciest apples.

"Nma," her mother called her. "Your father and I are going on a trip. You have everything you will ever need. Promise me that you will never leave the house while we are gone. And, you must never go to pick apples, especially at full moon. That is when the ghosts like to pick their apples."

"I promise, Mother," Nma told her mother.

When her parents left, Nma invited her friends over and they made a feast of the apples and foods. By late night of the following day, Nma, having exhausted her stock of food, became so hungry that she forgot what her mother had told her. She ran to the big apple tree to pick more apples under the light of the full moon, not realizing the ghosts were already there.

One of the ghosts picked some juicy apples and dropped them at her feet. Excited by her luck, Nma picked them right up.

She was about to eat them, when the ghost asked her to marry him.

"Marry me, Nma," the ghost proposed, "and take these apples as a sign of my love!"

Nma was afraid. She looked around. "Where did that voice come from?" she wondered. But she didn't see anyone about. So, she took the apples and ran home.

When her parents returned the next day, they were very happy to see their daughter. They hugged her and gave her lots of treats they had brought for her.

Later that night, at the stroke of midnight, a sharp rap at their door broke the calm glow of the bright moonlight and the serene quietness of the night. *Trap, trap, tratatatap*! The door rapped.

Nma's father walked slowly to the door and opened it. On the other side of the door was a weird looking old man. Nma's father could barely see the old man's face, as the moon cast the latter's shadow upon him.

"May I help you?" asked Nma's father.

"I have come to take my wife," growled the old man.

Meanwhile, Nma's mother had awakened when her husband left the bed. She walked up to her husband and stood behind him, holding on to him in fear and sadness. As she realized what her daughter had done, her heart raced within her like a stampede of wild African elephants.

"Please, stranger, don't take my only daughter away from me," she begged him. "I will give you all the gold in the whole world. I will even add any of my lady servants you like."

The old man shook his head. Nma's mother couldn't change his mind.

Then Nma's mother went to her daughter's room to talk with her for the last time, before the old man took her away to the never-never land.

"If you ever want to see your father and me again," she told her, "listen to me very carefully. You must run away when the old man goes into a deep sleep. You will know from his snore.

"When he snores 'grrrr fee fee fee fee...ghosts asleep, ghosts not awake,' don't waste any time. Run back home, for he has fallen into a deep sleep. Do you hear?"

"Yes, Mother," Nma nodded, as she sobbed.

Then Nma's mother dressed her in torn old clothes and dressed her lady servants in the beautiful clothes and jewelry she had bought for Nma. Then she took the servants to the stranger hoping that he would mistake them for Nma. But each time the old man refused. Nma's mother knew her tricks had failed. So she gave Nma to the old man, who took her to the never-never land of the ghosts.

The trip took them through seven forests and seven seas and they did not arrive at their destination until late the following night. When they finally lay down to sleep during the wee hours of the morning, Nma was very scared. Although she was very tired, she couldn't sleep. Finally, she was about to doze off when she was awakened by a loud snore:

Grrrr fee fee fee fee!
Ghosts asleep, ghosts not awake!
Grrrr fee fee fee fee!
Ghosts asleep, ghosts not awake!

Quickly, Nma jumped off the bed and ran away. She wandered about the forest in the waning moonlight of the early morning. She became even more tired and lay down by a big oak tree to rest. Then she dozed off and slept. As she slept, she heard footsteps getting closer, and closer.

"I will catch her soon enough," said one voice. "And I will make her mine."

"But she is my wife, remember?" said the other.

Nma forced her eyes open and noticed that it was already daybreak. Quickly, she stood up and started running again. She looked up at the sky and saw a big Hawk searching for food.

"Please, Hawk. Help me out of this never-never land," Nma begged hopelessly.

Just as the ghosts were about to catch her, the Hawk swooped down. It scooped Nma up, and carried her to a very big oak tree.

That made the ghosts very mad. They started to chop down the oak tree with machetes and axes. As the tree was about to fall down, the Hawk picked up Nma again. It flew toward her village. When it crossed the boundary between the living and the ghosts, the ghosts realized they could not catch up with them anymore. They gave up and went back to their homes.

When the Hawk arrived at Nma's village it started to sing,

Nma was in the land of the ghost!
Nma was married to the ghost!
Nma is now in the land of the living!
Which mother bore this lovely human being?

Nma's parents couldn't believe their ears. As they listened, the song became louder. Then they ran outside the yard and were amazed to see their daughter.

"She has come home at last," they sighed in relief.

Nma's parents were very happy to have their daughter back. They hugged her and thanked the Hawk. They offered the Hawk gifts of food and gold. But she wouldn't accept any. Her eyes were all the time fixed on a chicken and her brood scratching for worms in the corner of the yard.

"If you want those chicks, they're yours!" said Nma's mother.

That made the Hawk very happy. Nma's mother packed a basket of chicks for her, and the Hawk thanked them and flew home with her basket.

As she flew home, one of the chicks fell out of her basket. Not wanting to chance losing the rest of the chicks, she let it go.

"Keep that, farmers of the world!" she cried. "Let it be my loan to you. But I will be coming back to collect on the interest!"

That is why Hawks prey on chicks all the time. They believe they are the offspring of their great-great-grandmother's chick.

Why the Kite Chases Forest Fires

The Kite tricked the Sunbird out of his flute and when the latter managed to reclaim it, the Kite became enraged. In his anger he killed his own mother. Now the Kite, his anger subsided, must find a way to bring his mother back to life.

In the beginning, the Sunbird and the Coucal were the best of friends. They were so close that you never saw one without the other.

The Sunbird was a very clever, small, fast-flying bird. It was so small that people coined the saying "one wouldn't go in the midst of birds and pick out the Sunbird for game." Though it would certainly be proof of good marksmanship to be able to kill a Sunbird! Its long beak is adapted to feeding on nectar and small insects or ants that frequent the flowers. Its high-pitched shrill chip-chip sounds and long beak make the Sunbird unmistakable.

The Coucal, unlike his friend the Sunbird, was rather lazy and sluggish in flight. A much heavier bird than his friend, he was more often heard making coo, coo sounds than seen flying. In fact, he preferred to glide rather than fly, except when disturbed. For a change of position, he would glide to a tree and hop up to its top and then glide to another. He was not known in the bird kingdom to be very bright.

As the story goes, there was a famine in the bird kingdom. The only way any bird could get enough to eat was if it owned a flute made from bones. These special flutes were used to serenade worms and hypnotize grasshoppers. When the worms crawled out to listen to the music, especially after a thunderstorm when everywhere was quiet and fresh, or the grasshoppers gazed at the musician, the birds made a feast of them.

One day as they were horsing around, the Sunbird dared his friend the Coucal to three market weeks of fasting in a tree hollow full of tailor ants. "I say I can beat you in a fasting contest for the next three market weeks."

"I double dare you that you cannot," countered the Coucal.

"As small as you are, you'll die before the sun goes down the first day of the contest."

"Okay! During the next three market weeks we shall see who will be the first to say, 'stop, I've had it,'" warned the Sunbird.

So the Sunbird put his friend inside a tree hollow filled with tailor ants and took residence in the one filled with harmless nectar ants. While the tailor ants swarmed all over the Coucal and bit his eyes and legs and body, the Sunbird had a feast of the harmless nectar ants.

A market week later, the Sunbird called out to his friend to check on him.

Chi, chi, chi, li chiiiik!
Nda!
The Sunbird and the Coucal had a bet!
Nda!
That no one must eat or drink even a bit!
Nda!
For three market weeks!
Nda!

And in a faded and distressed voice the Coucal responded:

Coo, coo, coo, loo cooook!
N-nda!
The Sunbird and the Coucal had a bet!
N-nda!
That no one must eat or drink even a bit!
N-nda!
For three market weeks!
N-nda!

By the second market week the bites from the tailor ants, coupled with the starvation, had taken their toll on the poor Coucal. He could barely respond to the call of the Sunbird. By the middle of the second market week his response had degenerated to a mere "co, co, co," and by the end of the week, he was dead. By the middle of the third market week, the Sunbird was still as fresh as he had been when the contest began. The Sunbird knew that his friend could not have taken the punishment for this long, but just to be sure, he called on him again:

Chi, chi, chi, li chiiiik!
Nda!

The Sunbird and the Coucal had a bet!
Nda!
That no one must eat or drink even a bit!
Nda!
For three market weeks!
Nda!

But there was no response. At the end of the third market week, the Sunbird left his feasting hollow. He flew to the Coucal's nest of tailor ants and retrieved his bones. He chiseled a very beautiful flute out of the Coucal's leg bone and blew it as he joyfully flew about. As he was flying, he came upon the Kite and his family hard at work on their garden. He started singing for them with his flute.

Mr. Kite at work!
Nda!
Mr. Kite at work!
Nda!
The Sunbird and the Coucal had a bet!
Nda!
That no one must eat or drink even a bit!
Nda!
For three market weeks!
Nda!
The Coucal lost and died weak!
Nda!

"Whose bone is that flute made from?" the Kite asked the Sunbird.

"It is made from the bone of a stupid bird," he replied. "It is the Coucal's bone. And anyone who thinks he is stronger than me can come and take it from me."

"May I take a look?" asked the Kite. "That is an awfully nice flute."

"No. I know that you are not going to give it back."

"Sure I will. I just want to try it."

"Okay—but I must hold on to your wings so you don't fly away with it."

"Come on! You've got to trust me. If you hold on to my wings, how am I going to test the flute? I need my wings for balance."

"Okay! How about I hang on to your legs?"

"If you do that, how am I going to hold the flute to play it? Here! Hang on to my tail feathers instead."

So the Sunbird held on the Kite's tail feathers and handed the flute over to him. *Pilim*! The Kite wiggled free of the Sunbird's grip and left him with all his tail feathers in his beak. The Kite flew home and gave his blind mother the flute to save for him.

"Guard it with your life," he told her, as she felt and admired the flute. "Do not give it to anyone until I come back for it."

"Alright, my son. Run along and complete your work."

The Sunbird, who had been spying on the conversation, went back and dipped his feet in very thick and sticky mud. Then he piled it on to make his feet heavy. Satisfied with his makeup, he flew back to Mother Kite. When he landed and asked for the flute in a disguised voice, his landing and voice sounded like that of the Kite. So, Mother Kite thought that the Sunbird was her son and gave him the flute back.

"What type of food did you bring home for your mother today?" she asked. "A rabbit?"

"Noooo!" replied the Sunbird.

"A squirrel?"

"Noooo!"

"Come on, tell me and don't tease your mother like that. That one sounded rather heavy so I know it is not a chipmunk."

"Ha! Ha! Ha! Ha!" the Sunbird burst into uncontrollable laughter. "It is mud," he replied, still laughing as he knocked the mud off his feet and flew away to safety with the flute.

A little bit later, the Kite came back home and discovered what had happened. Filled with anger, he didn't even give his mother a chance to explain before he killed her. He then took her body and dumped it in a forest fire. By the time he came back home, his anger had subsided enough for him to realize what he had done.

"What have I done?" he asked himself. "I lost all my tail feathers, and now my mother. All because of a lousy flute made out of a Coucal's bone?"

In order to atone for his shame and bad temper he went on a self-imposed exile. Besides, his fellow kites were teasing him. They said that without his tail feathers, he looked like the chicks they preyed on. So, he needed time both for his tail feathers to grow back and to mourn his mother.

He was in exile from one dry season to another. Within this time, his tail feathers grew back completely. He also had enough time to mourn his mother and face the world anew. When he returned from exile, the dry season was in full force. The forest fires burned more than ever before. On seeing the fires, the image of the death of his mother came back to him again. He started circling the fires, hoping to find his mother.

"If only I can find her," he cried, "I will hug her and tell her how much I love her. I really didn't mean to hurt you, mother! Please forgive me."

The Kite searched all over the fires, once in awhile diving when he saw something that looked like his mother. But it was never her. Still he keeps searching and hoping that some day he will find her. Even today, the Kite chases forest fires, gliding around in search of his mother.

Why Mosquitoes Buzz

The Mosquito is the culprit in this Igbo tale of a chain reaction. The Hen's eggs were broken and she and the Rooster went into mourning. Then the Rooster would not wake up the sun and the creatures were without daylight for several days. The Lion King pleaded to Agbara to give them back the sun. But Agbara told the animals that it was the Rooster who was derelict. The Rooster then had to explain his case to the Lion King and Agbara.

One day, Nwankwo and his wife went to harvest some palm nuts for oil. They searched all over the farm but couldn't find palm nuts mature and ripe enough to harvest. It was getting dark and the sun was about to go to sleep. So, they gave up and headed home along a back snake road. Then Nwankwo saw a palm tree with four clusters of red palm nuts. *Osukwu*!—the most delicious and meaty kind of palm nuts. The palm tree was so lanky, though, that Nwankwo wondered how it could hold such a load of palm nuts.

Nonetheless, Nwankwo couldn't resist the temptation. He ran to the palm tree right away and flung his *ete* climbing ropes around it. With his machete dangling in its sheath around the waist cord of his g-string, like a hyperactive dog on a short leash, Nwankuo began to climb the palm tree. As he climbed, the palm tree swayed like the pendulum of a grandfather clock.

"Nkwo!" his wife called out. "Maybe you should come down. I'd rather we don't get the palm nuts and their oil than be a widow."

"I can make it," said Nkwo. "The river never flows backward, you know. Besides, the God that gave a child a wild yam must give him the fire with which to roast it."

Eventually Nwankwo made it to the top of the palm tree. He pulled out his machete from its sheath and began to cut the clusters of nuts. But, no sooner had he dealt several blows to the first cluster head of palm nuts than a Mosquito accosted him.

"What are you doing?" asked the Mosquito.

But Nwankwo was so busy cutting the nuts that he could not hear the Mosquito. So the Mosquito flew closer to his ear. As he did, the flapping of his wings buzzed Nwankwo who was already scared by the swaying of the palm tree.

"Bzzzzzzzzz! What are you doing here?" buzzed and asked the Mosquito.

"Shoo! Shoo!" Nkwo said, startled. Sham! Sham! went his hand as he slapped around for the Mosquito.

As he chased the Mosquito, his machete slipped. It headed toward his wife, who had been watching the whole encounter. She quickly jumped away from the path of the falling machete, clutching on to her own machete. She landed on the tail of a Python, who was resting after a very heavy meal of deer. The Python was so startled that it quickly uncoiled itself and dashed into a nearby Rabbit burrow for cover, hissing.

The Rabbit was petrified to see the uninvited guest coming at her with its mouth wide open. Thinking that the Python was chasing her, the Rabbit dashed out of her burrow through the rear escape hatch. She ran faster than she had ever run through the meadows, knocking down all the shrubs in her way. As the elders say, "When you run for dear life, you do not pause to catch your breath."

In her escape, the Rabbit ran through a clump of dried elephant grasses in which a Guinea Fowl was brooding her chicks. The ruckus scared the living daylights out of the Guinea Fowl. She flew off in a wild rage, letting out a shriek as her brood ran helter-skelter for cover.

Meanwhile, the black Monkey who was the night watchman of the animal kingdom was alerted by the Guinea Fowl's cry. The Monkey yelled out a shrewd cry. He crouched, stretched, peered between the branches to get a better view of the danger. He jumped about the branches to grab his talking drum so he could alert the whole kingdom. In his excitement, he jumped on a weak dry branch, which snapped.

The branch fell and landed on the nest of Mother Hen, breaking all her eggs. "Caw! Caw! Caw! Caw-Caw! Caw-Caw," cried Mother Hen. "You have broken all my eggs."

On hearing the cry, the Rooster came running to protect his wife. "What is it?" he asked. "What is it?"

But Mother Hen did not say a word. She spread her wings over the broken eggs, her eyes heavy with tears. On seeing what had happened the Rooster was saddened. He and Mother Hen together cried over the eggs.

As we all know, it is the Rooster who wakes up the sun every morning with his crowing. On the first crow, the sun opens one of her eyes very slowly. Then a new day begins to appear. On the second crow, the sun wakes up, stretches and smiles. On seeing her smile and her stretched-out hands, the day comes. Then, the rest of the creatures wake up, too.

But for a very long time, maybe four market days, the sun did not wake up, so the day never came. The night just went on and on and on. The creatures opened their eyes and closed them again. They became worried and thought the sun had died.

Lion, the king of the creatures, called a meeting of the animals before Agbara, the great god of all.

"Great One," said the Lion. "What have we done that you have taken away the sun from us?"

"I didn't take the sun from you," Agbara said in a bellow. "The Rooster forgot to wake her up."

"Why didn't you wake up the sun, Red?" the Lion asked the Rooster. "She has been asleep for four market days now."

"It was the Monkey," cried the Rooster. "He jumped on that branch and it fell and broke all Mother Hen's eggs. I have been in mourning—that was why I did not wake up the sun."

"I see!" said the Lion.

It was the Monkey,
Who jumped on a branch,
Which fell and broke all of Mother Hen's eggs.
Now the Rooster is in mourning and does not wake up the Sun,
And day does not come.

Turning to the Monkey, who was now a nervous wreck, the Lion said, "Monkey, as the watchman of the kingdom, you should know better. You don't harm what you are charged to protect. Why did you jump so hard on the branch that it should snap?"

"The King shall live forever," answered the Monkey. "It was the Guinea Fowl. She shrieked so loud that I thought we were all in danger. So I was running to beat my talking drum when I jumped on the branch."

On hearing this the Lion said to Agbara:

It was the Guinea Fowl,
Who shrieked to alert the Monkey,
Who jumped on a branch,
Which fell and broke all of Mother Hen's eggs.
Now Rooster is in mourning and does not wake up the Sun,
And day does not come.

Then the Lion asked the Guinea Fowl, "Why did you shriek so loud as to alert the Monkey?"

"Oh, King," said the Guinea Fowl. "Blame it on the Rabbit. I was in my nest with my brood when I heard his ruckus. Then he charged at me, knocked down my nest and threw my brood and me into a panic. I was scared. That was why I let out the shriek that alerted the Monkey."

The Lion found that made perfect sense. He played the whole incident back in his mind and reported to Agbara, saying:

It was the Rabbit,
Who scared the Guinea Fowl,
Who shrieked to alert the Monkey,
Who jumped on a branch,
Which fell and broke all of Mother Hen's eggs.
Now Rooster is in mourning and does not wake up the Sun,
And day does not come.

The Lion commanded the Rabbit to step up and speak for himself. The Rabbit hopped forward. His whiskers at ends, ears stretched upwards, and nose jiggling.

"Long live the King," said the Rabbit. "It was the Python. I was in my burrow when she lumbered in uninvited, with mouth wide open! I was petrified. What was I to do but save myself? I ran as fast as I could through the meadow. I did not mean to startle the Guinea Fowl. "

The Lion then turned toward Agbara and reported:

Your Greatness, it was the Python,
Who petrified the Rabbit,
Who scared the Guinea Fowl,
Who shrieked to alert the Monkey,
Who jumped on a branch,
Which fell and broke all of Mother Hen's eggs.

Now Rooster is in mourning and does not wake up the Sun,
And the day does not come.

Now, it was the Python's turn to say why she lumbered into the Rabbit's burrow.

"It was Mrs. Wine Tapper. I was minding my business when she stepped on my tail. She startled me with her machete. She was going to kill me. But I quickly uncoiled myself and ran into the Rabbit's burrow for safety. I was not going to eat the Rabbit."

Then said the Lion:

Your Greatness, it was Mrs. Wine Tapper,
Who startled the Python,
Who petrified the Rabbit,
Who scared the Guinea Fowl,
Who shrieked to alert the Monkey,
Who jumped on a branch,
Which fell and broke all of Mother Hen's eggs.
Now Rooster is in mourning and does not wake up the Sun,
And day does not come.

Mrs. Nwankwo, who had been patiently watching all the proceedings, stepped forward to defend herself.

"Put away that machete," said the Deer. "It gives me the creeps."

Mrs. Nwankwo put aside her machete and turned to the Lion and said, "It was my husband. I was standing under the palm tree when he dropped his machete. If it weren't for my quickness, that machete would have landed on my head.

"I told you," said the Deer. "Machetes are dangerous."

Then the Lion turned to the Wine Tapper. "You humans are always coming here to bother us. Now you want to kill your own wife? What do you have to say for yourself?"

"We did not come to bother anyone," said Mr. Nwankwo. "I was cutting some palm nuts for my dinner when the Mosquito came to buzz my ears. I told it to go away but it would not. I was chasing it when my machete slipped. I was not trying to kill or scare my wife!"

Oh! It was the Mosquito,
Which buzzed in the ears of the Wine Tapper,
Who dropped the Machete,
Which scared Mrs. Wine Tapper,

Who startled the Python,
Who petrified the Rabbit,
Who scared the Guinea Fowl,
Who shrieked to alert the Monkey,
Who jumped on a branch,
Which fell and broke all of Mother Hen's eggs.
Now Rooster is in mourning and does not wake up the Sun,
And day does not come.

The Lion then turned to the Mosquito. But the Mosquito, who was perched on a twig, said nothing. His legs trembled. He was too scared to say a word.

"Why did you buzz his ears?" Agbara intervened in a bellow.

The bellow rattled the twig and the Mosquito flew off. He circled around the court trying hard to say what happened. But he was so scared that when he opened his mouth no words came out. All the animals heard was the bzzzzzzz of his wings.

All the creatures shouted, "Let justice prevail. Punish the Mosquito."

Agbara was very mad with the Mosquito. So he put a curse on the Mosquito, saying, "Because you are disrespectful and refused to answer my question, you will no longer be able to speak. From now on, you will only buzz."

Then the Great One faced the Rooster. "You must never again refuse to wake up the sun. If anyone offends you, bring him to your King so that justice can be served."

The Rooster was satisfied that justice had been served. Directly he lifted his head, curved his neck downward, turned to the east and cried, "Koko ro Oko o." And almost immediately, the sun woke up and the day came. Since that time the Rooster never has failed to call the sun, and neither has the Mosquito regained his speech. He can be heard buzzing people's ears and blaming them.

Even today the sun remains awake so long as the Rooster calls him. Sometimes though, the Rooster does not pay attention and forgets to call the sun. The sun then goes to sleep early, even when it is still supposed to be overhead. Then the creatures get confused and run for shelter, thinking that the world is coming to an end. I think this is what the white man calls "eclipse."

You Asked for It

According to an Igbo proverb, one should always be mindful of the dangers of a gun, whether it is loaded or not. The Baboon forgot this proverb when he decided to play a trick on the Tortoise. Of course, no one plays a trick on the Tortoise and gets away with it.

The Tortoise and the Baboon were good friends and often shared a meal or two together. The animal world was reeling from a bad famine and no one had enough to eat. One day the Baboon decided to play a joke on the Tortoise and invited him for supper.

Knock! Knock.

"Who is there?" asked the Tortoise.

"It is me," answered the Baboon.

"It is 'you' who? Don't you have a name?"

"It is your pal the..."

"Which one?" the Tortoise teased.

"I didn't think you had any friends, much less several," retorted the Baboon.

"Come in, Boon. I was just teasing."

"How are you surviving the famine?" asked the Baboon.

"Barely. It is suicidal. My barn is empty and even tree bark tastes good to me now."

The Baboon grinned as though he just won a wrestling match with the Gorilla. He laughed so hard inside of him that the laughter escaped from him for the Tortoise to hear. "Uh! Uh! Uh! Uh!" he laughed, jumping up and down in excitement. "Today is your lucky day, pal. How about supper at my place tonight?"

"Great, Boon," answered the Tortoise excitedly.

"Skip lunch so your family can have more to eat. That way you will be famished and have enough space for the meal I plan to prepare for supper. It is a special recipe and has been in the family for generations."

The Tortoise's mouth watered with every mention of food. He couldn't wait to sink his teeth into the Baboon's dinner.

"Stop torturing me, Boon. Run along and I will see you at supper time."

The Baboon scampered back home as fast as he could to gather his ingredients. Meanwhile the Tortoise followed him immediately. The Baboon's house was quite a distance from the Tortoise's, so he figured he better start out early.

As he crawled in the sweltering heat, he thought of giving up and heading back home. But, he kept on whenever he remembered the food he was promised. Finally he arrived at the Baboon's house.

"Welcome, pal," said the Baboon.

"Thanks. Is the food ready?" asked the Tortoise.

"No. I was waiting for you to arrive first before I put in the final ingredients. Besides, I didn't want it to get cold. Keep yourself busy, while I get to it."

"Can I help?" asked the Tortoise.

"Not at all. Just relax. You are the guest."

So the Tortoise made himself comfortable as the Baboon went to finish preparing the supper. As the Tortoise waited, he could smell the most delicious foods. "Could that be chicken broth and corn meal?" he wondered. "It has been ages since I tasted those."

After some time the Baboon came in and announced, "Supper is served."

"Already? You lead the way. I am famished from that long trip. I say, you live quite a distance from me—or was it just the heat and hunger that made it seem that long?"

"Well, not to worry. You are here now. There! Just go up and get it," the Baboon said pointing at the fork in a tree where he had set the supper. While the Tortoise was thinking of how to get up the tree, the Baboon was already in the tree eating.

"Just throw some down for me, pal," said the Tortoise.

"Nooo! I could miss you and I don't want to waste such good food."

"I cannot get up there fast enough. You know that."

"What a shame. The food stays only on this forked part of the tree, which is my table. If you want it, come and get it."

"That is cruel," thought the Tortoise as he desperately tried to climb the huge tree. Before he could climb the tree, the Baboon had already eaten all the food. "That should be me doing that to him. How did I get myself into this?"

After the Baboon was done, the Tortoise picked up his walking stick and painstakingly walked back to his house. He wasn't sure whether it was the heat, the hunger, or the trick that bothered him most. As he walked home, dehydrated and his feet scalded by the hot desert sand, he concentrated long enough to map out a plan for his revenge.

Several market weeks passed before the Baboon got an invitation for supper at the Tortoise's. At first he thought that maybe the Tortoise was trying to get back at him. But then it had been quite some time and he thought the Tortoise was such a good sport that he should have taken the joke for what it was—just a joke. "Besides," thought the Baboon, "there's nowhere the Tortoise could set the food that I could not reach it." So he decided he should at least honor the invitation.

It was a long walk to the Tortoise's house. The Baboon, like the Tortoise, was driven to make the journey only by his desire to taste the delicious food the host promised him. The heat was equally unbearable for him. In fact, it was worse now because of the raging forest fires. Much of the dried vegetation had been scorched and the ground was charred black by the fires.

Midway between his house and that of the Tortoise was a strip of lake, which the Baboon crossed without any difficulty. But it was still quite a distance across soot-covered ground from the lake to the Tortoise's house.

"At last," exclaimed the Baboon as he finally approached and saw the Tortoise stirring what seemed to be porridge. "You are quite a cook I'd say."

"Hello Boon. I see you had no difficulty getting here on time," replied the Tortoise. "I am glad that you could make it. Have a seat. I was just about to serve the supper."

"He is quite a sport after all," thought the Baboon. "He is honestly inviting me for a real dinner."

The Tortoise dished out the food and set it on a tree stump and started to eat. Then the Baboon sat down next to the tree stump. He was about to start eating when the Tortoise exclaimed and slapped his hand.

"Stop! Where are your manners? Didn't your mother teach you to wash your hands before eating? Look at them. They are as black as the back of my pot. Even my two-year-old knows not to eat with those."

The Baboon quickly pulled back his hand from the food and gazed at it. "Those are dirty," he thought. "But I got them dirty when crossing the fire-scorched fields," pleaded the Baboon.

"Sure you did. Just run down to the lake and wash up. When you come back I will have supper ready for you."

The Baboon ran down to the lake as fast as he could, through the soot-covered grounds and washed his hands. But as he started back to the Tortoise's, he picked up the soot again, now even more than before because his hands were wet.

"You are dirtier than ever, pal. What is the matter? You seem to have taken a liking to the soot. Did you wrestle or swim in it?" the Tortoise teased him. "Run along again and get cleaned up. And you better be fast about it because I am about to finish the food."

The Baboon ran back to the lake again to wash up, hungrier than he had ever been. But every time he crossed the charred fields to get to the Tortoise's, his hands became coated with the soot again. Meanwhile the Tortoise was having a feast at his home and the food was fast disappearing.

By the time the Baboon came back to the Tortoise a third time, the food was all gone. Then he realized that the joke was now on him. Angry and hungry, he scampered back to his home, calling the Tortoise names.

The Tortoise finished his food and took a well-deserved sunbath and reveled in his revenge. "You don't play a player, pal, nor should you ever pick up a tiger by the tail. You have a lot of nerve. All my life I have conned people who spent the rest of their lives plotting to con me back. And you conned me first? Hmm! What nerve!"

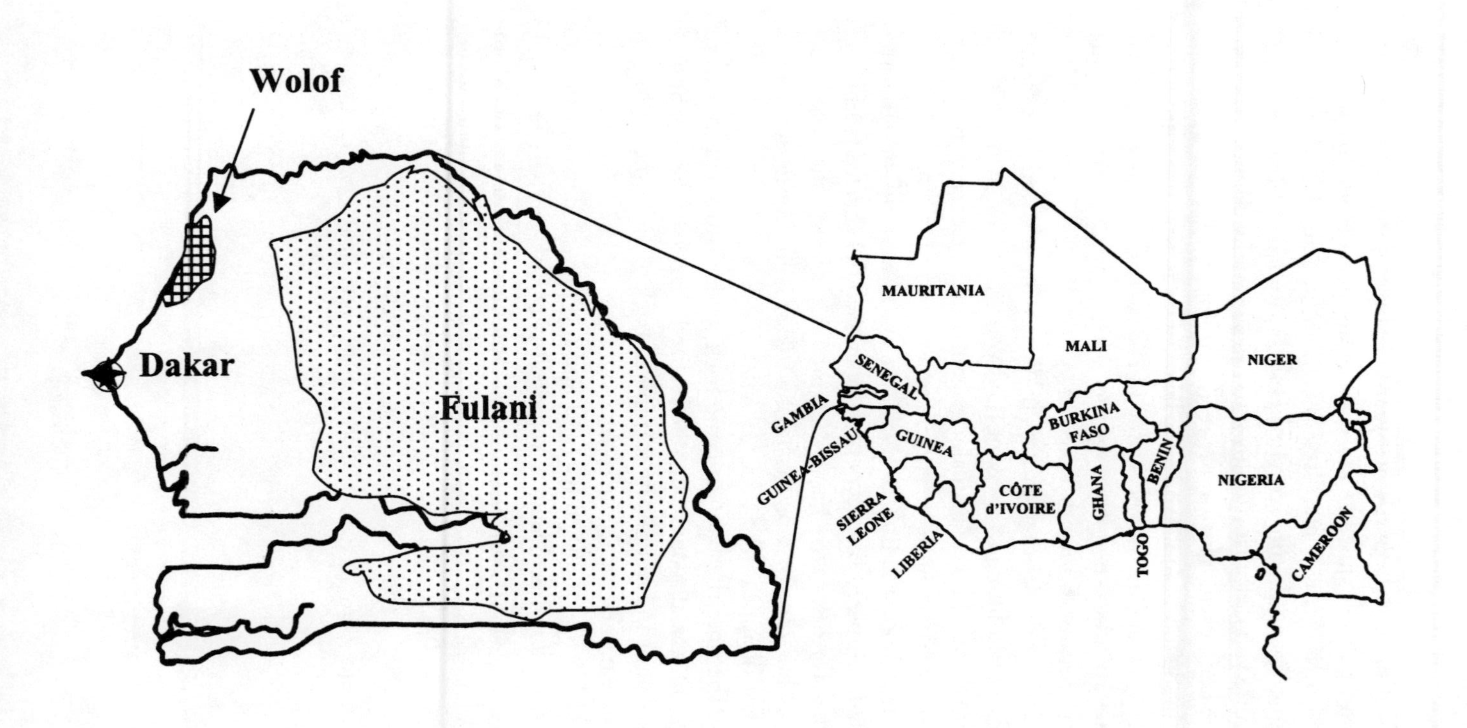
Wolof
Dakar
Fulani
MAURITANIA
MALI
NIGER
SENEGAL
GAMBIA
GUINEA-BISSAU
GUINEA
BURKINA FASO
SIERRA LEONE
LIBERIA
CÔTE d'IVOIRE
GHANA
TOGO
BENIN
NIGERIA
CAMEROON

Senegal

COUNTRY

Formal Name: Republic of Senegal
Short Form: Senegal
Term for Citizens: Senegalese
Capital: Dakar
Independence: April 4, 1960 (from France); August 20, 1960, federation with Mali dissolved

GEOGRAPHY

Size: 75,951 square miles (196,190 km^2)
Boundaries: Bordered to the north by Mauritania, east by Mali, south by Guinea and Guinea-Bissau, and west by the Atlantic Ocean

SOCIETY

Population: 10.1 million
Ethnic Groups: Wolof (43%), Pular (24%), Serer (14%), Diola, Mandingo, among others
Languages: The major languages are Wolof, Senegalo-Guinean, Mande, Pular, and Mandingo. French is the official language.
Religion: 92% Islam; 6% local religions; 2% Christianity

The Majestic Fish

The saying that one never quite knows the value of what one has until one loses it is illustrated vividly in this story. The Fulanis tell of a small pond and a Big Fish who became tired of the dull life of that pond and decided to take up residency in—of course—a bigger pond.

There lived a school of little fishes in a small pond very far away from the river. Because the river was far from the pond, the little fishes never had to worry about the bigger fishes coming into the pond to bother them. The only times the fishes felt bothered was when the local village boys cast their hooks into the pond hoping to snag one of them. But, the fishes knew this, so they seldom thought it was a bother. Indeed, they took a liking to the boys because they brought them worms to feed on. The boys' hooks were too big for the fishes to swallow, so they just nibbled on the worms, ate around the hooks and left them bare. To get more worms, they tugged on the lines and swam back to watch the boys pull them in with all their might. Finding no fish, the boys baited the hooks again and sank them back into the pond.

The fishes lived happily together in their own little world until one rainy season. It had rained so very heavily on one of the days that an upstream river had overflowed, flooding neighboring farmlands—and the little pond. When the water receded, the mud settled, and the water cleared, the little fishes found themselves sharing their pond with a much bigger fish.

The little fishes tried to make friends with this Big Fish, but he would not respond to their overtures. The Big Fish just kept to himself.

"Would you tiny ninny wits stop disturbing the water," he snapped at the small fishes one day. "I am trying to enjoy the sun and grab a nap." Then he turned away and faced the bank of the pond. Since he was so big, his movement swished the water so hard that the little fishes rammed into each other and against the bank of the pond.

The Big Fish's relationship with the little fishes never got any better. The little fishes tried to ignore him, but the pond was so small and the Big Fish so big that they couldn't help running into him. So, one day one of the little fishes said to the Big Fish, "You know, don't you think that you might be better off going down to the big river. As big and majestic as you are, probably mixing with other fish of your stature would do you some good. It is obvious that you don't like it here, and I don't blame you."

The Big Fish's ego was stroked. He puffed himself to be even bigger and more majestic.

"Oh! Yeah?" he asked, sizing up himself and watching his every move in his shadow.

"Sure," the little fish continued, "Isn't it obvious? It is easy to see you are of royal descent and we ninny wits are not even fit to groom your fins much less share a pond with you. Your whiskers and the grace with which you move your tail have royalty written all over them."

For several days, the Big Fish was the subject of discussion in the pond as the little fishes praised him and puffed his ego. The Big Fish decided that the advice was the best thing he had ever heard from those little fishes. So he decided to take it.

"You know," he said to the little fishes, "I think you are right for once. I believe that good can come out of those puny heads of yours after all. I have really had it with you little fishes and your childish jokes. So, the next time the upper river overflows and the floodwater arrives, I'll be out of here. I need to be down in the big river with fish of my own size and majesty."

The little fishes couldn't contain their joy, even though some of them thought that the Big Fish might be making a big mistake. While some urged him to rethink, others puffed him up for having come up with such a brilliant idea.

Several market weeks later the rains came again, followed by the floods. The pond and all the surrounding land was covered with water for as far as the eyes could see. Some of the fishes somersaulted above the water level to check out the extent of the flood. As they fell back into the pond, they anchored their fins to the bank to keep themselves from being swept downstream by the flood, but not the Big Fish. This was his opportunity! He slowly swam to the surface of the pond, bid the small fishes goodbye, and allowed himself to be swept down to the sea by the flood.

As he went with the flood, he began to notice that everything was larger than in the pond. The shrubs stood as tall as the trees at the ponds, and the rocks were towering over him like mountains. Even the water was different. It tasted funny, he thought.

"Wow!" he exclaimed, filled with excitement for the new life he was going to lead. "Why didn't I think of this sooner? I can't wait to see all these other majestic fishes!"

As he was thinking about his new life, he found himself between two giant rocks. Since he was now tired, he decided to catch his breath for a minute. But as he rested, he noticed that the water current had increased to a swirl. As he turned to anchor himself, he found himself staring into the eyes of a fish much, much bigger than he. He was still trying to recover himself when other, even bigger fishes swam by.

"What is a little fish like you doing here?" the much bigger fish asked him. "Get out of the way before we run you over."

"Can we eat him?" asked the first fish.

"He is too small, even for you," said the biggest one, who must have been their mother. Then one of the fishes chased after him. The Big Fish swam as fast as he could and hid between the rocks.

As soon as he noticed that they were gone, he cautiously came out from between the rocks. No sooner had he come out than another big fish dove for him. As he swam faster and faster, he wondered why he ever left the serenity and quietness of the pond for this war zone. How would he survive? He couldn't even settle down long enough to find something to eat. All day, he was busy running so that he wouldn't be some other fish's lunch.

"I must find a way to get back to that pond," he said to himself. "And I'd better do it now before the water recedes or I end up in another fish's stomach."

When the water calmed somewhat, he quietly swam upstream in the direction of the pond. "I hope that I can find that pond," he said to himself. "And if I do, I will cherish and appreciate it. I must make friends with those fish and live in harmony with them."

The swim upstream was more difficult than his ride downstream on the current had been. He laboriously swam below the current, digging his fins into the mud as he did. But eventually he came to familiar surroundings. Finally, he was in the pond, and he collapsed on its bed, exhausted and panting.

"Look who is back," said one of the little fishes. "I can see that the big river wasn't big enough for you either."

But the Big Fish just lay there out of breath. He thought to himself, "You win. You can talk all you want. If I had known what life in the big river was like, I wouldn't have left in the first place."

From that day on, the little fishes played to their heart's content. The Big Fish never bothered them; nor did he feel any more majestic than they. He played with the little fishes and they all lived happily ever after.

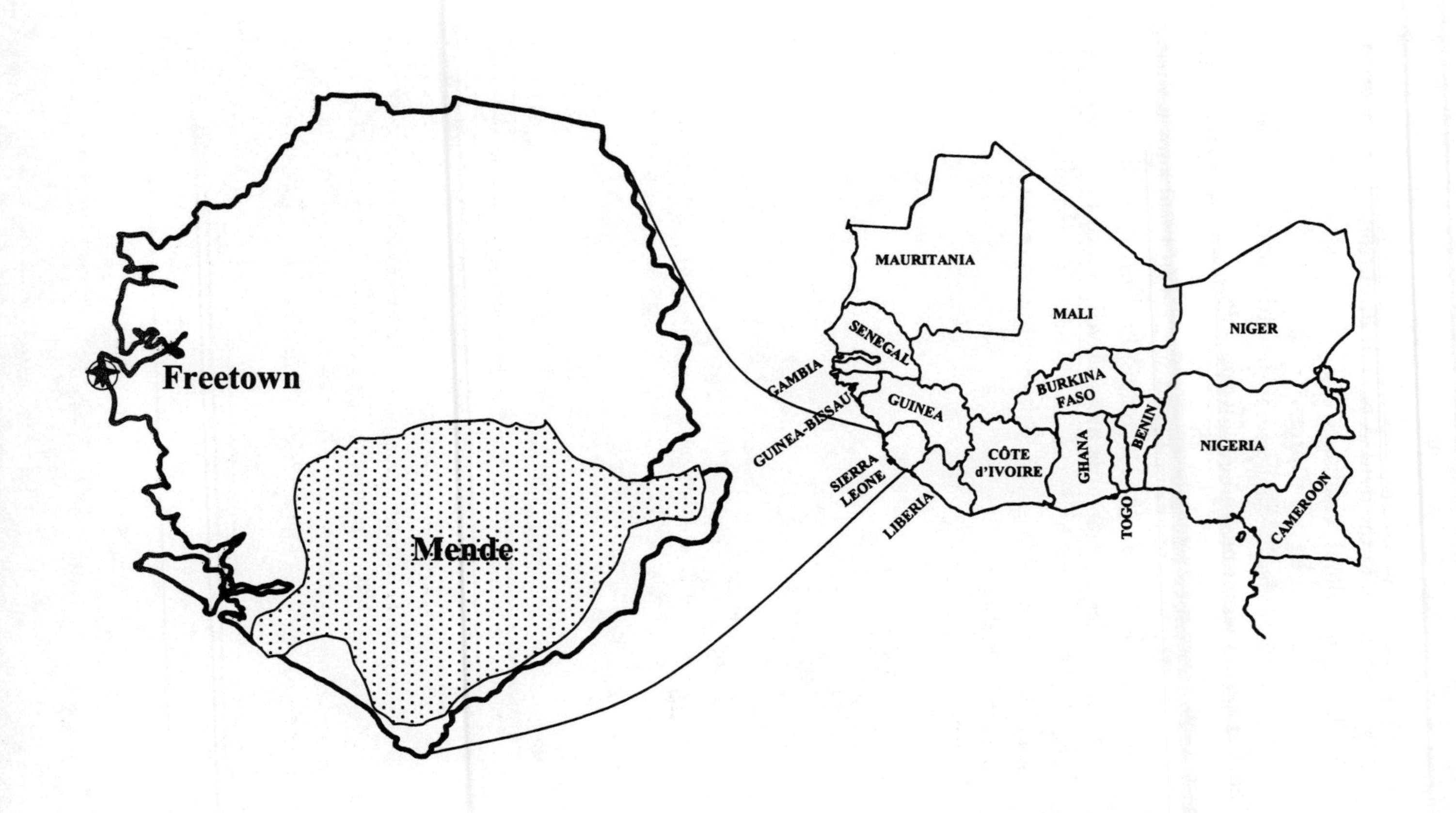
Freetown
Mende
MAURITANIA
MALI
NIGER
SENEGAL
GAMBIA
GUINEA-BISSAU
GUINEA
SIERRA
LEONE
LIBERIA
BURKINA
FASO
CÔTE
d'IVOIRE
GHANA
TOGO
BENIN
NIGERIA
CAMEROON

Sierra Leone

COUNTRY

Formal Name: Republic of Sierra Leone
Short Form: Sierra Leone
Term for Citizens: Sierra Leonean
Capital: Freetown
Independence: April 27, 1961 (from United Kingdom)

GEOGRAPHY

Size: 27,699 square miles (71,740 km^2)
Boundaries: Bordered to the north and northeast by Guinea, southeast by Liberia, and south and west by the Atlantic Ocean

SOCIETY

Population: 5.3 million
Ethnic Groups: Several African tribes including Temne (30%), Mende (30%), and others (30%). The rest are Creole, Europeans, Lebanese, Asian, and others.
Languages: The languages include Mende, spoken mostly in the south; Temne, spoken mainly in the north; Krio, spoken in the Freetown area. The official language is English.
Religion: 60% Islam; 30% local religions; 10% Christianity

The Mother in the Clouds

The Mende people tell this story about a pact the animals made among themselves to help them survive a severe drought and famine. They each agreed to sacrifice their mothers for food and the betterment of the younger generations. The Rabbit, though, loved his mother so much that he devised a plan to save her—despite all the other animals.

There was a great famine in the land of the animals. The rain had not fallen for a very long time and all the animals were skinny to the bones. As a means of surviving the famine and preserving their species, all the animals agreed to offer their mothers for food.

By the time it was deep into the famine, many animals had taken their turn offering their mothers to be killed for food. Although of course they loved their mothers, they felt it was a necessary evil.

"They'd want it this way," some of them justified their actions. "After all, it is customary for the child to bury his mother."

"Yeah," said the Rabbit, "but not to eat her."

The Rabbit loved his mother very much. He soon became ambivalent about the whole pact. Somehow, the idea of offering his mother up for food didn't appeal to him. The more he thought about it, the more deplorable it sounded. Then and there he decided on a scheme to save his mother.

One day the Rabbit told his mother, "As you know, it will soon be my turn to offer you for sacrifice. But I won't do it."

"But they will come after me," said his mother.

"Yes! But I have a plan. I will hide you up in the clouds. There you will be until the famine is over. Take this rope up with you. When I get you some food, I will sing to you and you will throw down the rope for me to come up with your food. When I have left, you must pull up the rope very quickly."

The Rabbit's mother loved the idea. She was glad that she wouldn't be killed after all.

Very late that night, the Rabbit took his mother to a secluded part of the forest. There they climbed a tall tree into the clouds where the Rabbit hid his mother. Together they rehearsed their secret signals for his mother to throw down the rope. Satisfied, the Rabbit came down, chopped down the tree, and went back to the rest of the animals.

From then on, whenever the animals ate someone else's mother, the Rabbit split his portion in two halves. He ate one half and saved the other. When all the animals left, he took the half to his mother. Then he called her with their secret song:

Mother Rabbit! Mother Rabbit!
Send the rope! Send the rope!
For your son has come with food for you.
Mother Rabbit! Mother Rabbit!

On hearing the song, Mother Rabbit threw down the rope. The Rabbit grabbed on to it, and when he was sure he had a good grip, he sang again:

Mother Rabbit! Mother Rabbit!
Pull the rope! Pull the rope!
For your son has come with food for you.
Mother Rabbit! Mother Rabbit!

Then Mother Rabbit pulled up the rope. When the Rabbit disappeared into the clouds, he offered his mother food. He told her how bad things were on earth, how the famine didn't seem to want to stop.

This continued for a long time. One day, the Monkey said to the Rabbit, "It is your turn to offer your mother tomorrow." (It was the Monkey's job to keep track of whose turn it was to offer their mother.)

"Again?" asked the Rabbit. "I have only one mother, you know, and we ate her long time ago."

"No, we didn't," said the Monkey surprised.

"We did too. It has been so long that you have forgotten about it."

The Monkey was sure that the Rabbit's mother had not been eaten. Furthermore, none of the animals remembered eating her. So they were suspicious of the Rabbit and decided to spy on him. Then they called on the next animal in line to sacrifice his mother.

Later that evening, the Rabbit took some food to his mother as before. He called on her to throw down the rope. And as soon as he got hold of the rope, he called on her to pull him up. Meanwhile, the rest of the animals were hiding in the bushes and watched him, but he did not know it.

"Now we know where he hides his mother," said the Monkey. "When a cunning person dies, he should be buried by one as cunning."

"He ate everyone else's mother but won't offer his own," said the Squirrel. "Now we've caught him. I am sure his mother is fattened now and will be quite juicy."

They waited patiently and before long, the Rabbit came down from the rope. When he walked out of sight, the rest of the animals caucused and decided to take the Rabbit's mother the next day. Then they quietly went back to their homes.

The next day the Monkey called on the Chipmunk to offer his mother. He did this because the animals wanted the portion to be too small. They had also agreed that they should not finish their portions. This was to allow them time to leave while the Rabbit tried to gather the leftovers for his mother. Soon after the animals took a few bites of their food, they went ahead of the Rabbit to the spot where he called his mother.

"You call her," the Lion whispered to the Hare, "your voice is close to the Rabbit's."

Mother Rabbit! Mother Rabbit!
Send the rope! Send the rope!
For your son has come with food for you.
Mother Rabbit! Mother Rabbit!

Immediately the rope came down from the clouds. All the animals grabbed onto it and the Hare sang again:

Mother Rabbit! Mother Rabbit!
Pull the rope! Pull the rope!
For your son has come with food for you.
Mother Rabbit! Mother Rabbit!

As soon as she heard the signal, Mother Rabbit began to pull on the rope. But the weight was much too heavy for her. She pulled harder, thinking that her son must have brought her more meat than ever. She dug her nails into the clouds and pulled even harder.

But, the more she pulled the heavier the load became. Just as she was about to reel in the Lion, who was leading the troop, the Rabbit came and saw what was happening. Immediately, he began to sing at the top of his voice:

Mother Rabbit! Mother Rabbit!
Cut the rope! Cut the rope!
The animals have come to kill you.
Cut the rope! Cut the rope!

Directly his mother took a sharp knife and cut the rope. All the animals fell from the clouds. Some of them broke their legs. Some broke their hips. And some died. Then the Rabbit sang to his mother to throw down the rope. He picked up as many of the dead animals as he could and went up to the clouds, where he and his mother stayed until the famine was over.

Who Is the Greatest Thief?

In this story the Mende people tell of two thieves who got into an argument about which of them was the best. To settle the argument and demonstrate his prowess, one of the men performed the incredible feat of stealing from the sharp-eyed eagle. How will the challenger respond?

Once upon a time, the Chief of a village sent word all over his dominion saying, "It is good that we conduct a census to know what everyone in my dominion can do. It doesn't matter what. Everyone has his powers, good or bad. We must know these powers, for they will surely be needed in time."

So it was that every man was assembled according to his trade. There were iron smelters, farmers, woodcutters, and so on. There were also liars, thieves, and the like.

Out of a village in the east came a man. He had been driven away from his village for stealing everything from people's crops to their silver. Out of a village in the west also came a man who was known for his thievery.

Soon the thieves began to argue among themselves.

"No one can steal better than me," the thief from the east boasted. "I am so good I could steal even from the Chief and neither he nor his guards would know it."

"If you are that good," said the one from the west, "how come they chased you out of the village? I am the best of the best."

"Well," said a bystander. "We all claim to be the best in what we do in our respective villages. If you believe you are better than he, you will have to prove it."

Meanwhile, a crowd was beginning to form to listen to their argument. Presently, the Chief called for order and told the people why he had called them to the meeting.

"The Chief shall live forever," the thief from the east greeted in obeisance. "This man has come here to waste your time. I am the best and you should send him back to his village."

The Chief listened as the two men argued about who was the best. As they argued and pointed at each other, the thief from the east saw an eagle perch in its nest atop a very tall tree. Realizing that the eagle was sitting on her eggs, he said: "The Chief shall live forever. To settle this case once and for all, I shall climb that tree, steal the eagle's eggs, and bring them to you."

"Do that," said the Chief, "and I will declare you the best thief in my dominion."

With that, the thief from the east set out. He carefully and quietly climbed the tree. One by one, he stole the eagle's eggs and put them in his pockets. The eagle didn't even know that he was there. Then as quietly and slowly as he climbed the tree, he came down, and with pride said to the Chief: "Behold, in my pockets are the eagle's eggs, which I have craftily stolen from its nest."

"Indeed you have," said the Chief. "Display the eagle's eggs before me and my counselors so that I may proclaim you the best."

Then the thief reached into his pocket for the eggs. But in place of the eggs, all he could find were rocks. He searched all over, but couldn't find the eggs.

"Who are you that you should make a fool of me," thundered the Chief. "Put him in chains. He must pay for his deception."

As the Chief was about to proclaim punishment for the thief, the one from the west reached into his own pockets and pulled out the eggs.

"Here are the eagle's eggs, your honor," he said, as he laid the eggs gently on the ground. "I stole them from his pocket and replaced them with the rocks."

The Chief and the crowd were surprised and confused. Of the two thieves, who do *you* think was the greater?

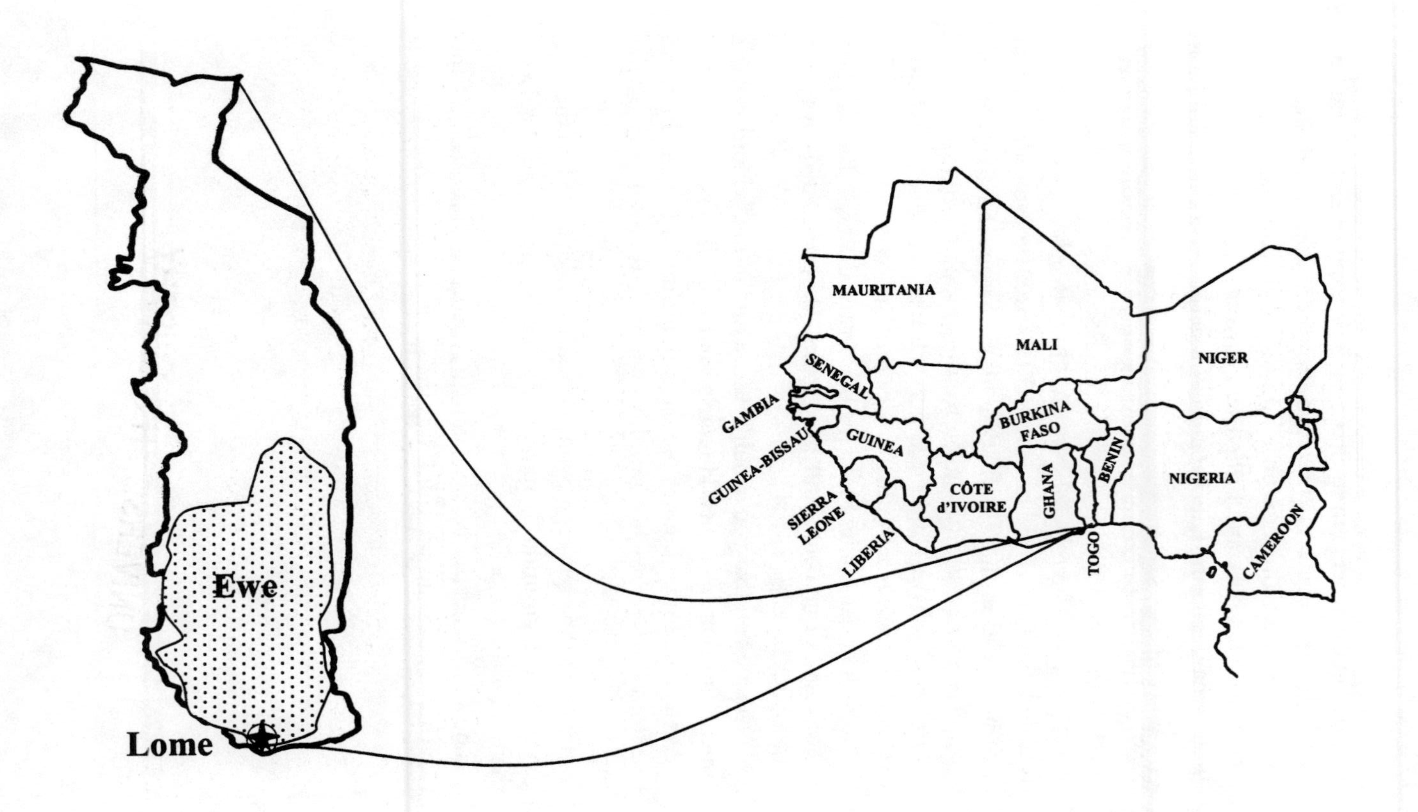
Ewe
Lome
MAURITANIA
MALI
NIGER
SENEGAL
GAMBIA
GUINEA-BISSAU
GUINEA
BURKINA FASO
SIERRA LEONE
LIBERIA
CÔTE d'IVOIRE
GHANA
TOGO
BENIN
NIGERIA
CAMEROON

Togo

COUNTRY

Formal Name: Togolese Republic (formerly French Togo)
Short Form: Togo
Term for Citizens: Togolese
Capital: Lome
Independence: April 27, 1960 (from French-administered UN Trusteeship)

GEOGRAPHY

Size: 21,925 square miles (56,790 km^2)
Boundaries: Bordered to the north by Burkina Faso, east by Benin, south by the Atlantic Ocean, and west by Ghana

SOCIETY

Population: 5.1 million
Ethnic Groups: The major ethnic groups are Ewe, Mina, and Kabre, which, with other smaller tribes, comprise about 99% of the population. The rest are Europeans and Lebanese.
Languages: Ewe and Mina are the major languages in the south; Dagomba and Kabye in the north. French is the official language.
Religion: 70% local religions; 20% Christianity; 10% Islam

How the Pig Got its Snout

According to an Ewe legend, the Pig once had a trunk just like the elephant. This story of how the Pig lost his trunk also explains why the Spider always lives between the cracks of a wall.

In the old days, the Pig was often mistaken for a baby elephant, for he had a trunk just like one. And, although his ears were not as large as those of the elephant's, his body was as flabby and his tail just a little shorter.

Also in those days, the artistic Leopard designed different patterns for himself and members of his family. Sometimes, when the animals went to important functions, like dances and marriage ceremonies, they asked the leopard to design special patterns for them. Some of these patterns he later wove into various articles of clothing, which his family sold for money.

One day the Leopard made a very beautiful cloth from a special dye he had brought from a distant land. Several days later, there was death in the home of Mr. Spider. So the Spider came to borrow a piece of cloth from the Leopard.

"Hello, Mr. Leopard," greeted the Spider.

"Who greets?" inquired the Leopard.

"It is just me."

"Why do you look so gloomy, my friend? Cheer up."

"You are just asking that," said the Spider. "You don't really want to know."

"Sure I do. What's the matter?" continued the Leopard.

"You must be the only one who has not heard that my father passed. Poor man. Such an honorable man and I have no way of paying my last respects."

"Don't be silly," the Leopard said. "Sure you can. You are a hard worker and your father must have left you a fortune."

Then the Spider told the Leopard how poor he was and that his father died a pauper and owed more than he cared to remember.

"I need something decent to put over my body so I can at least attend the funeral. I know you are quite an artist. That piece of cloth of yours on the line will really do the trick. But, I cannot afford it."

The two animals talked for a while. Finally, the Leopard decided that the best he could do was to loan the cloth to the Spider.

"Please," said the Leopard, "take good care of it. It is a special piece of work. The dye is from far away and I am sure that I will fetch a premium price for the cloth."

The Spider was overjoyed and jumped up and down with excitement. Then he thanked the Leopard and promised to guard the cloth with his life if necessary. The Spider took the cloth and went to his father's funeral. Everything went well and the Spider was the center of attention. Everybody liked his cloth.

After the funeral, the Spider bid farewell to his father's wives and set to go home with some of his friends who had accompanied him. After they had traveled for some distance it began to rain. So the Spider rolled up about one half of the cloth over his head with the other half barely covering his body. It was such a heavy downpour. The Spider and the cloth were soaked through. As he wiped the water off his face, some of it dripped off the cloth to his lips. He unconsciously licked off the water and noticed that it was quite tasty. Then he licked the water off the cloth. Then again, and again, each time faster and with greater sense of purpose than before.

"Gentlemen," he called his entourage. "I need to be excused for just one moment."

With that the Spider went into the forest and took down the cloth. He bit off a piece of the cloth and noticed that it tasted even better than the water that dripped into his mouth. He took another bite, then another, then another. Before long, he had eaten the whole cloth. Then he realized that he was naked. Not wanting to show his nakedness in public, he walked alone. When he heard someone coming he ran into the bushes. Then the Elephant came by.

"Pssst! Pssst!" he tried to catch the Elephant's attention from behind a thick shrub.

"Who goes there?" asked the Elephant.

"It's me! The Spider!" the Spider said in a low tone.

"Why aren't you showing yourself?" asked the Elephant in a whisper. "I can barely hear you. Are you wanted by the law?"

"No! I am naked," The Spider whispered.

"Don't make me laugh," said the Elephant. "Ha! Ha! Ha! Ha!"

Desperate to gain the Elephant's sympathy, the Spider told him that he was in a fight with the Leopard, who had ripped his clothes to pieces. Then he begged the Elephant to give him a piece of his ear to cover himself. He promised that he'd return it as soon as he got home and changed into his spare clothes.

The Elephant had pity on him. So he gave the Spider one of his ears. The Spider was very grateful. He took the ear, covered himself up and went home. When he got home he found his wife making his favorite soup. The aroma of the soup made him weak at the knees. But, the Spider had spent all he had on his father's funeral. So, he was not surprised when his wife told him that the soup would not be as tasty as before because there was no meat to enrich the flavor.

"We are in luck," said the Spider. "I happen to have what you need." So the Spider gave his wife the Elephant's ear. She singed it, cut it up, and added it to the soup. They both swore that they had never eaten a soup that tasty before.

Meanwhile, the Elephant couldn't wait any longer for the Spider to return his ear. The flies were getting the better of him. He flapped his one ear here and there. He stumped his feet, trumpeted and shook his body. But the flies kept coming. "I must go myself and get back my ear."

The Spider was expecting him, of course. So, he plotted with his family, saying, "The time for me to return Mr. Elephant's ear has come and gone. I expect he will come for it soon. When he comes, we shall all hide in my snuffbox. Then leave the rest to me."

"Pooh! Pooh! Pooh!" the Elephant trumpeted.

"Welcome, my friend," said the Spider. "I have been expecting you. Have a seat while I get you some kola nuts and snuff."

"I am not here to socialize," the Elephant warned. "I have come for my ear. He that borrows and repays shall live to borrow another day, you know!"

"I know, my friend, and I am sorry I am late. It was on account of my mourning. You know. I will fetch your ear right away."

Then, the Spider said to one of his children, "Go and get some snuff for our honored guest. It is not always that one is honored by the presence of Lord Elephant."

That was the cue the Spider's child needed. He left and hid in the snuffbox. Since he didn't come back with the snuffbox, the Spider sent another of his children. This he did until all his children had hidden inside the snuffbox. When the Elephant became impatient, the Spider sent his wife. But she didn't come back either.

"Children these days," said he, "they never do what you ask of them. But a wife too! Our elders were right. If you want something done right, do it yourself. I must go and fetch the snuffbox myself. Those children and wife of mine, I must teach them a lesson."

The Spider went and joined his family in the snuffbox. The Elephant waited, and waited, and waited patiently, even as the flies bothered him. Then he snapped and burst into the room shouting, "Where are you? I need my ear, and *now.*"

But there was no answer. The Elephant searched all over the house, looking for the Spider and his family, but they were nowhere to be found. He searched all over for his ear but couldn't find it either. Then he searched for something of value to take. But the Spider was quite poor and had nothing. Then he came across the snuffbox.

"Only a measly snuffbox!" cried the Elephant. "I will take it if that's all he has." So the Elephant took the snuffbox. He put it in his pocket and left.

When the Elephant had walked a good distance, the Spider and his family began to sing:

Mother Elephant!
What a lady!
She died a miserable death!
And her son is nowhere to be found!

The Elephant searched for the voices. When he figured out that the song came from the snuffbox, he took it and smashed it on a rock. The snuffbox shattered into pieces and the Spider and his family ran out, escaping into the crevices of the rock. The Elephant was very mad when he found out that it was the Spider playing a trick on him. He tried to get the Spider out from between the rocks but couldn't. Then he asked his cousin the Pig and his friend the Hyena who, with some other animals, were now gathering and watching the spectacle.

"Oink! Oink! Oink!" said the Pig. "Come out now and I will make it easy on you."

But, the Spider would not come out. Instead he brandished a very sharp knife, warning that he'd use it on anyone who tried to force him out of the rocks. But the Pig didn't take him seriously. He charged the rock, with his trunk taut and ready to dislodge the Spider from the rocks. With one swipe of his sharp knife, the Spider cut off the Pig's trunk.

Seeing what the Spider could do with his sharp knife, all the animals were afraid. None of them was bold enough to force the Spider out from between the rocks. So it is that even today, the Spider can be seen living between the cracks in the rocks. He is afraid that if he lived elsewhere the Elephant would catch him.

Since this incident, the Pig's snout has remained flat. And the Hyena can still be heard in the forest crying for his friend the Pig.

Glossary

Agbusi	Black stinger ant
Agbo	A thickly woven cotton cloth used as a blanket, loincloth, or chair cloth
Akpa Uche	The seat of wisdom. Literally, bag of wisdom
Akwasa	Wonderful. Often used to express euphoria
Apunanwu	Heat averse. Often used synonymously with beauty
Chi	Personal god
Chineke	God the creator
Chinyelu	A gift from God
Ego ayolo	Cowry shells, once used as money
Ekwe nwunyedi	A shrub-like plant, often used for crop rotation, with a notoriously tough root system that does not lend itself to easy cultivation
Ete	A thick strong rope made from special vines and used for climbing palm trees
Eze nwanyi	A female leader. Literally, queen
Foo foo	Cassava or yam that has been pounded into dough and is eaten with stew (locally called soup)
Idu uno	A process by which a master helps his graduating apprentice go out on his own by giving him or helping him secure tools he needs for the trade
Ikenga	Figurine of a personal god; often more revered than *okpensi*; often holds authority within a family
Iku aka	The first official visit of the family of a prospective groom to that of the prospective bride for the purpose of negotiating a marriage agreement. Literally, to knock on the door
Inu	Proverbs or riddles
Inyinya igwe	Bicycle. Literally, iron horse
Iputago ula	Good morning. Literally, "Have you woken up?" or "Have you come out from sleep?"
Kotma	A corrupted short form of court messenger or court man
Mammy water	Mermaid
Na anu bar	To drink at a bar
Na eli hoteli	To eat out in hotels
Nkasi ani	Tuberous plant that women grind into pulp and use to decorate their bodies

Nna anyi ukwu i mee	Thank you father. Literally, Our big father you have done it.
Nwam	My child
Nwannem	A neutral gender used to designate kinship. Literally, my mother's child
Obi	Special quarters where the head of a household receives and entertains visitors
Oche agada	An easy chair or recliner made with *agbo*
Ogbanje	Repeater. Literally, a child who is reincarnated over and over
Ogbolodo	The woman's equivalent of *obi* (generally refers to a woman's house)
Oji afo eje ugwo	One who eats too much. Literally, one who accepts repayment of debt with his stomach
Ojiefi	Short form of the title name *Ojiefi agba ncha.* It is the equivalent title name for a woman whose husband is titled. Literally, one who serves beef while others serve meat of lesser status, such as fish or chicken.
Okpensi	Figurine of a personal god
Omenuko aku	One who entertains in times of scarcity
Ono n'ikpo gbuo agu	One who has performed an incredible feat. Literally, one who killed a lion from the comfort of his couch
Onu aruru	Ant burrows, which according to legend were the homes of spirits called masquerades
Osukwu	A meaty and delicious type of palm nut
Pam putu, pam putu	Onomatopoeia for drumbeat
Shekere	A musical instrument made from gaud and beads. The beads are usually strung and tied loosely around the gaud to create the desired musical sound when shaken. The gaud then becomes quite smooth with use as the beads rub against it.
Udala	The fruit of a special type of rubber tree known by the same name. When mature and ripe, the fruit is gold-colored with succulent reddish-gold gummy tart meat.
Ugba	Sliced fermented oil bean seed. Often eaten with miniature eggplants and stock or smoked fish
Uli ogbu	Juice of a special rubber plant that females use to decorate their bodies
Uli oku	Palm-oil lantern without any protective glass casing; also called a naked lantern
Unu dum	Everyone, everybody, or all of you
Yagham	Onomatopoeia for raffia, or loincloth, around the waist

Index of Stories by Subject

ADVENTURE TALES

TALES ABOUT THE GODS

TALES ABOUT THE FAMILY

TALES ABOUT INGRATITUDE

TRICKSTER TALES